The 12 Days of Christmas

Poppy Alexander wrote her first book when she was five. There was a long gap in her writing career while she was at school, and after studying classical music at university she decided the world of music was better off without her and took up writing instead. She takes an anthropological interest in family, friends and life in her West Sussex village (think *The Archers* crossed with *Twin Peaks*) where she lives with her husband, children and various other pets.

Poppy's first novel, *25 Days in December*, was published in the UK by Orion and the US by William Morrow and has been translated into several languages. Her second, The Littlest Library, and third, *The 12 Days of Christmas*, have also been published by Orion in the first instance.

Poppy Alexander is always happy to chat with readers on social media. Search for Poppy Alexander Books on Facebook, Instagram and Twitter. Her website is Poppy-Alexander.com where you can also sign up for her author e-newsletter

Also by Poppy Alexander

25 Days in December
The Littlest Library

The 12 Days of Christmas

POPPY ALEXANDER

ORION

An Orion paperback

First published in Great Britain in 2021 by Orion Fiction,
an imprint of The Orion Publishing Group Ltd
Carmelite House, 50 Victoria Embankment,
London EC4Y ODZ

An Hachette UK Company

5 7 9 10 8 6 4

A CIP catalogue record for this book is
available from the British Library.

ISBN (Paperback) 978 1 4091 9642 6
ISBN (eBook) 978 1 4091 9643 3

Typeset by Born Group
Printed and bound in Great Britain by Clays Ltd, Elcograf S.p.A.

www.orionbooks.co.uk

For my Alex.

Chapter One

A Partridge in a Pear Tree

It was Christmas Eve and the High Street was teaming with last-minute Christmas shoppers, bundled up in winter coats and scarves, brightly coloured bobble hats and gloves, all pink-cheeked and happy. And warm. Freya shuddered and wrapped her denim jacket a little closer around herself. Looking up, she spotted a girl she knew from school. Ducking her head, she pulled her thin hoodie further over her all-too-recognisable burnished gold hair and slid silently by.

Sunset was still an hour away but already the streets had taken on their night-time identity, the shop fronts – like theatre sets – glowing into the intensifying gloom and enticing Christmas shoppers with open wallets. Freya wasn't there for the usual shops, though. Instead, out of habit, she was prowling around the food stalls in the market, the fruit and vegetables piled high, the butcher's wares on stainless steel trays, the row of game birds hanging from hooks above. At each stall Freya appraised, assessed, asked questions, allowing her imagination free rein in a desperate attempt to crowd out the thoughts she couldn't bear to think. This was familiarity to her. Comfort. The selecting and packing away of the parcelled and paper-bagged goods into the rucksack slung on her shoulder.

On the cobbled triangle at the base of the hill, where the High Street split into two, a Salvation Army band in their black uniforms with polished silver buttons, played carols, filling the cinnamon-scented air with glorious, triumphant sound. Behind them, the lights of the deli, with its little café area, shone invitingly into the rain-slicked street and – almost before she had had the thought – Freya slipped behind a man going inside and followed him in.

The little shop was crowded and heavy with a fug of wet dog and humanity. There was a snaking line of shoppers in front of the main till, each carrying their carefully selected choices – brightly wrapped panettone, stacks of nutty Florentines in their cellophane and ribbon parcels, special bottles of single-source virgin olive oil in green glass flagons with cork stoppers. As always, Freya was diverted and soothed by the sight and thought of food – what she would eat, how she would cook it – but her food shopping was done for the day. What she sought, urgently now, was warmth. And coffee, to keep her sleep-deprived brain going just a little longer – long enough to make a plan. She joined a loosely organised queue in front of the till by the café section, inhaling the aroma of excellent Italian coffee as the coffee machine belched its steam. She blew into her cupped hands. They were mottled blue and red with cold, her fingers stiff and numb.

The little clutch of café tables in the corner was filled to capacity with chattering, laughing shoppers advertising their shopping triumphs with the brightly coloured bags and parcels crowding the floor. There were no seats. She might have to settle for a takeaway, which would be disappointing; she needed a chance to sit, think and gather her resources, to work out – in a world that had just shifted on its axis, a world where she could no longer ask her mother – what she should do next.

She was staring unseeing at a wide back in a donkey jacket, when the man moved away and she found herself at the front of the queue.

'Fred?' came a deep voice. 'Fred! Wow, I can't believe it's you!'

Freya reluctantly raised her head to meet the gaze of a swarthy, handsome man with laughing green eyes, thick, wavy black hair and pronounced five o'clock shadow.

'Well, whaddaya know,' he said, sounding delighted. 'It's Fred Wilson herself, after all these years . . .'

'Finn,' she said, smiling thinly. 'How are you? And I am – as you know - "Freya", not "Fred".

'Whatever you say, Fred,' he agreed amiably. 'Tea and cake then, is it? Carrot cake's your favourite, right?'

Had carrot cake ever been her favourite? Possibly. A hundred years ago. 'Can I get a double espresso?' she enquired, robotically.

'At this time of day? You'll be awake 'til the middle of next week.'

'Actually, make that a triple,' said Freya, with a flash of defiance. 'No cake. Thank you.'

'Quick, grab a table,' he said, nodding towards a just-about-to-be-vacated table in the window. 'I'll bring it over.'

The window gave her a panoramic view of the market, and Freya, in her extreme fatigue, was quickly hypnotised by the ebb and flow of shoppers trudging past outside. Time drifted.

Beckoning a member of staff to take over from him, Finn gazed thoughtfully at Freya's hunched back as he made her coffee. Her deep blue eyes were dull, he observed, with fatigue at the very least, plus there was a watchful reserve that he didn't recognise from the Freya he knew of old.

A minute later, sliding the tray onto the table, he shuffled into the seat next to her, close enough for their thighs to be touching, making her shrink away, clamping her legs together tightly.

'I got you some cake anyhow,' he said, plonking a plate in front of her. On it was a large slice of carrot cake, studded with fat raisins and oozing with cream-cheese icing. 'You look like you need it.'

'I'm not really a cake eater nowadays,' she admitted.

He gave her a long, appraising look, noting the sharp collarbones, the bony wrists poking out beyond her cuffs, the child-sized hands wrapping gratefully around the little coffee cup.

'You've shrunk,' he said.

'I'm just not fat. Not anymore,' she replied, not meeting his eye. Despite being surrounded by food for every waking minute of her life over the previous ten years, she had become fitter to cope with the physical challenges and lean too, although that was more because she was usually too exhausted to eat at the end of a draining night's service.

'You were never fat,' Finn protested. 'You were just little, jolly, happy Fred.' He looked at her again, wistfully. 'You were perfect.'

She took a sip of her coffee, cradling the cup for warmth and looking out of the window, avoiding his gaze.

'So, what brings you back?' he went on. 'After all these years?'

'I'm . . . I don't know,' she mumbled, hanging her head, shaking it, looking away.

'OK,' he said carefully, recognising the omission and drawing back. He pulled the carrot cake towards him and broke off a piece, chewing it thoughtfully. 'Not bad,' he said. 'You don't know what you're missing.'

4

Freya allowed herself to say nothing further. He would think her odd – rude – but that didn't matter too much. What mattered more was avoiding complete breakdown, emotion slamming into her like a tsunami, leaving annihilation in its wake, right here in this shop, in her home town of Portneath, surrounded by the ghostly memories of her childhood and the all too alive people who inhabited those memories. Like Finn.

Instead, to distract herself, she replayed in her head the brief but fierce row between her and head chef, Andre, the one when she told him, just yesterday morning, that she needed to go home right now. The timing was terrible, of course, with the restaurant booked up solidly over Christmas and the new year. It had been that way for months and even the PAs of their most powerful and influential clientele were being turned away disappointed when they called for a table. No one in the tight-knit *brigade de cuisine* ever asked for time off over Christmas. For ten long years Freya had missed out on spending Christmas Day with her mum. Every single one. It had seemed an acceptable sacrifice at the time. The boss would, if he liked you, let you off a shift, or perhaps two shifts, over the Christmas week – not long enough to get home – but woe betide anyone who actually asked. And then, yesterday, Freya *had* asked. Worse still, she had been less than completely truthful about the reason, muttering something about family responsibilities, unable to share aloud the awful reality.

His wrath had been biblical. She had left the kitchen with the instruction never to return ringing in her ears. And being sacked by Andre was the equivalent of being sacked by the industry. None of the other restaurants in Paris with three Michelin stars would give her the time of day now. It was over.

'Going home?' Finn said, tugging her back into the present in a rush.

She nodded.

'Want a lift?'

It was getting on for five o'clock on Christmas Eve and she hadn't booked a taxi.

'Yes,' she said. 'Yes, please.'

Finn's car couldn't have been the same old banger he was driving ten years ago but the muddle of boxes, papers and parking tickets on the floor and seats was familiar enough. He chivalrously swept the contents of the passenger seat onto the floor for her.

The freezing rain was falling heavily now. He whacked the heating up full and waited, engine ticking over, for the windscreen to clear.

Soon they were out of the little seaside town and on the dark, winding country road leading to Middlemass, her mother's village.

'So,' said Finn, 'home for Christmas, eh?'

She nodded, twisting the string attached to her door key obsessively through her fingers. She had kept it with her throughout her decade in France, finding it occasionally in the top of her chest of drawers when she was looking for something else – a lip balm, or a comb. Each time she would take it out and look at it, feel the weight of it, knowing she could go home – just for a visit, and always a brief one – but hardly ever doing so, for reasons she did not fully understand herself.

The house was in darkness as they turned in to the drive and parked with a scrunch of gravel.

'Nobody in,' said Finn, reaching into the back and swinging her rucksack onto his shoulder.

'I'm fine,' she said, coming around to his side and trying to take it from him. 'Thanks for the lift.'

'I'll see you in,' he said, brooking no argument.

She drew the key out of her pocket now, opened the door and reached around the corner for the light switch, flicking it on in a gesture of habit.

Nothing.

'Blown fuse?' he said. 'Where's the fuse box?'

'Under the stairs,' said Freya, reluctantly.

Efficiently, Finn was there, reaching into the spider infested void with his phone torch on in his outstretched hand.

'No blown fuses,' he said. 'Look.'

'Misunderstanding over the bill probably,' said Freya, trying to sound insouciant. They had pushed a wedge of post to one side as they'd opened the door. There had been a general impression of window envelopes with red text on them.

'Where's your mum, then?'

'She's – she's away.' Again, there was the impossibility of saying the words. Telling the truth.

'OK,' he said as he walked confidently through the dark hall to the kitchen. 'Brrr. Aga's off. Fallen out with the gas people too then?'

'Probably.'

By the time she caught up with him Finn was running his torch beam around the room, highlighting swags of cobweb trailing from the ceiling, dead flies scattered on the windowsills and on the kitchen table too, desiccated, like dark confetti. He blew on a kitchen shelf and dust rose in a choking cloud.

'Jesus wept,' he muttered under his breath.

Freya stood in the centre of the room, breathing in a musty, pervasive stench of entrenched damp and desolation.

The smell of home, of warm bread, cotton sheets being ironed, of furniture polish and flowers, was gone. There was no sound, just the wind in the trees outside and the plink, plink of the kitchen tap.

'I don't know what's going on, Freya,' Finn said firmly. 'But you're not staying here.'

'It's fine,' she replied through clenched teeth, trying not to cry. Not in front of Finn. 'I just need to light a fire, find some candles . . . I'll call the gas and electricity companies in the morning.'

'It's Christmas Day in the morning,' he said, taking her elbow and leading her to the front door. He still had her rucksack and clearly wasn't giving it up. 'You're coming home with me.'

Back in the car, Freya allowed her head to fall wearily against the passenger window. The heating was still on full and the warmth made Freya feel that the next time her head hit a pillow she would sleep for a million years. All the adrenaline of the last twenty-four hours was spent, and even the coffee she'd drunk wasn't enough to counteract her exhaustion. New battles were to come but perhaps tonight – just tonight – she could rest.

'Right,' Finn said, when he had got Freya up the narrow stairs into the apartment above his little shop. He dumped her rucksack on the hall floor and walked her straight to the bathroom.

'Hot bath,' he instructed, opening the old-fashioned taps on a deep, roll-top bath. The steaming water, thundering onto a generous swig of Badedas, turned the water a startling, algae green.

'Wow,' he said, checking out the livid colour and peering at the bottle with awe. 'I never knew it did that.'

'Not yours, then?' queried Freya.

'What, bubble bath? Me? No, funnily enough – it's a girlfriend's,' he explained. 'Ex-girlfriend, I should say. Not that it's . . .' He trailed off. 'Towels,' he declared, changing the subject with obvious relief, and pulling a couple of rough, ancient towels which used to be white, from the airing cupboard and handing them over.

'Hang on,' he added, disappearing into his bedroom, then quickly returning with a pair of fleecy grey joggers, a navy-blue sweatshirt with 'Exeter Saracens' printed faintly on the front and some thick, woollen socks.

'Now, tea? Or something stronger?'

Freya raised a lopsided smile at last. 'Stronger?' she hazarded.

A minute later, the door opened a crack and a hand carrying a large glass of red wine, snaked its way through the gap, plonking the wine expertly, blindly, onto the little stool next to the bath.

Finn moved with the economy of habit around the room, flicking on cosily glowing wall lights and straightening feather cushions. The main living space of the flat was a large rectangular room with a high ceiling, fancy plaster-work and a pair of elegant, sash windows looking straight up Portneath High Street towards the little, ruined castle on the hill. The deli, with its flat above, was in an island of buildings at the foot of the town where the High Street split into two, the last row of buildings before the docks and the sea. It was a fantastic location commercially, perfect for the town's inhabitants and superbly placed to attract the attention of the many summer day trippers too.

He drew thickly lined, aubergine velvet curtains to shut out the cold and knelt to light the fire.

9

This room had been one big dark, cluttered stockroom when Finn had taken over the lease and it had been back-breaking work clearing it, revealing the elaborate Georgian cornicing and the wide, oak floorboards. It was now a haven of calm, and he needed it to be. He worked long hours with relentless energy but when he climbed the stairs – often late at night – the little apartment was a refuge, a work free zone.

There was an ancient, low-slung chestnut leather sofa, deep-seated and piled with feather cushions in jewel-coloured, knitted covers positioned opposite the fire; behind it, occupying the space at the other end of the room, was a long, trestle dining table and a mismatched collection of wooden dining chairs, standing out against the matt, plaster walls which were painted below the picture rail in a dark, complex green – almost black by candlelight. The only adornment on the scrubbed pine tabletop was a row of candles stuck in old wine bottles, so encrusted with stalactites of wax they were welded into place.

Among Finn's close-knit, loyal circle of friends, the apartment was the venue for many a rowdy Saturday night supper, with eating, drinking and shooting the breeze sometimes going on long into Sunday morning.

The firelight flared, illuminating his strong features, his brow furrowed thoughtfully as he mused on the re-emergence of Freya in his life. Always tiny in stature – something he had ribbed her about relentlessly – she had been so funny, feisty and brave then, he remembered; fiercely loyal, with a quicksilver wit, equally happy to laugh or to launch into battle for anyone she cared about. He had become fond of her – more than fond, if he was honest – thinking of her at first as a kind of cute, kid sister, four years younger, which was a lot when he was still in his teens himself; and then, later, it would be fair to say, his interest had been piqued in an entirely more disturbing way and while he was no monk, not then and not now, for some reason that made sense at the time, he had kept his distance. Biding his time.

He'd got used to her just always being there on those hectic summer nights, on the periphery of the loud, rambunctious gang of teens living it up as far as the sedate, town of Portneath would allow, getting into trouble, but none of it serious, all high spirits and no ill intentions. Freya – Fred – was never seen without her close friend and partner in crime, Hattie. He saw her often now, buying coffee from the café, exchanging smiles with him that acknowledged an acquaintance, nothing more. Freya, on the other hand, he had never seen, not once, in ten years. Over those long, long years with little news of her, he had often thought back to those days, regretting his failure to declare his interest, make a move . . .

He smiled as he crouched there, his hands held up to the fire to warm them, recalling vividly how he had once incited her wrath, with some affectionate teasing about her Halloween costume. There she was, dressed as a pumpkin, laughingly attempting to pummel him and Ciaran for their insolence as he held her effortlessly at arms' length. Those had been carefree days. He gave a low chuckle at the memory, but then his expression darkened.

That was then. She was quiet, wary and watchful now. Clearly much had happened to her over the last ten years and he was guessing that at least some of it was bad; but she would tell him in her own time. He would wait.

This was no opportunity to make up for his own regrets, he told himself sternly. He sighed, as he patiently fed kindling onto the fire, coaxing the flames into brighter, dancing life. She had changed, and he had changed too. Gone was the daft, irresponsible young man who thought nothing of turning up for milking at five a.m. after staying up all night, drinking beer and swimming naked in the lake at the farm. Now, apart from the occasional Saturday night dinner with friends, sleep was sacrosanct, because his business was a taxing mistress, and it needed his full attention. Which wasn't to say he wasn't interested in having what his brother had, a wife, children, a dog . . . all the accoutrements of family life. That was a definite ambition for one day. But now, coaxing his business into growth, into profit, was a hundred times more taxing than lighting this fire. There was no time for romance. Not now.

Chapter Two

Freya woke up to discover the bubbles were gone, her fingertips were white and wrinkled and the water was no longer the piping hot temperature she needed to warm her deep into her bones. Shivering, she dried herself and scrambled into the clothes Finn had left her. The sweatshirt and joggers swamped her, but they were warm and soft and the thick socks were cosier than slippers although she was nervous about slipping on the polished wooden floors as she sought out her host.

She found Finn in the sitting room, wine glass in hand, caressing the chin of a scruffy, black-and-white cat which had draped itself across his knee like a shaggy rug. The room was lit only by the fire and by the candles on the table now. It was warm and peaceful and Freya wanted nothing more than to curl up with her glass of wine in a corner of the sofa.

'What do you call him?' she asked, reaching out to stroke the disgruntled cat as it mooched past her, annoyed at being tipped off Finn's lap as he stood to refill Freya's glass.

'I don't call him anything,' admitted Finn, laughing as the cat stalked over to Freya, tossing a filthy look over his shoulder. 'He makes a point of not coming when I call, so I don't bother any more. But his name's Rafferty – Raff; I inherited him with the building.'

Freya sat down so the cat could climb onto her lap. She was taken aback to find she could feel his ribs through the thick, slightly matted, fur.

'I don't starve him, honestly,' said Finn, hastily, putting the bottle down on the hearth after refilling his own glass. 'He's a bit decrepit, but he's probably about a hundred years old in cat years, to be fair.'

'Don't you know how old he is?'

Freya was faintly condemnatory, but Finn gently rejected her reproach.

'Nobody knows. He's just been living here for as long as anyone can remember. And we tolerate each other. Are you hungry?' he added. 'I can do us some beans on toast, if you like?'

'Let me cook for you,' she replied. 'To say thank you for your hospitality.'

Finn looked taken aback. 'Really? Nah, there's no need. Plus, I've not got a lot in,' he admitted.

Freya wasn't listening. She grabbed her rucksack from where Finn had put it down in the corner and looked around. 'Your kitchen?' she asked, pointing enquiringly in the most likely direction.

She was acutely aware of his nearness as he leaned against the kitchen doorpost watching, with a bemused smile, as she carefully took out the paper packages she had bought in the market.

Rafferty had not deigned to join them, curling up on the hearthrug in front of the fire instead.

Underneath the food she had taken out of her rucksack was a roll of leather, tied with a thong. Reverently, she laid it on the counter and unravelled it, revealing a set of kitchen knives, razor-sharp and glinting evilly on the countertop.

'Welcome home, Sweeney Todd,' he joked. 'I hope I'm going to last the night.'

Freya rewarded him with a ghost of a smile, but she wasn't listening, not really, she was concentrating on the task ahead.

'Smells amazing,' he said, half an hour later as he peered into the sauté pan, to see four little oval pieces of meat, sizzling deliciously.

'It's ready,' she said, ushering him out of the way, hating being watched while she plated up. Taking the hint, he apologetically put his hands on her hips to move her sideways so he could open a drawer, revealing knives and forks with horn handles. They reminded Freya of the cutlery from home, she remembered with a painful twist of recall.

'The washing-up is all mine, by the way,' he said.

Freya looked guiltily at his sink, now piled high with virtually every pan and implement he possessed. Not that that added up to much. If this were her kitchen, she would seriously be buying some more kit. He was clearly no cook.

Facing each other across the table, with the candles lit, Freya was suddenly shy as she sipped from her glass, acutely aware of her make-up-bare face, and hair lank with steam.

'This looks amazing,' Finn said, looking admiringly at his plate, as he tucked in. 'Talk me through it.'

'So, partridge breast,' she said, pointing to her own plate to illustrate, 'on a bed of root vegetable mash. And that's caramelised pears, on the side.'

'Ha, very good,' he said, rolling his eyes.

'What?' she said.

'Partridge in a Pear Tree,' he said, looking confused now. 'You did that on purpose, right?'

Freya hadn't. She had just thought the pears would complement the delicate, gamey meat and she certainly hadn't been thinking about Christmas. In any case, if they were following the words of the carol properly then the first day of Christmas wasn't until tomorrow, she thought, deciding it might be pedantic to point that out.

'You're a bona fide chef!' he went on. 'It looks like something from a really fancy restaurant, but why am I not surprised? That's exactly where you've been, right?'

'You're a Facebook fan?' she ventured. It was the only way he could possibly know about her work. Not that she posted often.

'I wouldn't say a "fan",' he said, 'I mean, who's into Facebook these days?' He paused, checking her face for a reaction. 'Oh, OK, busted,' he admitted, with a self-deprecating grin. 'Not that I was stalking you, or anything. Honest.' He didn't press for details and she was grateful for that.

Freya realised she was starving. Of course, she was. She had left Paris yesterday straight after she read the text. She was in too much of a hurry – and too distressed – to eat before she set off. There was no incentive to eat on the train, because, even in the French part of the trip, the standard of refreshments was so bad. And then, once she had finally arrived in Portneath, food was the furthest thing from her mind, even though the lovely staff at the hospice had pressed her in vain to eat something.

And so here she was at last with – if she said so herself – a perfectly balanced plate of food and a sinful, second glass of wine. Andre had always insisted that the team try everything on the wine list so they knew the flavours and could understand the pairings. Of course, that was work. A relaxed, off-duty glass of wine was a rare thing, not least because being off duty was a rare thing.

Almost everything in her Paris life had been about work. Food was work. She had no time for friends, let alone romance. Let alone family, even, half the time.

But now she was home.

She sighed, a deep, weary sigh that came right up from her core.

Finn stilled, glanced up and then, clocking her unseeing gaze, returned to eating without comment.

Freya allowed her mind to drift. She still remembered the desperation to escape from Portneath ten years before, the sense of suffocation and stagnation, and yet, like rediscovering a much-worn and much-loved teddy, it was reassuring to be back. Finn was reassuring too. He was clearly happy to get on with eating quietly, letting Freya find her equilibrium. Finn had always been nice. He and his big brother Ciaran, she remembered, were always in the thick of the action, at the centre of the rowdy in-crowd, so confident and loud. They had been like a pair of handsome puppies, unaware, apparently, of their own good looks, effortlessly attracting the most glamorous girls, moving from one to another, but never cruelly, at least not deliberately. Being about four years older than Freya, with Ciaran older still, she had assumed he barely noticed her at the edge of his kingdom, not with her puppy fat and her painful self-consciousness over teenage spots.

That was then.

Freya woke shockingly late, having slept deeply and dreamlessly.

Finn was already up making coffee, but the sleeping bag was still on the sofa and the dark shadows under his eyes confirmed he had had an uncomfortable night.

'I feel terrible taking your bed,' she said, yawning and stretching her arms.

'No problem. Merry Christmas!' he replied, handing her a foaming latte, and dropping a kiss on her cheek.

She blushed at the sudden contact. 'Merry Ch-Christmas,' she dredged up in reply.

'So,' he said, looking at his watch, 'we're not due at my brother's until midday, that leaves the rest of the morning to have a chat and a catch-up.'

'I'm not due at your brother's.'

'Yeah, you are, I spoke to him this morning. He remembers you – can't wait to see you. Plus, you get to meet his wife Martha, who's just lovely.'

Freya's stomach was sinking at the thought of having to put on a brave face for strangers all day.

Finn was leading her to the sofa, moving his sleeping bag out of the way and bundling it up as she sat down.

'So, what's going on?' he said gently, once he had settled himself beside her.

'What do you mean?'

'Well, where's your mum, for a start? It was clear from your house last night she's not been there for a while. And then there's the fact you've been absent for years – wildly successfully cooking in Paris, we all gather – and suddenly you're back here on Christmas Eve with barely the clothes you stand up in. Need I go on?'

Freya gave a shaky sigh, put her mug down on the coffee table, and sat back in her seat.

'She died,' Freya said quietly. 'Mum. She passed away. I was there.'

He bowed his head. For long seconds he said nothing. 'I'm so sorry,' he murmured at last. 'Come here.'

Before Freya knew what he intended, she had been swept into a strong, all-encompassing hug. She could smell him, a fresh, comforting aroma of warm body, with a hint of shampoo and lemon and washing powder. It was too much. She couldn't bear it. She couldn't be comforted for a grief she couldn't possibly allow herself to feel, even for a moment, or she would simply splinter into a million pieces. She froze, almost stopped breathing, her heart clenching into a tiny fist inside her chest.

Several seconds into the embrace, seeming to realise she was stiff and rigid in his arms, Finn gently let go and took both of her hands in his own. She looked down at his big hands, warming her cold fingers. They were strong hands. Capable.

'When?' he said, softly.

Freya was still not certain she could trust herself to speak. She swallowed. 'Yesterday,' she said, in a voice so quiet he had to lean closer to hear. 'She died yesterday in St Bart's Hospice, up past the railway station.'

'Christ!' he exclaimed, his grip tightening. 'How are you holding it all together?'

An excellent question, thought Freya. How *was* she holding it all together? She didn't cry when it happened, she hadn't cried since. Instead, she felt frozen, physically, emotionally . . . God, she must be a cold bitch. And she was, of course. How else could she explain the last ten years? Barely half a dozen lightning-quick dashes home, for just a day or so at a time, her mother packing her off again – pushing her to get back to her exciting career – where she was storming up the kitchen hierarchy. Job first – family a very poor second. Yep, she was a cold bitch all right.

Thankfully, Finn seemed to realise she had no desire – no ability – to talk. Now was not the time for him to press her to confess how she had raced off to that first, lowly job in Paris, desperate to get away after her mother's first fight with cancer. She had waited until they'd had the 'all clear', of course. She wasn't a *complete* monster. But after the stress of studying at the same time as being at her mother's side through surgery, chemotherapy and radiation she could hardly wait to escape, could she? And anyhow, it had been the opportunity she had dreamed of for years, a Michelin-starred chef prepared to take her on as a pot washer with a chance to join his apprentice scheme. It was a one-time offer, made on condition she dropped everything and came straight away. And why wouldn't she? It was the golden ticket and it all came about because of some bloke her mother had been at university with. He got her in. Her mother must have been embarrassed, Freya thought, realising only now, how she had asked a favour she had no right to, prepared to charm a man she had not spoken to for years, just to get her daughter that first break. Worse than that, her mother had been horrified when she heard she herself had set off a chain of events that would cause Freya to insist on dropping her A levels just before she took her final exams. There had been rows, of course, tears, even – but Freya had been adamant.

Unbidden, memories of when she had walked into the room at the hospice flooded back. Ever since she'd received the text from her godmother, Diana Fuller, she had been furiously willing the journey to go faster, resenting each train stop, convinced that she would arrive too late.

Breathless, anxious, she had pushed open the door to her mother's darkened room. There had been a pool of light, illuminating the far-too-small bundle under the bedclothes, Anna's head turned away from her, looking out into the little courtyard garden. For a long moment, her mother was so still Freya thought the worst, but then her head turned, and her face lit up.

'You're here,' she breathed, and her voice was like the rustling of leaves. 'What absolute heaven to see you.'

Freya was worried about crushing her mother's delicate frame, but the hug she was enfolded in made no allowance for that.

'Mum,' said Freya, in anguish, her face pressed to her mother's frail, bony shoulder.

'It's all right, my darling,' came the reply, murmured into her ear. 'Everything is all right, now.' Her mum drew back at last, slumping exhausted against the pillows, but reaching up to wipe away the tears from Freya's face before clasping both of Freya's hands in her own, with all her failing strength. 'You're really here,' Anna said in wonderment.

'Why didn't you say, Mum?' choked Freya, sobbing. 'Why didn't you tell me the cancer had come back?'

'What would have been the point, darling? It is what it is. Until I absolutely had to, I didn't want to interrupt your exciting life . . .'

'That's why you told me your camera wasn't working, wasn't it?' said Freya, remembering how their regular FaceTimes had reverted to phone calls over the last couple of months – a broken camera on her mother's phone apparently. Supposedly. She should have guessed. She would have known instantly, if she had seen her for herself, seen how the flesh had melted away from her mother's bones, leaving her so ethereally fragile and frail.

Anna smiled her apology at the deceit.

'Did you already know in the spring? When you came to visit me?' Freya persevered, doggedly, searching her memory for signs she had been so oblivious to at the time.

But all her mother would do was smile. So that was a 'yes' then, thought Freya. How had she missed it? She must have been too wrapped up in herself to see what was right in front of her. Unforgivably.

'And anyhow, it's fine!' her mother insisted, as she slumped back against the pillows, all energy spent, her skin waxy and pale.

'It's *not* fine,' Freya had protested. 'Nothing about this, is fine!' She flung out her arm to incorporate the room – the whole world – rage and despair following close on the heels of grief.

'Shh, shh,' soothed her mother. 'I'm in this marvellous place, where they've been looking after me so well, and now you're here too. I want nothing more than this in all the world, believe me, darling.'

'But . . .' Freya gulped, swallowed and clenched her fists, summoning up the will to ask the unspeakable question.

'How long have I got?' Her mother said the words for her.

Freya nodded, her eyes squeezed closed.

'Not long now, darling.' She said it soothingly, as if she was announcing the end of some great endurance, rather than the end of her own life. 'Not long now.'

'But surely there's something?'

'Nope,' Anna went on, in matter-of-fact tones. 'All been tried, nothing worked. There you are,' she announced. 'And at least it was quick this time darling. Really, it's been so mercifully quick.' Her voice – barely there – was a mere shadow of brisk. 'Now, did you go and speak to that genetics person I found for you?'

Freya nodded. Her mother had been so insistent when she had come over to Paris but Freya had been slow to persuade. Serious stuff, like her chances of getting ill at some indefinable point in the future, was the last thing she had wanted to talk about in their precious time together.

'And?'

'All good, Mum,' she lied. 'All good.'

Chapter Three

'Freya?' Finn said gently, his face flooded with compassion. 'Are you still with me?'

She nodded, dumbly, sitting up straighter and tucking her heavy, blonde hair behind her ears. 'I'm fine,' she said, her lips closing into a straight line, daring him to press his case.

'You're not fine,' he replied. 'No one would be.'

They sat in silence while they drank their coffee, Finn's hand comfortingly close to Freya's but not touching.

They reconvened in the sitting room after going through the rigmarole of washing and dressing, politely arguing over who should use the bathroom first.

'Ready?' said Finn, looking up as Freya came back in. He was texting as he was talking.

'What for?'

'The chaos which is my brother's house on Christmas morning,' he explained, pressing 'send' and slipping the phone into his pocket.

'Oh no,' protested Freya. 'You can't seriously mean it. I am *not* going to crash your family Christmas. I haven't got presents or anything, Finn, and they don't want me there, not really . . .' she gabbled. 'Can't I just stay here?' She gave him a pleading look.

'Nope. Sorry. Not leaving you on your own on Christmas Day. And they're expecting you. I told you, I called this morning.'

'I just feel – after the last couple of days – all the stuff, you know?' God knows if she couldn't play the 'I want to be alone' card now, when could she?

'I do know, and I'm sorry,' said Finn. He paused. 'But we're still going to Ciaran's.'

'Fine,' muttered Freya sulkily, accepting defeat. 'Have it your own way.'

'So where does Ciaran live these days?' she asked as Finn drove.

'He's taken over my parents' farm, just the other side of Middlemass, but you know the old place, of course?'

Freya shook her head.

'Did you never go up there?' he said, incredulous.

Why would I have gone up there? thought Freya.

Mind you, there had been one time, when they were piling out of the pub one Saturday night at closing time – a whole crowd of them from Portneath High – and the talk was that the after-party was going to be at Holly Tree Farm.

Somehow, she and Finn had ended up next to each other on the pavement outside the pub. 'See you there?' he had asked. Freya, stupefied into silence, had nodded, blushing. Then, somehow, she and Hattie had got left behind, too awkward to come straight out and ask any of the older kids – the ones who were already nineteen and twenty years old – for a lift.

'So, you've never been to the farm?' said Finn, bringing her back to the present as they drove past the pond in Middlemass, the little village lane, so painfully familiar, deserted, except for the ducks who seemed to have multiplied since she saw them last.

'I could have sworn you knew it. Anyhow, so Mum and Dad have gone back to Ireland and we go over and see them every summer. Ciaran's been running the farm for a few years now, since just before he got married to Martha, who came to Middlemass after you left, so you won't have met. He got to know her when he was off travelling, a few years ago. She's great. You'll love her. We all do.'

Turning abruptly off the lane, Finn bumped the car down a pitted track, the ruts still solid from the overnight freeze. Freya's teeth chattered, whether from the rough terrain or the cold or her shyness, she couldn't say. Only her best friend Hattie, and her mum, really knew how insular she really was, how much it cost her to present the jokey exterior she pasted on to hide her insecurities. And now it was just Hattie. Oh God, Hattie! That was another thing she needed to feel agonisingly guilty about, because, if she had not seen enough of her mother over the last few years, her friendship with Hattie had been the other unforgivable casualty of her ambition. She couldn't remember the last time they had had contact; even their WhatsApps had dwindled to nothing long ago. And Hattie had always been so loyal, such a true friend. Hattie and Anna had been her guiding lights and she had treated them both shamefully.

Freya cringed inwardly at her thoughts as they pulled into a farmyard. Along one side was a lofty, open barn, piled high with hay and sacks of feed. There was a small tractor in there too. On the other side of the yard, the building was a run of low, slate-roofed brick, with little windows and stable doors, the woodwork painted a soft, olive green. They came to a halt next to a filthy red pickup truck with several bales of hay in the back. Finn came round to open her door but she was already out, on trembling legs, looking up at the handsome Georgian façade, with its lollipop-shaped holly trees on either side of the porch. Just then, the cobalt-blue front door flew open and two identical boys with shocks of thick, dark hair like Finn's piled out and flung themselves around his legs.

'Finn!' shouted one. 'We got Scalextric for Christmas. Come and see!' He tugged at Finn's hand.

'Give the poor man a chance,' said a deep voice, and Freya looked around to see Ciaran standing in the doorway, holding a chubby blond toddler with denim dungarees and a very dirty face. 'Freya,' he went on, coming over to her and enveloping her in a powerful one-armed hug. 'I am bloody horrified to hear your sad news. So, so sorry for your loss,' he said with fervour.

He let her go and pecked her formally on both cheeks. Like Finn, he was just as she remembered him from her teens, handsome, hazel-eyed in contrast to Finn's green but, like Finn, brown-skinned and powerfully built. Close up she could see fans of fine lines around his eyes when he smiled. Of course, it had been ten years and, as the older brother, he must be in his mid-thirties now.

'Come and have a drink,' Ciaran went on. 'You've got a better excuse for one than anyone else I know.'

Freya didn't know what she said in reply, but nothing much seemed expected of her. She had forgotten they were such lovely people.

Hovering behind Ciaran was a tall, willowy woman with dark smudges under her eyes and the kind of glossy, thick fair hair that Freya could only reproduce with effortful blow-drying. In this woman's case she suspected it was natural. She was wearing slim, dark jeans and a deep purple Sloppy Joe sweater with the type of navy-and-white striped apron Freya wore over her whites in Andre's kitchen. The sight of it gave her a frisson of anxiety. What would the team be doing without her this morning?

'I'm Martha,' the woman said, coming towards Freya and hugging her fiercely. 'Finn just texted us. I can't imagine . . .'

she said, drawing away but only far enough to rest her hands lightly on Freya's shoulders. Freya was touched to see her eyes were brimming with tears. It was good *someone* was crying, she thought irrationally. 'Now listen,' Martha went on, intensely, 'you have carte blanche to do or say whatever you want today. You're among friends, OK?'

Freya nodded dumbly.

'Come and have a drink with me in the kitchen, away from the chaos.'

'It feels a bit early,' she said guiltily, as Martha led her through to a large, homely kitchen at the back of the house and handed her a flute glass, brimming with bubbles.

'We've all been up since sparrow's fart this morning,' Martha explained in her defence, 'so it definitely feels like wine o'clock to me.' She chinked Freya's glass with her own and took a deep, reviving swig.

'What can I do to help?' said Freya, looking around her. The kitchen was a large, square, quarry-tiled space with an oak-beamed ceiling. It was warm and homely, with an engine green Aga in the chimney breast at one end of the room, a massive dresser packed with mismatched china at the other and a long refectory table in the middle, already partly laid for lunch. Half of the wall at the table end of the room was an enormous blackboard, with scribbled shopping lists and aide memoires. The rest of the space was given over to a huge corkboard, barely visible below pinned rosettes, children's drawings and certificates. Freya read the ones nearest to her; there was one awarding first prize for a school bake-off and another, covered in cartoon fish, celebrating a twenty-five metre swimming achievement. Quite a few were for 'Star of the Week', which seemed to be won with monotonous regularity by someone called Daniel.

'Shall I . . .?' Freya picked up the pile of cutlery that had been dumped at one end of the table and started to lay it out.

'That's brilliant, thanks,' said Martha. 'There's only eight of us this year, and that's presuming I can get our reprobate sons to actually sit down long enough to eat.'

'How many children have you got?' asked Freya.

'Four, can you believe?' said Martha, eyebrows raised. Clearly, she could hardly believe it herself. 'Four boys in a row. I actually had four under five years old at one point, but then I did start with twins, to be fair.'

'Good grief,' said Freya faintly. No wonder it was so hectic. Her experience was as an only child. It had just been her and Mum together throughout her childhood and she couldn't have imagined – or really wanted – it any different, although there had been times she had had an abstract longing for brothers and sisters.

'And no, it wasn't that we kept going hoping for a girl,' Martha continued, giving her an 'I've heard it all before' smile. 'Four was always the plan for both of us. That said,' she went on, 'I wouldn't mind being less outnumbered in the gender balance some days. The only girls in the house are me and Nelly the sheepdog. There was a goldfish once, which we thought was a girl, but I had my doubts and anyhow, she or he didn't last long.' All the while Martha was chatting, she was efficiently peeling and chopping potatoes, before dropping them into a large pan of water.

That task briskly dispensed with, Martha put on oven gloves and pulled out of the Aga the biggest joint of beef Freya had ever seen.

'They eat for Britain, my lot,' explained Martha, basting it with a ladle. 'We always have beef at Christmas and it's our own meat, reared on the farm. I hope you're not one of those people who longs for turkey at Christmas?'

'Not me. It smells amazing,' said Freya, her stomach growling. 'It's half a cow!'

'The intention is leftovers,' said Martha, topping up Freya's glass. 'I can absolve myself of responsibility for cooking for at least a couple of days if I can point Ciaran at a loaf of bread and a hunk of cold beef. I've got Christmas books to read and a bottle of Bailey's to get through – oh, it's such bliss to be done with breastfeeding! This is my first Christmas in years that I can actually have a drink,' she said.

'So, who are they all?' asked Freya trying to take stock, which was a challenge with children all running around, thoroughly overexcited.

'Rufus and Joe – seven years old. The twins,' said Martha, pointing as they charged past, 'they're the oldest; then that's Daniel, he's five, and the youngest one is Alexander here,' she said, scooping up the adorable toddler and planting a kiss on top of his little, blond curly head, before releasing him to totter after his brothers. 'And they've all got December or January birthdays,' she admitted, ruefully. 'Luckily, our wider family are all brilliant about not giving joint Christmas and birthday presents, which are such a swizz.'

'All Christmas babies!' said Freya, in awe.

'I know, what can I say?' said Martha. 'Except maybe "beware the Ides of March".'

Freya almost giggled. This noisy, chaotic home was the opposite of what her own had been. She and Mum used to have memorable Christmases, just the two of them – special times – something she would never have again. She swallowed hard, braced for tears that didn't come. Luckily, if there were any outward signs of distress, Martha was distracted by the reappearance of the twins, each with a large Nerf gun, fully primed with bright orange polystyrene bullets.

'Where the heck did they come from?' said Martha with some irritation. 'What happened to the "no guns" rule?'

'Guilty,' admitted Finn, coming back into the room behind them. 'I couldn't resist, especially when I saw they had flashing lights and sound effects.'

'Better and better,' said Ciaran blandly, standing apparently impervious as either Joe or Rufus – Freya couldn't tell – emptied his entire bullet stash into the back of his father's head at point-blank range. The orange bullets bounced off in all directions, sending the little boy scurrying to reload.

'Oh, my goodness, is that . . .?' Freya said, as she saw something moving in the open doorway of the Aga's warming oven.

'Born this morning,' said Ciaran, going over and pulling out a very small, very leggy black woolly lamb that tottered on its tiny hooves and then collapsed, sprawling, onto the quarry-tiled floor.

'A bit early for lambing, bro?' queried Finn.

'I know, I know,' said Ciaran as Martha shot her husband an 'I told you so' look. 'I don't know what I was thinking, to be honest. Martha and I had "words" on the subject,' he admitted, acknowledging Martha ruefully, 'although this one's a bit early even by my schedule. I was aiming for the New Year. Hopefully, it can go back to its mum in a bit.'

'Shall we feed it, Daddy?' lisped Daniel, earnestly.

'That's a good plan, mate,' said Ciaran, scooping up the little creature and standing up. 'Let's go and sort out a bottle.'

Somehow, with a fair bit of noise and bustle, the adults and children were finally all seated around a table groaning with food. The glistening, side of beef – a five-rib roast, Ciaran informed Freya – took pride of place as he sharpened a long, ferocious-looking carving knife. It was a Sabatier, she clocked expertly. Not a bad brand, although the true chef's knives were the Japanese Shun set she had in her rucksack. The tools of her trade and the first, nearly the only, thing she had packed to come home. There was no logic to her decision to grab them, just instinct. Perhaps she knew – or hoped – she was never going back.

Freya had been plied with champagne for more than two hours without food by this point and was woozily grateful to sit down at last. She watched Martha as she pushed her hair back from her face wearily and slumped in her chair, happy to let Ciaran take over.

'I can't eat all that,' she gasped in horror as Finn put a loaded plate in front of her. Several thick slices of pink, tender beef were the foundation on which Brussels sprouts with lardons and chestnuts, honey-glazed carrots, buttered peas and a tower of crispy, golden roast potatoes were piled, along with an impressively puffed slab of Yorkshire pudding and a lake of unctuous port-wine gravy.

'Try,' Finn replied. 'You might surprise yourself. Holly Tree Farm beef is an event. You'll not have eaten better anywhere, I promise.'

'Don't hector her,' intervened Martha. 'You leave what you can't manage,' she told Freya, who looked at her gratefully. 'It's not a competitive eating competition,' Martha went on. 'It's Christmas lunch, and,' she added to the twins sitting opposite, 'I'll have you using knives and forks please, not fingers. We're not animals.'

'We *are* animals really, though, aren't we Daddy?' said one of the twins, brightly, with a wicked look at his mother. 'And animals just eat with their mouths, don't they?' He lowered his head to his plate and hoovered up a few peas to demonstrate his point.

'Rufus, that'll do,' said Ciaran mildly, but with authority.

Freya smiled at the boys. They were cheeky but funny too. They clearly had a healthy respect for Ciaran, but it looked like Finn was the fun uncle, the one they got up to mischief with.

After that, to Freya's relief, and as if pre-agreed, the family benignly ignored her, making sure her plate and glass were filled but otherwise letting her be. She was grateful.

'Did you make this?' Freya asked Martha, moved to speak at last. It was the best Christmas pudding she had ever tasted, rich, moist, boozy, filled with juicy dried fruit and singing with orange zest.

'I confess not,' answered Martha. 'It's a Paynton's one, a local firm; do you know of it? When they do puddings this good, I'd be mad to make my own.'

Freya thought she vaguely remembered the name. At the time she had been dismissive of anything mass-produced and often she would have been right, but Freya was humbler and more open to be persuaded otherwise these days. She was older. Wiser. Sometimes, at least.

'Nerf gun war next?' said Finn, cocking an eyebrow at the twins as the meal wound its way to a close. 'Fight to the death? You lot versus me but I choose my weapons first?'

'I think, after a lunch like this, the last thing people should be doing is haring around shaking everything up,' suggested Martha wearily. 'I had board games in mind. Or maybe a film or something?'

The twins rolled their eyes at their mum and giggled into their plates.

'Clear up first, though,' said Ciaran to groans.

Finn nodded, but Freya saw him catching the twins' eyes making the classic, 'I'm watching you' gesture.

Chapter Four

Stomachs laden with food, and with Finn taking charge of the washing-up, Martha and Freya retreated to opposite ends of the comfortably saggy sofa in the sitting room with mugs of tea on the coffee table and a box of chocolates on the seat between them. Not that Freya had room to eat or drink another thing. She had astonished herself by ploughing through a huge plate of superb roast beef followed by a substantial portion of Christmas pudding with cream *and* brandy butter, more than she would eat in a week back in France. The team she worked with all ate at the end of the lunchtime service, but Freya had always struggled to eat a big meal then, just wanting to go back to her digs for a shower and a couple of hours rest before the evening. And then, at the end of the evening shift, she was even more exhausted and disinclined to eat. She had become increasingly slight, to the point of being too thin, even though she was eating healthy, substantial breakfasts which she cooked for herself in the tiny flat in the 4th arrondissement. The little attic flat was rented with a couple of her favourite waiting staff. Even with the three of them sharing, it was a struggle managing the stratospheric rent, but they all worked insane hours and valued having a short commute above everything else. The work was punishing, exhausting and – with Andre bellowing at every misdemeanour – electrifying. She loved it. Correction: she *had* loved it.

Sitting down, opposite a glowing log burner, Freya's eyes were drawn – not to the flames – but to the wall of glass opening out onto the most glorious view of Devonshire countryside. There were green fields dotted with sheep, interspersed with arable fields – now just neatly tilled brown earth – with thickets and hedgerows patchworking the landscape. Already, the sinking sun was setting the sky alight with the same reds and yellows echoed in the little stove inside.

'It's so beautiful out there,' Freya said. 'Is this all your farm?'

'We are the custodians of all we survey,' intoned Martha mock solemnly. 'Every blade of grass. Every cow. Every sheep. It's a headache, and the workload is brutal, but we both appreciate how lucky we are. And bringing the boys up on the farm, too . . . It's all I ever wanted, and Ciaran thinks the same way. It's pretty much the only thing we agree on, now I think about it.'

'You're Australian?' queried Freya. There was a definite accent that she couldn't quite place.

Martha laughed. 'You and everyone else,' she said. 'I'm actually from New Zealand. The wild wastes of the north island, to be exact.'

'So, how did you end up here of all places?'

'You can't help who you fall in love with,' said Martha, cradling her mug and looking into the fire, dreamily. 'I was grape picking in France, one summer in a break from uni. I spotted Ciaran across a crowded vineyard and the rest is history.'

'Do you miss home?'

Martha shook her head. 'I miss family, sure, but this is home now. I swapped rolling hills and sheep for more rolling hills and sheep. Mind you, what Ciaran and I are trying to do is a whole different level of intensity here.

34

I'm permanently exhausted . . .' She smiled, but it barely reached her tired eyes.

'So, love at first sight, though! That's so wonderful. I can't imagine.'

Martha nodded. 'We had this amazing relationship, the first summer. It was intense, just felt so right, you know?'

Freya nodded, although she didn't.

'So, I left at the end of the season to finish my degree,' Martha went on, 'and it was hard to go, but in a way it was a test to see if what we had was real.'

'Then what happened?'

'I barely made it through the year. Couldn't think about anything or anyone else. Next summer, straight after graduation, I came over to the UK and there was Ciaran, waiting for me at the airport. He was a different man, in many ways. He'd matured. His parents had moved back to Ireland that year and he'd taken over running the farm. He had Finn helping, but the deli was open by then, so it was a stretch for them both. Sometimes I wonder if he married me because it was cheaper than employing staff!'

She laughed and Freya joined in dutifully.

'Finn and Ciaran's parents have such a lovely marriage,' Martha went on. 'Do you know them?'

Freya shook her head.

'They were an inspiration for Ciaran,' Martha continued, 'and they set the bar pretty high. I moved in with him and within months I was pregnant with the twins. I guess, when you know, you know.'

'It must be lovely,' said Freya wistfully, 'to just absolutely feel you're in the right place, at the right time, with the right person. That certainty . . .'

'I'm not saying it's not tough, though,' said Martha. 'We argue constantly about business, how to run the farm. I'm

35

in charge of certain things, Ciaran's in charge of others, but neither of us lack an opinion about what the other one is up to.' She barked with laughter. 'I can't recommend it. That said, how about you and Finn?' said Martha, giving Freya a nudge. 'He's kept you secret, the dark horse.'

'What? Oh, good God no!' squeaked Freya. 'Me and Finn? There *is* no me and Finn.'

'Really? I'm so sorry, I just assumed . . .'

Then, Freya felt like an interloper for the first time in this lovely, warm family home. 'I'm here under false pretences,' she admitted. 'Finn found me yesterday and took me home,' she said. 'It was so kind of you both to have me here today. I don't know what Finn said . . .'

'Nothing, nothing,' Martha gabbled. 'He phoned this morning and just said you needed somewhere to go. And then, of course, he texted us with your terrible news. He's a kind man, always picking up waifs and strays.'

Then Freya felt even worse. She was just a passing problem to be pitied and chucked a bone. Of course, she was. Why would it be anything else? 'He's been *really* kind,' she said to Martha, who was now pink with mortification at having put her foot in it. 'So have you.'

'I hope I'll see you again,' said Martha, earnestly. 'And - I'm just going to say it – you look good together, the two of you. I'm sorry I've made you feel awkward. I shouldn't have jumped to conclusions.'

Just then, Finn came charging backwards into the room, closely followed by the twins at full pelt, both carrying weapons, along with Ciaran's sheepdog Nelly, who was barking hysterically and getting under everyone's feet.

'I concede!' panted Finn, wiping away the faint sheen of sweat on his brow. 'You've killed me, fair and square. Can I play dead for a bit while I get my breath back?'

'Hey, you lot,' interceded Martha, 'how about a nice, quiet game of Cluedo before everyone's lunch makes a dramatic reappearance?'

Despite Martha's intentions, the Cluedo was nearly as chaotic as the Nerf gun battle. Daniel, being too young to understand the rules, played alongside Martha, who whispered constantly to him as he beamed from ear-to-ear at having his mother's undivided attention. The twins' strategy consisted of making wild accusations of everyone, including themselves, regardless of whether it was their go, and Alexander kept grabbing the brightly coloured characters off the board to put them in his mouth and then no one could remember where they had been. The whole thing was a riot and only ended when Finn, the dark horse who had been paying attention without seeming to, made a play and got all three cards right first time. It was also Finn who noticed Freya's eyelids beginning to droop.

'Someone's ready to go to bed,' he observed. 'I should get you back to the flat.'

'Or you could just go upstairs and have a kip here?' suggested Martha.

Freya was embarrassed to have everyone's attention on her. So much for having a crafty snooze without people noticing. 'I don't want to drag you away,' she told Finn, uncertainly.

'I've been dying for an excuse to leave, if I'm honest.'

'You only had to say, mate,' chipped in Ciaran, with a totally un-insulted grin.

'No, joking apart, it's been great but I've actually got a ton of work to do,' said Finn, 'shelf-stacking and stocktaking. The glamour.'

'You're not opening the shop tomorrow, are you?' said Martha. 'It's a bank holiday.'

'Not tomorrow, but Thursday I am. The day after Boxing Day was huge, last year, nearly as good as my sales leading up to Christmas. I don't want to miss out on an opportunity like that.'

'You work too hard,' said Ciaran.

'You'd know,' Finn shot back.

'You're *both* workaholics,' agreed Martha.

'Just as well,' said Finn. 'Come on, sleepyhead,' he added, grabbing Freya's outstretched hand and helping her up out of the sofa that seemed to have sucked her in permanently.

'Martha thought we were an item,' said Freya as they drove back to Portneath.

'Hah,' barked Finn, amused. 'She's determined to get me paired up and Ciaran's as bad. He's a zealous convert to married life, although he and Martha are constantly bickering, as you'll have noticed. There's nothing he'd like better than to see me happily settle down with a good woman.'

'And do you know any?'

'What? Any good women?'

Freya nodded. It was intended as a light-hearted tease, but suddenly the answer seemed important.

'I've "known" a few good women, if that's what you're asking,' he said, rolling his head towards her as he drove.

'I bet you have,' she replied, sourly.

'Ouch, Miss Judgemental,' he laughed. 'I'm sure you've not been holding back in your glamorous Parisian world, with all those hunky men. Or women. I'm not making assumptions.'

'*I'm* not a tart,' she snapped. 'And, as it happens, I'm not a lesbian either,' she added primly.

'I'm pleased to hear it,' responded Finn. 'On both counts.'

There was a silence, before he went on, 'Listen. I've always been completely honest in my relationships that my business is the most important thing in my life now. I've got ideas I want to develop, things to do . . . I don't have the time or mental energy for commitment at the moment,' he glanced at her, 'so don't get any ideas.'

'*Me?*' she squeaked, outraged. 'You flatter yourself,' she went on, blushing scarlet, feeling like her teenage crush on Finn *and* Ciaran was written all over her face. 'And I'm definitely not looking for a meaningless fling.'

'Sounds like the bed's all yours then,' said Finn, infuriatingly calm. 'You should go and get your head down,' he added as they went through the shop and up the stairs to his apartment. 'Seriously. You're shattered – and I've genuinely got some work to do in the shop.'

'I can't take your bed again,' protested Freya. 'I'll sleep on the sofa tonight.'

'Sorry, can't allow it,' insisted Finn. 'If it makes a difference, I'll be up for hours anyway, and when I do turn in, I'll be able to sleep on a clothesline so the bed's wasted on me.'

'I'll be out of your hair tomorrow.'

'Where to?'

'Home.'

'With no car? And no power? Listen, I've been thinking. There's somewhere – nothing fancy – where you can be for a few weeks, or for as long as you need. You need to stay in the middle of Portneath where you've actually got a bit of public transport too; you'll be stranded otherwise.'

'O-K,' said Freya, slowly. 'Where, exactly?'

'I'll show you tomorrow. Now get some rest.'

Chapter Five

Two Turtle Doves

When Freya woke again, it was dark and silent outside. Even the single street lamp just outside the bedroom window had gone out now, but the moon in the cloudless sky cast a wash of silver light across the bed.

Damn! She was completely awake. She knew from experience there would be no more sleep for hours. Suddenly the loss of her mother hit her again like a physical blow, leaving her reeling, her heart pounding as if she had been running. She was truly and absolutely alone in the world now; no one watching her back; no one whose job it was to cheerlead, comfort and advise . . . all that was finished now.

She breathed in and out deeply several times. Who was it who'd said grief felt like fear? It was true, it seemed. There were still no tears, just this nameless terror. This was how she felt when she was being screamed at by Andre, a common occurrence for all the team. The one thing that might work, she knew from experience, was distraction. Freya's ability to lose herself completely in a book had proved a lifesaver over the years she'd been away and so, resolving to find herself something diverting to read, she tiptoed into the sitting room. If she could just use her phone torch to have a look at the stuffed bookshelf without waking Finn . . . She had clocked it the day before and it had looked like mostly recipe books, which was perfect. Food was obviously as endlessly fascinating to Finn as it was to her. There was always something new to learn, some new method or combination of ingredients that sparked imagination.

'Freya?'

She jumped and spun around, stubbing her toe on the coffee table.

'Ouch. Damn,' she leaned down and rubbed her smarting foot.

'What are you doing skulking around in the dark, in the middle of the night?'

'Couldn't sleep,' Freya admitted, hanging her head, as Finn snapped on the light. 'I just thought I'd quietly get a book. I'm so sorry I woke you.'

'I was waking up anyhow. Cup of tea?'

He was so kind, thought Freya for the hundredth time as he handed her a steaming mug.

'I should have made hot chocolate really, to help us sleep. I would have needed to go downstairs for more milk. Perks of living above the shop.'

'This is fine.'

There was a silence.

'Thinking about your mum?'

Freya shook her head. 'I mean, yes. I was, of course, but I was also thinking about my job. Not that I've got a job.'

She related a brief version of the final conversation she and Andre had had, concluding with her being summarily sacked.

'The bastard!' said Finn. 'He can't do that, surely? What about employment laws? Probably different in France, but they must have some?'

'Andre can – at least he does – do what he likes,' Freya said. 'I left him in the lurch, to be fair. With Andre, people have been fired – nay, killed – for less.'

'Are you sorry?'

She sighed. 'Honestly? Coming home and losing Mum like this? I don't think I know what I want, any more. It was an amazing job though. I worked *so* hard, learnt *so* much . . . but it was tough.'

Finn nodded, listening.

'. . . and it took a while at the beginning for them to believe I was worthy of the opportunity. I was young, I'm really small, I'm a woman.'

'I have noticed these things about you,' said Finn with mock gravity.

Freya walloped him gently with a cushion. 'Yeah, but it shouldn't matter, though; I was as good as the men any day,' she insisted.

He held up his hands in surrender. 'I'm sure you were. I wouldn't want to meet you on a dark night, for sure.'

'I really *was* as good as any of them,' she went on, tilting her chin up, 'and I learned to be tough too. I never cried. Never in front of the team anyhow. Never.'

'I can't imagine how brutal it must have been for you. He's got a hell of a reputation, that guy. Even *I've* heard of it.'

'Yeah, Andre's got a way about him,' she admitted. 'But it's not just him, to be fair, it's the whole macho thing in the industry as a whole, it's endemic. The women have to be twice as resilient, twice as good.'

'And you're done with that?'

'Yeah, maybe,' said Freya. She was staring into the glowing embers of the fire, talking as if to herself. 'I was hanging on . . . and on . . . and on . . . meaning to come home. Always telling myself "just one more month". I was

42

head of my section, but I wanted to make deputy chef. If you've been deputy to a head chef like Andre, you can pretty much go and work in any other three-star restaurant you want. And once I made it, I was going to pack it in and leave. And I earned it. I deserved it,' she said fiercely, turned to Finn, as if she had just remembered he was there.

'Tell me more?' he prompted gently.

'Well, I'd worked my way around all of the sections over the years, just to learn, so I wouldn't have been ready until I'd done that, but the deputy position came up twice during the time I was *chef de partie*,' she said, her eyes flashing in anger, 'and *twice* he chose someone else. The first time? Yeah, OK, fair enough . . . The second time, it was a man who was junior to me, younger *and* less experienced. He'd been there half as long so basically he leapfrogged over me.'

'Was he better than you?'

'No,' insisted Freya. '*I* was better. But he was a man.'

'Sounds like you've got a case for constructive dismissal.'

Freya sighed wearily, shaking her head. 'Why bother?' she said, realising the facts as she said it. 'If I have to go to those lengths to be seen for who I am, for what I can do, then let's face it, there's no point, is there? If I kicked up a fuss it would get me nowhere, plus it would be impossible for me to carry on working there afterwards even if I did – technically – win the argument.'

Finn nodded slowly. 'So, what will you do? Will you stay in Portneath now?'

'It's hard to imagine there's genuinely any sort of life for me in Portneath,' she sighed listlessly, and took a gulp of tea. 'I don't even have family here now.'

'No family at all?' asked Finn. 'No aunts, uncles, cousins?'

'Nope. I'm an only child, Mum was an only child too and I never met my grandparents because they both died before I was born, my grandmother from the same cancer that killed Mum . . .' Her existential aloneness struck Freya afresh like a punch in the guts.

'She raised you as a single parent, I remember that,' reminisced Finn. 'I remember being impressed, she was great, but where's your dad?'

Freya shook her head. 'No clue.'

'Ever wondered?'

'Nope,' she said, briskly. 'Not really. Once or twice, when I was a stroppy teen and Mum and I fell out, I suppose.' *And now I will probably never know*, she thought, with a jolt. What if she *did* have family out there? Not just a father, but half-brothers and sisters perhaps? Had she missed her one chance to find out by not asking her mother before she died? It had been the last thing on her mind and now it felt as if it was the most important question of all.

Finn gave her a considering look. 'OK. So, say you stayed in Portneath,' he said, returning to his original point, 'what do you want to do? For work, I mean.'

'Oh, still cooking,' she exclaimed. 'I can't ever imagine doing anything else. It's just – and I don't mean to sound disparaging – Portneath isn't exactly the beating heart of high-end cuisine.'

'Don't be too hasty with your judgement,' said Finn. 'It's been ten years, remember? The deli's been going for seven of them, and I've got a growing core of pretty discerning customers. They'd all eat in a posh restaurant if there was one. There's money here now, seriously, and not just from the second-homes crowd. Plus, don't forget the tourists; they come here with good money to spend so they could account for a big chunk of your custom between Easter and autumn half-term. After all, look at what Rick Stein's done with Padstow.'

'Fair point,' she conceded.

They were silent for a while, drinking their tea. Finn watched her out of the corner of his eye. She looked so vulnerable, despite her tales of toughness and self-reliance which he didn't doubt for a minute. There she sat, curled up on his sofa, alone now, with the most important person in her life gone for good. His heart ached for her in every sense of the word. It was as much as he could do not to reach for her, to pull her against his chest, drop a kiss onto that golden, blonde hair tousled with sleep, wrapping her in his arms and . . . And the rest.

'So, what will you do for money?' he asked, determinedly clearing the image from his mind.

'I'll get a job. I *need* a job actually. Any job will do, just to give me an income stream straight away. There's so much to think about and I-I can't . . .' She swallowed, suddenly unable to speak.

'One step at a time,' said Finn, gently. 'It's Christmas. The world's asleep for a few days. Chill. Find your feet.'

It was true, thought Freya. Christmas was a golden time away from normal life, a magical hiatus where the world held its breath. Her shoulders dropped, just an inch.

Finn looked thoughtful as he sipped his tea. 'Here's an idea,' he began. 'What do you do to calm yourself when you need distraction? What's your "go-to"?'

Freya didn't hesitate. 'I cook,' she said.

'Right, so cook.'

'Cook what?'

'Why not challenge yourself to cook around the Twelve Days of Christmas?' he suggested. 'Let the song be your inspiration. You said you didn't do it on purpose, but your partridge with pears was amazing. What's next?'

'Two Turtle Doves,' said Freya, reluctantly, but she felt the slightest stirring of interest. It wasn't a terrible idea.

Creating new recipes was the most absorbing thing of all. She loved it. She had gained so much knowledge in the last ten years; the patisserie – her favourite specialism – and then the preparation of meat, fish, soups, sauces. Her skills were encyclopaedic now, but to repeat what she already knew felt like the worst kind of retrograde step. She had ducked out of life as she knew it, and here she found herself, staring into the void. No family, no job, no home . . . Maybe Finn was right; she should take her foot off the pedal and focus on her core passion. It could be the mental distraction that might allow the way ahead to become clear.

'OK,' she said slowly, 'but where?'

'My kitchen is at your disposal.'

'Like you said on Christmas Eve, you don't have a lot in. Not even those baked beans you offered, from what I could see.'

'Aha, but you are wrong, because I have the finest ingredients Devon can offer and more besides. My deli is at your service.'

Freya nodded, slowly and consideringly, her mind coming alive.

'So – right now – waddaya want to do?' he went on. 'Are you cooking or sleeping?'

She was light-headed with sleep deprivation, but she knew she couldn't go back to bed now. Finn was right, this was what she needed. And she already had an idea for her Boxing Day challenge.

'I'm cooking,' she declared.

Chapter Six

'Come with me,' Finn said, giving Freya a little bow and gesturing towards the door.

She followed him down the stairs. He ushered her into the storeroom and then through into the back of the deli, with its marvellous, complex smells of cured meats, vanilla, spices and cheese. She sniffed appreciatively as she looked around her. The light was dim, conferring an intimacy and mystery that would have been romantic in any other circumstances.

Freya gave a deep sigh of satisfaction. 'You go to bed. I'll cook,' she said.

'Sleep's overrated, I've decided,' he replied, rubbing his hands together. 'How about some coffee?'

God, what she wouldn't do for a good coffee. She peered at the large, shiny chrome coffee machine behind the counter in the café corner. 'I wouldn't know where to start.'

'It's easier than it looks,' he said, 'but allow me.' He brushed past her, his hands lightly touching her shoulders. He smelt of clean hair and cinnamon, with a hint of fresh, honest sweat. 'Latte, no sugar for you, right?'

In no time at all he handed her a large, steaming mug and made himself a double espresso which he gulped appreciatively with his eyes narrowed.

As she made her way around the delicatessen with a basket, assessing her potential ingredients, Freya was absorbed and even more impressed than she had expected to be. Since that first night such a short time ago she had been pining to explore further. The wine bottles glinted in their serried rows, and, studying the labels, she was intrigued to see many were produced from local vineyards; there was local cider too. She was a fan of cooking with cider – her mussels with cider, leeks and bacon were one of her favourite dishes – something humble, simple and perfect. She wasn't interested in cooking with rare and expensive ingredients just for the sake of it.

The cake and biscuit section had no boring digestives or custard creams, instead the shelves were piled high with Florentines, macarons, chocolate bonbons, and those little amaretti biscuits in twists of tissue paper like big, boiled sweets. The Italian shelf was stacked with dried pasta of every conceivable size and shape, tiny orzo, linguine, nests of fettucine and bricks of lasagne sheets. The bottles of olive oil and jars of antipasti; the whole garlic cloves with peppers, artichoke hearts and fat, green olives stuffed with almonds, gleamed pale gold and green in the low light. Although the shop was small, the number of product lines he stocked must run well into the hundreds. She had to hand it to him, Finn knew his food. She was impressed from a professional point of view, but also personally touched to see his obvious passion. She even, with a tug of nostalgia, noticed the gentleman's relish in its little white ceramic pots with black writing, reminding her of sitting with her mother in the afternoons, having round after round of hot buttered toast with the salty, anchovy paste scrapped sparingly on top of the pools of melted butter. They had sat side by side, in front of the Aga in their cosy cottage kitchen, chatting and eating companionably.

All the time in the world . . .

A lead weight of loss settled in the centre of her chest and, sighing, she looked around for a distraction.

As well as many delicious-looking local cheeses and breads, there were cured meats, oils and a host of more exotic ingredients. The real treasure trove was the meat cabinet where Freya finally hatched a plan for something to cook. Two pairs of pigeon breasts were the initial breakthrough, then she quickly collected together some unsmoked streaky bacon, some plump, herby pork sausages, a packet of lard, some unnecessarily posh-looking organic plain flour and, as a bonus, she even managed to dig out a large jar of crab apple jelly that said it came from Holly Tree Farm.

Finn finished his coffee and took Freya's basket from her so she could drink hers. 'Lard, eh?' he said, peering into the basket. 'Niiice.'

'There is a place for lard sometimes. You'll see.'

'Cool,' he said reaching for a pad of paper and a pen. 'I need to take a note of what you've got.'

'Oh of course!' Freya's stomach sank. 'I need to pay you for it. Can I owe you?' Andre hadn't paid her final pay packet, so it had left her pretty much broke. She was going to need to find that job. Any job.

'Don't be silly,' said Finn, dismissing the idea with a wave of the hand. 'It's for stock levels and reordering, that's all. And in any case, I wouldn't rule out selling in the shop whatever you are planning to make. What *are* you planning, by the way?'

'You'll see.'

Back in the flat, he stood, leaning on the door frame watching as she worked, absorbed in the task ahead.

'Here, now stir this for me as I pour the water in.'

She slid a large pottery mixing bowl over to him and handed him a wooden spoon.

'What are we doing with this?' he asked peering into the bowl at the lard, now roughly chopped.

'Pastry. Just add boiling water, then put it in with the flour and salt.'

'Really? Are you sure?'

'Wait till you smell it,' she laughed, measuring water from the kettle into a jug and emptying it into the bowl, being careful to avoid splashing him with the boiling liquid.

'Argh,' said Finn, pulling his head back rapidly as the stench of melting animal fat hit his nostrils.

'I know, gross,' laughed Freya, shaking the flour into a big mixing bowl and chucking in a small handful of salt. 'But when you taste it, all crunchy and golden brown? You'll forget what went into it then.'

She took the bowl of water and lard back off him and poured it into the well she had made in the centre of the flour.

'If the fat doesn't block your arteries, the salt will give you a stroke,' muttered Finn as she stirred it into a thick paste with a wooden spoon, 'Honestly, seeing what goes into it makes me think twice.'

'It's good, honest traditional food,' she said, unrepentant. 'Nothing the matter with it, once in a while.'

It was companionable having him sitting there while she worked. It felt good to be doing something, using her skills – skills that she had acquired over ten year's hard graft with Andre. Despite his terrible temper, the man was extremely talented and had been an inspiring teacher, Freya had to admit, with a pang of guilt. She was incredibly lucky to have had the opportunity. She had let so many people down, people who were important in her life, who cared for her . . . Andre, her mother, her few remaining friends in Portneath who she had not kept in contact with. The litany of sins threatened to overwhelm her.

'Hey,' said Finn, quietly, noticing. 'Everything's fine. Just cook.'

'I've never been in a kitchen so poorly equipped,' she complained mildly. 'What do you even eat?'

'I manage,' said Finn, without rancour. 'I'm up at the farm a lot. To be honest, Martha keeps me fed most of the time.'

'I like Martha.'

'She likes you. You could do with more people like Martha in your life,' Finn said. 'She's wise.'

Freya had been wondering what on earth she was going to cook this creation in and had stumbled, with relief, on a large, round cake tin with a removable bottom. It wasn't a proper raised pie tin, but it would do, she thought as she lined it with the hot water crust pastry, pressing it into the corners, making sure it was thin enough to be lovely and crispy but thick enough that it would hold its shape when she took it out.

Now she was neatly lining the inside of the pastry with streaky bacon before pushing in a layer of the herby sausage meat that she'd got Finn to squeeze out of the casings into a bowl.

'The things you make me do, Fred,' he had complained, following her instructions.

Now Freya was swiftly and expertly trimming fillets of smooth, pink meat with one of the knives from her precious knife roll.

'You're so sensible just to stock the breasts,' she commented as she worked. 'The rest isn't worth bothering with, really.'

'I'm glad you appreciate it,' he said. 'It's the real deal. I've got a friend who's a beater on a pheasant shoot on Broadmoor. I get pheasant from him – although I don't sell much – but he brings me a few brace of pigeon every once in a while and I stick them in the shop. They're a pest, basically. He keeps the numbers down so it's a win-win. Local wild meat? Nothing tastier. Or healthier.'

'Happy meat,' said Freya, understanding him perfectly.

Finn nodded. 'And the more local it is the better, if you're worried about the planet.' He grinned apologetically. 'Sorry, I do go on. But it's true.'

By now she was pressing in another layer of sausage meat before rolling out the circle of pastry she needed to create the top of the pie, crimping the edges all around to make sure the filling didn't leak out, and then pushing a wooden spoon in through the middle to make a steam hole.

'Is that it?' asked Finn.

'Not quite. Here comes the artistic bit. Don't laugh.' She was deftly cutting the remaining pastry with a sharp knife.

It was only when she had put the little shapes on the pie, that he saw.

'Cute!' he exclaimed. 'A pair of pigeons beak to beak.'

'They're kissing,' she said. 'And they're not pigeons, they're turtle doves. Same thing, nearly.'

'Ah yes, the twelve days. So, two turtle doves – the love-birds – and then, what's next?' asked Finn, remembering and singing softly, '"Three French hens . . ." So, what are you going to do for that?'

'I don't know yet, but I'll cook supper tomorrow night. As a thank you for all this,' she said, waving her hand.

'No need, but thank you,' said Finn. 'It's good to have you back, Fred,' he said quietly.

Freya made eye contact and was mesmerised by the intensity of his gaze. She dropped her eyes and, to stem the feeling of freefall, busied herself with the final touches to her pastry doves before sliding the pie into the gas oven that was humming purposefully in the corner of the kitchen. With the oven door open there was a blast of heat and the sudden warmth made Freya shudder. She had hardly noticed while she was making her pie, but the flat was cold and she was chilled through.

'Go have a hot shower and get dressed, while your pie cooks,' said Finn, noticing.

Dawn had fully broken outside now and, even though it was Boxing Day, the community in Portneath was beginning to stir. It was too late to go back to bed now. She would have to battle through the day in a sleep-deprived haze. Again.

'What are you going to do now?' she asked.

'Go back to bed?' he hazarded, yawning and stretching. Freya's eyes were drawn to the little strip of washboard stomach below his T-shirt. 'Actually, I can't do that, tempting though it is,' he groaned, lowering his arms. 'I haven't forgotten that thing I promised,' he said. 'Ask me tonight. And, in the meantime, *you* should get some more sleep. Help yourself to my bed.'

'Should I be worried that you keep inviting girls into your bed?' she teased half-heartedly. It was a pretty tempting offer though. 'You'll get a reputation if you're not careful.'

'Too late,' he grinned.

It came easily, this banter between them, thought Freya. She was less in awe of him than she had been as a teenager, because she was his equal now. She had seen the world and experienced things outside the little Portneath bubble that she had returned to. In that moment, with a twinge of regret, she remembered the camaraderie of the kitchen team in Paris, all of them competing of course, but looking out for each other too, teasing, playing pranks, sharing post-service drinks . . . That had been the upside. The downside was darker; she was always being required to be a certain way, say a certain thing, do things a certain way, and if she got anything wrong, there was Andre to rage at her for her stupidity. She couldn't imagine sitting with any of her old work friends – could she even call them that? – in her pyjamas in the dawn light, just chatting like this.

'It's Boxing Day,' Finn went on. 'What else do you need to do but rest?'

'Go back to the house, for one thing, I've got to start clearing it,' she said, and then kicked herself. She needed a lift and he knew it.

'I'll drive you,' he said, quickly. 'I need to pop up to the farm so I can drop you off on the way and then pick you up later. How would that be?'

'You're busy.'

'It's fine,' he said, not looking at her, his mind clearly on his plans for the day.

Chapter Seven

Seemingly sensing her need for space, Finn dropped Freya off in the road outside, promising to collect her at sundown. In daylight, the bleakly neglected state of the house was even more apparent. There was a pair of stone pots on either side of the entrance, the occupants long dead, with just a few brown stalks remaining. A gutter dripped from above the front door, pooling in a green puddle on the doorstep.

Freya's stomach sank as she pushed open the door and stepped inside. The familiar smell of home – roses, furniture polish and cooking – all that was gone now, replaced with dust, damp and a peculiar stillness as if the house was in a state of suspended animation.

Sighing, Freya pushed the heap of mail on the mat to the side with her foot. The letter was almost certainly in there somewhere, lurking amongst the pizza menus and unpaid bills. She had wimped out of getting it sent to her Paris address, reasoning she was bound to be making one of her lightning trips home in the spring – after the Christmas rush. Getting it sent here meant she and her mother could face the news – good or bad – together. That had been her plan. Now she would have to face it alone but later. Not yet.

Scrabbling in the desk drawers in the study she swooped on a pack of coloured stickers. Perfect. A brief rummage in the drawer of the dresser in the kitchen produced a roll of black bin bags, in their usual place. That hadn't changed in her entire life, she realised with a pang, and soon that 'place' would not exist any longer. How much of her old life could she salvage? How much of her old life *should* she try to keep? Maybe her future life would be here in Portneath, maybe many miles away, perhaps in a city or a country she had never been to. She felt as though she was standing, swaying in the wind, on top of a cliff edge of uncertainty.

She took a deep breath and began.

In the study, the process was easy. She put a blue sticker on everything to go into store for the distant day, in the almost unimaginable future, when she had a place of her own. So, that was the old oak desk with the leather inlaid top, the little swivel office chair her mother had always used and one of the filing cabinets – the rest could go to the auction house or, more likely, the tip, but what about the paperwork inside? Her mother had always been meticulously organised; it was one of the qualities that made her such a treasure everywhere she had worked.

'Right,' said Freya, aloud. The files were in alphabetical order and most, surely, could be thrown away? She started at 'A' and got stuck in.

You couldn't call the succession of jobs Freya's mother had taken to support them both a career. For several years she worked at Freya's primary school, so she could have the school holidays off and finish in time to take Freya home. She started as the school receptionist, and ended up as the business manager, working alongside the head teacher, with responsibility for pretty much everything except the teaching itself.

As she got older, Freya had been embarrassed about her mum working in the school and would refuse to go to the school office at the end of the day. Instead, her mum would have to come and stand in the playground to collect her just like the others. She felt bad about that now.

Then, when Freya was at Portneath High, Mum took a job at a solicitors' firm in Portneath, where she also made herself quietly indispensable. She was a clever woman, Freya knew, too good for the admin jobs she did, but she was not willing to do any work that required her to travel, or to work more than a minute past five o'clock. Her priority was Freya.

Freya had been a bit of a problem child. Bright, but not interested in school, to the frustration of her teachers; what she had loved most of all was her cooking. Her favourite memories were of being safely ensconced in the warm, cosy kitchen at home, teaching herself the essential skills of French cuisine while she waited for her mum to come home from work; all the pastries and classic sauces – bearnaise, hollandaise, béchamel; choux pastry and shortcrust – food had been a welcome escape from her not exactly stellar academic career. She remembered vividly when her mother had arrived home with a second-hand copy of *Larousse Gastronomique*, the bible of French cooking, and how she had vowed to work her way methodically through it. And she had, too. No wonder, eating the results, she had got a bit tubby.

They had been a team of two, always, with Freya well trained on her household duties from an early age. There had been no slacking and it wouldn't have occurred to her to moan and try to get out of her chores even though she knew many of her friends would whinge about having to do much less. It had been fun, in any case, the two of them turning the radio up loud on a Sunday morning and dancing to the cheesy eighties pop music as they hoovered and mopped.

The house was orderly. There were systems and a routine, the shopping done weekly by home delivery from a list on the kitchen noticeboard. And, because of that, when her mother became ill the first time, too ill to run the house herself, Freya had been able to take over. She was already chief cook in the house, working tirelessly to find something to cook that her mother felt able to eat when she was battling through chemotherapy. It had been a heavy burden, especially coming right in the middle of her GCSEs. Her schoolwork suffered because of it, and she came out with mediocre exam results but a wealth of cooking experience.

Having no father or siblings had already marked her out as strange to her friends from big families but her situation had also been, in some ways, enviable. The kids Freya hung out with always knew they were welcome at Freya's. They called Freya's mother by her first name and they would congregate in the warm, welcoming kitchen during the school holidays, lured by her sense of fun and propensity for turning out teetering piles of bacon sandwiches: thick wodges of buttered white bread with plenty of crispy, salty bacon and brown sauce or tomato ketchup on the side.

Freya's closest friend, Hattie, had more or less moved in there during their mid-teenage years with Anna delicately counselling her through her stormy relationship with her own mum, cajoling Hattie to appreciate her mum's point of view when another argument had seen her turning up at Freya's with a hastily stuffed rucksack.

Whatever had happened to her friendship with Hattie? How had they lost such a precious relationship? They had hugged fiercely when Freya had left for Paris, promising to keep in touch, come what may, and yet the texts and WhatsApps had tailed off as the years went by. And then, somehow, the conversation had stopped altogether. Months passed. Hattie had simply disappeared and, as for Freya? Well, she hadn't even noticed at first, had she? And then she had just not got around to making contact herself to find out what was wrong. Her life in Paris was just so vital, so all-consuming. Home friendships, even the one with Hattie, had felt so distant. If anything, she admitted to herself, perhaps the need to be tough and resilient, at least as tough as the men she was surrounded by, had made her dismiss thoughts of home for fear of being overwhelmed with homesickness. She had needed to appear tough at all times. There was no room for vulnerability or sentiment.

During the shamefully short and infrequent visits home, Freya had always meant to catch up properly with Hattie. The first couple of times she had made sure she did, but the meetings had seemed awkward, strangely devoid of the giggles and chatter at the core of their friendship before. A gut clench of guilt followed this reminiscence. She had been a bad friend to Hattie. And a bad daughter too, spending too much time away, pursuing her dreams.

Still, she should tell Hattie about Mum, at least – she would give her a call. No, maybe she would just send her a text. Later.

Pushing those uncomfortable thoughts to one side, Freya stood and tied the top of another bin bag, looking around. She was making decent progress. Ploughing through the alphabet, chucking out ancient tax returns that were filed under 'T', keeping the last few years' worth, just in case, her hand hovered over 'W' for 'Will' and hesitated. There was a slim file there – the last in the filing drawer. Freya pulled it out and looked inside. It was empty other than for a white envelope, addressed in her mother's strong, black unmistakeable writing. 'Freya', it said, with a kiss underneath it.

The envelope was not sealed, and Freya pulled out the single sheet of paper with a shaking hand, wishing Finn was there with her for solidarity. It was dated June that year – just weeks after her mum had made her magical, final trip to Paris.

My darling, darling girl,

You are reading this so I must have gone. I am so sad to leave you already. I hoped I would stay alive longer, just so I could see a little more of your story, to see you settled. I tried so hard, but that was not to be. I am sorry.

Only know, I love you so, so completely, in a way that only a mother can love her child – something I hope you will know yourself some day – and I am hugely proud of you, my lovely – your extraordinary talent, your bravery and your big heart that will serve you well whatever path you choose in your exciting, wonderful life.

I have left a proper will, of course, just to make sure but all you need to know about it is that everything of mine is now yours. Only keep what matters to YOU, and give everything else away, rather than be burdened by it. There is still a mortgage on the house, I am sorry to say, but there should be something left after you sell that will help you with your next steps. You need to go to the solicitor in East Street, John Makepeace. He is a good man and he will help you sort things out.

Godspeed, my darling, go and be amazing in everything you do. Be bold – but more than anything, be happy.

All my love, always,
Mum Xxx

Freya swallowed hard, folding the letter and sliding it carefully back in the envelope. Looking around, her eyes lighted on the mother-of-pearl inlaid box her mother used for random but important scraps of paper – receipts, lists, takeaway menus. Emptying it, after a cursory search for anything she should keep, she laid the letter reverently in its velvet-lined interior. Surely now the tears would come? She blinked, experimentally. Nothing. Did she not care? Was she not human?

Three hours later, the group of filled bin bags outside the front door had become a mini-mountain and Freya's stomach was rumbling. Two polite little bips on the horn heralded Finn's arrival. Freya watched through the kitchen window as he parked and climbed out, holding a brown paper bag aloft.

'Rations,' he said, coming from the hall into the kitchen where Freya had been listlessly sorting through the pan cupboard. He plonked a paper bag on the table and next to it he chucked the slew of envelopes and leaflets he had gathered up from the doormat, en route.

'You read my mind,' said Freya gratefully, looking at the paper bag and averting her eyes from the post. 'What have we got?'

'Salt beef and pickles with mustard, on rye,' he said, getting out two doorstop-sized sandwiches and handing her one. He took an enormous bite and, chewing, nodded for her to do the same.

Freya held the sandwich appreciatively, sniffing, examining, analysing. Finn noticed, and laughed. 'I know it's impressive, but I want you to eat it, not frame it.'

She slid out a slice of green, gnarly gherkin and nibbled on it. The vinegar hit the back of her throat and made her splutter slightly. The salt beef was still warm and there were generous, juicy slices of it, crammed into dense, nutty rye bread, with the top piece stained egg-yolk yellow with plentiful mild American mustard.

'Cured meat is dangerous in large quantities,' she said repressively, rebuking his sarcasm, 'it's been linked to cancer.'

'Yeah, well, I'll take my chances,' he grinned, unrepentant.

Freya took a bite. God it was good, though. She couldn't remember the last time she had eaten an actual sandwich. As always, the simple things, done well, were the best.

'So,' he said, standing up and brushing the crumbs off his hands. 'I've got a load of stuff for the tip in the boot of the car. I'll add those bin bags by the back door, shall I?'

'That would be amazing. What are you chucking out?'

'Just rubbish,' he said. 'Having a bit of a clear out. You've inspired me. I've got that surprise for you when I take you back, later, remember.'

'Actually, don't worry about picking me up. I was thinking I could stay here tonight.'

'We've had that conversation,' said Finn, his face brooking no argument. 'This place isn't liveable. Not without power. Anyhow, like I said, I have a surprise. Trust me. Now, shall I chuck this stuff away too?' He was gathering up the junk mail he had put on the table earlier.

'Hang on,' said Freya, shuffling quickly through the double-glazing flyers, pizza menus and red inked bills. She put the latter to one side. She must pay them and get things switched back on before the house went on the market. What she would pay them with was a problem she shelved for the time being. She dared not use her debit card as she was pretty sure her Paris rent had just gone out, which would have left her boracic broke. Andre owed her some money, of course, but she somehow doubted she would get it and was too overwhelmed with other priorities to fight for it. Plus, he scared her. An angry Andre was a formidable figure. She didn't think she could face that just now.

She was just wondering if perhaps the envelope wasn't there, when she saw it. Yellow, with the distinctive franking mark. Sight of the logo was enough to spark a wave of nauseating fear and dread. She picked it up by its edges, as if the paper itself could burn her and looked around her for somewhere safe to put it. To contain it. As Finn watched she lifted the lid of the inlaid wooden writing box she had taken from the study and put the envelope carefully inside, on top of the letter from her mother.

'Nice box,' he observed, tracing the ebony and ivory inlay in the lid.

'I've always liked it,' Freya admitted. 'I can't remember a time we didn't have it. I'm keeping it. For old time's sake.'

'Good,' he said. It was clear his mind was already on the next task. 'I'll pick you up on the way back from the tip,' he said, scrunching up the paper bag the sandwiches had come in and chucking it into the open mouth of Freya's current black plastic rubbish bag.

'I – that's kind, but I need to put a few more hours in here, really.'

'You're tired,' said Finn firmly. 'And it's nearly two o'clock already. You'll be losing the daylight in not much more than an hour in any case.'

'True enough,' conceded Freya. 'OK, I'll come back with you. Thanks.'

Finn was right. She was tired and that was why, when she heard his horn again an hour later, she had to admit to herself she had achieved little more.

63

She went out, with her mother's inlaid box under her arm, and slumped gratefully in the car seat, the box cradled carefully in her lap.

'So, what's my surprise?'

'Can't tell you,' he teased, tapping the side of his nose. 'It wouldn't be a surprise then.'

'I'm too tired for this,' she replied, grumpily but then pulled herself up short. He was being so kind. It was more than she deserved.

Chapter Eight

Arriving back in Portneath, Finn swooped seamlessly into a parking space on the High Street as its previous occupant left. Freya was glad there wasn't far to walk. She was knackered. They went up to the flat where Freya headed straight for the kitchen to check on her pie. It was cooled now, and looking delectably burnished and brown, with its cute pair of turtle doves shining with egg glaze.

'It looks amazing,' said Finn, 'when can we eat it?'

'Not quite yet – can my surprise wait while I do just one thing?'

'Sure,' said Finn, taking up his now customary position, leaning on the kitchen door frame so he could watch.

Freya looked at the pie consideringly as she tied on Finn's blue-and-white striped apron. It wrapped snugly around her hips as she tied the ends into a bow at the front. It was a movement of complete familiarity. Second nature. Taking down a small pan from the shelf she opened the small glass jar of crab apple jelly she had found in the shop, shaking it vigorously so the contents flopped out into the pan.

'What on earth are you doing now?' said Finn, intrigued.

'Finishing touch,' Freya explained. 'Jelly in through the hole in the top, so there's a layer between the meat and the pastry.'

'Like in pork pies?'

'Exactly.'

'But that's Martha's crab apple jelly. It's from the farm.'

'It looks like amazing stuff,' said Freya, sniffing the pan as the jelly heated through and liquified. 'Perfect, in fact. It would be a waste to just use a meat stock jelly. This is so beautifully sweet and tart, it complements the richness of the pigeon breast and sausage meat really well,' said Freya, rummaging around for the measuring jug she knew Finn had somewhere.

'That's so creative. It would never have occurred to me,' he said, wonderingly.

As Finn watched, she directed the ruby-red fluid into the hole under the beaks of the kissing turtle doves, pouring in a steady stream of now liquid and steaming crab apple jelly, filling the pie slowly and steadily until the very last moment before the jelly backed up through the hole.

'What now?'

'So, stick it in the fridge for a couple of hours and we can eat some this evening – if you like?' she looked at Finn anxiously. 'Some salad and maybe some chutney with it would be good,' she ventured.

'White or red wine?'

'Not sure,' said Freya, doubtfully, washing her hands and then taking off his apron, hanging it on the back of the door. The sommelier at Andre's would probably say a fruity, full white wine. A Viognier, perhaps. She didn't want to suggest something really expensive – she owed Finn enough as it was.

'I'm on it,' said Finn. 'Now, that surprise . . .' He ushered her ceremonially back to the little hallway of the flat and opened a door she had barely noticed before. Open, it revealed ascending wooden stairs, so steep they were practically a ladder.

'I don't actually like surprises,' protested Freya as they climbed the stairs, Freya first, making her conscious that Finn was looking at her bottom as he came up behind her.

'And also, by the way, I'm grateful you're letting me stay but I have to insist you let me sleep on the sofa tonight.'

'You can if you like,' said Finn with a crooked smile, 'but you don't have to. Look.'

They were now standing on a tiny square landing under the steeply sloping roof, where a skylight framed the darkening sky. In the twenty minutes since they had arrived back in town, the light had faded away and the stars were visible in a sky shading from navy to violet over the Portneath rooftops.

Finn pushed open a wooden door door with flaking paint and stood back for Freya to go past.

The little attic room was enchanting. There was a fluffy sheepskin rug on the floor, covering swept, bare wooden floorboards. Along one wall, tucked into the eaves, was a white-painted wooden bed, with a heart carved out of the headboard. It was piled with cosy patchwork quilts and blankets and had a pair of plump feather pillows in smooth, white cotton covers. In the middle, curled into a perfect circle, was Rafferty. He opened one yellow eye, observed them both with suspicion and then closed it again, tucking his nose firmly under his fluffy tail.

Freya, suddenly realising how tired she was, imagined being cocooned under the blankets, her hot, heavy head sinking into the downy pillow.

Next to the bed was a worn, grey-painted wooden chair, doubling as a bedside table. The sole item on it was a small table lamp, the single bulb glowing from within a dusky pink shade, creating a circle of warm light and throwing the corners of the room into darkness. There was little other furniture in the room, just a low chest of drawers under a single dormer window, topped with a foxed, pivoting mirror with little drawers in its dark wooden base. Next to it was a small, square bookcase, filled with recipe books; all the classics from Claudia Roden to Nigella Lawson. Freya recognised some of them from the bookcase in Finn's sitting room. He had clearly chosen them just for her. A two-bar electric fire was doing a good job of warming the little space too. It was all so cosy and inviting it reminded Freya of her old bedroom at home. She swallowed hard, trying to get rid of the lump in her throat. She wasn't going to cry. Not now. Not in front of Finn.

To distract herself, Freya went to stand in the window alcove, gazing out up the length of Portneath High Street, the road rising up to the ruined castle on the hill, its ramparts long rendered obsolete by the lack of need to watch for seaborne invaders through the night.

'I hope it's OK?' said Finn, leaning against the door, making the clutch of wooden clothes hangers hanging on the back of it rattle like bones. 'It was full of junk a few hours ago.'

'Hence the trip to the tip?' She smiled, with an effort.

'Exactly that,' he admitted. 'The bed's my sister's old one. I got it from Ciaran's loft. The mattress is new, though. It's not a bad one, I don't think. You should be all right . . .'

'It's brilliant,' said Freya, turning away from the window and sinking onto the bed.

Finn came and sat next to her, bouncing experimentally. Rafferty slid off, in a huff, and slunk out of the room. 'It's one of those memory foam ones,' he offered. 'They're supposed to be quite good.'

'I'm so grateful,' said Freya, feeling exhaustion pulling her down into the bed, her bones aching with tiredness now. 'It's incredibly kind. What can I do in return?'

'Well,' said Finn, tapping his cheek, 'there is one thing . . .'

'Thank you,' she said, leaning over to peck him on the cheek, just as he turned towards her, his mouth open to speak. Their lips collided and time stopped in its tracks; a powerful wave of lust pulsed in her core and rolled outwards, sweeping her away in its wake. But then – what was happening? – Finn was pulling away from her and jumping up off the bed like a scalded cat.

'Ker-ist,' he said, panting. 'What just happened?'

'Sorry,' gabbled Freya, a crimson flush of humiliation bursting out onto her cheeks. She too leaped to her feet, forgetting about the sloping ceiling. Finn reached out and pushed her head down just in time to avoid her slamming it against the wall. 'Watch out,' he said reflexively before snatching his hand away again and taking a step back.

'I was just going to say you can let me have my bed back,' blurted Finn. 'And then you—' He waved his hand at where they had just been sitting. 'Listen, I'm sorry if I gave the wrong impression,' he said, 'and obviously, you're a very attractive woman, but I would never ask . . . never expect . . .'

'No, OK, so,' said Freya, aiming for briskness to dismiss her embarrassment, 'totally understand . . . business and pleasure and all that.' God! OK, it was an awkward moment, but that was an earth-moving kiss – surely he had felt it too? Obviously not, though. He was clearly horrified and now she was pretty horrified herself. Her face felt as if it was on fire with mortification. She pressed her hands to her cheeks, feeling the heat. 'How much do you want for it? The room, I mean.'

'Nothing,' yelped Finn, but then, seeing her expression, he relented. 'OK, pay me some rent for it, if you must. Bed and board, fifty quid a week, how does that sound?'

'Ridiculously low,' said Freya, thinking that she couldn't even afford that, at the moment. 'Call it sixty and it's a deal.' She held out her hand.

Finn reached for it and pumped briefly. 'Done,' he said.

'Good grief,' he murmured to himself as he left her to settle in, 'what the hell just happened?' He hadn't known her well before she went away, not nearly as well as he had wanted to, he reminisced – but where had that come from? That kiss, that vortex . . . he wasn't sure he had ever felt that intensity before with anyone. He'd been attracted to women, of course he had, and was careful to make sure the women he got involved with had the same objectives that he had and were not in the market for anything serious and permanent. He was too busy for that.

Maybe this had been a mistake, he mused, letting Freya into his life where – somehow – chatting, cooking, sharing ideas, felt so much more compelling and intimate than anything he had experienced with any other woman. She was good company – hell, they were good together, he wasn't denying that, but it didn't have to be a romance. That was a bad idea.

He was starting to hatch a plan, a business partnership, strictly work, so avoiding romantic attachments – any distractions at all – was critical. He wasn't going to make that rookie error, however much his brother and Martha thought they would love to see him and Freya together. He knew the pitfalls of mixing business and romance. Hadn't he seen Martha and Ciaran argue constantly over how to run the farm? It was exhausting to watch, plus it was the last thing he wanted to put Freya through, with all the other stuff she was having to deal with. Clearly, Martha and Ciaran had demonstrated that business was better kept well apart from love.

It was chilly in her little attic room – she had switched off the ruinously expensive heater for the sake of Finn's electricity bill – but Freya didn't mind the cold. Under a pile of blankets and quilts in her narrow child's bed, she felt safe and cosy, but sleep eluded her. She ought to have been able to nod off because she was exhausted and well fed too. She and Finn had both had a fat slice of her 'Two Turtle Doves' pie with a warm salad of roasted new potatoes, squash and fennel on mixed leaves. It had been delicious – and if she carried on eating like that, she was going to start putting on weight. She prodded her hip bones experimentally. They definitely seemed a bit more well covered than before. Freya wasn't vain about her weight or any other aspect of her personal appearance, but she knew she could do with gaining a few pounds. Her punishing work life had taken its toll. She had pined pointlessly for longer legs as a teenager, but she was used to being short now. No, she would definitely never be glamorous – not glamorous enough to interest someone like Finn, anyhow. He had made it clear he had zero interest in all that. No, the one flaw in the evening was that the conversation had flowed a little less easily after their unexpected and deeply disturbing clinch. Neither of them could quite meet the other's eye. She groaned at the memory, furious at herself for giving in to a ridiculous impulse. Not only was Finn mortifyingly uninterested, but neither should *she* be with such enormous questions and challenges facing her. Freya hugged herself, tears pricking at her eyes. With all big life decisions before, she had relied on her mother as a sounding board. They would drink gallons of tea together, turning the issue under consideration this way and that, talking it through endlessly until Freya had complete confidence in what she had decided to do. But that was all over now – she was on her own in the world. The future was bleak.

Her mother's inlaid box now sat on the little chest of drawers, the yellow envelope burning a hole in her soul, reminding her of her lie at her mother's deathbed. She wasn't ready to face what was inside that letter, the potential bombshell with the possible devastating effect on her future, ranging from how long she might live and how she might die to the potential impact on her children – or even whether she had any children . . . But she had enough to think about without that. She needed to work out what to do next about her career. Never mind her career, she just had to find a job. And soon.

Lying there, she tentatively probed her anxieties over Andre and her life in Paris. Replaying their final conversation made her wince nearly as much as the accidental clinch with Finn. She had been wrong to frame the urgent return to Portneath as 'family issues', then refuse to elaborate, but frankly, she had known she could not repeat for Andre what her godmother, her mother's lifelong friend, Diana had told her by text: that her mother was desperately ill, that she should return now or risk never seeing her again. Freya had never shown emotion in front of Andre. Girly tears, or any other display of vulnerability, had always been a complete no-no. With the benefit of distance, though, she could see she had been unfair to Andre by not being truthful. No wonder he had lost his temper and sacked her on the spot.

She had left immediately, of course, hastily packing her bag in the cramped, shared flat because she had wanted nothing more than to flee to the warm familiarity of her childhood home town, to her schoolfriends, to the house, to her memories of her life with her mother . . .

Who had she been kidding?

In her ten-year absence the world had evolved and her previous life here was just a memory now. Surely there was no going back? She was so glad she had seen her mother one last time, but she was just beginning to be angry that Diana had not texted her sooner. And why had her mother hidden the cancer's return? She should have been there for her mother's final illness, after a decade – a lifetime – of her selflessness, of putting Freya first. 'Your career's the key thing,' she would say, in their all too brief, all too infrequent phone calls and meetups. Not that her mother would ever call her, except on her birthday. She never wanted to intrude, to interrupt or interfere. Now Freya just wished she had called home a bit more often herself.

She had had a huge clear out of her childhood things before she left for Paris, she remembered. Now, the majority of her worldly belongings were still in her flat in France. There wasn't much, though. A few clothes, an armful of precious cookery books. Her second-hand copy of *Larousse Gastronomique*, a couple of favourite recipe books by Julia Child . . . Irritatingly, she had left her phone charger behind too but hadn't bothered asking Finn if she could borrow one. It hardly seemed to matter, not having a phone when the only person she wanted to speak to would not be calling her. Never again. She no longer had anyone she needed to call either. Not even Hattie. Especially not Hattie, actually, as she had let her old friend down so badly she couldn't face taking responsibility for that just at the moment either. No, her life was a mess. It was official.

As for her possessions, she would have to arrange for some things to be sent on, but most could just be donated to the other flatmates. Her worldly possessions in Portneath consisted, more or less, of the clothes she wore, plus a spare set, a phone without a charger and a debit card for a bank account with nothing in it. To survive in Portneath without being totally reliant on the generosity of friends, she was going to have to find a way to get hold of some money. Tomorrow, the job search was on.

Chapter Nine

Three French Hens

Next morning, she found Finn in the storeroom at the back of the shop. He was stocking the shelves, ready for opening for the first time since Christmas Eve. He looked preoccupied but greeted Freya warmly. Awkwardness at the disastrous kissing incident had dissipated, at least for now, it seemed.

'I've made you a coffee,' he said, inclining his head in the direction of the vast coffee machine.

She fetched it and gratefully inhaled the steam. 'Perfect, thank you. How did you know I was up?'

'It was either you or a herd of wildebeest in the bathroom,' he teased.

'Rude,' she replied, taking a blissful gulp of coffee. She would forgive anything of a man who made coffee this good.

She refused breakfast, even though the croissants, just delivered and still hot, were piled into a basket in the café area and smelling heavenly. 'God knows what time Brian the baker had to get up to do these,' said Finn. 'One of these with unsalted butter and cherry jam? You're turning down heaven on a plate,' he complained, but Freya was resolute. She might need to gain a pound or two, but it was going to be a stone or two at this rate. And in any case, she had to get on.

Freya left Finn to finish setting up shop for the day. He was

74

expecting to be busy, with all the post-Boxing Day malcontents spurning yet another turkey sandwich and seeking something more exciting to tempt their jaded palates. He had happily accepted the remains of the turtle dove pie and planned to sell it by the slice in the deli for a premium. It would wipe out Freya's debt to him for the ingredients and he would pass on the profits, he had insisted, intuiting that Freya was desperate for a chance to even up what she clearly saw as the 'score' between them. In short, Freya didn't like being beholden to people. Not even him. Actually, especially him. She had made that clear.

The High Street was nearly empty as Freya wandered, with no particular plan, up the hill. Here and there, shop lights were on and there was bustle inside them as, like Finn, proprietors prepared to open. Surely one of these shops would be looking for staff? There was the burger bar that Freya remembered opening to the glee of the young people and horror of the reactionaries who were terrified the town would turn into a massive drive-through. She could maybe get a kitchen job there. Or even waitressing.

Then, there were antique shops that didn't let you in if they didn't like the look of you. These rarefied emporiums were standing side by side with what were basically junk shops whose owners were happy to take anyone's money. Freya had loved poking around them for hours with her mum, spending pocket money on one treasured find or another. Her room had been cluttered with her finds, but she had cleared the lot away, doing a car boot sale of everything except bare necessities once she knew she was going to Paris. She had dumped her life in Portneath and walked away without looking back, she remembered. Now, here she was again, as if nothing had changed. In truth, everything had.

Freya walked past the tea shop with its towers of cakes and scones, and the funny little stationers with the beautiful leatherbound notebooks lined with marbled paper and the covetable novelty Post-it notes that Freya amassed a huge collection of to help her with schoolwork. After deservedly mediocre GCSE results, she had buckled down and become the model pupil for A levels, at least for a while. Of course, to the chagrin of her teachers who were encouraging her to pick universities, she had obeyed the siren call of haute cuisine just after her eighteenth birthday, gleefully emptying her rucksack of her textbooks without a second thought. She had quickly packed the barest of her possessions, dumping her A-level studies with just months to go, setting off for Paris to pursue her love of food instead. Her mother had been concerned, of course she had, but Freya had been adamant. Consequently, now back in the real world, her CV was looking very thin indeed. She was qualified for nothing, except a very particular style of cooking that seemed to have no place in parochial little Portneath.

The town clock, in the arch across the High Street, showed a few minutes to nine o'clock, she noticed as her calf muscles started to burn with the incline. The clock was a strange little feature that set Portneath apart from other towns and Freya had always loved it. It was halfway up the steep, ancient High Street, lined either side with a hodgepodge of buildings, the frontages ranging from Tudor to Georgian, all leading to the ruined castle on the summit. The clock tower structure itself stretched from the Star Cross Tea Rooms on one side to The Book Mine second-hand bookshop on the other. The span in the middle incorporated the clock itself and, behind it, a strange little room, suspended in the air above the High Street, with windows on both sides. At sunset, Freya remembered, the little room was suffused with a golden glow, the rays of the low sun slanting right through from one side to the other. She would daydream about what it would be like to live there, poised above the hustle and bustle. But this was morning, the empty room was shaded, and the High Street was all but deserted.

Freya had no idea who would be open today and who would be gratefully taking a break for the entire time between Christmas and the New Year. She needed, in no particular order, a job, an estate agent and, remembering her mother's letter, a visit to this solicitor, John Makepeace.

Maybe she could tackle that first. The solicitor's office, which was right where she'd thought it was, on the corner of the High Street and East Street, looked dusty, dark and very closed. She could imagine the John Makepeace, Esquire, of Makepeace, Morley and Bulmer Solicitors as an elderly, portly gentleman, sitting with his feet up and his slippers on, eating mince pies and watching *It's a Wonderful Life*. Fine, the legal stuff would have to wait for another day, she thought, pushing her hands deep into her pockets to keep them warm and thinking hard for a moment. What she needed was a job centre or employment agency but there was nothing like that in Portneath. She glanced back down the High Street, towards the little deli at the base of the hill.

Damn. Now she was thinking about Finn again, when she had other things to deal with. As well as her many other issues, she felt an urgent need to get her situation with Finn onto a more formal footing, so as not to take advantage of his kindness. She was glad he had agreed to her paying him rent for the little attic room. That was as it should be. In her world, you didn't get something for nothing. A flush surged, burning, up her neck to her face as she remembered pressing her lips onto his, the mortification of him politely unwrapping her and recoiling to get beyond her grasp! How would she ever live it down?

The answer, she soothed herself, was evident in the easy, normal chat they had returned to this morning, of course. Everything felt easy with Finn. He was just that kind of person. He was someone who would naturally be kind to an old friend – barely an acquaintance really – that he had bumped into, soaked through on a winter's night, with nowhere to go. It was nothing. It meant nothing.

By now, continuing up the hill as she thought, she found herself nearly level with the bus stop at the top, by the castle gates. Maybe she should check out the timetable, to see if she could get to Middlemass and do some more clearing at home? She was holding the key inside her pocket, its deeply familiar weight and curves like a talisman, warm in her hand.

There was a figure huddled in a dark anorak standing at the bus stop with its back to her. As she approached, the figure turned and, even with the anorak hood up, the recognition was instant.

'Hattie!' Freya called, crossing the road, her heart thumping nervously. 'Omigod, Hats, this is unbelievable!'

Hattie's eyebrows shot up, then they lowered and she gave Freya a thin smile.

'Hi, Freya,' she said, in a strangely unemotional voice. Not 'Fred' then. She'd only ever been 'Freya' when Hattie was annoyed about something.

'I can't believe it's you,' enthused Freya, doing her best to maintain her upbeat attitude in the face of such antipathy.

'I didn't know you were back,' Hattie said dismissively.

Freya could tell she was lying – but why?

She felt off balance at her old friend's obvious enmity. 'Yeah, no,' she stumbled. 'I've not been here long. I was going to call but my phone . . .' She trailed off. 'It's been a really long time. How long's it been?'

'Since you left, or since we lost touch?' sneered Hattie. 'Although actually, never mind, cos it's pretty much the same thing, isn't it?'

'Oh God, Hats, I know,' said Freya, hanging her head. 'I've been rubbish. A terrible friend. It's been . . .' She trailed off again, chilled by her old friend's lack of enthusiasm for their reunion.

'I did text,' said Hattie. 'Quite a bit. At first, that is.'

'Yeah, I know,' admitted Freya. 'And I said – one time – that you should come out and join me and have a holiday in Paris, didn't I?'

'Yeah, you did,' said Hattie. 'And you said you'd send the money for the ticket. But . . .'

'. . . but I never actually did,' said Freya, remembering with shame. She shuffled her feet, staring down at the ground. 'I'm really, really sorry, Hats.'

'Naturally, when you offered, I assumed you were earning a mint and it would be no problem, what with your stellar career,' Hattie went on. 'Stupid of me, I know. I ought to have paid for it myself, of course, but money doesn't exactly grow on trees if you're stuck in Portneath.'

'Listen, Hats, come and have a coffee, with me,' said Freya, brightening as she saw the Osteria owner turning his 'Closed' sign to 'Open'.

'I can't,' said Hattie, miserably. 'I'm waiting for the bus. I've got a shift.'

'Where?'

'The industrial estate, out of town. Paynton's.'

'The cake place? Is that still going?'

'Puddings. It's a major employer here now,' said Hattie. 'There's not much else going around. Not in the winter. Listen, there's my bus. I've got to go,' she said, turning to the bus that was rumbling up the hill.

'I'm not losing you again that easily,' said Freya, catching her friend's coat sleeve as the bus's brakes screeched on. 'Are they hiring?'

'What, you? Working in a pudding factory?'

'Why not,' said Freya, swinging onto the bus and peeling off one of her last two tenners for the fare. The driver laboriously counted out a heavy handful of change, scowling.

She flung herself down next to Hattie on the narrow bench seat, making Hattie shuffle along closer to the window, shrinking away from her, her body rigid with tension.

'I really am sorry about not keeping in touch,' said Freya. 'It's totally amazing to see you again.'

Hattie turned. 'You can't seriously want a job at Paynton's.'

'I can.'

'What about the whole fancy chef thing?'

'Am I in Paris being a fancy chef?' Freya enquired, looking down at herself and holding her arms out from her sides. 'What do *you* think?'

'Are you back to stay, then?'

'Dunno,' admitted Freya, 'but what I *do* know is: I'm here now, I'm broke, and I've got rent to pay. Plus, I love a pudding, who doesn't?' she added, remembering the amazing Paynton's Christmas pudding Martha had given her on Christmas Day.

Hattie looked unconvinced.

Was this the time? thought Freya. She knew she had to tell Hattie about her mum. They'd been close and she deserved to know. That said, Freya didn't think she had it in her to upset her old friend even further at the moment. There would be time enough for bad news later. She would do it soon, just not today, she decided cravenly.

Hattie's body language had thawed slightly by the time they were getting off, along with several others, at the edge of the industrial estate, north of the town.

'So, *are* there vacancies, do you know?' asked Freya a little less confidently, as the bus pulled away and they walked towards a low, vast, flat-roofed factory building with 'Paynton's Puddings' looped in red writing down the side.

'There's always vacancies,' shrugged Hattie. 'You'll need to go and ask for an appointment with Sharmayne. She's the boss's daughter so she's Head of – oh, well, everything she fancies being head of, basically.'

Freya wasn't liking the sound of this woman.

'You'll recognise her from school,' Hattie went on. 'Actually, you might not, she looks a bit weird nowadays.'

'What? Do you mean "Sharmayne" the one who got suspended every other week for stapling her skirt up to crotch length?'

'That's the one,' said Hattie, 'but shhh,' she added, looking about her nervously, 'she has her spies everywhere.'

'Doesn't do to upset the management before I've even started,' admitted Freya, not bothering to lower her voice. 'OK, well, wish me luck?'

Hattie nodded shortly.

'Right, see you later,' said Freya, rubbing her hands together.

'Sure,' said Hattie, seemingly without enthusiasm, but the corner of her mouth quirked into a smile, and, for the first time since they had bumped into each other, she met Freya's gaze properly. 'Good luck,' she said.

It was obviously shift-changeover for the entire factory; people scurried around, those leaving shouting goodbyes at each other and those arriving disappearing behind the respective Women's and Men's changing-room doors across the hall from the entrance.

Freya approached a reception desk. There was a formidable, middle-aged woman sitting at it, filing her nails whilst holding a phone between shoulder and ear and talking loudly to someone called Linda.

Freya waited for her to end her call, and then cleared her throat politely. 'I think I need to speak to Sharmayne?' she asked.

'Appointment?' the woman barked, looking Freya up and down suspiciously.

'No.'

'Sit,' instructed the woman, pointing to a narrow bench running along the wall.

Freya sat.

She whiled away several minutes, looking around her, reading the health and safety announcements and the lottery sweepstake results for the previous week. It seemed the workforce were keen amateur gamblers as there was a bingo night and tickets for a raffle at the New Year's Eve party too. Clearly, working in a pudding factory was quite the social whirl.

Just as she was summoning the courage to tell the fierce receptionist she was going to leave the woman nodded sharply at her and jerked her thumb towards the door on the left.

'In there,' she ordered, before returning to filing her nails.

Hattie was right. Sharmayne looked nothing like she had at school. Granted, their schoolmate had always had a thick layer of forbidden foundation and equally thick mascara and that bit was still true, but things had gone a lot further since then.

Sharmayne, wearing a grey business suit that was a little too tight, was sitting poised behind a capacious desk. It was bare apart from a rose-gold MacBook and an arty black-and-white photograph of herself pouting ostentatiously. Freya briefly wondered at the personality of someone who thought it was normal to have a photo of herself on her desk.

In the photograph, and in real life, Sharmayne had an enormous mane of expensively blonded hair with extensive hair extensions – she had been mousey at school – and eyelashes that were so exaggerated and so apparently heavy that her eyes seemed to be being forced half closed, making her tip her head back slightly to meet Freya's gaze. Either that or she was looking down her nose at her.

'Hi, Sharmayne,' said Freya. 'It's nice to see you again.'

'So, back from your fancy Paris restaurant, then?' Sharmayne sneered. 'Didn't work out? Your big chance?'

'I suppose not,' laughed Freya. 'But you know what they say . . .'

'No,' said Sharmayne sharply, as if she didn't like admitting not knowing the answer. 'What do they say?'

'Oh, I dunno, "You're only as good as your last" whatever,' said Freya, waving it away. Her shattered career was the last thing she wanted to talk about. Especially to this scary, ex-schoolmate who had never been a friend for reasons that were now coming back to Freya quite clearly.

This nugget of empty wisdom seemed to satisfy Sharmayne, who gave a little nod. 'We're looking for hard workers. Zero-hour contracts,' she barked. 'No slacking, no tardiness, no unauthorised absences. You'll work eight-hour shifts, five shifts a week, six when we're busy, which we are,' she went on, 'otherwise don't flatter yourself I'd be taking you on.'

Freya stifled a laugh. God, she was a monster. Even worse than she and Hattie had thought when they were all at Portneath High.

Sharmayne was still talking. 'Paynton's was the fastest growing FMCG in the Food Manufacturing Awards, three years running,' she barked. 'Cakes and Pastries category. We've become quite an international success story since I came on board,' she declared, smugly.

'Your dad was pretty successful when we were at school, from what I remember,' said Freya.

Sharmayne looked at her, infuriated. 'It needed bold strategies to get us where we are today though,' she persisted.

'And that'll be your influence, I'm sure,' said Freya. Maybe a bit of sucking up was called for. She wanted the job, after all.

'Right. No time like the present,' said Sharmayne. 'You can start your induction now. I'll get Hattie to show you around. You'll remember her. I seem to recall you spent quite a lot of time in detention with each other.'

'Ah, those were the days,' said Freya. It was true, Hattie had usually been her running mate when they were getting into trouble. It was nothing heavy – they would never have dared to bunk off or get into a fight, but they had played some legendary practical jokes, largely targeting the teachers with the least highly developed senses of humour. They had even got detentions just for laughing – huge, helpless, breath-stealing giggling sessions at the slightest thing. Freya couldn't remember having laughed like that with anyone since. Not since she left for Paris. The French sense of humour was a very different creature.

Within twenty minutes of her interview, Freya was kitted out with a hideous hairnet, blue overalls rolled up several times at ankle and wrist, and some seriously clumpy rubber clogs. She looked like an Oompa Loompa. She shared this observation with Hattie, who bestowed another reluctant smile on her.

The factory was the size of a couple of football pitches, high-ceilinged, echoey and noisy. People in identical garb trotted around the massive stainless-steel vats and others stood at an assembly line, packing cloth-wrapped Christmas puddings into rapidly constructed cardboard boxes from a high, flat pile on the end of the conveyor belt.

The air was redolent with spices and fruit.

'It smells like Christmas,' shouted Freya into Hattie's ear. 'Amazing.'

'You get a bit fed up with it after a while,' Hattie shouted back.

'This is next year's batch, I suppose,' said Freya. 'People won't be buying them 'til next winter, surely? What do you do with them until then?'

'We keep them for at least ten months,' said Hattie, pulling Freya out of the way as two burly, bespectacled men holding clipboards walked past talking earnestly. 'It's on the wrapper. You must have seen? They improve with age, apparently.'

'Sharmayne hasn't improved with age,' said Freya.

Hattie gave her a scandalised look. 'Shh,' she said, suppressing a genuine grin at last. 'She's our boss now, remember.'

'I don't think she's going to let us forget it,' Freya responded, relieved that Hattie was now at least speaking to her a bit more normally.

Looking around the factory, Freya's heart sank. Sharmayne had mentioned a pretty lousy hourly pay rate, and an eight-hour shift was going to feel like a very long time indeed. That was the one thing you couldn't complain about, working for Andre; the work was so intense the time flew by. Still, this represented an income, something she urgently needed, and it meant she could stay in Portneath, paying her way, until she decided what to do with her life.

Chapter Ten

Ciaran came into the shop backwards, carrying a large cardboard box, which he put on the floor behind the delicatessen counter.

'Cheese?' queried Finn, after he had finished packing his customers' purchases into her basket and wished her goodbye.

'Yep,' said Ciaran, standing up straight and holding his lower back with both hands. 'Two of the smoked Cheddar, plenty of the next batch of sheep cheese – you said you were running low – and one block of extra-mature Cheddar too, but that's the last of that for now. How's it going?'

'You've just missed a big rush. I knew I'd be glad I opened today,' said Finn.

'No peace for the wicked.'

'Talking of which, how's lambing?'

'Up since three this morning,' admitted Ciaran, yawning and stretching hugely. Finn reached out and diverted his brother's arm from sweeping jars of chutney off the shelf behind him.

'Well, if you must do this farming business,' he said, but there was sympathy in his tone. 'Coffee?'

'God, yes.'

Finn busied himself with the coffee machine and Ciaran watched him thoughtfully as he worked.

'So,' said Ciaran as Finn handed him an espresso cup, 'What about Freya turning up like that, eh? Just in time for Christmas.'

'Just in time,' echoed Finn neutrally.

'Martha's got some interesting views on the subject.'

'I bet she has.'

'Rarely wrong about affairs of the heart, my wife.'

'And here's the exception that proves the rule,' insisted Finn evenly, refusing to rise.

'Wouldn't do you any harm to give a bit of attention to that side of things,' Ciaran pressed. 'You're not getting any younger.'

At this Finn laughed, explosively. 'Speak for yourself, older brother, I'm only thirty-two.'

'Yeah? Well, time flies and you don't want to be "that guy", going after the younger women with the bigger and bigger age gap.'

'Age gap? For heaven's sake. What are you like?'

'Just saying, you haven't got forever. Being a dad's a young man's game, I tell you, those kids are giving me grey hairs.'

'Yep, you're really selling it. Listen, Freya and me, it's . . .' He cast around for something that would make his brother understand. 'You remember when we found the kittens, at the farm, and it looked like they'd been abandoned, all cold and wet, curled up in that tractor tyre, looking up at us with those wide eyes?'

'Yeah, sure, we stuck them in a box in front of the Aga and fed them with a pipette. They all survived, I remember.'

'That,' said Finn with finality.

'So, it's your rescue reflex kicking in?' said Ciaran.

'Exactly,' said Finn again, glad his brother was being successfully diverted.

'You always were wanting to rescue the women you sleep with – or was it sleep with the women you rescue?' Ciaran pretended to scratch his head in puzzlement.

'That's rubbish,' snapped Finn. Clearly his brother was *not* being successfully diverted. 'And I'm not sleeping with her. What's more, I'm not *going* to sleep with her. That's the last complication she needs at the moment. She's just a friend. Plus, well . . .' He hesitated, wondering whether to share. 'I might have a business proposition for her, not sure, at this stage, so I don't want anything getting in the way of that or making it complicated.'

'Something we should be discussing?'

'I'll run it by you. Soon,' Finn promised.

'Don't let work be the only thing in your life, little bro,' counselled Ciaran.

'Don't do as I do, do as I say,' needled Finn. 'You're one to talk. When did you and Martha last have a date night?'

'Never you mind,' said Ciaran, looking uncomfortable. 'She's a trojan, my wife, she knows the score. That's why I married her.'

'Can't see you having any more children with an attitude like that,' teased Finn.

Ciaran paled. 'I don't bleeding *want* any more children, thanks. Four's at least one too many as it is. Especially when two of them are the terrible twins.'

'I feel your pain,' said Finn, deciding to let him off. He meant well, his brother, but he – Finn – was perfectly capable of running his own life without interference; and a girlfriend, especially someone with Freya's issues, was a complication he could do without.

Work was all consuming, and that wasn't a bad thing, Finn thought, once his brother was gone and he was unpacking the cheese. Business was brisk, sure, but profits were hard won with the supermarkets constantly expanding their ranges and dropping their prices.

He was working hard to carve out a niche in the Portneath community, with his carefully selected local foods. He was pleased with his decision to get a license to sell alcohol, too. He had some interesting English wines in stock now, even some from Devon vineyards. He had been meaning to go and explore a few of them and maybe he could take Freya with him. He would value her opinion.

Finn was happy to admit he enjoyed spending time with Freya. The initial instinct, when he bumped into her, might have been a mercy mission, but he felt surprisingly content at the thought he was going to see her that evening. She had promised him supper on the theme of three French hens. Whatever it was, it would be delicious, and he would enjoy her company just as much as her food.

'That smells a-mazing,' said Finn when Freya put the casserole dish down on the table. She had even lit the candles and poured them both a glass of wine. It was late, and he was famished.

He sat down opposite Freya and enjoyed the view. The flames danced in the faint draught, lighting up Freya's face, scrubbed clean and glowing, definitely a little less pale and drawn than it had been when they met. Had it really been only three nights earlier? She looked adorable, he thought. And also, about twelve years old, he told himself sternly.

'So, what's this?' he asked, ladling a generous amount of casserole onto his plate to join a mound of buttery mashed potato and some baby broad beans.

'You should be able to guess,' she teased. 'Remember my Christmas challenge?'

'Of course! Three French hens?'

'Correct.'

'So, this is . . .' He stirred the contents of the casserole, analytically. 'Chicken. French chicken? With bacon and mushrooms? No, I don't get it.'

'Coq au vin.'

'Oh, hilarious,' said Finn, heavily but with a smile playing around his lips. 'Very good. You've been thinking that through for a while, haven't you?'

'I might have been, yeah,' she admitted.

'We haven't got three chickens in here have we?' he said, eyeing the pot. 'I'm hungry, but I'm not that hungry.'

'I wasn't quite that literal,' she reassured him.

'So, how was your day?' he queried, waiting while Freya shovelled in an enormous mouthful and chewed thoughtfully.

'I packed Christmas puddings into cardboard boxes for half my shift,' she told him, when she could speak again. 'A dozen at a time. It's quite a sight, that many Christmas puddings, I can tell you.'

'I'm sure.'

'I also did online courses on first aid and heavy lifting, got given my own pair of clogs, overalls and an extremely fetching hairnet, and met up with a friend I have unforgivably neglected for ten years. She's pissed off with me. Big time.'

'Busy day,' said Finn, raising an eyebrow. 'So, you've landed a job . . . I take it you're staying then?'

'I didn't say that,' said Freya, uneasily. She was staring miserably at her plate now, her knife and fork frozen in her hands. 'I do need to work, but I've got a house to sell and a funeral to organise, although the hospice said there was no rush.'

'I agree. Plenty of time to worry about all that. So, who's your neglected friend then?' he went on, in a bid to distract her.

'Hattie. We were at school together.'

'Hattie with the short, curly red hair and the baggy dungarees?'

'You make her sound like Ronald McDonald,' said Freya, 'but yes, that Hattie. I'm surprised you know who she is.'

'Of course, I know. Both of you were very – how shall I put this? – memorable. Partners in crime.'

'Why does everyone say that?' complained Freya. 'We weren't *that* naughty. Anyhow, I'm still amazed you noticed us.'

'You were trying quite hard to *get* noticed,' Finn teased gently. 'During those wild weekend nights out?'

'Ah, the Fox and Hounds . . . it was the place to be on a Saturday night,' said Freya, remembering.

'And this New Year's Eve,' said Finn. 'Be there or be square this Friday night. Karaoke and everything. It's going to be a blast. You coming?'

'Wouldn't miss it for the world. For old times' sake,' Freya replied. Friday night was a million miles away. She would have thought of an excuse to duck out by then.

'It was lucky you were allowed in at all, the age you were,' Finn reminisced. 'You're what? Four years younger than me?'

'Twenty-eight now, so yeah, I suppose we were fifteen when we started going there,' admitted Freya, nodding. 'We were only drinking coke. Well, most of the time we were,' she said, remembering the illicit half bottle of Bacardi that Hattie kept in her voluminous pockets to top up their drinks when no one was watching. There had been some riotous evenings.

'Hang on, it's all coming back to me now,' laughed Finn, remembering. 'Wasn't it you and Hattie who streaked naked through the bar and out into the street one night, running away from Gavin the barman? He was horrified. Reasonably enough. Plus, you must have caught your death of cold.'

'You're such an old woman,' chided Freya, blushing as she remembered. It had been silly, ribald fun. She and Hattie would do anything for a laugh then, and – if she was honest – it was the attention of older, glamorously handsome boys like Finn and Ciaran they were after.

The two girls had just wanted to be part of the cool crowd. It was an escape for them both. For Hattie it was about getting away from her self-centred single mum who barely noticed Hattie disappearing until late on a Saturday night as she was usually out herself. Freya's mother, on the other hand, made it clear she relished every minute spent with her daughter but was delighted she was finding a way to have some fun, far away from a home life that was muted by the silent mantle of illness. Her mother had been struggling to get over her first bout of cancer then and they had both known, all too well, what might lie ahead. It had been then, too, that the oncologist had explained her mother's cancer had not been a random event but a near certainty due to a defective gene, so a cancer that might well return. And a gene that Freya might have too.

Chapter Eleven

Four Calling Birds

Freya overslept. Up in her cosy attic room she could hear little of what Finn was up to in the flat below, so the silence was complete, other than the creak and groan of timbers in an old building. She couldn't remember the time she last slept so soundly. Opening her eyes, she was shocked to see it was nearly nine o'clock. She didn't notice Rafferty was on the bed until she flung back the covers, hearing him land heavily on the floor and catching a flash of black-and-white fur as he stalked past her, disgruntled. She tumbled down the stairs to the bathroom, relieved that Finn was already gone. He was probably in the shop getting ready to open, or in the storeroom out the back.

Barely twenty minutes later, she was washed, dressed and ready to go. However, sneaking through the shop to the door, not wanting to interrupt Finn's chat with his customers, she suddenly found an arm barring her way.

'Breakfast,' Finn said, simultaneously ushering the customers out of the door and grabbing Freya by the scruff so he could steer her behind the counter.

'Coffee and pain au chocolat,' he announced, pushing her gently towards a plate and a steaming mug.

'Very Parisian,' said Freya. 'I'll be the size of a house if I live with you for much longer.'

'Rubbish,' he replied. 'Have you ever seen a fat Parisian? Anyhow, that pain au chocolat is the best in Portneath.'

'Well, I suppose it would be rude not to,' she conceded, taking a huge bite and chewing, eyes closed with bliss.

'It would. Terribly. So, what are you up to today? Christmas puddings?'

'Not 'til tonight. I'm on the late shift.'

'Until then?'

'I've got to find a solicitor.'

'Why? What have you done?'

'Not a criminal solicitor, a normal one. My mum left me a letter. She told me he's got the will.' And that he would help her, she remembered silently, this John Makepeace who she had never met and who, as far as she knew, owed her nothing.

Taking a deep breath of the sharp, frosty air Freya raised her chin and pushed back her shoulders. She began to wonder if the solicitor's office would still be closed – who would blame him for taking an extended break until the new year, but this morning, the lights were on, the door yielded to her push, and a bell clanged to announce her arrival.

The little room was dark and cluttered. A broad oak desk was covered in stacks of paper and a grandfather clock gently clunked out the seconds, marking the passing of time in a room that didn't look as if it had changed in a hundred years.

The doorway at the back darkened with the figure of a tall, stooping man, signalling with his hand for Freya to sit.

'Hi there,' he said as he sat down in a high-backed swivel chair, placing both large hands on the desk in the gaps between the stacks. 'John Makepeace. How can I help?'

She blinked. He was not the elderly gentleman she had been imagining. The stoop was clearly more to do with being a tall man in a very old building than about age. He might be wearing a conservative old green moleskin jacket, with the kind of checked, button-down shirt she associated with some of the more staid teachers at her school, but the top button was undone and his hair was mostly dark, albeit thinning on top, with touches of grey just at the temples. He was in his late fifties perhaps, she reckoned. A rugby player, at least in the past, she guessed.

'My name is Freya Wilson,' she told him. Did she imagine it, or did he stiffen at hearing her name? He looked at her sharply and then his eyes dulled with an emotion she couldn't fathom.

'Freya,' he said quietly. 'It's lovely to meet you.'

'My mother has died . . .' she faltered, swallowing hard at hearing her own words, needing a moment to gather herself.

'Yes . . . yes,' he murmured, as if he had already known, clasping his hands tightly together now. 'I am so sorry to hear it.' His brow knitted with distress.

'Thank you. So . . . my mother asked me to come to you. I don't know what to do about things – the will, probate, selling the house,' she said, her voice steadying as she spoke. That was what she needed to hang onto. Don't think about the crushing emptiness of bereavement, not in front of strangers, focus on the practical.

'Of course,' he said gently, steepling his fingers under his chin in a considering, almost prayer-like gesture. In that attitude he looked, Freya thought, like a bird of prey, a hawk, or an eagle. The dark brown eyes, with the fan of creases at the corners, looked kindly enough though.

'So, she left me a letter,' Freya went on. 'I gather you have the will?'

'I do. Hang on.'

He stood, gave her a little nod which was almost a bow, and went back through the archway in the wall behind him to a further office. This one, Freya could see, was less well-appointed but more workmanlike. She could see several tall filing cabinets. He went to one of these and inserted a small key. Once unlocked he pulled out the bottom drawer and searched, talking under his breath as he rifled through.

'She was so young, your mother,' he said, as he came back holding a dark green drop file in his hand.

'Fifty-four,' Freya confirmed.

He handed her a single sheet of A4 and bowed his head, patiently waiting, as she read, *I hereby revoke all former Wills and Testamentary dispositions heretofore made by me and declare this to be my last will . . . I appoint John Makepeace of Makepeace, Morley and Bulmer, my dear and loyal friend . . .*

It was a brief document, simply declaring Freya to be her sole beneficiary, with a handful of specific instructions at the end, asking that various close friends be remembered with some little keepsakes. There was a particular 'bee' pendant for her great friend Diana. In clearing the house, Freya had already found this, and she was sure the other bits and pieces would turn up as she went on. It helped to think that she could do these simple things to honour her mother's wishes. It was not too late for that at least. The process of clearing away a lifetime's possessions would seem even more ineffably sad without that thread of purpose. It also reminded Freya that she needed to somehow get in touch with Diana, although that was easier said than done. After getting the devastating text from Diana and fleeing Paris for home, she was now in possession of a useless phone, so completely flat and dead she couldn't even switch it on to see what Diana's number was. She added that to her list of things to sort out. She somehow doubted John Makepeace's services extended to that.

Suddenly she was aware of letting her mind drift. How long had she been sitting, staring at the will, unseeing?

'What do I do next?' she asked him, handing back the will.

'Paperwork, I'm afraid. There's a lot of it around this sort of thing, sadly – death certificates, probate, the funeral, of course. You might have noticed,' he coughed discreetly, 'that your mother states in her will she wants to be cremated. Have you appointed an undertaker, by any chance?'

'The hospice said something about that. I think they've done it. I said I didn't mind who.'

'It's probably Mortimers. They're a good company. There's no rush, that's the first thing to remember. Take your time.' He looked at her thoughtfully, his hands steepled under his chin again, in what was clearly a gesture of habit. 'I am so sorry to see you having to cope with such a sad situation so early in your life,' he said. 'When did your mother pass away, if you don't mind me asking?'

'Christmas Eve,' said Freya, looking beyond him into space. 'It was cancer,' she added, although he hadn't asked. She sighed, thinking about her mother's letter and the yellow envelope at that very moment boring a hole in the bottom of the inlaid wooden box she had consigned it to.

He bowed his head again in a slow, sad nod. It was partly his measured, careful manner that made him seem older than he was, she decided. It was rather soothing, which she imagined came in handy in his line of work. The peaceful atmosphere, his clear interest and complete lack of any apparent urgency encouraged Freya to volunteer something she had discussed with no one else.

'I don't know if you knew, but Mum had a mutation on her BRCA2 gene. Of course, we didn't know about it until she got cancer the first time ten years ago.' She raised her eyebrows and paused, but he nodded for her to continue.

'My chances of having the gene too are fifty-fifty. So, if I have it, my chances of getting some sort of woman's cancer are – well, it would be almost inevitable unless I did something drastic to avoid it.' Now she had started, Freya found she couldn't stop. 'With Mum, we thought she had beaten it,' she blurted, 'but it was just waiting to come back, all this time. Ten years. And then . . . well. You know what happened.'

Finishing in a rush, suddenly feeling she had overshared, Freya blushed. He must have been thrilled to get an impromptu biology lesson. What was she thinking? She talked a good talk, it seemed, now she had started. Speaking to a counsellor about getting tested herself had forced her to look clearly and dispassionately at the issue, but making the decision to get tested had been one thing – summoning up the courage to look at the results was something else.

'Just before she died, I told my mother I'd tested negative. But I lied,' she admitted, flushing deeper in shame. 'At least, I've had the test, but I actually don't know the result yet.'

If he was surprised at this confession, he didn't show it. 'Perhaps you *will* test negative?' he ventured gently. 'Hopefully you will?' This time it was his turn to raise his eyebrows in enquiry, but Freya made no reply.

After that, he ran her through the next steps, insisting on 'tidying up loose ends' as he called it, without charge, which was extremely kind of him. She couldn't imagine he made much money if he took that attitude with everyone, but somehow his gentle but firm insistence had made it easy to accept.

'Will you tell me when you know your plans for the funeral?' he asked as she prepared to leave, at last. 'I'd like to attend, if you have no objection?'

'Of course,' Freya replied. 'I'd like you to be there.'

*

John Makepeace watched Freya close the door behind her and walk back down towards the High Street, gazing at her back until she rounded the corner and disappeared from view. Still not moving, he mused on their meeting. He had been expecting it, of course. With intense concentration, as he sat motionless, he committed their encounter to memory, replaying their conversation in his mind and savouring every nuance. He wanted so much more than he could ask for – or expect. Briefly, he allowed himself a well-rehearsed little fantasy – him and Anna together throughout the years, raising a child – their child – a child like Freya . . . The dream faded and he shook his head. Instead, he made the most of what he could have – just as he always had.

Her voice was so achingly familiar though – he hadn't been expecting that. And in so many other ways, she was her mother's daughter, too. He'd seen it instantly in her build, her eyes, even the determined angle of the delicate chin; he hadn't needed to be told who she was, or that Anna had died. The moment he saw her, he knew. Along with the exquisite sadness of loss, there had been a kaleidoscope of sweet memories from many years ago, when they were young and everything was possible. But, of course, just months ago, he had experienced the pain of seeing Anna so diminished, but still with her eyes burning bright, when she came to see him, as she told him what she needed him to do.

It was a privilege to be able to fulfil his promises to her at last.

Chapter Twelve

Freya's meeting with John Makepeace had taken a load off her mind, and with her pudding factory shift not starting until the evening she strolled down the High Street, engrossed in diverting thoughts about the day's cooking challenge. It was 'Four Calling Birds', but not only was she getting a bit fed up with all the dishes to date involving poultry of some form or another, she didn't really know what a 'calling bird' was. And she was pretty sure she didn't want to eat one. The other preoccupation was how little equipment Finn had in his kitchen; for a man with such an interest in food, it was obvious he didn't cook very much.

Not a lot had changed in ten years on the High Street, but as luck would have it, one of her favourite junk shops had been replaced by a fabulous-looking kitchen shop, with a window display full of everything you would need for recreational baking. There were also some serious-looking Sabatier knives. Although not as good as Freya's treasured Japanese Shun knives, this was clearly a shop with a proprietor who knew what they were talking about and now she was employed again, Freya felt slightly less worried about spending a little of the cash she had with her. To be truthful, she struggled to ignore a kitchen shop at the best of times. Maybe she would just let herself have a little browse. In pride of place in the centre of the window was a cluster of cute little blackbird pie funnels, designed to let the steam out through a hole in the pie crust. They were adorable – and they gave Freya just the inspiration she needed.

'What is that amazing smell,' said Finn coming up to the flat hoping to put together some lunch, to discover Freya had beaten him to it and was in the kitchen, wiping down the floury work surfaces.

'What do you think that smell might be?' she teased, chucking the cloth in the sink and folding her arms.

'Mm,' he said, eyes narrowing as he sniffed the air. 'It's caramelly. And there's vanilla . . . and . . . actually, is that apples?'

'Very good,' she replied. 'Go and sit down, I'm just about to take it out of the oven.'

Finn went without protest and shortly afterwards she followed him, proudly bearing a magnificent round pie, with a sparkling sugar coating on the pastry and four yellow beaks piercing the crust in each of the four quarters.

'It's my Twelve Days of Christmas challenge for the day,' she said, breaking into the crust and spooning generous portions of pie into two bowls. The apple filling was steaming fragrantly. 'I thought the various bird life we've been eating our way through since I got here needed to stop and I can assure you that no birds were hurt in the making of this pie.'

'Ah, I get you; well, I'm glad it's apple,' said Finn. 'It's my favourite, actually. Oh right, good thinking,' he exclaimed, as Freya came back out of the kitchen with a carton of cream from the fridge.

'It's not a particularly balanced nutritious meal on its own,' she admitted.

'I disagree, this is definitely one of my five a day,' said Finn, pouring a stream of thick, yellow cream over his pie, before tucking in.

'Wow,' he mumbled around a mouthful. 'This is seriously good.'

Freya's mouth was too full for her to answer. The apple was part caramelised and perfectly fluffy, the pastry – only a basic, enriched shortcrust – was crisp and buttery and even Freya had to admit it had turned out well.

'This cream is from the farm,' said Finn, indicating the now half-empty carton. 'It's just about the best you can get. Ciaran's got a tiny herd of Jerseys and it makes no economic sense, really, but people do pay a premium for the milk. And the butter.'

'Holly Tree Farm just seems like this magical place where everything delicious comes from. No wonder Martha looks so exhausted. And Ciaran. It's great that you've got the shop to sell the produce.'

'We need to branch out, really,' he said, putting down his spoon for a moment. 'The shop shifts a lot, especially in the summer when we've got all the visitors, but we could do with other outlets for the cheese and butter. Hotels, restaurants, maybe a couple of carefully chosen delis in Exeter. Or Plymouth, even. Nothing too far away because we have to get it there. We've got a couple of places already under our wing but there's lots more to do once we're sure we can keep up with the quantities we would need. We don't want to start supplying and then not be able to meet demand.'

'I'd love to see what you guys do up on the farm.'

'I'll take you,' said Finn. 'Soon.' He gave her a long, considering look. 'Now listen, if you're working the night shift you had better go and get some rest.'

The graveyard shift at the factory was the toughest thing Freya had ever done. The first part of the night was in the cooking room, a hot steamy environment redolent with

Christmas spices. It was like being in a Christmas-themed Turkish bath. Freya was surprised to find she really did feel she had had enough of Christmas now. She wasn't sure, even with nearly twelve months to go, that she would be ready to eat Christmas pudding next Christmas. Or ever again, come to that.

Talking to the other staff, there was a possibility they would be commissioned to produce treacle sponges in a few days, which Freya wouldn't have minded. There was even talk that they would be taking a break from Christmas puddings and switching to sticky toffee pudding for a week, but that was only a rumour.

She was disheartened that Hattie wasn't with her on this shift, although the upside was that it gave her longer to summon up some balls and tell the closest friend she had ever had about her mum dying, something she was still dreading having to do. She saw Hattie on packing, but her old friend didn't look her way. It seemed the slight thawing of relations had frozen over again. Freya hoped to catch up with her at break time, but their breaks didn't overlap and she ended up spending the entire session listening to Jim, who had been there for twenty years, ruminating about the poor performance of his favourite football team, which had been relegated, to his great distress. Freya was so weary she didn't feel like eating the cheese sandwich that Finn had made her take with her. What she really craved was another slice of that amazing apple pie. She loved to cook the simple things, but to do them really well. It took longer to fry the apple chunks in butter and sugar first, but it was that kind of detail that made the ordinary transcend to another level. She supposed, if she thought about it, that was something she felt strongly about, transforming what might be dismissed as banal into something memorable and extraordinary.

Her shift finished at two in the morning. The last couple of hours had been the toughest, the only bright parts were having a wage packet handed to her and Jim offering her a lift back to town. It would have been a long, cold walk.

Letting herself into the shop quietly, she was surprised and pleased to see Finn in a pool of light at the cash desk, sorting through till receipts.

'Hello, stranger,' said Finn, barely looking up from his work. 'Off to bed?'

'With you still slaving away? It wouldn't feel right,' Freya replied.

'Too wired, eh?'

'Actually, yes,' she admitted. 'I am a bit.'

'Make me a coffee? And I think you should have some hot chocolate to help you sleep.'

'Hot chocolate? What am I? Six years old?' scoffed Freya, although now he had mentioned it, she really, really felt like one – a big, delicious mugful, just like the hot chocolate she had drunk with her mother as a child, with a swirl of whipped cream and a sprinkling of cocoa, maybe with a handful of mini marshmallows or, best of all, a little meringue kiss sweetly melting away into nothing.

She went over to the café area and nervously tackled the monster of a coffee machine, but there was a vending machine, prefilled with milk and chocolate syrup, for the hot chocolate which was easy enough. She gave it everything she'd got, dolloping in a spoonful of whipped cream from a bowl in the fridge and accidentally chucking chocolate everywhere with the chocolate shaker Finn used to finish cappuccinos. Then she made the espresso for Finn.

'Brilliant,' he said, straightening and putting his hands in the small of his back before taking the little cup from her.

Freya sat down on the high stool by the till and took a sip of her hot chocolate.

'Good, eh?' said Finn. 'I can tell by your cream moustache.'

Freya wiped her mouth with the back of her hand, unselfconsciously. 'It is literally the best thing I have ever drunk.'

'That's Ciaran's Jersey milk, too.'

They drank in companionable silence for a moment.

'So, market day tomorrow,' said Finn, conversationally. 'Or today, technically.'

'Brilliant! Every third Saturday in the month,' she recalled. She and her mum had always gone into Portneath for market day. 'I love market day,' she said. 'I wonder if it's as good as it was all those years ago.'

'It's better,' said Finn, fishing out his phone as he finished his coffee. Then, 'Damn!' he exclaimed, staring at his notifications in dismay. 'That's the last thing I need.'

'What?'

'Nothing. Go to bed, you look terrible.'

'Thanks. And what is it?'

'Oh, it's just the lady who helps me out staffing the deli on market day has texted to tell me she's ill. I didn't hear it come in over the noise I was making shifting boxes earlier and it's too late to get anyone else now.'

'Me?' suggested Freya, pointing to herself.

Finn looked at her doubtfully and sighed. 'Really?'

'Why not?'

'I suppose I'll have to.'

'Thanks for the vote of confidence.'

'Sorry,' he said, shaking his head. 'I – that would be great, thank you. It's only for the morning. I'm doing a stall at the market or I'd be here.'

'You run a stall?' said Freya, surprised.

Finn nodded. 'It's just a bit of theatre really . . . tastings, mainly, which draws people in, but then, of course, I need staff to cover the shop.'

'What time do you want me?'

'Half eight?' he said, wincing at his own suggestion.

'Done.'

'Now, *definitely* go to bed.'

Chapter Thirteen

Five Gold Rings

Freya's phone alarm seemed to go off just moments after she had set it. Yawning and shivering, she managed to wash, dress and stumble down to the deli for half past eight to find Finn was already there.

'You're a star,' he said, rapidly showing her how to use the till, which was luckily simple enough for Freya's sleep-deprived brain. 'Just take a quick look around the shop and familiarise yourself – most things have price labels on and apologies for the ones that don't. For them you'll have to check the price on the shelf edge. The main thing is to learn the deli counter stuff, because all the price information is facing towards the customers. Listen, I've got to dash, are you sure you'll be all right?'

He had loaded up boxes with various nibbles and anti-pasti to entice the crowds but was so full of concern and last-minute instructions Freya practically pushed him out of the door. She didn't envy him having to stand out there in the piercing wind for several hours because it was a bright, chilly day with a high, blue sky, frost on the ground and a pale yellow sun bringing little warmth.

The first hour after Finn left was quiet. People were thronging the market stalls, showing little interest in the shops they could visit every other day of the month. There was a clutch of stalls at the front of the shop, on the triangle of cobbled paving where the High Street split in two.

Nearest the deli door there was a table piled with goats' cheeses, some rolled in herbs, others in ash. Another stall was selling fresh fish and boiled crabs from Brixham, and another selling nothing but various delicious-looking bottles with jewel-bright chillis and sprigs of rosemary glowingly suspended in olive oil. They were offering samples of the green-gold oil in little ceramic bowls with cubes of ciabatta to dip in and they always seemed to have a little clutch of people gathered, sampling hungrily. Around the corner there was a stall selling roasted chestnuts, creating delicious wafts of scented smoke which blew into the deli every time someone opened the door.

Despite crowds teaming outside, the shop was so quiet at first that Freya had time to wander around in between customers, checking out prices and trying to commit them to memory. But it was an impossible job. The place was crammed with everything from designer spaghetti in richly decorated paper sleeves to Spanish smoked paprika in gorgeous little red, embossed tins. Whenever she had time to explore, she found more treasures. Paynton's puddings were in good supply too. Obviously, they were top quality, or she was sure Finn wouldn't stock them, so at least she was involved in making something decent at the factory – the job would be even more soul-destroying if they were rubbish. In Finn's shop there were no Christmas puddings left, naturally, but the sticky toffee puddings and raspberry jam sponges stacked in pyramids made her mouth water.

By ten o'clock the place was beginning to fill with people escaping from the cold. They came in, stamping their feet and blowing into their cupped hands. Soon, Freya was in full flow, tweaking levers on the coffee machine and pounding on the till buttons, racing, in the increasingly rare lulls between queues of customers, to round up dirty plates and cups for the dishwasher. Hot chocolate with whipped cream, chocolate powder and marshmallows was the top drink of choice and stocks of the syrup-drenched Italian lemon cake and the fruit-studded flapjacks, which she knew Finn had made locally, were both getting alarmingly low. Soon, the little seating area was filled to capacity and still people came, even standing in the aisles to eat and drink, getting in the way of the customers queuing to buy groceries, but the mood was jovial and buzzing with good-natured conversation.

Finn had been right about customers coming in for coffee, but staying to buy from the deli, she saw. A good half of those finishing their drinks and cake queued again patiently to buy a chunk of cheese, or some olives, and a loaf of good sourdough bread to have for lunch, perhaps with one of the crabs from the fishmonger outside. Freya managed to work out how to use the scales but was hopeless at identifying which cheese was which, let alone remembering the prices. If they were French cheeses, she would have been more confident but, in keeping with his principles, Finn stocked solely English cheese, including several from Holly Tree Farm, not least a couple of amazing-looking sheep cheeses that she made a mental note to ask Martha about. Luckily, customers were amiably helpful in providing names, pointing to the ones they wanted and reading the prices for her from their side of the counter.

Short of wearing a wig and a false moustache, there was no escape from being recognised and exclaimed over. Having to put up with a barrage of questions about life, love and career news from old school colleagues was not much fun, though. Everyone was polite, but the truth leaked out of the little pauses in the conversational gaps, while they processed the obvious conclusion that she was back from Paris with her tail between her legs. Freya stopped putting them right on the strict accuracy of this as it would lead, inevitably, to her admitting she had come home to see her dying mother, causing awkward conversational hiccups of its own. Bereavement was too difficult and weighty a conversation to have in between decisions about whether to have a cappuccino or a flat white. She was starting to get used to coping with people's distress, whilst still feeling numbly devoid of sadness herself and felt like a fraud in the face of their sympathy. In the end she just stopped mentioning it and found that people were more than happy to talk about themselves instead.

The most astonishing conversations were the ones she was having with her former classmates, many of whom had babes in arms and toddlers in tow. In one case, the child was at least ten, reminding Freya that a few of her contemporaries had got off to a very early start. She made polite noises about the attractiveness of all the offspring, privately thinking no toddler was at its best with a stream of snot coming out of its nose. Imagine if she was one of these mothers? It could, so easily, have been her. In the absence of the Paris opportunity, early parenthood would at least have felt like moving forward.

Despite being an idyllic part of the world and a magnet for holidaymakers, the truth was that job opportunities for young people in Portneath weren't brilliant. The aim, for the most resourceful and determined, was to 'get out' and – in the face of Freya's ignominious return – she detected a distinct whiff of *Schadenfreude*.

At the tail end of a rush, a tall young man came in with a woman and baby. Freya recognised him instantly – a classmate, initially from Middlemass Primary School, who had been filtered off into the low-achieving streams of everything as soon as they were separated by ability at Portneath High. They were friendly strangers and Freya half expected him not to recognise her when he came to the counter.

'Hi, Freya!' he said, his eyebrows rising in recognition. So much for being incognito then.

'Jake,' she acknowledged in reply. 'How are you? Is that one yours?' she inclined her head in the direction of the tot who was gazing over its mother's shoulder in her direction.

'How's your mum?' he asked, nodding in answer to her query.

Damn. Here we go again, Freya thought. 'Sadly, she's just died,' she replied neutrally, looking away, braced for the sympathy and embarrassment. It didn't come.

Long moments passed and she shot a look at Jake who, to her alarm, was mouthing silent words and colouring violently, his eyes suddenly glassy with tears.

'No!' he choked, his mouth working and his hands shooting to his face to cover his distress.

'I'm so sorry to just blurt it out like that,' said Freya, mortified at having triggered such distress. She came around the counter and put her hand on his arm. The woman with the toddler, was looking concerned now, making to get up and come over.

'No . . . no, I'm sorry,' he choked, grabbing a paper napkin from the pile on the counter to mop his tears. 'I'm so sorry,' he went on. 'She was . . . she was this incredible woman. I loved her,' he went on, meeting her eye at last.

'You knew her?'

'Of course. She was my literacy tutor. Basically, the most important teacher I ever had.'

Freya didn't know what to say, feeling powerless in the face of his unexpected grief.

'I'll bring it over,' she told him when he eventually managed to stutter out his order.

Jake made introductions to his wife Kylie and daughter Mabel. Freya, her eye on the till and the door, sat down with them for a brief break.

'My mum was a literacy tutor?' she repeated, astonished, as Jake and Kylie sipped their coffee.

'I thought you must know she was,' said Jake. 'You remember I wasn't much cop at school? The truth is, I never really learned to read properly at Middlemass. Not the teachers' fault, I was too busy messing about, but also, we had a lot going on at home during that time – my dad wasn't too reliable . . . Anyway, no excuses, but I struggled at Portneath and didn't come out with much in the way of exams. It didn't matter in some ways, I did my plumbing training – I'm a plumber now, gas certified and all that – but I was working for a big firm until a year ago. There were loads of us, ten at any one time. It's the type of firm that got the contracts for factories, offices, new housing estates and stuff like that, more than domestic repairs. Anyhow, the pay was a flat daily rate and it wasn't great. But my problems with reading and writing were what stopped me going it alone as an independent because I'd never have managed the paperwork. Anyhow, when Kylie and I got together I decided it was time to sort it out.'

He and Kylie looked at each other with smiles and she patted his arm encouragingly. Freya was touched at the obvious love and respect between them.

'I tell you, I nearly bottled it, walking into the adult literacy class that first time,' he went on. 'Your mum was there; funnily enough, she was learning too, just finishing the training to be a tutor and, luckily, she was assigned to me. Anyhow, she recognised me from you and me being in the same class at primary school. I was amazed she remembered. She was so nice, and she – well, she made it clear she really believed in me. I hadn't had that before, not from family and definitely not from any of my teachers. And I don't blame them,' he added, hastily. 'I was a little git at school, I don't deny it.'

Freya wasn't going to deny it either. She had definite memories that whenever there was mischief going on, Jake tended to be in the middle of it, but the cheeky demeanour of his schoolboy self was transformed now into calm assurance and self-belief.

'She had a way of explaining things that really made sense,' he said, 'and she was never impatient or annoyed. Actually,' he corrected himself, 'she was, but not with me, it was only because she was reminded how let down I had been by the people who were supposed to be supporting me at school. It made such a difference, that attitude. Plus, for the first time in my life what she was teaching actually felt relevant because I could see how much I needed it.' He shook his head, clearly abashed at this outpouring, but Freya nodded him on, eagerly.

Encouraged, he carried on. 'Once I basically knew how to read, she spent ages teaching me stuff like invoices and receipts and tax stuff. I do all my own paperwork now,' he said, proudly. 'And I even read books – sometimes – just because I can. And also, completely thanks to your mum, I gave in my notice so I could set up on my own, just a few months before this one came along,' he finished, gently pinching Mabel's nose and making her giggle.

Kylie, all the while, had been smiling proudly as he spoke and now she covered his hand with hers before turning to Freya. 'I'm so sorry for your loss,' she said. 'Your mum was an amazing woman.'

'And full of surprises,' said Freya, heartfelt, as she dashed back behind the counter to serve a customer looking at the cheeses.

There was another rush of customers then and, by the time she had sorted them out, Jake and his little family had gone. She was idly wondering how on earth she could have not known her mother was an adult literacy teacher and was trying to imagine being one of these young women with multiple children, when a familiar face popped up in front of her.

'Martha!' she exclaimed, delighted. 'How are you?'

'"How am I"?' responded Martha with a weary smile. 'How I am, is gloriously alone for some precious "me time". I have been sans all my delightful little children for a couple of hours of freedom, and,' she said, hauling up a wicker basket full of filled paper bags, so Freya could see, 'I've been busy.'

'I can't understand why you *wouldn't* want to bring four children shopping with you,' responded Freya with wide-eyed innocence. 'Can I do you a little child-free cappuccino?'

'You most definitely can,' Martha said, with a contented sigh. 'Me and Ciaran are basically tag-team parents,' she explained, checking her watch. 'I've got about forty-five blissful minutes left.'

It was then Freya noticed Martha's eyes were red-rimmed and her face even paler than when she had seen her last. 'Are you OK?' she asked. 'You look tired.'

'Yup, always tired,' Martha admitted, turning away, but not before Freya had noticed her eyes flood with tears, which she brushed away, hastily.

'Martha!' Freya said, with dismay.

With terrible timing, Finn walked through the door at that precise second. He was loaded up with a stack of boxes from the market stall, but at least he seemed too distracted to notice Martha's distress which she was desperately trying to hide from him.

Freya was also embarrassed to have him walk in at exactly the moment the café area looked as if it was in the aftermath of a hurricane. 'Just catching up with the clearing,' she said, guiltily, piling up dirty plates and cups and carrying teetering stacks to the dishwasher.

'I've really left you in the lurch,' he said, greeting Martha absently, dumping the boxes behind the counter and grabbing a cloth to wipe down the tables. 'Sorry you've been so busy on your own, but I'm good now. Why don't you girls sit down and have a coffee and a catch-up?'

Freya was torn but Martha seemed to need her more than Finn, who was restoring order swiftly and efficiently.

A short time later, sitting opposite each other with steaming mugs, Martha gave Freya a wobbly smile and sighed, fiddling with her teaspoon.

'What gives?' Freya asked. 'Is everything all right with you and Ciaran?'

'Me and Ciaran? Who knows?' said Martha, shrugging. 'Ciaran and I don't exactly communicate much nowadays,' she admitted. 'We're both too busy, what with the kids and the farm.'

Freya nodded. 'I don't know how you manage everything.'

'It's brutal, but that's not news,' Martha shrugged. 'And you're right – I am really tired at the moment. I've been struggling for months, actually. Even when I go to bed at the same time as the children, I'm still exhausted the following morning.'

'Are you ill, do you think? Maybe it could be an iron or vitamin deficiency?' asked Freya with concern.

Martha shook her head. 'Not ill.' She paused, still fiddling with her spoon. 'So . . . um . . .' She hesitated again. 'It actually turns out, I'm up the duff.' She glanced up at Freya for her reaction.

'But that's amazing!' said Freya loudly, wondering whether it was or not. If it were her, child number five would be daunting, to say the least. 'Totally amazing,' she added, in a lower voice, glancing at Finn who was still clearing up, apparently unaware.

'Astonishingly, *I* think it's amazing too,' said Martha. 'I surprise myself, but here's the problem: I'm not sure Ciaran would think it was quite such good news,' she muttered, glancing around distractedly. Finn was now out of earshot in the storeroom.

'Of *course*, he would,' said Freya, lowering her voice to a hiss, just in case. 'Why wouldn't he?'

The tears had returned. Martha brushed them away impatiently. 'Grr. Hormones,' she exclaimed. 'No . . . see . . . we definitely decided four was enough and it's more than enough, most days, so I don't think he'll be thrilled and,' she looked up at Freya again, with desperation in her eyes, 'I'm worried he won't want to keep it.'

'Oh! B-but surely . . .?' said Freya.

Martha shook her head, emphatically. 'We disagree on everything nowadays. I actually realise . . .' She stopped and pressed her fingers hard against her mouth before continuing, 'I actually realise, I daren't tell him because it petrifies me that we won't agree on this either. And if we can't agree . . .' Her chin wobbled precariously, on the brink of a sob.

'How far along are you?' asked Freya, casting about for something comforting to say. Martha was extremely slim and there was no hint of a bump that she could see, although it was such a cold day, she was swathed in a thick pink sweater.

'Quite far,' Martha admitted. 'I think – in retrospect – about twelve weeks already, but I was really slow to realise this time, which makes me look idiotic, I know. With the other ones I could tell straight away. With this, it was only that my boobs were sore and I was getting worried I should get a mammogram or something. Anyhow, I did a test because – what the hell – and then I was blown away when it was positive.' Martha chewed her lip anxiously. 'In fact, it feels *so* different this time, I'm actually really worried something's wrong.'

Freya reached across and squeezed Martha's hand. 'What are you going to do?' she asked gently.

Martha straightened. 'I've decided not to tell Ciaran,' she declared. 'Not yet. There may be no point if it's not going to work out.'

'But surely you'd want his support if it was bad news?'

'Normally, yes, but if it *isn't* bad news, then I need to be far enough along that there's no longer a decision to be made. I just couldn't bear it if he said . . .'

Freya nodded thoughtfully. Secretly, she thought *not* telling Ciaran was going to cause more trouble in the long run than telling him, and she couldn't imagine he would be the ogre Martha was suggesting, but it wasn't up to her.

'I'm really sorry you've got this going on,' she said, quietly, although Finn had yet to reappear and the shop was empty of customers. 'If you need a chance to talk to Ciaran – properly, without the kids – then let me babysit for you soon.'

Martha's face lit up. 'Now there's an offer. But are you actually going to be around?' she added, her face falling again. 'I thought you were just here because of your mum. Oh God, here I am loading you with my problems,' she wailed, fresh tears rolling down her cheeks.

Freya handed her another napkin. 'That's a point,' she admitted. 'I'm not sure if I *am* going to be here for long. But any time soon, I can. Just ask.'

Chapter Fourteen

'Bed,' said Finn firmly, reappearing when Martha had gone.

'You've talked me into it,' joked Freya, 'yours or mine?'

She enjoyed the look of confusion followed by mild alarm on his face. 'Anyhow I have absolutely no time for that,' said Freya, who had had an idea, 'food to buy and cook. I'm doing supper tonight, no arguments.'

'I wouldn't dream of talking you out of it,' he said, putting his hands up in surrender. 'It's a pleasure to eat your food, any time.'

Freed from her responsibilities at the deli, she grabbed her rucksack and headed out into the market before the stallholders shut up shop for the day. The fish stall was her first target. She had spotted some squid which she had a yen to cook. Plus, there was her Christmas challenge, which she had not forgotten.

Once she had the lovely fresh squid, well wrapped in paper, at the bottom of her bag, she browsed the other stalls for inspiration. There was an intriguing stall selling seaweed harvested from just down the coast in Cornwall and she bought a small amount, with a view to experimentation. It was a far cry from conventional French cuisine, but she had a great interest in Japanese culinary influences and this was just what she needed to explore some ideas. She just hoped Finn was feeling adventurous.

These purchases took a significant chunk out of her slim pay packet, but she still had just enough left to pay her rent and she was determined to do that this evening too.

She only wished the pudding factory work paid better. There were some thick, woolly hoodies with a cosy fleece lining on sale at one of the market sales and she craved the bottle green one. It wasn't that the colour would match her eyes – although it would – mainly she was desperate for the warmth and comfort of it, to beef up her tiny wardrobe of inadequately warm clothes. She had travelled light to Portneath and now, as the bitter wind blew off the sea, she was suffering in her thin denim jacket.

She was looking at them regretfully when a hand grabbed her arm.

'There you are, at last!' came an accusing voice, and the next thing Freya knew, she was embraced in a fragrant, woolly hug. Released, finally, she saw it was Diana, her godmother and favourite of her mother's friends. Diana was the one who had sent her the text imploring her to come home before it was too late to say goodbye to her mother. The text which, in her confusion and alarm, she hadn't even replied to.

'Where on earth have you been and why have you been so profoundly incommunicado?' Diana's tone was indignant, but her hand rubbed Freya's back comfortingly. 'I tried to call, and when that didn't work I sent you a text – a lot of texts, actually. I had no way of knowing whether you even knew to come home.'

'I got your text thank you,' said Freya. 'I'm so sorry I didn't reply, I just dropped everything and came back.'

'Well, I know that now but why haven't you answered my calls or responded to my messages?' wailed Diana, sweeping Freya back into a hug again.

'I didn't get them, apart from the first one,' Freya admitted apologetically, detaching herself. 'My phone's dead. I need to buy a new charger from somewhere, but Portneath's not brilliant for things like that.'

'Ah well, I've found you now, at least. Oh, what is the matter with me? The first thing I should say is how sorry I am about your mum,' Diana exclaimed, slapping her forehead. 'Really, darling, so, so sorry . . .'

'Thank you for letting me know she was ill.'

'You put that politely, but you must want to slap me for leaving it so long,' admitted her godmother. 'I pleaded with Anna to contact you sooner, but she was adamant. She wanted you to be able to get on with your life in Paris, not moon around here waiting for the inevitable. And then, when she was too ill to contact you herself, I just thought – damn it! – and I did it behind her back. I was terrified you wouldn't get here in time.'

'Don't worry,' Freya told her, and she meant it. She wasn't angry with Diana – she was angry with herself. Deep down, if she admitted the shameful truth to herself, she had doubts that, even if she had known earlier, she would truly have come sooner anyhow. There was no need to admit such dark thoughts to Diana. It was nice that the older woman thought fondly of her and if a little less truthfulness was the way to preserve that, then Freya was starting to get used to lying. 'I understand why she – you – didn't tell me. I do. You were such a good friend to Mum,' she assured her. 'I am so glad you were there for her.'

'You are a darling girl,' said Diana cupping Freya's face in her hands. 'Now, where on earth are you staying? I've been up to the house several times, so I know you're not there. If the girls at the hospice hadn't told me you'd been there with your mum when she died, I would have assumed you were still in France.'

'I've shacked up with a friend.'

'Details?' barked Diana. 'I'm not going to risk losing you again. We need to sit down and talk about the funeral.'

'Can we?' said Freya with relief. 'I'd love that.'

Diana nodded sharply. 'We will.'

'I'm staying with Finn above the deli,' Freya offered.

'Are you now!' Diana said, shooting her a shrewd look.

'Absolutely not like that,' Freya blurted. 'Get those thoughts out of your head straight away.'

'Must I?' Diana wheedled. 'I'd love to think that you and that lovely, handsome man were hooking up. It would make my day. And Mum would have been thrilled, I am sure.'

'We are *not* a thing,' said Freya. 'And I can't explain to you the extent to which I am absolutely not with him or planning to be. In a million years,' she added, for emphasis.

Promising to get a charging lead and to be in touch with her about funeral planning soon, Freya managed to persuade Diana to let her go. By the time she trailed back through to the stairs at the back of the shop with her booty, she was not only chilled, but yawning and dragging her feet. Maybe Finn was right. She should get her head down for a bit. She was finding the reality of shift work at the pudding factory pretty brutal, even after her tough working schedule in Paris. If she was really going to stay around Portneath while she tried to decide what to do in the long term, she was going to have to look for something better to do.

It had been late on that summer's evening, with the low summer sun slanted in through the kitchen windows at Freya's childhood home, dazzling her and bathing the world in golden light. She sat curled into the little Lloyd Loom chair by the Aga, cradling her favourite tea mug in her hands while she and Mum caught up on the news.

'I wish you didn't have to work so hard, darling,' her mother said, without reproach. 'You look exhausted.'

'I'm totally fine,' Freya reassured her, not wanting to say how utterly grinding the work actually was: getting into the kitchen first thing in the morning to start prepping; checking the refrigeration room to ensure the orders had been delivered correctly; having a hasty meeting, as head of her section, to talk about last-minute changes to the day's menus with the chef de brigade, who was only marginally less terrifying than her overall boss, Andre . . . And she didn't tell her mother how she would get back to the tiny flat with her workmates long past midnight, after finishing service and cleaning down every inch of the kitchen, only to get up just five hours later, ready to start all over again.

She looked at her mother contemplatively over the rim of her mug. She was smiling at her daughter as the iron dashed efficiently over Freya's trousers, already washed and dried, ready for her to go back to Paris with a rucksack of clean, pressed clothes after her lightning visit.

Freya never came home for weekends – those were a prime time in a restaurant's week. Instead, she would occasionally be excused Sunday evening's service which was always quiet, shooting off to the train station after Sunday lunch, getting into Portneath on the very last train and then – blissfully – home to Middlemass in the dead of night. Generally, she would sleep right through to lunchtime the following day, spend a lazy afternoon and evening with her mother, being fed and chatting idly, then the race was on the following morning for her to tightly co-ordinate her trains back to Paris, arriving just in time for Tuesday evening's service. It was punishing.

'What would you like to do while you're here?' her mother would ask her, every time. 'Shall I get someone over for supper? Some of your old friends? Hattie, perhaps? You haven't seen her for ages, darling,' she would gently suggest. And she was right, but the thought of having to be switched on, to be entertaining *and alert, for anyone more than her own mother, felt like too much. She wanted – however briefly – to be allowed to be a child again. To greedily guard her precious time with her mother. To drink her in. To be spoilt. To be lazy.*

Freya slept heavily, waking confused and dry mouthed, wondering for a moment why she had her clothes on and the low winter sun in her eyes, just like it had been in her dream. Getting out of bed and standing at the little dormer window, she could see the whole High Street, rising steeply before her, with the fiery red sun hovering on the horizon above the castle ruins. It was just past four o'clock in the afternoon and dusk was descending fast, as the twinkling Christmas lights stretching across the High Street began to weave their magic. She had slept profoundly for more than two hours. No wonder she felt groggy.

Going down to the flat, she splashed her face with water and brushed her teeth. There was no sign of Finn, which was good. She didn't generally mind having him watching her while she cooked his supper, but when she was experimenting she liked to be able to focus completely, plus, working in someone else's kitchen always needed a bit more mental energy. She was short of that these days.

First, she needed something she could deep-fry in. Fortunately, Finn had a decent-sized cast-iron enamelled pot that would do. She dealt with the seaweed first, chopping it rapidly into ultrafine strips and dropping it, one mound at a time into groundnut oil that was just the perfect temperature. It only took a minute to cook before she scooped it out with a slotted spoon and drained it on a thick wad of kitchen towel. Once it was blotted dry, she seasoned it and then tasted it thoughtfully. Not bad, but next time she would try it in a salad with a Japanese-inspired vinaigrette.

She loved the clean, complex flavours of Japanese cuisine, the miso, yuzu and chilli and – although it hadn't featured at all in Andre's essentially traditional French kitchen – it was something she had always promised herself she would explore further.

This was the kind of cooking she wanted to do, she thought happily, finely chopping another batch – it was exciting to be allowed to go beyond her own classically trained comfort zone. There would be no such thing as a mistake in the kitchen she would like to run, just experimentation, hard work, and intelligent innovation. Of course, she had not the slightest idea how she was going to create this magical kitchen she was after, unless Finn was right that, even in Portneath, there might be a chance to set up something new and exciting.

Daydreaming, she cleaned and prepared the squid the way she wanted it. It was too soon to make the light, delicate tempura batter. She would do that only when she and Finn were ready to eat.

By the time Finn came up to the flat, having closed up the deli and restocked the shelves, Freya had laid the table and stoked the fire where a blissed-out Rafferty lay on his back in front of it like a shaggy, black-and-white hearthrug. She lit the candles and opened a bottle of Chablis, flinty, citrusy and full of delicate, light, flower fragrances. For Freya, it was the perfect pairing for the precise and delicate flavours of Japanese food. Some flowers would have been nice for the table too, but the overall effect she was aiming for was simple and pure – austere, even. She could have picked up a bunch of paperwhite narcissi from the market that day, but Andre had taught her to ensure that no scents from candles or flowers should vie with the experience of the food she was serving. She wasn't going to be precious about it, the heavenly but overpowering scent of paperwhites would have been too much.

Under Finn's wine glass she had placed six, crisp tenners from her wage packet which had pretty much cleaned her out, leaving her just enough for the bus fare to work.

She saw Finn clock the money, but he said nothing.

'Just whipping up the batter,' said Freya brightly. 'Have a glass of wine, while you wait.' She filled his glass and sloshed a bit of wine into her own, as well. She had to be careful how much she drank or, even after her afternoon nap, she would end up snoring with her face in her plate.

He made appreciative noises and peered in with interest as she whipped up the batter with the flour and iced water. Luckily Finn's fridge had an ice dispenser. In fact, now she was getting used to it, she wasn't finding Finn's bachelor kitchen nearly as limiting as it might be. It was small, but she didn't mind that. She was a neat and precise worker, unlike Andre who always left a tidal wave of mess in his wake, to be cleared up by hordes of underlings.

'What are we having?' Finn asked.

'We're going Japanese with our Twelve Days of Christmas today,' said Freya.

'As you do,' he remarked quizzically. 'I love calamari,' he said, giving a nod to the prepared squid.

'Good. That's basically what it is – with a bit of a Japanese twist. Have you seen this amazing Cornish seaweed?' she asked, handing him a bowl of the crisp fried seaweed she had cooked earlier.

With concentration, he forked some out and ate it.

'Wow,' he said. 'Amazing. I'd definitely consider stocking this in the deli. From the market today, eh?'

Freya nodded. 'Now, go and sit down while I do this.'

Within just a few minutes, she brought out a serving dish piled high and carefully tonged five of the crisp little rings onto Finn's plate, arranging them carefully.

'What's that?' she asked him, pointing at her arrangement.

'Olympic logo?' he asked, deliberately obtuse.

She went to swat him around the ear, but he ducked, easily fending her off.

'Five gold rings?' he added, laughing at her.

'Exactly.'

She noticed the money under his wine glass had disappeared but that three ten-pound notes had now appeared tucked under her plate.

'What's this?' she said, pulling them out.

'Wages for the deli this morning. You really got me out of a hole.'

Freya wasn't going to argue. She needed the money. She smiled her thanks and tucked the notes into her pocket. 'We should have chopsticks, really,' she said, picking up her fork 'Bon appetit.'

'Amazing,' Finn said, pushing his plate away at last, nothing but crumbs left on the serving platter in the middle and a smear of dressing in the dipping sauce bowls. 'So few ingredients, such an incredible result. You are a seriously talented chef.' He chuckled.

Freya looked at him sharply, her antennae out for teasing, but his expression was frank and honest. 'Seriously,' he said. 'I don't think you need to worry about your employment prospects, the world's your oyster.'

'Ah, but is Portneath my oyster?' mused Freya, laying her fork down regretfully. The tempura squid had been delicious, but it wasn't that filling. She was pretty sure Finn – having a big appetite – would want something more. She should have thought.

'Can I tempt you with pudding?' he said, as if he was reading her mind. 'I'll just be a sec.' At that, he went off down the stairs to the deli, returning almost immediately with a box which, Freya recognised, bore the Paynton's Pudding logo.

'I know it's bringing your work home,' he said, apologetically, 'but Sharmayne popped in this afternoon to give me this. I'd appreciate your opinion on it.'

'I can honestly say I have never eaten a Sussex pond pudding,' said Freya, reading the label. 'I've not been involved in making these at the factory yet either.'

'You won't have done. It's kind of a prototype.'

'What's Sharmayne doing asking *your* opinion on prototypes,' queried Freya.

'I can't help it if she recognises my talent for spotting culinary genius,' he said. 'It's what makes me such a rewarding person to cook for.'

'If you say so,' Freya retorted. 'Come on then, let's give it a go.'

She had not only never eaten one, she had never made one either, but she did know it had a suet crust that generally required long, slow steaming.

It was lucky that Paynton's puddings were sold already cooked and microwaveable, so it didn't take long for Finn to marshal two large portions, along with the remains of the jug of cream from yesterday's apple pie.

There was silence as they spooned in mouthful after heavenly mouthful of deliciously golden suet pastry surrounding a 'pond' of caramelised butter and sugar, mixed into the most extraordinarily delicious sauce. The whole lemon in the heart of the pudding had completely disintegrated from cooking, into a heap of candied peel with just enough sharp juice taking the edge off the sweetness. It was utterly delicious.

'I can feel my arteries blocking,' Freya said, at last.

'Heart attack on a plate,' agreed Finn. 'But it's worth it,' he mumbled, his eyes fixed on his bowl as he scraped up the last of the amber sauce, mingled with thick, yellow cream.

'Oh dear God,' exclaimed Freya as she scooped up the last spoonful. 'How on earth did anyone decide packing a whole lemon into a suet crust with a tonne of butter and sugar would turn into that?'

'Is that how it's done? How do you know?'

'I knew it existed. I've just never quite wanted to give it a go,' Freya admitted. 'I'm not sure something as robust as this fits comfortably with the principles of fine dining.'

'True,' admitted Finn, 'but thumbs up to Sharmayne's new pudding though, no?' he asked. 'She should be even more grateful she's had your much more highly qualified opinion as well as mine.'

'Yeah, good idea to tell her she should be grateful,' commented Freya sitting back and folding her hands over her groaningly full stomach. 'Except don't, obviously. I need that job.'

While Finn washed up, Freya wandered over to his bookshelf and picked up the acoustic guitar leaning against it. Tuning it idly – it clearly hadn't been played in a while – she sat herself on the floor, holding the guitar against her and began to play softly.

Noodling around through half-remembered melodies, snatches of songs she had sung so long ago, she found herself quietly singing a Sinead O'Connor song her mother had loved – it had a haunting chorus, repetitive, persistent, wringing the heart out of the sadness and disappointments of life, love and loss.

It was only when she came to an end that she realised Finn was standing just behind her, a refilled wine glass in each hand.

'That was beautiful,' he said, handing down her refilled wine glass and taking the guitar from her, propping it back against the bookcase. 'It's a long time since it's been played – and an even longer time since it's been played that well.' He sank into the armchair opposite her. 'There's open mike at the Fox and Hounds on New Year's Eve, that could be your number.'

'Yeah, that'll kill the party mood,' she joked. 'I'm not sure I'm up for a big new year party this year.'

'Of course,' he said. 'That's understandable. Although there's a bunch of us going, all the old crowd.'

'As good a reason to stay away as I've ever heard,' she joked wryly. 'Why don't *you* play something?' she said, to divert him.

'Me?' he demurred. 'I know when I'm upstaged by a superior talent. I'm a three-chord wonder. If me and Ciaran are really drunk at new year we might just give it some. You never know your luck.'

Freya smiled in spite of herself.

'Talking of the "old crowd", how was it, this morning, seeing familiar faces while you were running the deli,' he went on. 'Must have been weird?'

'A bit,' she admitted. 'In a good way, mainly.'

'So, do you ever think you could actually live here again?' The question felt loaded.

'That's a tough one,' she admitted. 'Amazingly enough, maaaybe,' she said slowly. 'I couldn't wait to leave, but that was ten years ago . . . Now, seeing people I was at school with married, with children, it's the road less travelled, I guess. You can't help but think, "wow, that could be me".'

'Instead, you've been off in Paris kicking ass in the cooking world. Following your dreams . . .'

'Huh,' she said. 'Not sure I've exactly made my mark. And look where it got me. Unemployed – pretty much – and unemployable.'

Finn didn't comment but stretched his arms up languorously above his head and yawned. 'Are you working tomorrow?' he asked.

'No way, Sunday is a day of rest,' she declared. 'And even Sharmayne thinks so, thankfully.'

'So, you've got a free day?'

'Yup,' said Freya, having not the slightest idea what she was going to do with it. Maybe she had better go to the house and do some serious sorting and clearing.

'Give me a day,' he said, suddenly urgent, breaking into her thoughts.

'What?'

'Give me a day to demonstrate you could have a good life in Portneath. That you should consider staying permanently. Or for longer, anyhow.'

She blinked. 'OK,' she said. 'If it means that much to you?'

'It does,' he said, nodding slowly. 'Yeah . . . it does actually.'

Chapter Fifteen

Six Geese a-Laying

Freya overslept. By the time she woke up, her watch was telling her it was nearly nine o'clock. Not particularly late for a Sunday, perhaps, but, knowing Finn, he would have been up for hours. She had no idea how the man coped with so little sleep. He worked harder than anyone else she had ever met and never seemed tired. She hurried downstairs to the flat where she could hear him moving around. Taking a quick shower and putting on the warmest clothes she had – the frost was still white in the places the sun had yet to fall – she went and found him.

'Morning, sleepyhead,' he said, putting a steaming latte in front of her as she slipped onto what was now her usual seat at the dining table.

'"Day off", remember?' she reminded him.

'Nope. Does not compute,' he teased, going back into the kitchen. 'Now, I hope you're hungry,' he called.

'If I said I wasn't would it make any difference?' she called back.

'Not really,' he admitted, sticking his head around the kitchen door. 'Two minutes.'

Freya relaxed with her coffee. She really hadn't been particularly hungry, but the smell of bacon and eggs wafting out of the kitchen was changing her mind.

'Good grief,' she said as he placed a steaming plate in front of her. 'Where did you get the comedy eggs? An ostrich?'

'Yeah, cos on the sixth day of Christmas her true love sent her six ostriches a-laying,' he quipped.

'Ah, I forgot we were playing that,' she said. 'So, it's a goose egg, right?'

'Right. Not quite as big as an ostrich egg. Probably the size of three average hen's eggs.'

'I'm not sure I can eat three eggs in one sitting,' admitted Freya. It really looked daunting, although the yolk was beautifully golden and domed, on a perfect white circle of egg white. Thankfully the white was fully set; Freya had always had a horror of snotty fried eggs.

'What's the rest of it?'

'Bubble and squeak,' said Finn, 'but with parsnips and greens, not potato and cabbage. And the crispy bacon's from an amazing farmer up the road. He cures the bacon from his own pork and makes fantastic sausages too. They're in the shop downstairs.'

'Of course, they are,' said Freya. It was all delicious and – even though she wasn't a big breakfast eater – she astonished herself by finishing every bit and polishing off a slice of sourdough too, because not wiping up the last bits of egg would have been a sacrilege.

'Right, let's go,' said Finn, dumping their plates in the kitchen, 'but first, I've got a little present for you.'

'It's not my birthday,' said Freya, puzzled.

'Call it a late Christmas present,' he said gruffly, handing her a large, brown paper bag.

She reached in, encountering soft, woolly fabric. 'That is so spooky,' she said, amazed as she pulled out the exact thick, dark green hoody she had seen and longed for at the market the previous day.

'You need something substantial on,' said Finn. 'We're going to be outside a lot today.'

'It is absolute heaven, thank you *so* much,' she sighed, pulling it on over her head. It was big on her, but still snug, with its thick, fleecy lining. The sleeves were too long, allowing her to pull them right over her hands, doubling up as mittens, and it was long enough to cover her bum. For the first time since she had arrived, in her inadequate clothes, she would be properly warm.

Finn wouldn't say where they were going, but, climbing the hill out of Portneath and then taking the turn off to Middlemass, she quickly worked out they were heading for Martha and Ciaran's farm. It was on the top of the hill, overlooking Middlemass, and the view, with a clear, blue sky, was magical, the village just below them and the twinkling blue sea, a strip of sequins in the distance.

There was no one in sight, when they arrived, but a thin skein of pearly grey smoke was rising from the chimney. Finn parked on the grass next to Ciaran's yellow Land Rover.

'This frost is amazing – it almost looks like snow,' she said, crunching the hoar frost on the grass under her foot and then, like a six-year-old, jumping into a frozen puddle, shattering the ice into milk-white shards.

He watched, smiling at her simple pleasure. 'This is my favourite winter's weather,' he said sucking the sharp, cold air into his lungs. 'I'd rather have it a few degrees colder like this, but dry. I don't envy my brother, farming in the rain half the time.'

'He probably doesn't envy you, running the deli every hour of the day and night.'

'We've both got the right job then,' agreed Finn. 'He's not my only supplier, obviously, but I wouldn't have the deli business I have if I didn't have my brother slaving away up here. It's a brave business model he's got, producing such variety and on such a small scale.'

'So, that's unusual, right?'

'It's pretty much the opposite of monoculture farming,' he agreed. 'And that's become the norm in the last few decades.'

'Monoculture?'

'Yeah, one crop. Each farm – and they're usually bigger than this, too – only produces one thing, because everyone is trying to achieve a profit in a market where the supermarkets are pushing farm gate prices as low as they can possibly get. They're squeezing everything they can out of their economies of scale. It's no good for the land, in the long run.'

'So, what does Ciaran do instead?'

'That's what we're here for me to show you.'

They were in the farmyard now, with low, corrugated-roofed buildings around three of the four sides.

'That's the sheep milking parlour,' said Finn, pointing.

'Milking sheep? I know people must do it, but . . . seriously?'

'We didn't invent it,' he said, smiling. 'They're mammals. They produce milk. Come and see,' he said, walking her over to the double doors, which were open. 'Sheep cheese is a brilliant product. It's not a new thing at all, although other countries are more used to sheep milking than we are. It's good stuff, and it's perfect for people who are allergic to cow's milk, especially if they're not fond of goat's milk either.'

'I find goat dairy a bit – well, "goaty",' admitted Freya. 'Is the cheese made here too?'

'Yep, that's Martha's baby. It was Martha's idea to farm sheep, actually. It's more of a thing in New Zealand.'

'You don't say?' quipped Freya, remembering her old geography lessons. 'Aren't there ten sheep for every human there, or something?'

'Guys!' came a voice from inside the shed. 'How lovely,' said Martha, emerging from the gloom. 'I didn't know you were coming.'

'Didn't want to get you laying out the red carpet,' joked Finn.

'You wish,' she laughed, kissing each of them on both cheeks. She and Freya exchanged an intense look, remembering yesterday's conversation.

'I was just showing Freya what you do here,' said Finn. 'The guided tour.'

'Cool,' said Martha. She winked at Freya mischievously. 'What an innovative date.'

'*Definitely* not a date,' Freya mumbled. The woman wasn't *still* trying to match her up with Finn, was she? Diana was as bad, now she thought about it.

'When did you get here? Have you shown her the dairy yet?' Martha asked Finn.

'Just now, and not yet,' he replied. 'I was hoping to catch up with Ciaran. Would you do the honours?'

''Course. Allow me,' Martha said, ushering Freya towards another low building next door to the milking shed. Inside, the atmosphere was cool and damp with its whitewashed walls and grey, stone floor. There was lots of stainless steel too, a huge sink, shelves filled with large white plastic tubs and a stainless-steel rack on casters, consisting of smaller shelves filled with cricket ball-sized mounds, wrapped in white muslin.

'How are you?' Freya asked as soon as they were alone. 'Have you spoken to Ciaran yet.'

Martha looked anguished. 'I'm fine, just tired – and no, I've not spoken to him. I just don't know how to start.'

'You know you have to, right?' Freya pressed.

Martha nodded miserably. 'I do. And I will . . . Anyway,' she said, pulling her shoulders back and standing tall, 'on a lighter note, this is where we pasteurise the Jersey milk,' she explained, determinedly changing the subject and pointing to a large, stainless steel drum. 'Once that's done, I bottle however much we need for our clients – mainly the deli – and make the rest into butter and Cheddar. It makes *the* most divine Cheddar. It's really special stuff. Have you tried it?'

'The extra-mature Cheddar in the deli? Not yet, but I will. I didn't realise it was from here,' said Freya. 'I noticed in the deli it's—' She stopped herself, but Martha gave her an enquiring look. 'Well, I noticed in the deli it's quite expensive,' she said, apologetically.

'It's definitely for the afficionados,' agreed Martha. 'The price reflects the fact that it's time-consuming, and – of course – we are making on a small scale. We sell to the affluent second-homers around here mostly, but it's really, really good. If I say so myself.'

'I think you're absolutely entitled to say so yourself. What's that?' she asked, pointing at a huge steel bowl with a paddle turning slowly inside it.

'My next batch of butter. Finn stocks it in the deli too.'

'That's the stuff in logs, wrapped in the white paper with string?' She had seen them in the deli, and sold some too. It was pretty expensive, like the cheese.

'Waxed paper, yes, and a little label with our logo on, red checks for salted, blue checks for unsalted. Here's the salt I put in . . .' She showed Freya a tub of dirty-white flakes. 'Sea salt, the best you can get – it makes those little crunchy bits in the butter.'

'Like the French stuff,' agreed Freya enthusiastically.

She and her mother had bought it for special occasions when she was a child. On cold winter nights, they would pig out together on cinnamon toast made with great slabs of sourdough and really salty French butter. Freya's mouth watered at the memory. It was so vivid it was almost like a hallucination.

'Earth to Freya!' joked Martha, laughing at her glazed look. 'Try my sheep cheese. I call this "St Leonards" after the house I grew up in in New Zealand,' she explained, looking misty-eyed herself as she handed Freya a slice she had cut from one of the white-wrapped mounds on a tray. 'Quality control,' she explained. 'We eat one from each batch, to check it's up to standard.'

'Well, I don't know what standard you're aiming for, but this is delicious,' said Freya, with her mouth full.

'. . . which is the right answer,' said Martha. 'And I have to say, I agree. You and Finn can take this tray back with you if Finn's got room in the cold store. It's doing no good sitting here.'

After that, Martha showed her the beautiful Jersey cows who came to say hello and stood, in their frosty field, regarding Freya benignly and looking glamorous with their huge, liquid dark eyes framed by gloriously long lashes as she stroked their velvety noses.

The two women then walked around, away from the farmyard, to see the fields in the valley laid out below them, where Finn had grown the wheat for the flour Finn used for some of his bread. 'The one thing we don't do is mill it ourselves,' said Martha. 'There's an artisan miller up towards Exeter—'

'What, literally the windmill on the hill that you can see from the road?' asked Freya.

Martha nodded. 'That's the one,' she said.

'I love that windmill! I had no idea it actually worked. I'm glad there's something you don't physically do yourselves.'

'So am I,' said Martha, with feeling.

'And that's the orchard?' said Freya, pointing. 'Don't tell me, you make your own cider.'

'Well, it's funny you should mention . . .'

'You don't seriously,' laughed Freya.

Martha shook her head. 'Not quite. We bribe the kids to help pick the apples—'

'Child labour,' interjected Freya. 'Go for it.'

'Yeah, that's why we had 'em,' said Martha. 'And then we send the apples off to be juiced and bottled.'

'Of course, you do,' said Freya, remembering. 'That's the 'Holly Tree Farm Apple Juice that Finn sells in the deli?'

'You're catching on!'

'I envy you.'

Martha gave Freya a sweet smile. 'You say that, and you've been cooking with one of the top chefs in the world, living in glamorous Paris, and here I am, stuck here and permanently covered in mud?'

'Honest mud, though.'

'Hmm. I wouldn't mind being a bit more high-maintenance,' Martha went on, examining her rough hands and short, clean, bare nails in despair.

'But this is so . . .' Freya searched for the words. 'What you've got here is so special,' she said at last.

Martha nodded, understanding completely. 'With its early mornings and late nights, with the cold and the mud and the sheer, unrelenting grind of it – that's before you get me onto the childrearing with the washing and the constant feeding and the cleaning . . .' She broke off and put the back of her hand to her forehead, wonderingly.

'Talking of which – why on earth *haven't* you spoken to Ciaran?'

'I can't face it yet,' Martha admitted, pulling a face. 'I will though, I will.'

'And I'll babysit, remember?'

'Yeah, maybe,' Martha dismissed it, 'but anyway, back to my life and other problems, when dawn breaks and I'm standing here, looking down into the valley, across the fields, and I can see all the lights starting to come on in the houses below us in Middlemass – I don't know – it's the most beautiful place in the world and I wouldn't be anywhere else. I wouldn't be *with* anyone else other than Ciaran and the kids. It's everything I've ever wanted. I can't see why you wouldn't stay here for ever.'

'But you left New Zealand and came here,' insisted Freya. 'You escaped the place you grew up in. This *is* your wide world, your big adventure.'

'And my "happily ever after",' said Martha. 'When you're brought up in one place, I think it's natural you want to go out and explore the world. Paris is *your* big adventure.'

'I think Paris *was* my big adventure,' admitted Freya quietly.

Martha gave her a searching look. 'So, maybe your "happy ever after" is to come back here – to come home?'

'This is where you're hiding,' Martha declared, leading Freya into the warmth of the kitchen and discovering both men leaning up against the Aga with steaming mugs of coffee. 'I hope you've left us some.'

'"Left you some"? We made it *for* you,' said Ciaran mock obsequiously, pouring the two women each a coffee from the half-full cafetiére on the warming plate.

'This is our own milk,' Martha told Freya as she topped up her mug from a big, green jug on the table.

'Mm, it's so creamy,' said Freya, after taking a sip.

'Grass-feeding,' explained Ciaran.

'All year round? What about the winter?' asked Freya. 'What if it snows?'

'Good question,' said Ciaran. 'We do have to supplement in the winter, and we do our best to harvest enough hay to keep them going when it comes to it, but occasionally we have to buy in extra, which knocks a bit off the profits.'

'Off the extremely slender profits,' expanded Finn.

'Yeah, *well* slender. If I got a decent price for my cheese and butter from that dodgy bloke who runs the deli in town . . .' joked Ciaran.

'You mean the exploitative, big bucks retailer,' agreed Finn. 'They'll be the death of small-scale farms like this.'

'Oi, less of the "small scale",' said Ciaran.

'Size is not important,' quipped Martha. 'Or so Ciaran keeps telling me.'

Freya giggled, catching her eye.

'We'd have set up that online hampers idea by now if you had enough surplus to warrant it,' Finn reminded Ciaran.

'Fair point,' he admitted. 'Maybe in time for next Christmas, eh? Anyhow, I'm sure we're boring Freya rigid with all this stuff.'

'No, you're genuinely not,' Freya protested. 'I love it. And I love to hear your ideas for the future.'

Ciaran and Finn exchanged a look. 'Well, we've softened her up for you, bro,' said Ciaran, mysteriously. 'It's down to you now.'

Freya immediately asked him to clarify but he refused, shooting Ciaran and Martha quelling looks. Freya was then distracted by Nelly the sheepdog slinking into the room and pushing her cold, wet nose into Freya's hand, politely asking for a stroke, and the moment passed.

*

After coffee and a huge, warming lunch of home-made chestnut soup with soda bread, during which Martha insisted on Freya sampling all the different cheeses they produced, including a couple which were still 'in development', Freya was feeling exhausted, although all she had done all day was watch other people work and stuff her face.

When they were leaving, Martha pulled Freya into a tight hug. 'Take care,' she said fiercely, as if they were never going to see each other again. 'And tell me if you need me to do anything for the funeral,' she added. 'Anything. Just ask.'

Freya was touched to see tears in the other woman's eyes. There were none in her own. She and Martha might not have known each other long enough to become proper friends, but there was something in the other woman that made Freya think they could be. And she wanted them to be. She was certain she had never felt that way about any of the people she hung out with in Paris. In the team she worked with, intimacy was instant but as for loyalty? Freya was under no illusions. And, if she had found a friend in Martha, that was some comfort as she remembered with a pang that she seemed to have lost her friendship with Hattie. She must be brave and break the news about Mum to her. She was sure Hattie would want to come to the funeral, so telling her couldn't wait much longer. Perhaps also she could persuade her oldest friend to say what the problem was. They had too much history for Freya to let it all slip through her fingers.

Chapter Sixteen

Freya was so relaxed and well fed she was ready for an afternoon nap, but Finn was relentless. He insisted on driving her here and there, over what felt like the whole county, showing her the hotels and restaurants he already supplied – or would like to supply – with Holly Tree Farm produce.

They stopped at The Cow for afternoon tea. It was a low, thatched stone building, a traditional Devon longhouse, probably hundreds of years old, but kitted out inside with achingly hip interiors – all stone floors with Instagramable cowhide rugs and groovy light fittings with gleaming copper shades. Even Freya, in Paris, with little English language media available, had read about this small, select chain of pubs and hotels, making their mark with the top influencers and setting the trend for laid-back luxe. Freya had never eaten so much in her life as she had already that day, but the enormous fluffy scones, filled with juicy sultanas, and the epic Holly Tree Farm butter, along with home-made mulberry jam and Devonshire clotted cream, were so delicious she ate two, happy to fade into the background while Finn had a matey, backslapping chat with the chef, Colin. Freya had made Finn promise not to tell Colin about her own work, but, in any case, he more or less ignored her. Maybe he was another one who basically thought women were irrelevant, she pondered. Mainly, it seemed, he came out to wish Finn a merry Christmas and complain that Finn had still not brought him samples of the sheep cheeses to try for the restaurant.

'They'll be worth waiting for,' Finn promised him, leaving with a pledge to return in the new year and try out the new tasting menu Colin was excited about. She was relieved now that Finn had not mentioned her employment with Andre. If she decided she wanted to look for a chef job locally, she would admit to it then, and not before. That said, Andre had made it quite clear he would not be giving her a reference so she might be better off not mentioning him at all. She would be starting from the bottom again, as if the last ten years had not even happened, she thought, her heart sinking.

Freya fell asleep in the car on the way home and Finn stole glances at her as he drove. It was good to see her so completely abandoned to sleep, because he honestly wondered if she had slept deeply in all her ten years in Paris. The more she gradually let him know about her life there, the less he liked the sound of it. Andre was clearly a nightmare employer and Finn thought he might be starting to understand why the Freya he knew when she left – the confident, funny, loud, practical-joke player who would break into song at the slightest excuse – had turned into this watchful, reserved creature who rarely smiled. Briefly, he allowed himself to remember their awkward, ill-fated kiss. He wanted an action replay far too much, he realised – only better this time, and longer. He gave himself a stern talking-to for the remainder of the drive. 'Business not pleasure' was the unbreakable rule, he told himself – and when it came to business, he had a cunning plan he was keen to share with her.

She woke as they arrived back in Portneath, with Finn nipping skilfully into a parking space just around the corner from the deli.

'I've got one more thing to show you,' he said, as Freya got sleepily out of the car.

'Where now?' she said, secretly pining to just go back to the flat and sit in front of the fire.

'Right here,' he said, taking her through the deli to the storeroom at the back. Then, jangling his keys rather than opening the flat door as she expected, he moved a crate of vegetables, selected a second key on the bunch and opened a door she had not noticed before.

Flicking on the lights, Finn stood back and let Freya come past him. She found herself in a small, desolate-looking catering kitchen, with stainless steel units and metal shelves. There was a gas range and grill, a handwashing sink, and a larger one for washing-up. A tall and capacious fridge/freezer stood in the corner, switched off and empty, its doors left ajar. The work surfaces looked dusty and the floor was in need of a mop. Taking it all in, Freya pushed open a door to the front of the building and gasped. The last of the daylight was pouring in through a large, bay window fronting onto the cobblestones and then onto the High Street, with the same view as from the flat and the deli, stretching up the hill to the castle. The space was not huge, perhaps five metres across and about the same deep. Apart from a serving counter and a narrow stretch of worktop behind, the only furniture in the room, was half a dozen wooden tables with chairs piled on the tops of them. The floor was a black-and-white checkerboard of lino, the pattern quite worn in places, especially in the doorway.

'So, what did this place used to be?' she asked, going to the window to drink in the uninterrupted view of the sunset, casting low sunbeams that were catching the dust motes in the air.

'This is – was – the ice-cream shop and café.'

'Oh, of course, it was!' she exclaimed, remembering. 'An Italian couple ran it.'

'Julio and Sofia Marconi, that's right.'

'Tell me they haven't . . .' Freya dared not speak her fears aloud.

'Alive and well,' Finn reassured her. 'The café was getting too much for them, the busy summers especially. They retired at the end of the last summer season and moved to a lovely little bungalow in Middlemass.'

'So,' Freya was intrigued despite herself, 'who's the landlord for this place?'

'It's complicated,' Finn replied. 'Basically, it's me. I was sub-letting to them but the overall owner and landlord is the Middlemass estate.'

'I remember. That's your posh mate, Lord whatsisname.'

'Gabriel,' agreed Finn. 'Everything goes in front of him ultimately. He doesn't interfere, he just wants to see businesses that'll do well and benefit the overall community in here. He's got a useful business brain, actually. I value his input.'

Freya remembered Gabriel, whose actual title was something like Lord Middlemass, Earl of Havenwood. He had been a fixture amongst Ciaran and Finn's crowd, a dark, brooding presence, deeply loyal to his friends, mistrusting of strangers. She was pretty sure he didn't know she existed.

'What will you do with this, then?' Freya asked, looking around the empty space.

'It's been empty for a while, purely because I've been too busy to deal with it. There's been some interest from your boss Sharmayne actually – I've not seen the proposal yet – and Gabriel may favour it; I don't know, but I mean . . .' He paused, gauging her interest. 'I've been playing with this idea of setting up a restaurant, using the local ingredients I'm sourcing for the deli, but I can't do it alone. I can barely manage the work I have. In fact, I've even thought about moving my little café offering into here because it's become so wildly popular and it could do with a bit more space but . . .' he scratched his head '. . . the other thing that stops me doing that is, to be honest, selling coffee and buns is never going to turn over enough on its own to support the rent we *should* be charging for the place. I inherited the Marconis when I acquired the building, and I don't think they'd had a rent rise in thirty years.'

'And you didn't put it up? You didn't charge them what you should?'

'I didn't feel I could,' he admitted.

'So, why are you showing me?'

'Oh, come on Freya,' he chided, 'don't tease!'

'Who's teasing? Oh no, hang on – you can't seriously think . . .' Freya took a step away from him, holding up her hands in horror.

'Don't say "no",' he pleaded. 'Not yet anyhow. At least have the heart to tell me it's a "maybe"?'

'It's . . . it's impossible,' she said, shaking her head. 'I apologise if I have given you the false impression that I'm up for running my own business, let alone as a restaurateur, which is – just so we're clear – pretty much the most unstable sector you could ever enter into. I'd never be able to get up and running, paying you proper rent, and recruiting staff, and compiling menus . . .'

'OK, listen, listen,' Finn laughed, relenting, 'I didn't mean to spring anything on you and anyhow – to be honest – I've only just had the thought myself. Let's sleep on it. Alone, naturally,' he added, with a wicked twinkle and a look that lingered just a moment too long.

'Naturally,' said Freya, with a twisted smile. 'Anyhow, I am *totally* awake now, thanks to you and your big ideas.'

'I'm probably not even staying in Portneath,' she said once they were back in the flat, sitting with large glasses of red wine in front of the fire. 'Not once the funeral is done.'

'I don't think you should rush things,' said Finn. 'What harm would a few more days make? A month. Stay another month.'

It wasn't as if she had anything to go back to in Paris. Or anywhere else, come to that. Maybe she should try her luck in London. There were some great chefs she could learn from there, really inspiring people. It was worth a try, but, let's face it, there was no certainty and January was a quiet time for restaurateurs. It was pretty much the worst time ever to be looking for a job.

'I could . . .' she said doubtfully.

'Agreed,' declared Finn, deliberately prematurely, clinking her wine glass with his to seal the deal. 'You owe it to your mum,' he said. 'She'd want you to take your time.'

'I owed her a *lot* more of my time, while she was alive,' Freya said. 'More than I can ever give now. It's too late,' she swallowed miserably and hung her head.

Finn put a sympathetic hand on her arm. He didn't speak and she was glad. What was there to say that would change anything now?

They drank in companionable silence for a while, both watching the flames flickering hypnotically in the fireplace.

'If I was staying,' she said, pausing to listen to her own words, her head slightly on one side. 'If I was staying, then what you're suggesting, working with you and Ciaran and Martha – well, I just want to say, I can't imagine anything more inspiring.'

'So, say "yes",' said Finn. 'It's as easy as that.'

'We'll have to see,' she said, picking up her glass and his to take them to the kitchen. 'And I totally love you for asking.'

Shit. Had she just told him she loved him? It was the wine talking. She looked at her empty glass with dismay as she walked past. Hopefully, he hadn't noticed.

She put the glasses down on the draining board and, turning, found herself chest to chest with him as he reached for her arms to shuffle her around him in the narrow space. They did an awkward manoeuvre to swap places and then, when she reached the kitchen doorway, she made to bolt, but his hands remained on her arms, holding her gently but firmly. She looked up and their eyes locked. He really did have the most extraordinary eyes – definitely more green than blue – she thought, with dark lines around the irises that echoed the short, dark lashes, so thick it was almost as though he had eyeliner on. She gazed seemingly endlessly, losing herself, as his mouth worked in an effort to speak.

'You know, when . . .' he said at last, '. . . when you really mean to do something . . . to say something . . . but you don't, and then you discover it's too late, and you really, really wish you'd been braver and just said it?'

Freya nodded. She did. With all her heart.

'Well, there was a time . . .' he began, then paused, then squeezed her arms a bit harder, both to help him marshal his thoughts and to stop her escaping, 'There was a time when I wished I'd said something to you,' he blurted, looking into her eyes. 'And I didn't, and then I heard you'd found this job and just taken off to Paris, overnight, and I thought, well, I've missed my chance, and even if I'd taken it, why would she have turned her back on a career opportunity like that anyway? Staying in Portneath, versus becoming a top chef? It's not difficult to see which one a talented eighteen-year-old with the world at her feet would choose. So, it makes no odds.'

There was a pause while Freya processed what she had just heard. '*You*,' she said, remembering how glamorous and totally beyond reach he and Ciaran had seemed to her and Hattie all those years ago. 'I had no idea . . .'

'No? Well . . .' Finn trailed off, letting go of her arms and dropping his eyes. 'I don't suppose you did. Anyhow,' he said more loudly, 'doesn't matter now. Listen, I'm really glad you'll stay a few more days, at least. It seems mad coming all that way for such a short time. Stay. Spend time with your old mates, then, you know, if you do decide to stay longer, at least you've got an offer for something a bit more exciting than pudding making.'

Freya moved reluctantly to let him pass, the moment broken. 'You may think pudding making's boring,' she said, deliberately lightly, 'but I'll have you know, there's already talk of moving me up to treacle sponge, and – I'm sure I don't need to tell you – that's a stellar rise up the pudding hierarchy. It doesn't get much more exciting than that.'

Chapter Seventeen

Seven Swans a-Swimming

In the deli café, waiting for Diana to join her for a coffee, that Monday morning, Freya allowed herself a moment to dream. The memories played across her mind like a cine-film, Mum baking, Mum holding her hand and walking her to the little village school, Mum sewing the hem of her nativity costume as they watched a Christmas film together. Vividly, she saw the smiling face, the reddish-brown curls, she could even remember the smell of the kitchen at home, when, every Saturday, the stock bubbled and vegetables from Portneath market were piled on the scrubbed table, waiting to be cleaned and chopped and made into soup. She had been so ready to give it all up and go to Paris, to race on with her life. Now she would give anything to be back there, safe, cared for and unconditionally loved.

Diana arrived in a flurry of scarves and shopping bags and settled herself opposite Freya with a sigh of contentment. Freya had bagged the best table in the café, the one in the corner with the clear view up towards the castle.

'So, just to get things clear, tell me exactly what's happened, since the moment you got my text?' instructed Diana, once they had been given their coffee.

'I'm so sorry I didn't reply,' apologised Freya. 'I was shocked.'

'Of course, you were. You don't need to explain, darling. So, what did you do then?'

'I didn't handle it too well,' admitted Freya, recounting how she had failed to actually tell Andre about her mother, which might – to be fair – have made a difference to his decision to fire her on the spot.

'But that's appalling!' Diana exclaimed. 'He can't do that . . . I've got a good mind to tell him what I think.'

'Good luck with that.'

'But I suppose the main thing is you got there in time? In time to say goodbye?' Diana gazed at her anxiously.

Freya nodded, mutely. 'And then I came here, bumped into Finn and – well – you know the rest.'

They drank in silence for a while, and then Diana got out her diary. 'Now,' she said, 'I always think Friday is the best day for a funeral. It gives people an excuse to wrap up work early and they get a long weekend into the bargain. That's always popular. I've already checked with the church and the undertaker, and this Friday's fine.'

'*This* Friday,' said Freya in alarm. 'That's only five days away. Is it enough notice?'

'Plenty,' said Diana. 'In fact, I might have mentioned it to a few people already,' she admitted. 'They all think it's ideal.'

'OK, then,' said Freya. 'I totally need you to tell me who to invite. I'm . . .' she swallowed. 'I'm really out of touch with who was important to Mum.' She would never have known to invite Jake, for instance. Thank goodness she had his contact details now. Then she remembered again, with a twist of guilt, that she needed to break the news to Hattie and wasn't at all sure how she would take it. If it was anything like Jake, the answer was 'not well'. The emotional outpourings of other people were putting her to shame with her frozen deadness.

'I'm totally on the case,' said Diana, stoutly. 'Leave all that side of things to me.'

Freya might as well have left it all to Diana, she quickly realised, as a remarkably large amount of it seemed to be already in hand. They would all be at the little Norman stone church in Middlemass by half past three on Friday. There would be a service and then the coffin would go to the crematorium. Freya would collect the ashes the following week and make arrangements with the vicar to inter them in a plot in the graveyard a few days later. It was all such an alien experience to Freya, and hugely reassuring to have Diana telling her how things worked.

'I think the main thing now is to just think about some sort of wake after the service,' she told Freya. 'All food-related issues I'll leave to you, although if you're asking me, I would suggest tea and sandwiches at the cricket pavilion. I've checked, and it's free to hire on Friday too, although we would have to be clearing up by seven o'clock because there's a yoga class at seven thirty.'

Freya wrote some notes for herself on her phone – thankfully, Finn's recharging cable fitted it, so it was back in action again. And that also meant she had no more excuses to avoid calling Hattie. Perhaps she would be cowardly and just send her a text. But now there were other problems to solve. She chewed her lip anxiously over how to organise the refreshments. She felt she could – should – do better than tea and sandwiches.

'I'd like to do something hot,' she proposed, cautiously. 'But I'm pretty sure there's not much of a kitchen up at the cricket pavilion. Also, it's a funny time of day for a proper meal. I'll have to have a think,' she said, her brow furrowed.

'Think on, darling, I am sure you will do something splendid. Now, what are your plans for New Year's Eve tonight?'

'There's a party at the Fox and Hounds,' Freya admitted. 'Happy Hour, open mike, disco . . . all the glamour Portneath nightlife has to offer.'

'Not a patch on gay Paree?'

Freya smiled, in spite of herself. 'I wouldn't know. I was always working,' she admitted with a shrug.

'It'll be nice to catch up with a few old friends though, surely?'

'I suppose.'

Diana gave her an appraising look. 'Old friends matter,' she said. 'But I can see it might all seem a bit parochial . . . And your mum wouldn't want you to get stuck here, missing out, when you should be following your dreams in some teeming metropolis.'

'Well,' shrugged Freya, thinking of her conversations with Finn and Martha, 'maybe I *am* following my dreams. Maybe here is where I should be. As it is, I am horribly aware I should have come back sooner . . . come back more often.'

'Not for your mum's sake. Don't you dare beat yourself up over that,' said Diana, firmly. 'It's not what she wanted. Your career comes first. Always. Now,' she added briskly, 'back to frivolity, what are you going to wear tonight?'

'To the Fox and Hounds? Oh, I don't know,' Freya grimaced. 'I don't think I'm going. I've got to go home – to the house, I mean – I've got loads to do.'

'It's New Year's Eve,' said Diana. 'You *must* go.'

'Well, OK, for a start, I haven't got anything to wear. I was only supposed to be here for a few days. I've got my jeans and a couple of T-shirts. That's about it.'

'Have a rummage in your mum's wardrobe. No,' she said, laughing at Freya's expression, 'don't look at me like that – you'd be surprised what she's got tucked away in there. Retro's in, isn't it?'

'Yeah, proper retro, not just old,' Freya joked.

Breakfast had arrived now and Diana oversaw her eating a large bowl of creamy porridge with Greek yoghurt and blueberries. It was the best porridge she had ever eaten. Knowing Finn's zeal over ingredients, Ciaran probably grew the oats at the farm, she thought, inconsequentially.

'I'm so glad you're here, darling, truly,' Diana murmured, 'and I want you to go out tonight and have fun.' She squeezed Freya's hand. 'Promise me you will. Tell me all about it tomorrow, OK? I'll write down some more ideas for the funeral service, too. I've arranged for both of us to see the vicar about readings and hymns this Wednesday morning, so keep it free.'

'But the funeral's on Friday. Will that give us enough time to do the Order of Service?'

'Loads,' Diana reassured her. 'I'll do it on my PC straight after. The print shop'll run off copies there and then. It'll be fine.'

Freya had refused Finn's offer to take her up to the house. She knew he was busy. Instead, she called a taxi, giving the driver another of the precious ten-pound notes she had received in her pudding factory pay packet. Only a couple left, now. If only Andre would pay her the wages he owed . . . She was too nervous of his continued wrath to get in touch with him, though, but maybe, now her phone was back in commission, he would contact her. She swallowed hard, anxious at the thought.

A couple of hours of dusty, dirty work later, Freya was happy with her progress. Three more black bin bags of junk sat outside the back door and the furniture downstairs was marked up for the sale room, storage or Freecycle. Now for upstairs.

She went into her mother's room, shaded and secretive now, it was simultaneously familiar and strange. Here was her dressing table with its muddle of make-up and her mother's favourite cologne, the one that smelt of rain, dew-soaked roses and the seashore, the faceted glass and silver filigree label, so familiar. She sprayed a little on her wrist and sniffed. Surely the tears would come now? Dry-eyed, but with an ache in her throat, she turned to the wardrobe and flung open the doors. She buried her face in the clothes and breathed deeply. It was like mainlining memories. This wardrobe, and these clothes . . . her mother . . . soon, they would all be gone for ever. It seemed beyond imagining, as if the ground beneath her feet, would disappear and she would be left, floundering and alone in the world. Unthinkable.

Freya sat heavily on the edge of the bed, wrapping her arms tightly around herself. Refusing to allow chaos to overcome her, she turned her thoughts to John Makepeace, so calm and reliable, wading through the administration that was the inevitable consequence of death. She must find a way to thank him properly. Perhaps she should drop in on him again soon. She needed to tell him about the funeral, and she could ask if there was anything she could do to help. Perhaps he would tell her something about her mother, something she didn't already know – maybe he had his own lovely story to tell, like Jake had. There was clearly some sort of history between them – solicitors didn't generally work for free. It was compelling, this search for things she would have known about the last ten years if she had been here more.

To distract herself, Freya did as Diana had suggested and looked for something to wear for the pub tonight, even though she was increasingly certain she would be able to think up a convincing excuse not to go.

For a start, she thought despondently, clacking the hangers along the rail, the dresses would all be too long because it was a standing joke in their house that Freya had got to twelve years old and stopped growing. Plus, her mother's wardrobe was almost exclusively office clothes, and for an older woman too. Her always slim and elegant mother had always had an interest in looking good, but the types of jobs she took to support them meant her wardrobe leaned more towards the severe, formal end of things, so totally unlike her personality, Freya realised consciously for the first time. She rifled through without much hope but then a flash of glimmering light caught her attention. Crammed in between a pinstriped skirt suit and a navy blazer was a wisp of fabric that glittered and gleamed. She pulled out the hanger – it was heavier than she expected – and went over to the window with it.

It was actually two garments she saw now, essentially a twinset: a short cardigan, in a sheer, netted fabric, heavily encrusted with tiny beads in colours ranging from clear glass through turquoise and green, shading downwards into a scalloped hem. It was like the water in Portneath harbour on a bright, spring day, the sunlight glancing and dancing off the waves. Underneath was a delicate silk camisole with spaghetti straps. It was covered in sequins ranging from oyster cream mixed with delicate shell pink at the top, turning to turquoise, matching the cardigan, as it went down. Freya held them up against herself and looked in the mirror, her head on one side, considering. They brought out the blue in her eyes and complemented the highlights in her bright blonde hair. With the long sleeves she would show only a modest amount of flesh – which was how she liked it. As for what she would wear on the bottom half, it would just have to be her faded, blue jeans and her trainers – the only shoes she had with her. Glamour and grunge. Well, why not? It was just the local pub, after all. She would go for a quick drink, see who was there, and then call it a night.

Reluctant to spend more of her dwindling cash – she needed a tenner to buy herself drinks that night – Freya walked the three or so miles back from the house into the centre of Portneath. On the way past Makepeace, Morley and Bulmer, she noticed there was a light on. On impulse, she pushed open the heavy door and slipped inside. At first she wondered if she had been mistaken, but after a short delay John Makepeace appeared from the back office like a genie from a lamp and seemed genuinely pleased to see her.

'Tea?' he offered.

'I'd like that. Shall I?' said Freya, instantly wondering if it was ridiculous to offer. If he saw her as a client – which she essentially was – then he would find the offer to make him a cup of tea in his own office very strange.

'Great, yes please,' he said, with only the briefest hesitation, standing aside so she could go past him into the back office where she saw a little kitchen area with a sink and a kettle.

'I think there might even be some biscuits,' he said. 'Have a delve in that cupboard above the kettle.'

Once they were settled, with Freya warming her hands gratefully on a large mug of tea, he shuffled together some papers on his desk and looked at her directly.

'I'm thinking now might be the time to give you a little more detail about your mother's estate?' he enquired, gently.

'I'd like that,' said Freya.

'OK, well, it is, essentially, very straightforward,' he went on, steepling his fingers under his chin in that familiar gesture of his. 'There are a few savings,' he said. 'Nearly two thousand in a savings account, a further five thousand in Premium Bonds,' he said, 'and your mother was careful with money, there are no major outstanding debts – perhaps there's the odd bill yet to resurface – but I'm sure nothing major.'

Freya thought guiltily of the red-inked envelopes at the house. She should have brought them down.

'Of course, the house is the principal asset,' he went on, 'although – as I warned – there is a mortgage outstanding on that. It's a pretty substantial one, I'm afraid, but I am certain there is also some equity in the house.' He paused, watching her face. Clearly, he was considering whether to tell her more.

She waited.

'Look,' he said, making up his mind, 'when I saw your mother last, she was quite distressed, talking about your inheritance, and how she felt she had let you down . . .'

'Of course she hasn't let me down,' said Freya, tears catching in her throat at the thought. 'I never had any expectations for an inheritance, I've never given it a moment's thought.'

'I'm sure,' he said hurriedly. 'I told her as much, but it was the issue of life assurance – at least to cover an amount that would have paid off the mortgage, so you could keep living in the house.'

'Live there without her? Alone?' Freya knew it was the very last thing she would have wanted to do. It was her childhood home, sure, but that was over now.

'I think she would want me to explain,' he went on. 'When you were born, she made sure her life was assured for a substantial sum. She felt – as a lone parent – that was important. Money was tight though and so I remember advising her the most cost-effective solution was term life insurance, a policy set to expire when you were eighteen. At that point, she would see what life assurance she needed next and it would have been natural to at least take out a policy to cover the mortgage. Of course, by that point, she had had her first brush with cancer and when she came to explore options she discovered no-one would take her on without specifically excluding a pay-out if cancer was the cause of death. She seemed to know the cancer would return,' he added, 'but she did feel she let you down in that way.'

'She didn't let me down,' said Freya fiercely. 'She never let me down, over anything, least of all this.'

'I told her as much,' he said quietly, shuffling papers, clearly hoping to distract Freya from the tears that she saw had filled his eyes.

He cleared his throat. 'So,' he went on, 'I have taken the liberty of appointing a chartered surveyor to value the property, and his initial estimate is that it should be put on the market at around three hundred and sixty thousand pounds, or thereabouts.'

'Three-sixty?' said Freya, astonished. Of course, she had no idea what houses sold for here – she had never given it any thought – but that sounded like a lot.

'There's a thriving market for second homes in the area, so that is the going rate for a modest, detached three-bed property, I am assured,' he confirmed. 'Do I have your permission to put the house on the market?' he asked, eyebrows raised.

'Of course,' nodded Freya. 'Thank you.'

He inclined his head and went on, 'I am waiting for probate, but I expect no significant delays there. I also took the liberty of acquiring a copy of your mother's death certificate. Actually, I got several copies as one tends to need them. Would you like to take one?'

'No,' said Freya, 'thank you, but no.'

He inclined his head again, respectfully. 'So – where was I? Ah, OK, marketing the property. I need you to be completely certain you don't want to live there. Of course, if you did, for reasons I have just explained, that would necessitate you taking out a mortgage.'

'I don't think I'm the sort of person who has a mortgage,' admitted Freya. 'Not at the moment, at least. I don't actually have a job, or at least not the kind of job I would need to borrow that sort of money,' she said briefly filling him in on the shifts at the pudding factory.

'Ah. Yes, I don't think the mortgage company would think much of that,' he agreed. 'Er, if I dare ask, what happened to your employment in Paris. Is that not ongoing?'

Freya explained, briefly, how she had lost her job.

'So, there is a chance you will stay here, perhaps?'

'Unlikely,' Freya admitted. 'Not impossible, though.'

'Well,' he said, after a pause, 'whatever it is you decide you would like to do next, I anticipate that you will have a lump sum from your mother's estate which will be comfortably into the five-figure range,' he said. 'Not a fortune, perhaps, but enough for a deposit if you find yourself in a better position with regards to a mortgage in the future. Or perhaps for a venture . . .? Or even an *ad*venture,' he added with a gleam in his eye that Freya now understood was the equivalent of a belly laugh in people who were less restrained in expressing their emotions.

Freya liked John Makepeace.

Chapter Eighteen

By the time she got back to the deli, Freya's feet were wet through and she couldn't feel them any more. The sun had dropped below the rooflines and dark had crowded swiftly in. Going to the Fox and Hounds was the last thing she felt like doing. Correction: the *very* last thing she felt like was spending the evening alone in her chilly little attic bedroom. The *second* last thing she felt like was going out. But, 'Ladies first,' said Finn, sweeping a low bow and gesturing towards the bathroom.

'I won't say no,' admitted Freya, who was dying for a long, hot bath to warm herself up. She had her mother's twinset in her rucksack and was shy about Finn seeing it. While she ran the bath, she tentatively probed her feelings about the evening ahead. She knew from the café on market day that she was going to attract interest, which was uncomfortable. It was likely she would see Hattie and all the signs said that wasn't going to go well. Now she thought about it, how many other characters from her past would give her a chilly welcome? But she should man up, she told herself, squaring her shoulders. This was an opportunity, a chance to get to the bottom of Hattie's problem with her. She missed her friend desperately, she realised, and even though it might be too late to resurrect their friendship, Freya cared too much about her old friend to let her be upset and angry if there was anything she could do to fix it.

A scalding hot bath turned her lobster-red. She had nicked a bit more of Finn's ex-girlfriend's Badedas and had a really good soak, then suddenly wondered if she had been in there too long and felt bad about hogging the bathroom. She vacated hurriedly, leaving billowing steam in her wake as she scampered upstairs to her attic room before Finn could see her in a towel.

It was cold up in the attic, but the hot bath was keeping her toasty from within. She found clean underwear and then shimmied quickly into her trusty jeans, breathing in a little more than usual to do up the zip. God knows how much weight she had gained in the last week! Now though, standing on the bed to see her rear end in the little dressing-table mirror, she quite liked the look of her jeans stretched just nicely over her bum. She had an actual booty! Cool.

Carefully she slipped the camisole on, slippery and cold, with its delicate spaghetti straps, and then the cardigan, heavy with beading, falling like water into place. She had never seen her mum wear such glamorous clothes, she realised. In fact, she couldn't remember her going out to enjoy herself much at all. And if she did, there was no money for new clothes when so much of what she earned had to go on ingredients and kitchen equipment for Freya – there had been a never-ending list of expensive kit to buy, which all appeared. Freya had totally taken that for granted. She had not been grateful enough at the time – or since – and now it was too late.

Of course, her mother had had no social life when she was ill with the first bout of cancer; the one that turned their lives upside down when Freya was taking her GCSEs – she had had no energy for it. The brutal treatment dragged on through the following year and, at the end of it all, she remembered her mother and herself raising a glass of champagne in defiance of fate and toasting the future filled with hope.

Freya had left shortly after and all too quickly the months, then the years, had passed. Her mother visited Freya in Paris just once, that last spring. They had the most magical, care-free few days together, with Freya showcasing the glamour and downplaying the negative, weaving a fairy tale version of her life to persuade her mother – and herself – that she was OK. They had clung together at the station, she remembered, and Freya had promised herself that she would come home for a holiday soon.

But after ten bonus years of life the cancer had come back to get Anna, silently. And her mother had borne it alone.

Feeling tears beginning to melt her tough outer shell, Freya gave herself a stern talking-to until they receded. She couldn't allow herself to cry once her make-up was on and she was going to go the full works on it too. She had loved using dramatic make-up as a teen but had barely worn it for years as anything remotely glamorous was just sweated off her face in the kitchen. She had allowed herself a rifle through her mother's make-up drawer at home that after-noon and now she was grateful to have all necessary weapons at her disposal. Rummaging gleefully, she found everything she needed for a full-on glamour makeover: there was a trusty lash-building mascara; an all-round wonder pencil in her favourite shade that could do blush and lips too; and a bodacious liquid highlighter that gleamed like the moonlight.

First she had done her primer and carefully sponged on the base, pressing it into her skin really well the way she and Hattie had taught themselves to do as teenagers, with a bit of help from YouTube. She then coated the whole eyelid with the highlighter and then shaded her eye sockets with a beautiful, radiant shell pink that reflected iridescent light like a hologram if it was put on thickly enough. Freya put it on thickly enough. Then, taking great care because she was out of practise, she drew heavy cat's eye flicks with her black eyeliner and for once she managed to make it look the same on both sides. She was right up against the mirror for close-up work, but she stood back frequently to check the full effect. The aim was balance, with one focus only, and for Freya, tonight, it was definitely her big, blue eyes. Once she had them thickly but perfectly mascaraed to her satisfaction, they looked huge. She quickly shaded her cheeks and lips with the pretty, natural-looking pink crayon, gave her cheekbones a light slick of highlighter and added a dot of lip gloss to her lower lip. The finishing touch was a pair of diamanté earrings she had found on her mother's dressing table – two tassels of silver light, they flowed like waterfalls nearly grazing her collarbone, and would be shown off to best effect if her hair was up. She twisted it loosely into a knot and fixed it with a few pins. She would be surprised if it stayed up for long, but it would do.

The trainers she was stuck with wearing were looking tired and grubby but she would give them a quick wipe over and they would be fine. They had to be. It was surprisingly nice to be glamorous for a change. She couldn't remember the last time she had dolled up to go out. Actually, she couldn't remember the last time she had gone out, full stop.

She came down the attic stairs tentatively, hoping Finn was still in the bathroom or otherwise occupied because there was a full-length mirror on the wall by the door and she wanted to see herself before he did. Even in the low light, the beads and sequins glimmered and her eyes were bewitchingly large and dramatic. As far as she could judge, in the gloom of the hallway, she seemed to look reasonable.

'Wow,' said Finn, making her jump. She tried to turn away from the mirror, but with him standing right behind her, there wasn't room in the tiny hall. 'I really didn't come all the way back to Devon to go out partying,' she complained, shuffling her feet.

'Could have fooled me. You look great,' he said, admiring her reflection over her shoulder. Their eyes met in the mirror. He stood a full head and shoulders above her and it was easier to meet his eye this way than it was face to face or, in Freya's case, face to somewhere around the third button on his shirt. Tonight, he was wearing jeans, teamed with a midnight blue shirt, open necked and with the sleeves rolled up. Beaten-up trainers like Freya's completed the look. He looked and smelt extremely fanciable, Freya's body told her, even as her mind firmly rejected the possibility. Complexity like that was the last thing she needed – and anyhow, Finn had made his views on romance more than clear.

'So,' she said, gesturing to the door. 'Shall we?'

'First things first,' he said. 'Preloading.'

'As in, drinks before we drink?'

'As in, "yes, but also, I've made you a snack",' he explained, walking away.

'I'm really not hungry,' she protested after him.

'No snack, no champagne,' he teased, coming back from the kitchen with a full glass but withdrawing as she reached for it.

'You win,' she smiled, taking it from him and having an appreciative sip. 'Mm. Lovely.'

'I'll take that as an expert view, from the uber-smart Parisian party girl herself.'

'Don't,' said Freya. 'Seriously, you have no idea how little fun I've been having in Paris. And I hardly ever drink champagne either.'

'Waste of an opportunity,' observed Finn. 'There you go,' he said, interrupting her disturbing thoughts and handing her a plate with a large piece of Christmas cake and what looked like a slab of cheese.

'It'll line your stomach,' he explained. 'Holly Tree Farm extra-mature Cheddar. It's legendary. And it's amazing with Martha's Christmas cake. What with you not being used to drinking – or so you claim – we don't want you getting pissed and carried away.'

'I'm not sure I need help to avoid making a tit of myself, tonight thanks. I'm pretty motivated not to anyhow.'

'Although, if you did, you'd remind me of my aunt, who was – still is – quite the partygoer.'

'Go on,' said Freya, sensing an anecdote.

'Ah, my Auntie Niamh,' reflected Finn, mistily, sitting back on the sofa and relaxing into his story. 'What a woman. She'd always have a cheese sandwich before she went out on the lash and then – three nightclubs, six hours of dancing like a loon, two bottles of wine and twelve cocktails later – she'd be chucking her guts up in the nightclub toilets, groaning "it must have been the cheese sandwich".'

Freya laughed in spite of herself. 'That *definitely* won't be me.' But he'd been right about the cheese and fruit cake combination: it was one of the most perfect pairings she had ever encountered, and it was impressive Christmas cake too, with no horrible, gritty currants, just fat raisins, juicy cherries and generous amounts of candied peel, with a thick coating of yellow marzipan. There was no fondant icing, which Freya often found a bit too sickly, but instead there was a jumble of roasted nuts and crystallised fruit, glistening stickily with a syrupy glaze.

She wondered what Martha and Ciaran would be doing to celebrate the new year. Perhaps they would have a quiet night in. It might give Martha that opportunity to have a proper talk with Ciaran. She needed to.

'Eat up,' Finn said, a moment later, breaking into her food-fuelled reverie. 'We'll be missing all the fun.'

The Fox and Hounds was just a stone's throw from the deli but on the short walk from the flat, Freya's nerves resurfaced. She hated the whole 'walking into a crowded room' thing. She could see through the windows, casting a glowing yellow light out onto the rain-slicked street, that the pub was absolutely heaving, too.

Finn paused, his hand on the door handle. 'Ready?' he asked, glancing behind and giving her a reassuring smile.

She took a deep breath and puffed it out. 'I'm good,' she said, with a little nod.

He held open the door, there was a blast of shouted conversation and heat, and in she went. Being short, she was instantly enveloped into the crowd, limiting her ability to see across the room and check out who was there. 'I'll get us a drink,' said Finn, putting his lips so close to her ear a shudder travelled down her spine, leaving her tingling and with a disturbing, hollow feeling in her stomach. The next moment he was gone. Freya stood, self-consciously, with a daft half-smile on her face, trying to give the impression of being engaged and happily waiting for Finn to return, rather than alone and totally out of her depth.

At the other end of the pub, where the dartboard had always been in her teens, there was an area that was up a couple of steps. The people there were high enough, and far enough away, to be observed without her drawing attention to herself. Some of the faces were unfamiliar, but most weren't. There was Gabriel, the local aristo – although he never put on airs. She didn't think she had ever actually been brave enough to speak to him, but he had been a fixture in Ciaran and Finn's crowd back in the old days, always with a leggy blonde in tow. There was one with him now, although she assumed it wasn't the same one as ten years ago. It couldn't be, could it? They didn't look 'together' enough. In contrast, the woman standing arm in arm with Aidan, the tree surgeon, was definitely 'with' him. She was new and unfamiliar, clocked Freya. A stranger. And they looked so in love. How wonderful that must be, just to know that there is another being on the planet who is totally on your side. Parents – good parents – were like that, of course. Freya's mum had definitely been on her side, always. But this was something else, meeting someone who started as a stranger, and forming that bond, possibly for life. Didn't swans mate for life? she mused, remembering the time there was a pair of swans on the village pond in Middlemass. They had stayed for several weeks before eventually moving on to more spacious quarters, but Freya had remembered vividly how they would canoodle on the little pond, necks twined around each other in elegant embrace.

'Oh my God, Freya!' came a cry from her left.

Taking a deep breath, she turned, smiling, in the direction of the voice, hoping her micro-expression when she caught sight of its owner didn't give her away. It was Natalie, one of the cool girls from school. Having always moved in far more elevated circles than Freya had, she was astonished the woman even knew who she was, let alone recognised her after ten years.

'Natalie,' Freya called back, smiling nervously, as the woman wove determinedly through the crowds to get to her, turning sideways to squeeze through the gaps. She was wearing the tightest of tight jeans, teeteringly high heels and a halter-neck gold top with a daring, virtually non-existent, back. Her hair was dark, shiny and long, just like it had been at school, and her face and nails were immaculate. Natalie and her crew had always been high rent and scarily mature, the first in Freya's year to do more or less everything

– dating, drinking, passing driving tests and immediately being given their own cars . . . They were a dauntingly sophisticated crowd but to be fair, Freya admitted, Natalie had been uninterested in bitching. In her perfect world, with her rich parents and privileged home life, there had been no need to bring down others around her. If there was a shortcoming it was a benign failure of imagination leading to a blank inability to register others were less fortunate.

'I thought you were in Paris,' Natalie said, grabbing her arm excitedly as she reached Freya's side at last.

'I am . . . I was . . . I mean, I am,' Freya blurted. Yep, being addressed by a member of the cool crowd still made her feel like the short, awkward, inky Year Ten. She had been all those years ago. Nothing had changed, not really.

'So totally cool,' Natalie went on, misty-eyed, 'I remember when we all heard you'd got a job working for Andre Boucher this, like, famous guy, and we were, like . . .' She paused, gazing at the ceiling, to think exactly what they were like.

Astonished, probably, thought Freya. Surely, as a chubby schoolgirl she would have won the 'Person least likely to get whisked off to Paris by a C-list celebrity' award in the High School Yearbook. In fact, having Andre spirit her away just months before A levels had got her out of being listed as anything in the Yearbook, which had seemed like yet another minor win at the time.

Natalie was now looking at her intently, clearly waiting for an answer to a question Freya hadn't registered. She guessed it was probably something along the lines of 'What the heck are you doing here?'

'My mum's just died,' she yelled, somewhere close to Natalie's ear, then ducked her head to hide the threatened tears. Damn, this was a terrible time for her weeping propensity to suddenly reappear, her elaborate eye make-up was not going to survive random crying spells. She had to get a grip.

'Oh my God, no!' exclaimed Natalie. She looked at Freya with horror. 'I am sooo sorry!' She threw her arms around Freya and squeezed her so tight she was relieved to come back up for air. She was astonished at Natalie's interest in her, but she supposed that was because, with exciting celebrity chef collateral, she was infinitely more interesting than she had been at school. Plus, to be fair, the compassion was clearly heartfelt, and Freya was grateful for it in a way she wouldn't have been just a few short days ago. Maybe the heart of the ice queen was melting at last.

Next, Freya was dragged by Natalie through the crowds back to her little gang, each of the women in the group hanging onto the arm of whichever slightly bored-looking man belonged to them. Natalie screeched the critical information at them all, and then offered Freya up to a chorus of 'Oh my God' and sympathetic head tilts. It was not actually unpleasant, Freya decided, being the main attraction for a group of women who might not be up to Parisian celebrity chef standards but were pretty glamorous for Portneath.

At the periphery of their noisy group Freya saw Sharmayne pressing forward with her eye on the little gathering. On seeing her newest employee, and clocking the glamorous transformation, she looked first perplexed and then annoyed. She said something sharp to the man following her, turned a hundred and eighty degrees and started fighting the crowds to go in the opposite direction. Freya couldn't say she was sorry.

Not having the advantage of height, in these crowds Freya had completely lost sight of Finn as he edged his way over to the bar, and he had no way of knowing that she had moved, but then he suddenly popped up beside her, handing her a glass of fizz. 'Not as good as the stuff I gave you at home,' he shouted apologetically in her ear.

It was reassuring to have him there, standing beside her. As the jostling intensified, he rested an arm around her shoulders, pulling her in to his side, to protect her from the crush. Just then Freya glanced up and locked eyes with Hattie, who was standing a few yards away, looking miserable. Seeing Freya, she glowered, and Freya was dismayed to see a look of rage and misery settle onto her face. What was upsetting her old friend so much? Was it really all because she had been a bit crap at keeping in touch? Detaching herself gently from Finn's arm she indicated with a nod of her head where she was going and edged over to where Hattie was standing.

'Hats,' she exclaimed, digging her old friend gently in the ribs.

Hattie nearly smiled, in spite of herself. 'No one calls me that anymore,' she complained without heat. 'You look nice,' she added grudgingly, gesturing to Freya's twinset. 'That some posh French designer, or something?'

'Vintage Portneath,' said Freya, shaking her head. 'I've upset you,' she went on, looking at her friend imploringly. 'I know I have. I've been rubbish . . .'

Hattie sighed. She opened her mouth to speak and then closed it again, looking away.

'Please talk to me, Hats,' Freya pleaded.

Hattie grimaced, shaking her head. 'You've done nothing wrong, not really,' she admitted at last, shouting into Freya's ear above the din. In the corner, on a raised platform two skinny men with long hair were fiddling around with cables and a huge amp doing sound checks, which raised the decibels even higher as well as generating blasts of agonising feedback.

Freya waited, giving her friend a sideways look.

'I know I'm probably expecting too much,' admitted Hattie over the din, 'but it's hard, you know?'

'You have a right to expectations,' shouted Freya. 'Believe me, my life is a car crash if you want a reason for me having been absent . . . but I know that's no excuse. Listen, can we go somewhere quieter and talk?'

Hattie paused, then nodded reluctantly. Together, they slipped through the crowds and out of the door onto the street outside where Hattie turned away, crossing her arms, seemingly newly unwilling to communicate.

The door to the pub closed behind them and the clamour dropped instantly. The relative quiet was a relief.

'Hats . . .?' prompted Freya. 'Please tell me what went wrong,' she went on. 'I'm sure it's my fault, but what happened? Suddenly you were just gone. No texts, nothing. Although I appreciate I should have made the first move, got in touch—'

'You. Are. Kidding!' Hattie exploded. 'You're pretending you don't know? That last text of yours? Offended, much? And you wonder why I broke off contact?'

'What? What did I say?' Freya was genuinely clueless.

'It wasn't so much what you said, it was the way you said it,' continued Hattie, persuaded and somewhat mollified by Freya's obviously genuine confusion, drawing her affronted dignity around her like a cloak. 'I mean, I know when I'm not wanted. I'm not going to just—'

'Seriously, Hattie, you're going to need to be specific,' interjected Freya, impatient now. She knew she hadn't done whatever she was being accused of. Had she?

'Well,' Hattie was unsure now, 'we were just texting, watching that Netflix thing together, you know – the one about the woman who committed all those frauds and kept changing her identity? Anyhow, I just said I needed to go to sleep, and you just – well – you just went "Fine." With a full stop. Really snippy and abrupt and I was only saying I had to sleep because I had work the next day.'

'I said "fine" though.'

'Yeah, but with a full stop.'

Freya sighed. 'Literally? A full stop?'

Hattie nodded, rubbing her toe against the ground, awkwardly. 'OK, I admit, it might not have been—'

'It definitely wasn't,' said Freya, firmly. 'But apologies if offence was taken.' Freya sounded aggrieved. Because she was.

'OK, so maybe I was being oversensitive,' admitted Hattie, looking away. 'But just look at things from my point of view for a moment,' she continued turning back to Freya, suddenly urgent. 'While you're swanning off to Paris to work with this fancy chef who's just plucked you out of obscurity so he can make you into this celebrity food person too, just remember I'm still boring my tits off in Portneath, trying to find an actual job with actual career prospects but there literally aren't any here, basically, so I end up working on a production line in a sodding Christmas pudding factory. So far, so glamorous, right?'

'Er, right?' echoed Freya, uncertainly.

'And that's before you even factor in that I'm hanging onto the roof over my head for dear life, because my useless mum's on her third boyfriend in a year, only this one's actually moving in, it turns out, and he and my mum would quite like to have the place to themselves. So that's really nice for me.'

Freya's heart ached for her friend. Hattie's mother had always been a catastrophe, living off the drama of endless soap operas, plus any aggro that she could generate in her own life, to keep herself amused. There was an ongoing parade of boyfriends, some fairly nice and some downright unpleasant, but even the more decent ones had rarely had time for poor Hattie. She had been subjected to constant insecurity and change, never knowing what mood her mum would be in or whether there would be food on the table. It wasn't a 'call the social worker' scale of neglect. If anything, it was more soul-deadening than that. Even if her mother remembered her at all and bothered to cook, Hattie would be lucky if it was anything other than something brown from the freezer chucked under the grill.

Mum had always encouraged Hattie to stay for tea when she came home with Freya after school, she remembered. Shepherd's pie, bangers and mash, lasagne, roast chicken . . . Freya had always been given a hearty meal in the evening – increasingly something she had cooked herself – and Hattie had eaten with them on countless occasions. At the weekends, she frequently had a sleepover on Saturday nights, with Anna being worried that Hattie was so often left on her own at the weekend, even at a young age. When Freya, with her burgeoning interest in food, was gradually taking over responsibility for cooking supper, especially when her mum was working late, she and Hattie would prepare food together and, when Hattie went home at last, Freya realised she was lucky to do so with a full stomach. It taught her to be grateful and curtailed the worst of her teenage sulks. And it wasn't just the food, either, Freya remembered, gazing at Hattie with compassion, seeing those memories afresh through the prism of her friend's experience. Anna had made time to talk to them both too, asking Hattie what she'd been doing at school, checking homework was done, engaging them in lively chats about life, the universe and everything. Both girls felt equally that they could go to her with worries and concerns. She had been a good mother to Freya and she had, Freya realised now, done what she could to compensate for Hattie's mum's deficiencies too.

'And you make it look so effortless, don't you?' Hattie was going on, cutting into Freya's thoughts, 'because whatever you decide you want it just falls into your lap, doesn't it? Even down to getting a man, because what happens is this: you come back home for the first time in, like, forever, and instantly – *instantly*,' she insisted, eyes blazing, 'you bump into Finn, your eyes meet, and the rest is history, right?'

'Erm, actually no,' said Freya, tentatively, for fear of getting her head bitten off.

'Nah, don't waste your breath,' said Hattie, bitterly. 'I saw you. You didn't see me, but I saw you both, in the deli café on Christmas Eve, and you'd have to be blind not to see the connection between you. The chemistry.' Hattie stopped, staring into the distance, conjuring up the scene in her mind's eye. Her scowl deepened. 'Not that he would ever give me a second glance, anyway,' she muttered, almost to herself.

Clearly Hattie's jealousy extended beyond Freya's career to include her imagined ability to pull hot men. She could put her old friend right on that score, at least.

'That?' she exclaimed, 'Listen, Hats, he'd just bumped into me. It was completely random. Honestly, that was . . .' She trailed off. What *had* it been, then? Definitely not romance . . . but what? They were friends, certainly, but more than that? Maybe. She looked at her friend in anguish.

'Look, Hats,' Freya implored, 'I've been a crappy friend, but believe me, it's not as rosy as it seems for me, I mean, for a start, this thing with Finn . . .'

Hattie sighed, seeming to deflate in front of her. She rubbed her forehead, wearily. 'That's not the point,' she admitted. 'He's hot, obviously, and I'm sure he's lovely, but he's not for the likes of me, I know that. And listen, I know I'm being unfair. I know. But it's hard – Freya with the incredible job, the amazing mum, the hunky boyfriend

– seeing you having it all, effortlessly, and, at the same time, I'm *so* clearly not a priority for you, you don't even bother to let me know when you visit. Yeah,' she said pointing triumphantly at Freya's guilty expression, 'if you want to make a secret trip home without letting your mates know, then don't post pictures of you and your mum's cosy little meet-ups on Insta, eh? Doh.' Her chin wobbled and she lifted it defiantly, knowing she had hit home. 'I thought we had something,' she went on, more quietly. 'I thought we had history. You and me and your lovely mum.'

'We did,' said Freya. 'We do.' Damn. How completely stupid of her not to realise she was giving herself away on Instagram. All she had wanted was to spend time with her mum in their lovely, safe, cosy world. How careless she had been of her poor friend's feelings! Hattie had every right to be angry. That said, Freya wondered how to put her straight about how very much not 'having it all' her life actually was – but maybe now wasn't the time to play the grief card, just to score a conversational point. Not like that. Although she wanted and needed her friend to know the terrible truth. But before she could steel herself to say it, Hattie spoke again.

'You know what?' she said. 'Let's just put it all down to me being an envious cow, shall we? I think it would just be best if you stayed out of my way, yeah?'

Before Freya could reply, Hattie yanked open the door and pushed her way back into the crowded bar, leaving Freya standing, alone, on the street. 'And I've got some terrible news to tell you . . .' Freya whispered into the night air as she watched her old friend disappear into the crowd.

Chapter Nineteen

Inside the pub, the open-mike session was kicking off. Resisting the temptation to slip back to the flat without saying goodbye to Finn, Freya sidled back into the melee, smiling politely, trying to ignore the double takes of people she recognised and who clearly recognised her. She was losing interest in the whole 'wow, it's you, so what's Andre Boucher like in real life?' conversation.

She wanted Finn.

'Looks like you got rinsed,' he shouted into her ear, turning up suddenly on her left side. He inclined his head at Hattie who was now fighting her way back to the bar, probably to drown her sorrows. 'Didn't go well?'

'It could have gone better,' agreed Freya, shouting back at him as someone threaded their arm through hers on her right.

'Ciaran!' she exclaimed, delighted, as she turned to see who it was.

'Looking gorgeous,' he said, kissing her on both cheeks.

'It's lovely to see you. Is Martha here?' Freya asked, looking around her hopefully.

He shook his head, sadly. 'Kids,' he said. 'We tossed a coin and I won. Or Martha won, depending on your point of view.'

'I'm so sorry,' Freya said. 'You should have asked me. I'd have babysat.'

'I couldn't condemn you to an evening with our rabble,' Ciaran said.

She should have thought to offer tonight, of all nights. Yet more proof she was a rubbish friend, she thought, despondently. Plus, it would have been a great excuse to duck out of this.

Up on the stage, an Elvis impersonator was making breakfast, lunch and dinner out of the last line of 'Are You Lonesome Tonight,' to bawdy cheers and enthusiastic applause.

'I think it's us,' said Ciaran to Finn.

'This could be our big break,' joked Finn.

'I sincerely doubt it,' said Ciaran.

'Actually, I might . . .' began Freya, looking longingly at the door. She was pining to get back to the flat just to get away from the noise. It was starting to make her head hurt.

'You're escaping?' said Finn, second-guessing her. 'Don't go just yet,' he said. 'I need a friendly face in the crowd.'

'What on earth are you going to do?'

'Watch,' said Finn over his shoulder as he followed behind Ciaran who was already weaving his way towards the make-shift stage.

Seemingly without nerves, Finn picked up his guitar and smiled at the expectant crowd. 'Here's a number that means a lot to me,' he said into the mike, strumming lightly and experimentally across the strings then tweaking the pegs as he talked, 'mainly cos it's the only thing I can play, but especially at the moment when unexpected changes in life are kind of making things a little weird,' he added, enigmatically.

'Not for me,' chipped in Ciaran, grinning. 'Nothing weird about *my* life.'

Finn gave him an eye-roll that made the crowd laugh, and then, with a quick count-in, they launched into an energetic cover of 'I Will Wait,' by Mumford and Sons. The crowd in the pub roared their approval and Freya smiled, despite herself. It was New Year's Eve, she was surrounded by people she had grown up with, all determined to have a great time, and there she was, buoyed up by feeling as though she was part of something bigger. It felt tentatively good.

Finn sang surprisingly tunefully, his eyes fixed on Freya. Some people in the crowd were following his gaze and whooping their approval. Freya felt like there was a spotlight on her, picking her out. She overcame the instinct to duck and manufactured a smile. They were all friendly, she reminded herself, and, in any case, her eyes were locked onto Finn's and she was finding it impossible to pull them away.

The song ended to riotous applause and whoops. The two men, so alike, so obviously brothers, bowed in unison. Refusing cries of 'encore' they left the stage, walking straight into Sharmayne with her Ken-doll man friend. Sharmayne was instantly all over them both and they politely returned her attention, although Finn briefly looked Freya's way, catching her eye with a micro-expression that signalled he was going to come over to her when he could.

But Freya couldn't wait. Suddenly she felt compelled to get out, a wave of adrenaline coursing through her like wildfire. Being already near the door, she turned, slipped between the bodies with her eyes down and the next second was expelled into the sweet, crisp night air.

The deli was a dimly lit and tantalising Aladdin's cave at night. Grabbing a few inspiring ingredients from the shelves – she would have to give Finn the list in the morning – she discovered her legs were shaking a little as she climbed the stairs to the flat.

It was barely eight o'clock. So much for seeing in the new year, but she had had about as much socialising as she could take that day. Cooking was what she needed to do now. Freya stood for a moment, gazing out of the window at the view up the High Street, her ears still ringing from the noise in the pub. Tonight the challenge was 'Seven Swans a-Swimming', such a beautiful image to capture, and she knew exactly how to represent it.

She made a simple batch of French meringue, the quickest and easiest. When she'd been working as patissier for Andre she would generally make Swiss or Italian, which was more complicated and more stable so better for a lot of things, but French was fine here. There was no piping kit, so she improvised, cutting off the corner of a small, plastic sandwich bag. She worked quickly, piping out her meringue shapes and getting them into the oven on a flat baking tray. They were small and delicate, so they wouldn't take long to dry out. The thick, yellow cream took no time to whip because it was so rich. It would have been very easy to overwhip it into butter instead – she had done that often enough, to roars of outrage from Andre – and she had learned the hard way when to stop. Concentrating, she whisked it by hand into soft, sumptuous peaks that smoothly held their shape. She flavoured and tasted it until the balance was just right and then she was done, for now. She would assemble them later, before Finn came back. She imagined he would stay to see in the new year with his mates.

At last, she was blissfully alone, with nothing to do.

She sat in the dimly lit flat with her thoughts and another glass of champagne from the bottle Finn had opened. The soft, velvet curtains were open and she could see the town Christmas tree on the triangle of cobbles outside, with its twinkling lights rivalling the bright moon and stars. Time drifted.

Comfortable on the sofa, in front of the dying fire, Freya stroked Rafferty the cat, who had draped himself across her lap and was now purring throatily and dribbling. She dreamily recalled the surprise trip to Paris her mother had finally made, just eight short months ago. She had always promised she would come, but as the years went by and their meetings were only ever those snatched late weekends in Portneath, Freya had stopped wondering if she would ever have the chance to show her mother Paris – her Paris. And then, suddenly, she was there. Thinner? Gaunt, even? Perhaps. In retrospect.

Freya had nervously taken her to meet Andre, who had turned on the full Gallic charm offensive, kissing her mother's hand and praising Freya to the skies. Better than that, though, he had given Freya two whole days off, and a glorious forty-eight hours had ensued. They drifted, almost like a couple in love, through the secret, cobbled streets of ancient Paris, the louchely romantic Paris of a thousand cinema montages. Eschewing the standard tourist fare – the Eiffel Tower, the Arc de Triomphe, and even the Louvre – they largely spent their time eating their way around the neighbourhood of Freya's tiny flat in Le Marais, the hip, fashionable quarter of central Paris, which was filled with cafés and boutiques; Freya delighted in showing her mother her foodie discoveries, the elegant patisserie where they ate millefeuille and opera cake with fine silver forks, the boulangerie where they bought almond croissants stuffed with frangipane and took them back to the flat for a lazy breakfast, dipping them in their bowls of coffee and scattering buttery, flaky crumbs on the floor. After that, they ventured out to get deliberately lost before taking fresh baguettes stuffed with charcuterie to a curly metal bench on the bank of the Seine, watching the river and the people as they ate. At the chocolatier they admired the myriad, delicate colours and flavours of the macarons, stacked neatly in rows, and watched greedily as the lady behind the counter tumbled dark, handmade chocolate truffles, flavoured with orange oil, into a gold, cardboard gift box, intricately folded then tied with spring green ribbon. They devoured the chocolates without ceremony whilst wandering in the gardens at the Rue Vieille du Temple, basking in the spring sunshine and admiring the cherry blossom.

On the second day, Anna, looking drawn, had guilelessly proposed a picnic in the little flat, where they lounged on the sofa together for hours, chatting about Freya's life and drinking endless milky mugs of the English tea Freya had missed but had teased her mother for bringing.

All too soon it had been time for her to go. There they stood in the Gare du Nord, with just minutes until Anna's train took her back home. Freya avidly relived those moments as she sat dreaming by the fire. It was just another lovely memory, nothing momentous, she had thought at the time, but she now vividly recalled her mother's intense gaze. It was as if she was drinking her daughter in, every detail, her eyes ranging greedily over Freya's face. And that hug of farewell, too – was it even more fervent than all the other goodbyes, brimming with motherly love? One more squeeze, extra tight, and her mother had turned to run for her train. Even then, she had stopped, swivelled and blown one last kiss, before reluctantly turning away. And had Freya seen – just in that microsecond as she turned – the mask falling and an expression of desolation settling bleakly into place? The Paris trip had been her mother's goodbye. She realised that now.

Anna had quietly stopped being the one to initiate contact after her trip and Freya's texts to her had been – well, definitely not blanked or ignored, but the level of engagement had been less. There had been – what? Detachment, Freya supposed. But it was not a rejection, she saw that now, more an act of compassion, inviting Freya to put in some practise at not having her there and perhaps, too, to spare her from living minute by minute those final, grisly, hopeless months.

The guilt of not guessing what was truly going on during that visit gnawed at Freya's soul. She wished, with fierce desperation, that she had seen her mother just one more time – but what would ever have been 'enough'? What could possibly have spared her from the pain of pining for more?

Freya got up stiffly, disembarking the cat from her lap, and stood at the window, gazing out onto the dancing lights of the Christmas tree outside. The hands on the clock across the High Street were saying it was a quarter to midnight – just a few minutes until a whole new year, a future that scared and excited her in equal measure. She was glad she'd got out of the pub – she was always mortified at being in the middle of a crowd at new year, not knowing who to hug and kiss. In fact, usually not having anyone to hug and kiss.

Freya had a pang of yearning to see in the new year with her mother. It would have been the first time in ten years and now it would be never. Confusingly, the one other person she wanted to share these new beginnings and anguished regrets with was Finn. She felt as if she was standing at a crossroads between her past and her future, with the new year already promising loss, but maybe – just maybe – some hope along with it.

She was so deep in thought, Finn made her jump when he arrived behind her, touching her arm gently to get her attention.

'You disappeared,' he said.

'I had something to do,' she replied, filled with joy that he was there, that she was not alone. 'Wait here.'

'OK, try this,' she said, a minute later, handing him a fork and one of two delicate white china plates. On each there was a little swan, constructed entirely from meringue in the palest, palest pink, its body filled with puffs of billowing whipped cream sprinkled with jewel-bright, ruby-red pomegranate seeds, its meringue neck arched upwards in an elegant, extended 'S'.

'Brilliant,' he said. 'I assume there are seven?'

'There are,' she nodded. 'I'm not expecting you to eat them all, but I'm not saying I wouldn't be flattered if you managed two.'

'It's a work of art,' Finn marvelled, looking from his plate to Freya's. 'Right, I'm going in,' he said, and Freya followed suit.

The meringue yielded instantly to Freya's fork. It was crisp on the outside but soft, melting, marshmallow in the middle and sweet as sin. The voluptuous sweetened whipped cream, with heady hints of rose and vanilla, and the sharp, juicy bursts of the pomegranate seeds, complemented each element perfectly.

'You're a witch,' Finn said, shaking his head in wonder. 'This is witchcraft – seriously, magically good.'

Freya inclined her head, but with no false modesty. 'I'm pleased with them,' she admitted.

Finn nodded, taking another bite, analytically. 'It tastes a bit like Turkish delight,' he observed.

'That's the rose essence. In summer, instead of pomegranate, I thought I'd serve them with just a few rose petals scattered – they're edible did you know? – and so romantic . . .' She ducked her head, shyly.

She couldn't believe she had just said the word 'romantic'. Awk-ward. She glanced up the High Street to the clock in the arch. Damn. The clock was reading exactly midnight. Now what? Was she supposed to fling her arms around him? Or not. Maybe he would hate that. He had recoiled the last time she tried. Freya's brow wrinkled in confusion. She felt like an inky sixteen-year-old again and didn't know what to do with her hands, but, in the end, Finn made it easy.

Silently, he took the empty plate and fork from her, placing it on the coffee table beside them. Then he turned her to face him, put up his hand to brush away a bright tendril of her hair, tucked it behind her ear and tilted her chin up with his finger so their eyes locked, like they had in the pub.

The world melted away.

'Little Fred,' he murmured. 'Who have I been kidding, with my "no time for romance" rubbish. Ten years I've waited for this, and that's long enough for anyone.' Then, with infinite slowness, he leaned down and gently brushed her lips with his own. Without conscious thought she pushed up towards him, planting her mouth on his, parting her lips, deepening the kiss, until – a million years, or a millisecond later – she broke away, breathless and reeling.

He clamped her upper arms to steady her and she looked up at him in astonishment, still feeling his lips on hers, her nose still full of the comforting, warm, earthy, lemony scent of him.

'Happy new year,' he said, softly.

Chapter Twenty

Eight Maids a-Milking

Finn wasn't great at lie-ins. Even having gone to bed in the early hours, he had snatched just a few hours of sleep and woken early, but that was fine; he had things to do and a lot to think about. Stocktaking and ordering were perfect activities for thinking along to, in his experience; they were just diverting enough to occupy the conscious brain while the subconscious got on with making sense of 'stuff' or, in this case and to be specific, Freya. Since she had stumbled back into his life on Christmas Eve it had been quite the emotional ride, culminating in what he hoped was the beginning of something with that kiss last night. He'd been warning her off, of course, telling her he didn't have the emotional space for a relationship, but he hoped he had the grace to admit when he was wrong. And he had been so, *so* wrong about this.

Despite appearances, Finn did not do romance lightly; he would never use a woman like that. That was not to say there hadn't been women, of course, but he was sensitive to whether a woman was interested in him for life or just for Christmas and he had avoided getting entangled in situations where they wanted the former. Plus, there had been no one – until Freya – he wanted to commit to, but, that said, what kind of a hot mess was he getting himself into now? She was clearly ambivalent about sticking around in Portneath and that was a problem: because if she left again, he was in trouble.

They needed to talk.

For the first time in as long as she could remember, Freya drifted awake on a feather bed of optimism and calm. Bluebirds sang. Fluffy clouds floated. Bubbles of happiness rose up inside her as she relived that moment – that kiss – which had come along so unexpectedly and yet with a deep sense of rightness and belonging that even soothed the pain of her bereavement, just a little, turning the raging storms of loss into a sweet sorrow that made joy seem all the brighter.

Freya was especially touched that the potentially awkward moment of 'whose bed' was made easy by Finn kissing her lightly on the forehead and wishing her goodnight. She had been relieved to go up to her newly familiar attic bedroom. Life was changing so fast she needed time to ground herself, plus there were other elements of her life that were less sunny, and these were quickly crowding back into her consciousness as she stretched luxuriously. It must be late. They hadn't got to bed until nearly two o'clock, after sitting entwined on the sofa in front of the dying fire, chatting idly. And kissing.

She reached lazily for her phone to see the time. Yikes, nearly midday, and double yikes! the text notification tab was showing. Oops. She had left her phone here in her room when she went out last night. Since the text from Diana just before her mother had died, seeing a text notification had brought nothing but stress. Still, it was bound to be nothing. It was new year in Paris too and friends – more acquaintances, really – would have been wishing her happy new year when they had got to the end of their shift. She should reply, though. Tapping on the icon, her heart stopped, and then pounded hard, filling her head with such force she could hear her own heartbeat.

There was a text from Andre.

It was long – very long – and written in his broken, ungrammatical English, but the gist was clear: Freya was an appalling person for not telling him the real reason for her sudden departure, he was devastated for her loss – he had loved her mother the moment he met her – she was deeply irritating for not telling him what was going on – was he such a monster that she felt she couldn't say? (yes, thought Freya, he was) – and he supposed that now she was expecting him to hold her job open for her and this was a massive inconvenience but – because he wasn't a monster (that same theme again) – he expected her back at work by absolutely no later than first thing on Monday the seventh of January and they would say no more about it.

So now she knew. She had just a few days more to enjoy her time in Portneath with Finn. She would get through her mother's funeral and then she would go back to Paris and normal life would resume. Of course it would. This wasn't just a job she was snatching from the jaws of disaster – it was her career.

She briefly pondered whether going back to Paris necessarily meant the end of her thing with Finn. After only a few moments she discounted the possibility of continuance. It was obvious no man as wonderful as Finn, with so many women after him, would be prepared to enter into a relationship where the couple were divided by a day-long journey and the English Channel. What kind of a relationship would that be? No. It was not going to work out and she needed to tell him that. Let him off the hook. In fact, there were myriad reasons why she and Finn couldn't really be a thing. Even though a Christmas romance always felt magical, that was just what it was – 'magical', for which read 'an impossible fantasy'. And, in any case, another excellent reason for it just being a fling was that – let us not forget – her genetic destiny was probably a disaster. That was the last thing she wanted someone she cared about to have to deal with. Her heart sank further at the thought of the yellow envelope still lurking with its life-changing news. It was too much to think about. She would get her mother's funeral over first.

In that moment, she desperately wanted to be in the same room as Finn. If she was going to have to say goodbye to him soon then she didn't want to miss a moment in his company. She was allowed that brief happiness at least, surely?

She had a quick shower – there was no sign of him in the flat – and then hurriedly got dressed.

She found him hunched over his laptop at the table in the deli window.

'Morning,' he said, turning to her with a smile. Then, his face dropped. 'God, what's the matter,' he said, standing up and starting towards her. 'You look grim.'

'It's good news, actually,' she said brightly, filling him in.

'The man's an arse. I can't let you go back to him,' he said, fixing her intensely with his gaze when she got to the end.

'Being sensible,' she said, 'I don't think I have a choice, unless I throw away my entire career!'

'Listen,' said Finn, pulling out a chair for her to sit down opposite him, 'I need you to understand something important.' He waited, leaning towards her, until Freya met his eye. 'This situation you told me about – being passed over for promotion because you're a woman?' He paused for emphasis. 'It's not going to change.'

'Coffee?' she hazarded, changing the subject.

'Caffeine's the last thing you look as if you need. All you're doing is *thinking* about going back to Paris and you're on edge, I can tell,' he counselled, turning to the coffee machine all the same.

'What's this?' she asked, looking at the laptop screen. Keen to distract him.

'The eighth day,' he told her. 'You wowed me with your swans. What are we doing for "Eight Maids a-Milking"? I was thinking these.'

'Sure. So, what are they?' she said, peering at the picture on the screen. 'They look like little custard tarts.'

'Maid of honour tarts – it was the closest thing, I thought. More like little cheesecakes than custard tarts, but you're close.'

'So, we're thinking milkmaids of honour, if that's even a thing.'

'Yes, milk – basically – but they're made with curds, actually. The first stage of cheesemaking, you add the acid – vinegar, in this case – and it makes the milk split into curds and whey.'

'You know about weird stuff,' marvelled Freya, brightening. She was instantly intrigued and diverted. 'Where am I going to get curds?' she asked, her dilemmas about work forgotten.

'If I'm honest,' Finn admitted, 'the only reason I know the curd thing is I had a refresher course on cheesemaking from Martha this morning. She's dropping in with some this morning so we can have a go.'

'You mean *I* can have a go?'

He nodded his agreement, grinning wryly. 'Yeah – you're definitely the patissier. I'm just the chief taster.'

'You do it so well,' agreed Freya, glad the serious mood

that had been engendered by her return to Paris had apparently passed. 'Oo, that reminds me,' she went on, 'I had an idea about a thing to commemorate Mum and say goodbye to Christmas. Actually, for *me* to say goodbye to everyone here, now I know I'm going back to Paris.'

'Shoot,' he said, letting the bit about leaving go for now.

'I really want to do something for all the people in Mum's life, so, more than anything, I'd just like to cook a meal for everyone, the day after the funeral. It can't be the same day, not really. Too much to do.'

'Excellent,' said Finn. 'Go on . . .'

'So, we've got the space next door, and it even has a kitchen, and I was just wondering if I could possibly use it – just for one day – and cook supper this Saturday. It's Twelfth Night.'

'As a beta test for my restaurant with local ingredients?' Finn said, hoping against hope.

'As a wake for my mother and a goodbye meal before I go back to my life in Paris,' she replied, firmly.

'Can't blame me for trying.'

For a moment, Freya didn't answer.

'I wouldn't expect "us" to continue if I did go back,' she said at last.

'Why not?'

'I just don't want you to think I have any expectations,' she continued, spreading her hands as if begging him to see reason.

'I *want* you to have expectations,' he said, sounding like he was consciously keeping his voice even.

'You specifically said you weren't looking for a relationship the other day,' she told him. 'You said you had too much to achieve in your career with the deli and the farm and now maybe the restaurant.'

'Yeah, yeah . . . OK, you're right. I said that,' he admitted. 'But that was then. I was in denial, seeing as − on the face of it − having a relationship with you is a nightmare because you're such a pain. In fact, talking about you being a pain, why don't you tell me more about this supper you're wanting to do? How many are coming and what about a menu? You've got to do your meringue swans, they're a winner . . .'

Diana and Freya were in the corner, hunched over their coffees, talking intensely. Finn brought the two women a thick slice of panettone each, the airy, pale-yellow cake studded generously with fat sultanas and big chunks of candied peel.

Finn liked and admired Diana and it felt good to have both of his favourite women there in his café, getting on so well. Perhaps Diana would become a mentor for Freya now? In loco parentis? Wasn't that literally what godparents were intended for? To step in if the parents died? He could hardly imagine what it must be like to lose your mother in your twenties. He was devoted to his, even though he only saw his parents once a year now. As far as he could see, it was important for the two women to bond. He had been told, in no uncertain terms, that he, solely, was not enough of a draw to keep Freya in Portneath so he was all about encouraging her to believe she could have a full life here. She needed to see she could have friends. Family. A career. If she didn't start to believe in these things really quickly then she would disappear. Finn wasn't sure he would be able to cope with that.

'What on earth did you say to him?' demanded Freya, once Diana admitted she had lobbied Andre on Freya's behalf. 'I'm surprised he even took your call.'

'He didn't at first. I left three messages with this flunky person who was answering the phone.'

'That would have been Muriel,' said Freya. 'She's used to politely getting rid of people.'

'You're telling me! So, I lied in the end. Said I was calling from the French food standards agency and there had been a report of a rat in the kitchen.'

Freya burst out laughing. 'They didn't think it was weird that you're English?'

'Naturally, I pretended to be French. I tell you, there is no end to my talents. So anyway, once I had him on the phone, it was easy. Turns out his own mother died only recently, so he even got a bit teary telling me about her.'

'You. Are. Kidding!' marvelled Freya. 'He never let on to us, but he confided in you?'

'And gave you back your job and paid your wages up to date. I did actually make a bit of a punt for a pay rise, but I don't think I managed to succeed there.'

'That's no surprise,' said Freya. 'He's as tight as a ferret's backside when it comes to money.'

'Ah well,' said Diana. 'It was worth a try. Now listen, don't forget, we've got to go and see the vicar together tomorrow morning to sort out the service.'

'I wish Mum had left some instructions about the funeral,' fretted Freya. 'It would have been nice to have a bit of a steer.'

'Funerals are for the benefit of the living,' said Diana. 'I wouldn't have thought your mother cared a jot about it, except for your sake.'

'I should have asked, though,' Freya continued. 'And it's not just that, I keep remembering things I wished we'd talked about when I was there with her at the end.'

They hadn't talked much. It was partly because her mother was so weak, but also partly because nothing seemed to matter at the time, only being together. 'I mean, did she ever . . .' Freya fiddled with her napkin, avoiding Diana's gaze, 'did she ever say anything to you about my father?' She raised her head and their eyes locked.

'Nothing,' said Diana firmly. 'But if she had anything to say she'd have said it to you, not me.'

Except that I wasn't there, thought Freya. 'I left it too late,' she said, heavy with regret. It hadn't been a subject of much interest to her in her childhood and, as an adult, it had never seemed the right time; anyhow, her mother had always been enough – but her conversation with Finn had got her thinking and now, newly alone in the world, it had started to feel like a big deal.

'If there was anything she wanted to tell, she would have found a way to tell you,' Diana said.

Freya thought back to her mother's final letter. She had read it so often she could recite it from memory. Had her mother left her a clue there? Maybe.

'OK, I just thought I'd ask,' said Freya, dismissing it, but Diana was looking concerned, pressing her hands together in a prayer position as she gazed sympathetically at Freya. Her concern was over a different subject, however.

'What's playing on my mind,' she admitted, 'is this thing your mother *was* talking about in her last few months. She was really concerned for you over this BRCA gene that's caused so much heartache. I have to ask: did you go and see the geneticist?'

'I did,' said Freya, examining her panettone closely, 'and I've got a confession to make.' She looked up at Diana who held her gaze.

'Go on,' she said.

Freya could barely get the words out. 'I told my mother a lie on her deathbed,' she admitted, squeezing chunks of panettone into doughy pellets. 'I told her I'd looked at the results and I was negative.'

'And . . . you're actually positive?' asked Diana gently.

'I don't know. I've got the results, I just . . .'

'You can't face finding out at the moment,' said Diana, nodding understandingly.

'I know it doesn't make sense . . .'

'It does,' said Diana. 'I understand, but I'm glad you told your mother what you did. She talked about it a lot, especially when the cancer came back. It was all she wanted, that peace of knowing that you wouldn't have to go through what she did.'

'Was it really OK to lie?'

'In this case, yes. But you *will* need to face it, my darling,' she said, gently. 'If you are positive, there will come a point – soon – when you need to know so you can get yourself screened regularly; to maybe make decisions over preventative surgery. And the whole thing about children too – the pregnancy risks, the risk of passing it on – I hardly need to tell *you*, but these aren't all decisions you'll have to make on your own. What about your relationship with Finn?'

'Hang on, what relationship?' said Freya.

'Oh, who do you think you're kidding,' laughed Diana. 'It's written all over both of your faces. And it's great.'

'It's just a fling,' said Freya sulkily. 'I'm going back to France now, anyhow. There's no future in it.'

'But of course, Paris,' said Diana in dismay 'I'm beginning to regret bouncing your funny little French friend into behaving himself.'

'Well, *I'm* really grateful to you,' said Freya, firmly. 'Now,' she said, desperate to change the subject, 'please tell me you'll do the eulogy? I'm terrified of having to do it myself, and you knew her better than anyone.'

'Of course, I will, darling,' said Diana, rounding up the last few delicious crumbs of panettone on her plate and popping them in her mouth. 'It would be an honour,' she declared stoutly, but her gaze flicked from Freya to Finn and back again, and her brow knitted with concern.

Chapter Twenty-One

Once Finn had poured Freya a glass of wine and she had told him all about how Diana had put Andre in his place, dinner – a fragrantly steaming steak and mushroom pie with more of the Holly Tree Farm beef – was ready. Sharing a meal together felt easy now. They dished up and laid the table as a team, weaving around each other in a well-rehearsed dance. They ate, as had become their habit, by candlelight and then, after supper, they sat on the saggy old leather sofa, in front of the fire. With Freya in Finn's lap, they kissed and cuddled languidly, staring idly, contentedly, into the flames.

'Get us,' laughed Freya softly. 'We're like an old married couple.'

'Is this what married couples do?' Finn joked. 'I thought they stopped all this nonsense on their wedding day.'

'Remind me never to get married then,' said Freya, stretching over to the coffee table for the maid of honour tarts, selecting another one and taking a large bite. Finn was already on his third. They had turned out well on her second attempt – the recipe on the internet had been completely wrong with its curd cheese quantity but, with her patisserie experience, she had worked it out for herself in the end. The little tarts, with their crisp pastry, light, cheesy filling, and hint of lemon were surprisingly moreish.

'I've porked out,' she observed, looking down at her gently curving tummy.

'You needed to. You were far too thin when I found you on Christmas Eve.'

They both chewed contentedly for a minute.

'Can we talk about the elephant in the room?' said Finn, at last.

'Rude. You literally just said I *needed* to gain weight,' answered Freya prodding him accusingly in the ribs with a sharp finger.

'Idiot,' he replied, catching her hand in his, laughing. 'Seriously, can we talk about the whole "going back to Paris" thing?'

'It's my career,' said Freya bleakly. 'It's as simple as that. And I'm lucky to have a job.'

'But what about the misogyny, the sexual discrimination? You've already said you're never going to get the promotions you deserve.'

'But nothing's going to change unless people like me keep trying.'

Finn growled in frustration. 'It's not your responsibility to change the world. What about the idea for the restaurant next door – your incredible cooking skills plus the local, fresh ingredients? The fish from the harbour, the cheese and cream from Holly Tree Farm?'

'That's *your* ambition not mine,' Freya reminded him gently.

'It could be ours?'

Freya briefly allowed herself to luxuriate in a daydream where she and Finn – and Martha and Ciaran – were running a thriving business as a team. The montage played across her mind's eye, the working together, the laughter, the sunshine, the happy, admiring customers, the reviews from notable restaurant critics who travelled all the way down to Devon specially . . . No, no! It was nothing but a silly fantasy. And anyhow, Finn would never want a relationship with her if he knew what a disaster her genes probably were. Something was making her unable to face telling him that just now, though. She winced as she remembered lying to her mother about it. She was a bad person, whatever Diana said to the contrary.

Freya gazed glumly into the flames. She needed to put Finn straight on everything soon, including the BRCA gene thing. It was crueller not to. Knowing she was a bad bet might help him to accept her leaving. He'd be glad to get rid of her once he knew. Plus, who was to say they *would* be a good team?

'Ciaran and Martha argue all the time because they work together,' she said at last. 'That's the reality.'

'That's just how they roll,' Finn insisted. 'Although, I agree with you, things don't seem great between the two of them at the moment.' He frowned, but Freya said nothing. She could hardly break Martha's confidence, especially not to Ciaran's brother of all people.

Finn sighed, settling Freya a bit more comfortably in the crook of his arm.

It was heaven, she thought, resting her head on his shoulder – what a shame it couldn't last. Real life was going to intervene soon enough. 'Eurgh. I've got a meeting with the vicar in the morning and then a late shift in the pudding factory. We'll have to have supper late, when I get back,' she groaned. She was not looking forward to going to work at the time others were planning an evening in front of the telly. She, in contrast, would be spending hours in a hairnet, heaving bags of currants around, and she didn't even need the job *now* – not if she was going back to Paris. Andre had paid the wages he owed into her bank account, which was a relief. At least she could afford to buy her ticket back to Paris now.

'The pudding factory?' said Finn, lazily. 'I think you should throw a sickie. That awful Sharmayne deserves it.'

'Hmm,' said Freya. 'Not very principled. Fancy suggesting such a thing, Mr Donaghue,' she said, although she enjoyed the mental image of Sharmayne possibly having to lug Christmas pudding ingredients, if she didn't show. No, that would never happen. Sharmayne kept normal working hours – probably part-time too – unlike her poor staff.

'Maybe I should ask for an emergency day off. I am genuinely knackered.'

'You should. And I should have thought you're due some compassionate leave too, with your mother and everything.'

'Let's not ruin a lovely evening, thinking about depressing things,' she suggested at last, cuddling up closer and leaning in for a kiss.

Freya went up to her attic bedroom alone again that night. There seemed no point progressing in her relationship with Finn, much as she wanted to – it was going to be hard enough to say goodbye to him as it was.

She would get through the funeral and do the supper in memory of her mother; the sooner she had done that and left Portneath for ever the easier it would be. She and Finn could be just a short, sweet Christmas romance, which was probably all it was ever going to be anyhow. Freya didn't flatter herself she would be more than a passing fancy to someone as handsome, kind and altogether lovely as Finn.

Chapter Twenty-Two

Nine Ladies Dancing

Despite their late night, Finn went down to the deli even earlier than usual the following morning. He needed to do the ordering, but more than that, he needed to do some thinking.

For everyone's sake, he had to be clear where his conviction that Freya should stay in Portneath was coming from. Was he being selfish? Was he just very, very much wanting this woman to stay in his life and so was therefore hoping she would turn her back on her career? Because if her chances of making the big time weren't as good as they ought to be in Paris, they were probably vanishingly microscopic in Portneath. But then, he only had to think of what she had told him about Andre's abuse of her and others to boil with rage at the damage the man had done. Andre had cynically tapped into a talented woman's hopes and dreams so he could exploit her for his own business objectives.

Finn needed to make sure he wasn't doing the exact same thing.

Somehow Freya had snuck in under his defences, with her wit, her talent and her feisty, brave demeanour all wrapped up in such a petite frame. *'Though she be but little, she is fierce'*, Martha had quoted at him yesterday – Shakespeare apparently – and it summed her up pretty well.

It wasn't just him who had become besotted. Martha was keen on him keeping Freya around and so was Ciaran; they had both let him know exactly what they thought about his love life, as usual. As the older brother, Ciaran had always told him what to do, and this time – maybe – he was right. Surely the law of averages alone said he had to be right eventually, didn't he? Finn mused.

Finn had ordered a smaller than usual batch of Danish pastries for today – apricot, apple, prune with almond paste and a dozen pain au chocolat. They would all go, or mostly, he thought, but it was too early in the new year for people on diets to have fallen off the wagon, so his sales expectations were lower than usual. There were still plenty of people coming in for his coffee, though. He had no interest in competing with the high street chains with their fancy, seasonal syrups, their six kinds of plant milk, and the poncy latte art in the foam on the top. Instead, he had earned a reputation for exceptionally good Italian coffee, strong, black and fragrant. Anyone wanting anything other than espresso, latte or cappuccino would be firmly directed elsewhere, although he did offer soya milk, acknowledging grudgingly that some people were genuinely dairy intolerant. He was confident he knew his coffee and maybe that made him a bit prescriptive, but he wasn't discriminatory.

The mood in the deli that morning was ebullient, with plenty of regulars to exchange new year greetings with. The early morning pre-work crowd were thin on the ground as most were taking a holiday in the break between Christmas and new year. Consequently, the morning rush was slower to get going with most people drifting in around mid-morning, to drink coffee, replenish the store cupboard and pick up a good loaf of bread for lunch, perhaps with some local cheese or a couple of Freya's maid of honour tarts which were giving his ever-popular Portuguese custard tarts a run for their money.

Finn made Freya stop for a coffee and a pain au chocolat before he would let her go to see the vicar, but although she chugged the coffee she only picked fretfully at the pastry. She had a challenging 'to do' list for the day and there was one item in particular that was stealing her appetite. It was something a lot more challenging than making nice with the vicar.

The meeting with the vicar, a slim, boyish man who insisted they call him Chris, went more smoothly than Freya had thought it would. The hymns and readings were chosen, which seemed to be the main thing, but then Freya realised, with horror, that she would have returned to France by the time the ashes were ready to be interred in their little plot in the graveyard. Thankfully Diana soothed her with promises she would do it herself but, increasingly, Freya felt as if fate was telling her to stay.

Diana loved Freya's idea of having a memorial supper on Saturday, the twelfth day of Christmas, rather than having the usual ham sandwich and tea thing right after the service, which – Diana informed her – were usually dire and depressing. Freya realised that somehow she had managed to avoid attending a single funeral in her life to date so it was lucky Diana had experience.

Freya glanced at her watch, fretfully. Chris didn't seem to notice but Diana did, giving her a piercing look. There was no hiding anything from her godmother, it seemed. Not that her godmother could possibly know what Freya was doing next, or why. Having spent half a restless night steeling herself to see John Makepeace she just wanted to get on with it. Her excuse for going to see him was that she was dropping in the details of the funeral the day after tomorrow and updating him on the house clearance. The real reason was a lot more anxiety-inducing . . .

Freya's heart pounded as she pushed open the stiff, brass-handled door. As before, the bell sounded and he came through the doorway from the back office, his face lighting up at the sight of her.

Once he had made the tea and brought two mugs out with a plate of biscuits, Freya's mouth was not so dry, and the trembling of her hands had stilled. She began by relating the details of the funeral service.

A brief silence fell and she took a deep breath. It was now or never.

'Are you my father?' she blurted.

His eyebrows shot up and his mug lurched in his hand, spilling hot tea across his desk in a wide arc.

Grabbing a handful of tissues from the box on the desk and moving papers out of the way, he dabbed at the spill conscientiously. At last, he balled up the tissues, tossed them in the bin and looked up to meet her eye.

'I'm not,' he said regretfully. 'I'm sorry to say that because I would be proud to call myself your father, believe me.'

Her heart plummeted. Now, it seemed, she would never know who her father was. As a child, she had no memory of it ever having bothered her. Until now. The regret at not having asked before it was too late weighed heavily again. Of course, she had occasionally been curious, but that was another thing. 'Curiosity killed the cat' her mother would say and distract her with something diverting. In the end, she learned not to ask for fear of suggesting their family was somehow less for having no father figure in it. Because it never had been. Never. In fact, if anything, she realised afresh with a new twinge of guilt she would have been jealous of having to share her mother's attentions with someone else. How selfish she had been, forever depriving her mother of the opportunity to find someone she could love romantically. And how selfless her mother had been to let her.

'I ask,' Freya went on, carefully, 'because – well, a) I don't know who it is, and b) if you're not my father then I don't understand why my mother asked you to do all this for me for free. Or, to put it another way, I don't understand why you are prepared to do it.'

There was a silence. She watched John's face as a series of emotions flickered across it, then he carefully placed his palms together and propped them under his chin in that now familiar prayer-like gesture.

'I loved your mother,' he said, smiling and shaking his head at himself. 'For my sins, I did, and she knew it.'

Freya waited.

'However, my best friend Darall was much more dashing than me,' he went on. 'It was inevitable that she would fall for him. Kismet.' He sighed, looking far into the distance as he remembered. 'And they looked great together, too. The gilded couple, clever, beautiful and funny. Your mother was so witty and quick – but you know that, of course. They tolerated me kindly. We spent lots of time together that summer, with me as very much the gooseberry. By the autumn your mother was pregnant with you and,' he hesitated, 'by Christmas . . . Darall was dead.'

He paused, watching her face anxiously.

Freya nodded, indicating that he should continue. Her heart was beating so hard in her chest she felt she was swaying with the force of it.

'He had an undiagnosed heart defect,' John continued, gently, 'so he simply died one day when he was out for a run. He was a fit man, in his twenties. Nobody could possibly have known that it would happen. It couldn't have realistically been prevented.

'We were all devastated, of course,' he went on. 'Darall's family didn't know about the baby because the two of them had been choosing their moment to break the news, what with not being married – Darall's family were quite conventional in that way. For some reason I never fully understood, your mother made me promise to keep it a secret that Darrall was the father. She said that, without Darall, she would rather go it alone. I agreed to – well, I would have done anything for her then. I still would.'

He sighed heavily and continued. 'When she realised that she was dying, she asked me to watch over you. I think, by then, she had started to regret her decision all those years ago and was troubled at leaving you alone in the world. I promised – was happy to promise – I would help you any way I can. It is my honour and privilege to do that. For her – and for you.'

He smiled sadly and offered her the open packet of biscuits for all the world as if they had been chatting about the weather.

With her probable return to Paris in just a few days, Freya was relieved John was dealing with the house sale and had even proposed using a professional house clearance company. That way she only had to mark up the furniture and possessions she wanted put in store for the far-off day she had her own place. She thought again about her mother's modest legacy to her. It made Finn's idea of opening the restaurant next door to the deli feel a bit more feasible, but Freya still couldn't allow herself to think too much about that. If she was sensible, she would gratefully accept Andre's offer and get herself back to Paris straight after the weekend. As far as Finn was concerned, that was exactly what she was doing. She didn't want to raise his hopes any more than she wanted to raise her own.

'What was your challenge today?' Finn asked, lining up the knife and fork on his empty plate with a regretful sigh. It was late for supper, nearly midnight, but Freya had only just come back from the pudding factory, starving hungry. She had been relieved that Finn already had some supper on the go – only beans on toast – but, to Freya, it was the most delicious thing she could have imagined. 'Although, I assume you've been too busy for the cooking thing?' he added.

'You assume wrong,' announced Freya. 'You've clearly not looked in your fridge since this afternoon,' she said, getting up. 'Now, you see if you can tell me something about this,' she added, coming back out of the kitchen.

'What even *is* that?' he wondered aloud as she carefully put a pudding plate on the table. On it, was a tall, elegant confection with a layer of upright sponge fingers encircling a coffee-coloured blancmange, with dark chocolate shavings on top.

'I know,' agreed Freya. 'I think it looks like something Jane Austen might have eaten – it's definitely not my usual style. Actually,' she said, consideringly, 'it reminds me of one of those puddings in an old gentlemen's club where they have an awful sweet trolley they wheel over and you choose from three different types of trifle or something.'

'You're not selling it,' laughed Finn. 'But it does look – erm – unfashionable.'

'It is. I found an old 1950s recipe for it amongst your recipe books, but I've updated it a bit.' As she spoke, she was cutting a generous slice and handing it to Finn with a little jug of cream. He poured the cream and then took a bite.

'Mm, coffee. It tastes like a tiramisu, in a way,' she said. 'I'm more of a fan than I thought I would be.'

'Yeah, the coffee aspect . . . That's my update.'

'I have no idea how it links in to the Twelve Days of Christmas though,' he admitted. 'Give me a clue?'

She gave him a sideways look. 'So soon?' she said. 'Don't you want to work it out? I don't want to spoil your fun.'

'Believe me, I've had as much "fun" as I can cope with today,' he replied.

'So, all right,' she said, relenting, 'what are those biscuits called?' She pointed at the ring of sponge fingers.

'Sponge fingers?'

'OK, what *else* are those biscuits called?' she persevered, patiently.

'Dunno.'

'They've actually got a few names,' she admitted. 'In Italian they're "savoiardi", but another English name for them is "ladies' fingers".'

'Oh yeah. I should know that because I've got them in the shop, haven't I?' he admitted.

'Where do you think I got them from?'

He laughed.

'So . . . "Nine ladies" – come on, you know this one – "Nine ladies . . ."'

'"Nine ladies talking"?' he suggested mischievously.

'Dangerous ground, mate,' she warned, but the corners of her mouth quirked up into a tiny smile.

'Nine ladies dancing?' he proposed at last, taking pity on her.

'Exactly. So, guess how many sponge fingers I used.'

'You've made your point,' he said, quickly counting them up. 'Seven, plus the two I just ate. Got it. And there's definitely something worthwhile in there. It's a starting point,' he went on, more seriously now. 'I mean, I'm all for short menus, but I can appreciate we can't open our restaurant with meringue swans as the only choice.'

She had to admire his tenacity, but constant talk about this fantastic project that would never see the light of day wasn't making her thoughts of leaving Portneath any easier.

Chapter Twenty-Three

Ten Lords a-Leaping

After another gruelling nightshift and a snatched few hours of sleep, Freya was dead-eyed with exhaustion. At least, thankfully, she now had a few days off. Her first job that morning, was to go to the print shop for them to copy the Order of Service while she waited. Diana had put it together on her own straight after their meeting with the vicar and it had been perfectly compiled with brisk efficiency.

That task accomplished, Freya got Finn to drop her off in Middlemass on his way up to the farm. She had said nothing to Finn about John Makepeace's revelation the previous day for reasons she hardly knew. Perhaps it was her way of getting used to her disappointment – disappointment that John wasn't her father – as well as the irrevocable and horribly final truth that she would now never get to know the man who was. As her mother had feared, despite her friendships with people like Diana and Finn, Freya was now essentially alone in the world.

At the house, she concentrated on marking up the handful of pieces of furniture she would like to keep: her mother's old brass bedstead; some chipped but beloved cast-iron enamelled cooking pots; the saggy, deeply familiar green sofa; the old, worn kitchen table with its mis-matched chairs, which she couldn't bring herself to dispose of . . .

Perhaps one day she would come back and have a little flat in Portneath and at least now she would have something to furnish it with.

Quickly, once she was done, she had a compulsion to get out of the house where even the walls seemed to now ooze musty sadness and regret. She needed to pin up the notices giving the funeral details on the village noticeboards, so that was her excuse for a walkabout. Diana had already told most people, as well as posting the details on the village WhatsApp and Facebook groups, but Freya wanted to leave nothing to chance. She hoped there would be a reasonable turnout but, realistically, it couldn't be great, she warned herself. She and her mother had done so little socialising when she was growing up, being perfectly happy in each other's company. She had no reason to think her mother had suddenly become gregarious after she had left for Paris, and yet it was sad to think of her alone and lonely, as Freya was sure she must have been. Having a chance to talk to whichever people had been involved in her mother's life over the last few years, when she had had so little contact herself, might fill the void in her and maybe assuage a little of the guilt that she had not been there. After all, she reasoned, there had been Jake, for one. She would never have guessed about him so perhaps there were more.

One person she knew she needed to break the news to was poor Hattie. Freya had tried to call her several times that day, but she wasn't answering her phone, whether it was because she was refusing to take the call or because – and Freya preferred this theory – her phone was in her locker at Paynton's Puddings was anyone's guess. Enough. Now she would have to make do with a text. It seemed a terrible way to tell her such awful news, but Freya composed a message, worded as gently as possible, and then pressed 'send' with a skipped heartbeat. Hattie was so sensitive and fragile – Freya and her mum had always known that they needed to be careful with her feelings – and this . . . Freya just hoped that one day she would have a chance to make it up to her. Maybe the funeral would be a turning point. Maybe.

It had been ten years since Freya had walked down the village street. Doing it now, for nostalgia's sake, was a bittersweet experience. Things seemed familiar but somehow smaller than she remembered. The old phone box by the pond had been turned into a little library, she saw with a smile, the pond was frozen and the ducks were skittering and sliding across the surface, pecking hopefully at the milky, opaque surface. Even in the depths of winter, the lemon-yellow sun was turning the grass from white to vivid green wherever it cast its thin warmth and here and there on the verges there were clumps of green spears, daffodils already thrusting their way out of the earth, promising spring one day soon.

The little village church nestled in the middle of the graveyard, the oldest graves, with their wonky headstones, lining the path between the old oak lychgate and the church door, but the newer ones, including the memorial garden where Freya's mother's stone would be, were behind, on a bright, open plot stretching towards the open farmland. She went up there and saw the little space already reserved, a small plastic sign with 'Anna Wilson' on it pushed into the grass. Freya stood quite still for some time, eyed beadily by a robin perched nearby on the lichen-encrusted wall. Her mother's ashes would lie in the sunlight, well beyond the shadow of the ancient yew tree shading the older graves and Freya was glad about that. Her mother had always craved the sunshine, getting outside at any excuse, gardening in her bikini on every roasting summer's day, to Freya's teenage chagrin. She had been so young, just fifty-four when she died, and that was no age, Freya saw that now. Yes, her mother had been a young, attractive woman, but she had avoided romantic relationships for all those years of Freya's childhood, giving all her emotional energy to her daughter alone. And what had Freya done to repay her? She had taken off to France at the earliest opportunity without a backward glance. But it was too late to change things now.

Freya was relieved to be distracted from her dark thoughts by the ringing of her phone and scrabbled clumsily for it in her pocket. Was it Hattie responding to her text?

It was Diana.

'You're to come here when you're done,' she instructed. 'I'm making supper for everyone – Gabriel and whatsername, his latest, Aidan, Jess and you two. Nothing fancy. Finn's going to meet you here, rather than picking you up at your mother's house.'

Freya's heart sank. The last thing she felt like, the evening before her mother's funeral, was having to present a sociable face. Diana and Finn were fine, but she knew Aidan only slightly and Gabriel even less, let alone the girlfriends, or whoever these other people were. She made assenting noises and then, when Diana had hung up, changed direction so she could walk up to Paddy's shop and grab a bottle of wine before it closed.

'Sure, and it's been a long old time since I saw that face,' Paddy declared as soon as she walked in. She hadn't expected him to remember her at all, although he and his shop were a definite part of *her* memories. He had been running the village general store for as long as she could remember and – as a fellow Irishman – she was sure he must know Finn's family from way back.

'Paddy,' she said, putting up a hand in an awkward greeting.

'I was so sorry to hear about your ma.'

She nodded her acknowledgement, not trusting herself to speak for a moment. She took a breath. 'Could I put up details about the funeral in the window?'

'Course,' he said, coming towards her, his hand outstretched. 'Give it to me. And I'll be there myself too. Tomorrow afternoon?' he said, reading the note. 'That's grand.' He stuck it up prominently on the glass door, just above the 'Open' sign.

Freya had a quick look at the wine he had on offer. Really, considering what a small shop it was, he had a pretty good selection available, nothing too pricey, but nothing completely undrinkable either. She wished she had asked Diana what they were going to be eating, but it might have sounded precious if she had. People were funny about cooking dinner for a professional chef, she had found, on the rare occasions it had happened, when she would genuinely have been more than happy to be given beans on toast. She picked out a decent middle-of-the-road Merlot. Everyone would like that, wouldn't they?

'Good choice,' said Paddy, deftly wrapping it in paper. 'There you go. And I'll see you tomorrow at the church. Take care, me darlin'.'

Chapter Twenty-Four

As a child, Freya had always thought Diana's house looked like one of those gingerbread cottages from the fairy tales – she had loved the steeply pitched roof, the curly bargeboards and the sweet little trelliswork porch with tumbling roses and honeysuckle, thrumming with bees in the summertime. Now, with the sundown dewfall starting to form ice on the grass and turning her breath to steam, Freya headed towards the glowingly lit windows of the little house with trepidation.

Diana had a beautiful Christmas wreath hanging on the door – grey-green eucalyptus entwined with trailing ivy and scattered with delicate pink physalis flower husks. Freya admired it as she waited for an answer, getting the subtlest whiff of menthol as she did so.

'Freya,' came a deep voice. It was Finn. She breathed a sigh of relief that he had arrived before her. She had been dreading arriving to a house full of near strangers without having him by her side. He hugged her briefly, dropped a kiss on her head, and showed her into the kitchen, which ran the width of the back of the house, with a dining table and chairs at one end.

Diana swept in for a kiss and then instantly handed Freya a large, empty wine glass.

'White or red?' she demanded.

'Red?' queried Freya, handing her the bottle from Paddy's.

'Good choice!' said Diana looking at it approvingly. 'I think we've already got one open though. Gabriel darling, would you?'

Gabriel, with courtly manners, had already stood up as Freya came into the room, and – still standing – he took the open bottle from the table and filled Freya's glass, simultaneously greeting her and commiserating over her loss. 'I meant to speak to you at New Year's Eve,' he said, apologetically. 'I saw you across a crowded room, but it was all such a bun fight I didn't make it over to you before you disappeared.'

Freya was touched. She genuinely hadn't expected Gabriel – Lord Whatever – to know who she was.

'Thank you – er – my Lord . . . sir,' she muttered awkwardly.

'Don't call him "Lord",' squawked Diana. 'He'll get thoroughly above himself.'

'Yeah, I felt for you in the pub,' Finn said to him, deftly steering the conversation away from Freya, who was now blushing scarlet, so she could recover herself. 'You were being pinned down by that awful Sharmayne woman,' he went on, clapping Gabriel on the shoulder. 'I thought I should probably come and rescue you – then I decided I couldn't be arsed.'

'Cheers for that,' responded Gabriel. 'I could have done with a hand. I was being subjected to a full-on business proposal, and she wasn't taking "no" for an answer. I'm surprised she didn't whip out a PowerPoint presentation. I think the estate office people might have been blocking her on it – they do a good job over things like that – so I can't blame her for taking the chance when she could.'

'Rather you than me,' teased Finn, unrepentantly.

'Well, it's funny you should say that, but it *does* involve you, actually,' said Gabriel with a mischievous glint in his eye. 'She wants to set up a pudding café next door to the deli and I actually don't think it's a bad idea. She wants to call it The Pudding Club. A simple concept, just the full Paynton's Puddings range on the menu served hot, with custard.'

Finn met Freya's eye. She dropped her gaze.

'I've been meaning to mention it to you,' Gabriel went on, with a hint of apology. 'We need to find a tenant at some point. Can't just leave it empty.'

'But I've told you about my ideas for the place,' said Finn, with an edge in his voice.

'You've not got the capacity to take on anything else at the moment. I mean,' Gabriel waved his glass, 'who would run it?'

'Freya,' Finn ground out the name.

'Nothing's been signed,' said Gabriel, evenly. 'Obviously, I was going to talk to you about it first, but I happen to think The Pudding Club is a strong, commercial concept that would fit in with what we already have in Portneath. It'll be good for the tourists, and it doesn't cannibalise trade for the tea rooms, burger bars, fish and chips . . . there's no point doubling up on what we've already got. It's a solid prospect. Sorry.'

'You don't think Finn's plan looking to showcase local food producers would work then?' said Freya, feeling she had to support Finn, who had now gone dangerously quiet.

'Paynton's Puddings *is* a local food producer,' said Gabriel, with finality.

He had a point.

Diana, sensing the atmosphere, put herself between the two men. 'No talking business at the table,' she declared. 'It's Thursday night, that's the start of the weekend – in my book, at least – so no more serious talk. Now,' she declared, taking Freya's elbow to turn her towards the table, 'have you met Charlotte, Aidan and Jess?'

Charlotte, according to Diana's indication, was the slim, elegant young woman with long blonde hair who had draped herself casually over the chair at the end. She was dressed in jeans and a faded denim shirt with the sleeves rolled up. It would look basic and unimaginative on anyone else, but on her model figure made her look as though she'd sprung, fragrant and perfect, from the pages of one of those clothes catalogues where everyone is always laughing and even the wellies are two hundred quid. Charlotte smiled sweetly and rubbed Gabriel's arm to further defuse the men's brief antagonism.

Of the other two people, sitting relaxed at the table, Freya knew Aidan slightly – he had been friends with Finn and Gabriel for years, part of the slightly older gang she and Hattie had gazed at in wonder from their teenage perspective. Aidan waved a greeting because getting up would disturb everyone, and he introduced her briefly to Jess, who Freya instantly warmed to. Jess was probably about her own age but not at all a familiar face to Freya, so it looked like she was a newcomer to the Middlemass community. She smiled shyly at Freya and patted the chair next to her.

'Come and sit at this end,' she said. 'Then, you're not in the middle of the boys' boring talk about business, farming and football.

'I was so sorry to hear you've just lost your mother,' Jess went on when Freya had sat down. 'I'm an orphan too, if it's any consolation – which I doubt it is.'

'How long have you lived in Middlemass?' asked Freya. 'Sorry, if that's unforgivably nosey – I've hardly been back here over the last ten years, but I'm still amazed to see an unfamiliar face.'

'Understandable,' said Jess. 'With childhood memories, everything is supposed to stay exactly the same or it's weird, isn't it? I've been in Middlemass a couple of years now. I lived at Ivy Cottage where Aidan's grandfather was but we rent it out as an Airbnb now I've moved into Quince Cottage with Aidan and Maisie, his daughter.'

So clearly Aidan's marriage didn't work out, thought Freya. He had married young, to a beautiful woman that Freya knew only by sight. She had been vaguely aware they had a little girl. Not so little now, of course.

'Ivy Cottage!' she exclaimed, sticking to safer ground. 'I remember Aidan's grandad. He was a sweetheart.'

'And you're working in Paris, right?'

'I am. I mean, I will be – I'm going back after the weekend.'

'I'm so sorry it's a short trip and for such sad reasons, but if you're going back, what's this thing Finn was mentioning?'

'Just an idea – not a serious one – but it looks like Sharmayne has scuppered it anyway.'

There were so many reasons why she couldn't entertain Finn's plans for them both, but having it end up not happening because of Sharmayne made Freya feel sick with envy. Which was unfair, she told herself, because it was hardly Sharmayne's fault Freya's and Finn's future together was untenable. What had Mum always said about situations like that? She was being a dog in the manger. She needed to stop blaming Sharmayne for things. After all, Freya should be grateful she had been prepared to give her a job. She had done her past classmate a favour, even if now it was coming to nothing.

Diana may have been in awe of Freya's cooking skills, but she needed to make no apology for the feast she produced. First there was a colander of tender purple sprouting broccoli, cooked to perfection, and a mountain of mashed potato, heavily buttered and peppered, served still in its saucepan without ceremony. Finally, Diana placed two, beautifully browned and delicious-smelling pies on the table alongside the vegetables.

'I didn't think one would be enough,' she said, plonking serving spoons into pans so people could help themselves. 'Finn told me it had to be inspired by "Ten Lords a-Leaping" so – if you hadn't already guessed – these are Lord Woolton Pies – very popular in the Second World War and, conveniently, meat-free as Charlotte is a "vegetable".'

Charlotte gave the other guests an apologetic look. 'You're so kind, Diana, but I'd have been happy with just the mash and broccoli, honestly.'

'It smells delicious,' said Finn, digging into the first pie, 'and I'm sure Freya and I would have survived if our little pledge had gone tits up for a day.'

'What pledge is this?' asked Gabriel.

Freya briefly explained. 'Really, it's nothing. Just a silly joke.'

'It's been great,' countered Finn. 'I've eaten really well over the last few days as a result.'

'It *has* been fun,' admitted Freya. 'A diversion.'

'Of course,' said Diana, gently. 'You've needed that, I'm sure.'

'So, what have you guys been eating then?' asked Charlotte, looking intrigued, as she helped herself to a larger portion of pie than Freya would have imagined, given her slim figure. Clearly, she was one of those thin people with huge appetites. There was so much about life that wasn't fair, she mused.

Finn was listing the dishes they had eaten since Freya arrived. 'If I say so myself, the bubble and squeak with crispy bacon and a goose egg was epic,' he told them all.

'Anyone can do bacon and eggs, darling,' said Diana, refusing to be impressed.

'What was your favourite?' Jess asked Finn.

He scratched his chin. 'It was all fantastic, to be honest – I mean, you know how serious I am about good food.'

'Always thinking of your stomach, you mean,' teased Gabriel.

'Far from it,' Charlotte jumped to his defence, 'we all know Finn is really discerning.'

'I am,' he grinned happily. 'I totally am, that's why it's so hard to choose, but – if my life depended on it – I think I'd have to say the partridge with pears. And then the meringue swans for pudding,' he added.

'Sounds amazing,' said Diana. 'I think you have your menu for the memorial supper then, don't you?'

'What's this?' asked Gabriel.

'We were thinking of using the café space for a supper on Saturday,' explained Diana. 'We were going to invite everyone who comes to the funeral, instead of having a boring old tea and fruit cake thing after the church service tomorrow.'

'That is, if Sharmayne has no objection,' said Finn, with the slightest hint of a hard edge to his voice.

'Never mind about that now,' said Diana, swiftly. 'Let's talk about your memorial supper, Freya. We've sorted out the menu now – very efficiently too – and you should leave the table dressing to me. Just something nice and simple, I think. White napkins and cloths, candles, flowers – nothing too fancy. I've got some little bud vases and I'll use them. How many tables are there, Finn?'

'Five tables, six chairs around each,' he said promptly.

'That's thirty covers,' said Freya quietly to herself, but Finn heard.

'Too much? It's not a big kitchen,' he said, anxiously. 'I don't want it to be a massive stress, there's no point in that.'

'God no, thirty's *easy*,' Freya reassured him. 'And it's only me in the kitchen so the size is no problem. As long as I've got the gas hob for the partridge and maybe I could borrow your oven in the flat for the meringues?'

Finn nodded. 'Are we doing a starter?' he hazarded.

'It would be good,' mused Freya. 'But there's nothing I've done so far that really lends itself . . . what are the last two days?'

'Of the Twelve Days of Christmas?' asked Jess. 'You've got eleven pipers piping tomorrow and then – the day of the supper – it's twelve drummers drumming.'

'I've got the pipers sorted already,' said Finn. 'Freya and I are having a quiet supper after the funeral tomorrow, just us – haggis, neeps and tatties – even *I* can cook that. And a traditional nip of Scotch whisky of course.'

'That sounds perfect,' said Freya, putting her hand over his gratefully. He was such a kind, decent man, as well as being seriously hot. It was such a shame it couldn't last, she told herself. Her eyes filled with tears and she bowed her head, dabbing surreptitiously. Doubtless, if the others noticed, they would attribute her tears to grief – which they were, in a way – only Freya knew that, as far as the loss of her mother went, her heart was still frozen in suspended disbelief.

'Twelve Drummers Drumming,' said Diana thoughtfully. 'That doesn't suggest anything food-related to me, except chicken drumsticks.'

'I hate being given chicken drumsticks at parties,' said Jess, diffidently. 'They're so greasy and difficult to eat, and you're left holding the bone.'

'Having canapés rather than a sit-down starter is a good idea, though,' said Freya, her mind ticking over. 'It's nice giving people a chance to have a drink and circulate, then they can all sit down, table by table, when the main course is ready. If not chicken drumsticks, then maybe cheese straws to represent drumsticks? And then perhaps vol-au-vents for the kettle drums? Oh, I don't know . . . it sounds a bit lame, is anyone going to actually get it?'

'Doesn't matter if they don't,' said Diana stoutly. 'The whole Twelve Days of Christmas thing is for our amusement, not theirs. Personally, I adore a cheese straw, and who doesn't love vol-au-vents?'

'Sorted!' said Finn. 'Make me a list, Freya, and I'll order everything in tomorrow.'

'Ahem,' said Charlotte, with a polite, pretend cough. 'You won't forget the vegetarians?'

Freya nodded. 'Of course, Charlotte, there's you, and probably others too. It's just the main dish that's the issue. The canapés and pudding can easily be animal-free. What sort of thing would you like?'

Charlotte, put on the spot, paused for thought.

'I hardly dare remind you,' said Diana, chipping in, 'but the pie I just gave you all is vegetarian.'

'I *thought* there was something missing,' teased Finn, putting his arm around Diana's shoulders.

'Speaks the man who had thirds,' she snorted. 'But, like I say, not up to professional standards.'

'I think it's perfect,' said Freya, quickly. 'It's hearty, honest, seasonal too. It's exactly the kind of thing I would put on the menu in my own establishment – not that I have one,' she added, embarrassed that she might be sounding like a despot. Or like, Andre, which was basically the same thing.

'There you go then,' said Diana, triumphantly. 'We've sealed the deal.'

'Freya?' said Jess, shyly. 'It's just a thought, but I could dig you some veg from my garden to make it, if you'd like? I've got everything you need I think – potatoes, parsnips, carrots . . .'

'That would be so lovely,' said Freya, so touched her eyes filled with tears again. Jess was a sweetheart. She and Freya could have become friends in any other life. Like in a life where Freya was not disappearing off to Paris, a thought that was making her sadder and sadder.

For pudding, Diana had bought in some really good quality chocolate and peanut butter ice cream which was quickly demolished by all – even the guests who had already declared themselves full to bursting.

As they were all noisily clearing and doing the washing-up while they waited for the kettle to boil for tea, Gabriel took Freya to one side.

'I really am sorry about renting out the café to Paynton's Puddings,' he said. 'I hope you can see the sense of what I'm saying.'

'You don't have to apologise to me,' Freya insisted. 'It's not my baby, this local ingredient restaurant thing.'

'Really?' he said, astonished. 'You and Finn look very united on the idea. In fact, you look very united, full stop.'

'Me and Finn? It's just a little Christmas fling,' insisted Freya, her lips feeling strangely stiff and unable to form the words. 'I'm back off to Paris next week, probably.'

'Really?' he said again. 'It's Andre Boucher's place, I gather?'

Freya nodded.

'I don't know the man personally,' Gabriel admitted, 'but we have mutual friends – really, I should say, "acquaintances" – and the *on dit* seems to be that the man's a proper arse.'

'Hmm,' said Freya, 'you may very well say that—' she began.

'Would you not rather work with Finn than Andre?'

'Well, as you say yourself, the café isn't available.'

'And that's why you're going back to France?'

Freya flushed. 'Yes and no,' she said, defensively. 'It's complicated.'

'And does Finn realise your relationship is "just a little Christmas fling"?' he fastidiously put quote marks around her words.

'He—' Freya looked away, lost for words.

'Listen, Finn's a mate,' Gabriel said, coldly. 'I have a problem with seeing him being used. Now I appreciate you're going through a hellish time – and Finn would always be the first to help a damsel in distress – but, if you're really not serious about this "thing", whatever it is in *your* head, I hope you won't be stringing him along any longer than absolutely necessary.'

He was right, of course, thought Freya, miserably, picturing that cursed yellow envelope in its box. She needed to tell him the whole truth. And soon.

'The twelfth day of Christmas is a pretty important date, you know,' said Diana to everyone, pouring the tea as they sat around the fire in the cosy sitting room with its patchwork layers of worn Turkish rugs and deep, encompassing sofas piled high with cushions and throws. 'We've largely forgotten, in our society, that Christmas doesn't actually end until Twelfth Night – January the fifth. It's the eve of the Epiphany.'

'I am *so* not religious,' admitted Finn. 'I don't even know what that means.'

'The Epiphany – you poorly educated person – is when the three Kings who had been following the star, arrived to see Jesus and declared him the son of God. Goodness, do they teach them nothing in schools?'

'*I* never knew that either,' said Freya, intrigued. 'Is there any particular food associated with it? I should include it in the menu if there is.'

'Well, there's wassail, for a start, which is always good – that's mulled wine to you heathens, or sometimes it's mulled cider or beer.'

'I was thinking mulled wine,' said Freya, with satisfaction. 'We can serve it with the canapés. It makes sense to keep it simple, to just offer one thing.'

'And, as for food,' Diana went on, 'there's not really anything in this country, I don't think, but in Portugal and some other places they have something called Bolo Rei – literally, "King Cake", which is a sort of bready bun made with port-infused fruit and candied fruit on top. That said – technically – we are feeding people on Twelfth Night not the twelfth day and some people believe the King Cake should be served the following day, King's Day . . .'

'It sounds fascinating,' said Freya. 'Let's look at how many people are coming and I'll see how I do for time.'

'Are you sure you should be doing this at all?' said Finn to Freya quietly, on the side. 'Cooking a meal for up to thirty people might be the last thing you feel like doing the day after your mother's funeral.'

'When I'm stressed, I cook,' admitted Freya. 'When I'm sad, I cook – actually, when I'm happy I cook too, I just—'

'Yeah,' he smiled, 'I get the picture. Listen, I'm sorry about Gabriel and The Pudding Club.'

'Don't be, on my account. I'm just sorry for you and your local ingredient restaurant thing. Maybe you can find another venue?'

Finn shook his head. 'That's not how I pictured it. Never mind,' he said. But he did mind. Freya could tell.

Chapter Twenty-Five

Eleven Pipers Piping

The morning of the funeral, Freya was glad to have the next day's supper to think about. She wouldn't know even roughly how many she was cooking for until after the funeral, but that didn't stop her getting prepared. She had double-checked with Finn over the ordering – aiming for thirty seemed sensible as that was how many people could be seated in the café. She would be amazed if that many people turned up to the funeral, so, even if they all came to the meal, that would be fine. Instead, half of her was expecting – and dreading – that there would be practically nobody there. How sad that would be. Again, Freya felt a pang of guilt over knowing so little about how her mother had spent the last ten years of her life, and with who.

'Come on,' Finn had gently encouraged her, 'you need to get cooking.'

He was right. There were things she could be getting on with. He had good stocks of eggs and sugar in the deli so she could get on with the meringues.

As always, cooking calmed her. By the time she had whipped and piped the meringue, delicately flavoured with its carefully balanced combination of vanilla, rose and lemon, onto several sheets of greaseproof paper in Finn's small kitchen, she was amazed to see a good chunk of the morning had gone.

Taking her time, she prepared the infusion for the mulled wine, tipping sugar, cinnamon sticks, cloves and star anise into a pan with sugar, water and fat slices of juicy orange. By the time she had let it simmer gently for a few minutes, the sugar syrup was delicately infused with flavour. And that was enough, she thought, putting it on the side to cool. It was important not to overdo it. The cloves, in particular, could easily dominate, making the whole thing taste like cough mixture. Now all she needed to do was add the wine, warm it through gently, chuck in a bit of good brandy and then serve.

There wasn't much else she could do after that. The rest would have to be done tomorrow, when the ingredients she had asked Finn to order had all arrived. She left the last sheet of meringue swan bodies and necks drying out in Finn's oven and went to get changed.

Martha had thoughtfully sent a selection of black clothes back with Finn when he left the farm the previous evening, and while everything was too long as Martha was so much taller, there was a slim-fitting mini-skirt that looked deliberately below the knee on Freya, and a soft, clingy black polo-necked jumper she was able to wear with the overly long sleeves pushed up, would do for the top half. Diana had insisted on lending her a pair of black, stack-heeled leather boots when she discovered they had the same shoe size. She had also lent her a black trench coat which she could belt over the top as it would probably be chilly in the church.

Everyone was so kind, but it was Gabriel's warning not to exploit Finn that kept ringing in Freya's ears. They had to talk. She couldn't take advantage of his good nature without telling him about her probable genetic destiny – the very thing that would put him off her. That way he would see her go back off to Paris without regrets. It would be an act of kindness.

Finn drove Freya up to Middlemass from Portneath with half an hour to spare before the funeral was scheduled to begin. She was touched to see he had cleared the rubbish out of the car, especially for the occasion.

Freya was unaccountably nervous when they arrived at the little stone church. She felt as if she was just about to go into an exam she had failed to prepare for. She stood in the shady churchyard, waiting for the undertaker to arrive with her mother's coffin, scared of what her reaction might be when she saw it.

In the church, Mrs Dunnant, who Freya remembered from primary school, had turned up to play the organ and was noodling through a series of sombre pieces. Freya recognised 'Jesu, Joy of Man's Desiring', Pachelbel's 'Canon' and something by Handel which she couldn't remember the name of, but it was in Italian and was something to do with tears falling.

Martha and Ciaran turned up first, arm in arm. Ciaran was looking handsome and clean-cut in a narrow-trousered charcoal suit, black tie and white shirt. Martha, in a black wool wrap-over dress to accommodate any hint of waist enlargement, was pale and tense. Freya exchanged meaningful looks with her. Had she broken the news of her pregnancy to Ciaran at last? By the almost imperceptible nod of Martha's head over Ciaran's shoulder as he swept Freya into a hug, she gathered the answer was yes. That was something to be grateful for. It was impossible to tell how it had gone, and Martha was hardly going to tell her all about it now, but it was at least encouraging to see them arriving together.

'That skirt looks lovely on you,' she whispered to Freya as they exchanged kisses and brief, tight hugs.

John Makepeace was next, looking more sombre and rigid than Freya had ever seen him, in a dark blue pinstriped suit.

He shook Freya's hand, bowing over it slightly, as was his slightly odd, formal manner, and then he flourished a large, white handkerchief to blow his nose, looking as if he was already overcome.

Freya and Finn had agreed they would explain about the Twelfth Night supper at the end of the service, and Finn had promised he would stand up and talk for her if Freya looked unable to manage it.

Diana and her great friend Mungo came along next. Freya had not seen Mungo for years, but he instantly came up with a fond anecdote about how he remembered doling out sparklers to Freya, Hattie and their friends several bonfire nights in a row on the village green. She was touched he remembered her from all those years ago – it probably helped that she hadn't actually grown much since then – but the mention of Hattie made her even more nervous. Hattie had not replied to her text, although she had been anxiously checking, almost every few minutes. Clearly, she was not forgiven. How sad. And how sad that her failure to be the loyal and sensitive friend Hattie deserved clearly meant that Hattie would not attend the funeral of a woman she had loved so deeply as a surrogate mother for years.

However, with a jolt of surprise, the very next person she saw was Hattie, wearing a huge, sloppy black jumper dress with thick tights and boots. Her face was pale, except for her red-rimmed eyes and she made a beeline for Freya, who was standing to one side on the path, watching warily as she approached. Freya was not sure she was up to another bout of Hattie's rage at that moment.

'Fred?' Hattie choked out on a sob.

Freya looked at her, compassionately.

'I've been a complete cow,' Hattie went on.

Freya was so distressed to see her ex-best friend crying that her eyes spilled over too, emotion overtaking her defences at last. 'Hats,' she said, reaching out.

'Can you ever forgive me?' Hattie went on, grabbing Freya's upper arms. 'I don't deserve for you to.'

In answer Freya threw her arms around her. 'Me forgive you? Of course I can. There's nothing to forgive.'

'I'm so sorry you lost your mum,' Hattie sobbed into Freya's neck. 'I don't know how you can bear it. Anna was so amazing, just the best – and she was so good to me. You were, too. I would never have survived my teens without you both.'

'It's OK,' said Freya, snuffling. 'Mum loved you. She really did.'

'And I've been such a horrible, selfish cow. I didn't even ask you why you were suddenly back here again. If you'd said . . . Anyhow, when I saw your text . . . Oh, I'd do anything to see your mum again, just one more time!'

Hattie was really sobbing in earnest now, her face blotchy and her nose running copiously. Finn was quickly at her side, handing her two large tissues from the pack he had brought and gently persuading her into the church with him, so he could find her a pew. He was such a kind man, thought Freya, guiltily recognising a twinge of jealousy seeing him so attentive to someone else.

Gabriel and Charlotte distracted her from her thoughts by arriving next, with Charlotte giving her a hug and Gabriel an austere nod and a formal kiss on both cheeks, his hands lightly resting on her upper arms. He was looking heart-breakingly handsome in an impeccable dark suit, with a double-cuffed shirt, crested gold cufflinks and highly polished black Church's lace-ups. He looked every inch the aristocrat.

Jake was next, with his wife Kylie, both of them nodding awkwardly at Freya as they sidled past. Kylie was already crying, dabbing her eyes with a crumpled tissue.

Mostly, people seemed to want to go straight into the church without talking much beyond 'hello' and 'sorry for your loss,' and Freya was glad of that. Now the hearse had arrived, she found she could look nowhere else and was only vaguely aware of more people walking past her into the church. The undertakers solemnly unloaded the coffin and walked slowly towards her, bearing it on their shoulders.

Finn, who had silently reappeared, wordlessly guided her to fall into line behind the coffin and follow it in. The walk up the aisle felt interminable. Freya's gaze was fixed on the coffin to the exclusion of everything else, except the hands coming out from the pews in silent support as she passed. The pew in the front was reserved for her and Finn. Freya was relieved that all the other mourners were standing behind. It meant she could pretend she was all alone in the church, with just her mother to the right of her and Finn to her left in this sombre, echoing space with its smell of age and decay.

If she could just keep imagining it was her and Finn alone with her mother's coffin, she would be fine, she told herself, gritting her teeth so hard her jaw started to ache.

The welcome tears that had spilled in the graveyard – not for the loss of her mother but in empathy at Hattie's distress – had drained away again, leaving Freya feeling as if the tide had gone out, with just that tight, grim blankness remaining, a state she had honed over so many years of not giving in, not crying, when she was getting the hairdryer treatment from Andre. Her head started to ache fiercely.

She watched Chris the vicar standing talking at the head of her mother's coffin, his hands held open in welcome. It was like watching television with the sound off. He was rocking backwards and forwards on his heels, becoming quite animated, and once he even laid his hand, in an overly familiar gesture, on the coffin itself.

Mrs Dunnant was striking up on the organ now, breaking through the silent barrier around Freya with the opening bars of 'Dear Lord and Father of Mankind'. It was her mum's favourite hymn and Freya had felt proud being able to retrieve that memory when Chris had asked. The two women had been unanimous on a veto of 'Abide with me'. 'The Lord's My Shepherd' was allowed on sufferance when Freya was persuaded by Diana that it was only the Crimond version she couldn't bear.

'What if no one knows the tune to this other one?' she had fretted, once Diana had hummed it to her.

'Then I'll sing it as a very loud solo,' Diana had reassured her.

And she would too, thought Freya, letting the voices from behind wash over her in the echoing space. Freya found she couldn't sing at all. Her throat seemed to have closed up and she knew that if she tried, the very most that would come out would be a croak. Also, she wasn't sure what would happen if she let herself make a sound. She had begun to suspect that once something started coming out, it wouldn't stop, and the noise – whatever it was – would go on and on. That had always been the unimpeachable rule when doing the 'not crying' thing in Paris. Say and do nothing, and the tight control of emotion would endure . . .

Mungo was standing up at the lectern now.

Freya tried not to listen. It was safer to be elsewhere, at least in her head, but Mungo had a lovely warm, comforting voice, and the words trickled past her defences into her brain.

'And God shall wipe away all tears from their eyes; and there shall be no more death, neither sorrow, nor crying, neither shall there be any more pain . . .' he intoned.

Freya took a deep breath. Mum's pain had gone but so had she, and Freya would never hear her voice again; never have another hug from her; never be told everything would be fine; never congratulated on an achievement, however tiny; they would never share another joke; bake another cake; chat over another cup of coffee, the 'never agains' tumbled through her mind like a monumental waterfall, fierce and implacable. Freya had been hundreds of miles away, wasting all those final chances to spend time with her mother. And for what? To work for a despot who would promote even the most incompetent man rather than give her, a woman, the chances she deserved? And now she could do nothing to retrieve the last ten years of her life. They were gone. Her mother was gone.

Freya gave a dry sob and took a deep, shuddering breath to ground herself. It emerged in another sob, and then a third, wrenching sound from deep inside her chest. She folded forward in her seat, astonished at the groundswell of grief surging upwards through her body. She was half aware of Finn putting a comforting hand on the back of her neck, but rather than helping her to regain her rigid control, somehow that simple human gesture stripped away all her dissociative defences, bringing her fully into the 'now'. The full, overwhelming experience of being at her mother's funeral, the finality of saying goodbye forever, hit her like a tidal wave.

Diana was at the lectern now, giving the eulogy. And she was the right person to do it, because Freya knew nothing of the memories Diana was leading the mourners through: her mother's contribution to the community choir;

her volunteer work at the school, helping with reading every Thursday morning and running the Wack-a-Rat stall at the annual school fayre. There was a ripple of laughter as Diana wryly recounted memories of riotous suppers with Anna and friends at her house, and Anna's erratic, but always entertaining, contributions to the pub quiz team that she made up with Diana, Mungo and Gabriel. There were murmurs of recognition and approval when Diana reminded them all of Anna's tenure on the Parish Council, leading the fight to reject the housing developers like a modern Joan of Arc, scuppering their plans to concrete over much of the farmland between the village and Portneath.

On and on the litany continued, and amidst Freya's pain at having missed this huge part of her mother's world, there was also the cooling, healing balm of relief; relief that Mum's life had not been empty without her, that she had had joy, challenges, triumphs and a host of really good friends, who were here today to give her a good send off. Freya saw now that it was egotistical of her to grieve over the last, lost ten years – at least for her mother's sake. She might personally regret being in Paris all that time, but it was wrong to beat herself up over some misplaced idea that her mother's life had been empty without her. She could let go of the guilt and this thought swept fully formed into her mind as if it was borne on a gentle breeze.

And now, as the tears began to trickle down Freya's cheeks at last, Diana mentioned her name.

'. . . and her greatest triumph, her greatest joy was, of course, her beautiful daughter, Freya.'

Freya looked up through a veil of tears and saw Diana smiling benignly down at her. 'Freya was never far from Anna's thoughts,' she said slowly, 'even when she was far away, blazing her trail, refining her talents and making her mother so, so proud.' Diana paused, and, for a long moment, gazed fondly down at Freya, who was now sobbing openly.

'She loved you more than anyone else in the world,' Diana went on, speaking softly now, not to the congregation but just to her, 'and I know she would want you to take that thought with you always, whatever you do and wherever you go.'

Freya sobbed helplessly through Chris's prayers and the final hymn, 'Jerusalem'. The next thing she knew it was Ciaran, not Finn, who was standing at the front of the church, issuing the invitation to her mother's memorial supper the following day. Finn had stayed by her side, holding her tightly against him as she wept. She was beyond stopping now. It was as if all the sadness of the world was flowing through her like a river and she was powerless against it. She felt her eyes puffing, her nose swelling and still the tears tumbled down her face, dripping off her chin where she had failed to catch them with the increasingly sodden tissues Finn was patiently passing her. She had to pull herself together if she was going to cook. But that was tomorrow. This was today, the day she said a final goodbye to her beloved mother; today it was OK for her to cry.

Now the undertakers were preparing to take her mother's coffin out of the church again. Finn whispered in her ear and she stood, preparing to walk behind it. She was now so abandoned to her weeping she was beyond deciding for herself what to do. As she turned, she saw through her streaming eyes, lids now so swollen she could barely keep them open, all the people gathered behind her in the church. The pews of the little village chapel were full. Faces were blurred by tears, but she could make out Diana, Mungo, Ciaran and Martha, and there was Aidan with Jess and Gabriel, scowling and fierce as always, with Charlotte looking stunning, at his side. There were other people too, all familiar faces and all smiling kindly at her as she trudged slowly after the coffin, tucked tight into Finn's side, feeling secure and warm there, even at this, the very bleakest of hours.

Driving back to Portneath, Freya, her tears spent now, rested her head against the car window and watched the dreary rain trickling down the glass. It reminded her of Christmas Eve, when she had been in Finn's car, driving through the sleet after sitting at her mother's deathbed and then visiting the empty family home. In that moment, as on Christmas Eve, she wondered when the losses would end.

Chapter Twenty-Six

'I'm just not ready to say goodbye to her,' she said numbly to Finn as he guided her gently up the stairs to the flat.

'You don't have to say goodbye,' he comforted her, pulling her into his arms in the narrow hallway and holding her head against his shoulder. 'She'll always be with you,' he murmured in her ear.

They stood there together, Finn rocking her gently, for a long, long while.

'You're cold,' he said, pulling back at last and warming her hands in his own. 'I'll run you a bath. And how about a cup of tea?'

Freya nodded dumbly.

He put her on the sofa and got to work. Freya stared, unseeing, as he bustled around, setting the bath to run, finding her a dry towel and then going into the kitchen to slide the kettle onto the hob. The homely routines, the already familiar sights and sounds in the little flat, were a comfort in themselves.

When he brought the tea, he had put a maid of honour tart on a little plate for her too.

'I forgot. What's the challenge today?' asked Freya dully. It felt important to hang onto these little details of life as they floated past her like pieces of wreckage.

'Eleven Pipers Piping,' he replied. 'Haggis, neeps and tatties for supper. Bagpipes optional, so I've decided against.

But never mind about that now. Drink your tea in the bath and then – if you can – you should try and get some sleep.'

'I don't want to be on my own,' she said, looking at him imploringly.

'Settle down in my bed then,' he suggested. 'I'll be right here, all the time. If not here, then just downstairs in the deli.'

Freya nodded.

Once she was warmed through by the bath and the tea, she put on a pair of Finn's pyjamas and curled up in his unmade bed. The pillow smelt of his aftershave and she pushed her nose into it, soothed by the familiarity. How odd that she should feel so at home with a man she had always admired from a distance. It felt so right for them to be together. Now, vulnerable and grieving, she wanted nothing more than to be with him. Close. Breathing the same air that he breathed.

Sleep overcame her.

Finn was relieved the funeral was over. It had gone OK too. Now, it was just his priority to make sure Freya rested and ate something, so she had the energy to shine when she was cooking for everyone tomorrow. It was a relief the Eleven Pipers Piping theme gave him an excuse to serve haggis. Not only did he personally really like it, even a non-cook like him could shove some haggis in the microwave and whistle up some mashed potato and swede to accompany it.

He had learned a few years earlier there was no need to actually make the haggis from scratch. That would definitely be beyond him. As he pottered, he revisited fond memories of meeting the deli's supplier of haggis at a food fair in Exeter some years back – larger than life, red-haired Scot who didn't speak so much as roar in broad Glaswegian, exhorting anyone and everyone passing his stand to have a try. Finn had done exactly that and had been impressed by Hamish's company's commitment to making the best possible haggis and black pudding in Scotland, if not the world. They had hit it off personally too – Hamish was hilarious and Finn had been the only stockist of haggis in Portneath ever since. He didn't offer it all year round though, just making sure he had a few in for New Year's Eve and Burns Night.

He weighed the hefty purple-brown lump experimentally. There was more here than he and Freya could manage, but he wasn't going to exhaust her by inviting anyone else to join them. She needed a quiet evening in, just the two of them. Tough as today had been, he was enjoying the quiet peaceful togetherness he and Freya had settled into. There was no drama and histrionics which he found exhausting and unnecessary, just a strong, unspoken commitment to each other that they could gradually build on in the year ahead. She would need to come to her own conclusions, of course, but he was certain they belonged with each other and, come what may, he was quietly excited for their future. Together.

When Freya woke up, the sky was darkening and she could hear Finn pottering around comfortingly in the kitchen.

She got up. Her heart felt leaden in her chest at what she was about to say.

'What?' asked Finn as she came into the kitchen, seeing immediately that something was up. 'Actually,' he added, 'hold that thought. I'm just finishing this whisky sauce and then I'm good to dish up. You can tell me while we eat, but – while you're there – bung some butter and pepper in the mashed swede for me, will you?'

In automatic pilot, Freya did as he instructed, and then laid the table whilst Finn brought out two plates, piled high – she really wasn't sure if she would be able to eat anything – but he put them down on the table and nodded at her to sit.

He sat down opposite her, giving her a puzzled look, inviting her to speak.

'So, I've been thinking about what to do next,' she began, carefully, staring at her plate, reluctant to meet his eye. 'Diana did an amazing job getting Andre to give me back my job but,' she sighed heavily, 'it's not definite, and I've pretty much decided to let the job in Paris go.'

Finn was still. His fork frozen in mid-air.

'I don't have a plan,' she went on. 'I just know that it's probably wrong to go back and – now I'm telling myself that – it feels like a relief.'

'For me too,' contributed Finn, quietly, his eyes fixed on her steadily as he rested his knife and fork askew on his plate.

'But there is, unfortunately, something else in the way of the two of us being together, and it's something I should have told you sooner, because it's rather – well – large,' she said, clasping her hands together and staring at them fixedly.

Finn was silent. Waiting.

'My mother's cancer was almost inevitable,' Freya went on, casting around for the right words, to carefully transmit the 'thing' she didn't want to say but had to. 'She has a mutation on a particular gene – it's called the BRCA gene and we all have one, but in people who have this particular mutation, the chances of their developing cancer are very high. Like Angelina Jolie?' Freya looked at Finn for a sign of recognition but his face was blank, so she carried on. 'Anyway, so she – my mum – first got breast cancer when I was sixteen. It was very aggressive. It was during her treatment for it that we found out why she had developed it. Once we knew, she took the decision to have her other breast, her ovaries and her uterus removed, to stop it coming back. She managed to have nearly ten years of healthy life after that and we thought everything was OK – well, *I* thought everything was OK; then I got a text from Diana. She told me it had come back and this time it was terminal. Diana said Mum hadn't wanted to tell me, to interfere with my life, but that she knew she didn't have long . . . And – well, you know the rest.'

Freya stopped. Her mouth working. She brushed away a stray tear that had edged its way past her defences and sniffed defiantly. Finn reached out to her, but she waved him away without touching him. 'I'm fine,' she said. 'I've got to get this out.'

Finn nodded, and waited, his brow furrowed.

'So,' Freya went on, 'this gene mutation, on the BRCA gene – like I say, it's hereditary. The chances of my having it too are fifty-fifty.'

Shock flashed across Finn's face.

'That's high,' he said. 'What does that mean, for us? If you have it, that, is.'

'Basically, it means I either have to accept a high cancer risk and face it if – when – it happens, or I have to decide how to mitigate that risk with surgery and/or extra surveillance. If I were to agree to a hysterectomy, to have my ovaries removed, my breasts . . . I could reduce my cancer risk dramatically.'

'I appreciate that's—' began Finn, but Freya shushed him.

'There's more,' she warned him, and he closed his mouth obediently. 'If I'm positive, I have really difficult decisions to make over whether – and how – I have children. For one thing, there's the issue of delaying preventative surgery, then the chances of my developing a cancer during pregnancy are higher or, at least, any cancer will progress more quickly in that hormone environment, and, as if that wasn't enough, I seriously have to think about passing this thing on to any children I have . . . That's a question in itself. Could I knowingly give birth to a child who bears a burden like this? In a way it was easier for my mother, because she didn't have that one to grapple with – the gene mutation hadn't been identified then. These are all things I would have to decide,' she said, rubbing her brow distractedly. 'Some women are having IVF so they can choose embryos without the gene mutation, so that's one way around, but it's a big thing . . .'

Freya had given *some* thought to these issues over the years, of course she had, but it had all felt hypothetical, something that would only matter at some unknown future date. But then she had finally steeled herself to get in contact with the geneticist her mother had found for her. She had had special permission to go through the obligatory counselling on the phone and then have the blood samples taken in the private Paris clinic before they were sent to the laboratory in the UK. It had been complicated and sorting it out had taken her mind off the magnitude of the answers she would be getting. And now, here she was, and it could not feel more real and relevant. The future had begun and what it held for her was contained in that yellow envelope inside her mother's inlaid wooden box.

'So, yeah, I potentially have a lot of decisions to make,' she said, giving him a wan smile.

'It sounds like *we* might have a lot of decisions to make,' ventured Finn, cautiously, reaching out to take her hand.

'Oh, no,' said Freya, leaning back in her chair, a little further away from him. 'This is me, mate, not you. I'm not dragging you into all this.'

'Do you seriously think that hearing this changes how I feel about you?' Finn sounded annoyed now. 'Of *course*, this is something we should face up to together. What kind of a man do you think I am?'

'It's too much,' whispered Freya, pushing her barely touched plate away and resting her elbows on the table, her head in her hands. 'We've only known each other a few days.'

'Well, that's crap, for a start,' retorted Finn. 'We've known each other for most of our lives. I've definitely known you since you were about fourteen.'

'I had such a crush on you then,' Freya smiled, remembering. 'I didn't think you even knew I existed.'

'Oh, I knew,' said Finn heavily. 'I mean, not in a creepy way – you *were* only fourteen, but later, when you were older. And then suddenly you were gone, just when I had started working my way around to you.'

'Working your way around to me? Charming. I suppose I should be honoured you were planning to give me the benediction of your attention,' said Freya, with a sniff.

'I was admiring you from afar,' smiled Finn, undeterred. 'I thought I had more time. I suppose we always think that, don't we? About everything. Just goes to show we should live in the moment more. That's what I believe now, anyhow.'

'Works for me,' agreed Freya. But that wasn't what she thought really, was it? She was more a 'put off until tomorrow what you don't have to do today sort of person'. That was why the yellow envelope was burning a hole in her conscience right now. She should at least open it, so she had a 50 per cent chance of enjoying some good news for a change.

'Anyhow,' she went on, 'these are things I *might* have to decide. I mean, we've all got a BRCA gene, it's only if there's this genetic abnormality on it. Obviously, if I've inherited a normal BRCA gene from my father's side instead, I'm OK.'

'So find out! No point agonising over things that might not even be a "thing",' Finn was incredulous.

'Sure. I will,' said Freya. 'Just . . . not right now.'

'I don't understand you,' said Finn, staring at her, shaking his head. 'Why would you not just face it – with me – so we can deal with it, if we have to?'

'I'm just doing it my way, OK? This isn't about us.'

'Yeah, it really isn't about us, is it?' said Finn, bitterly.

There was a silence.

'I think we should slow things down,' he said quietly, at last.

'Us?'

'Yep,' he went on, crisply. 'Like you said, it's only been a few days, really. I mean, you've just told me you're possibly not going back to Paris, but the stuff you're going through – Freya, I don't think you're exactly in the right head space to be making big career decisions like that. Maybe you should think again. Either way, clearly it would be better if we both took a step back. Before we get in any deeper.'

Freya's heart sank. She agreed with him, of course, but she didn't think she had ever felt lonelier than she did in that moment. She would be the first to appreciate he didn't want to saddle himself with a woman who couldn't easily do the things women did – like have babies without complication and risk, like have breasts. *That* was the real reason why he wanted to end it before it had even started. It was fair enough – she didn't blame him – but God, it hurt.

'OK,' she said, at last. 'I think that's sensible.'

'It's still fine for you to have the room,' he said, his expression softening.

'Thank you, I appreciate that,' responded Freya, as flatly and unemotionally as if they were discussing the weather. 'But I'll find something else soon if I stay. I can rent something. Somewhere.'

There was another silence.

'That sounds like a plan,' Finn said evenly, standing and collecting their plates to scrape them clean and put them in the dishwasher.

Chapter Twenty-Seven

Back in her attic room, the sinking feeling of dread and loss continued. How could they have gone from talking about the funeral one minute to ending their fledgeling relationship the next? What Finn said was fair enough, though. If she didn't feel comfortable involving him in decisions about the geneticist's letter – and she didn't – then clearly their relationship wasn't in the right place to continue. Plus, it was clear he had been looking for an excuse to bail. I mean, who wouldn't, under those circumstances? As for her desperate desire to climb back down the attic stairs and crawl under his duvet, to get him to hold her in his arms, well . . . that was just her selfishness rearing its ugly head again, just as it had with her mother. She needed to get over herself.

No, she was going to cope with this by herself, and maybe now was the time to get her big girl's pants on and open that yellow envelope lurking in her mother's writing box. After all, as she kept telling herself, there was a 50 per cent chance it would be good news, which would be a plus in her next relationship with – whoever – and maybe, after a suitable interval, perhaps she could even consider resurrecting her relationship with Finn one day. If he wanted to, that was. He was perfectly within his rights to go off and begin a thing with any one of the many girls who flocked around him, fluttering their eyelashes, flirting with him over their coffee order.

Freya was sure Hattie would be happier with a fancy, cinnamon-spiced caramel latte thingie with whipped cream and sprinkles than an uncompromisingly correct flat white from Finn, but she still went in and chatted with Finn every day. Maybe, despite what she said about him, it wasn't the coffee she was after. And why shouldn't Hattie have a crack at him? They would make a good couple. Freya's heart gave a painful twist at the idea. She thought about her text to Hattie, her confession and apology . . . thank goodness Hattie had been at the funeral today. She would have felt even more awful if her cowardice at breaking the news had led her closest friend to miss the chance to say goodbye to someone who had been so special in her life. But a text? What an awful way to find out someone important had died. Still, there you go, that was Freya all over, wasn't it? Doing a crappy job of being a friend as well as being a rubbish daughter. Hattie had had every right to never speak to her ever again. She was sure she would feel the same if the situation were reversed.

Lying there, on her little wooden bed, trying to summon up the energy to go and brush her teeth, Freya thought she had heard the doorbell outside the shop ringing, but she must be mistaken. It was nearly nine o'clock. No one would be arriving now.

Next, she heard footsteps coming up the wooden stairs. Two sets – one set unmistakeably Finn's – but there was a woman's voice, she could hear.

'Freya, it's Hattie to see you,' Finn called up.

Freya sat bolt upright, banging her head on the ceiling, a tiny flutter of hope flickering in her chest as she rubbed her head ruefully. Surely Hattie hadn't come to tell her what a crap friend she was? Not after the way she had been at the funeral. Maybe – just maybe – Freya was being offered a last chance to make amends, with Hattie at least.

She climbed down the attic stairs slowly, to find Finn and Hattie crowded together in the tiny hallway.

The two women looked at each other for a long moment.

'Same,' said Freya, pointing ruefully to her own puffy, tear-glazed eyes and then at Hattie's, which were worse, if anything.

'Fred!' Hattie's voice broke and she held out her arms.

'Hats!' Freya choked.

The women hugged fiercely.

'Why don't you two come and have a proper talk,' suggested Finn, shepherding them into the main room, where the fire was still glowing.

Finn sat them down on the sofa and offered drinks. 'Wine please,' they said, simultaneously, and then laughed.

'One mind,' said Hattie.

'Yeah, dipsomaniacs, both of us,' suggested Freya.

As they got themselves settled on either end of the sofa, Rafferty appeared and made a beeline for Hattie's lap.

'Oi, what about me?' said Freya, pretending to be affronted. She had been the one getting Rafferty's undivided attention recently.

'He's a shocking tart,' admitted Finn, coming back with two wine glasses between the fingers in one hand, and a bottle of Rioja in the other. He poured two generous glasses and then left the bottle on the hearth.

'I don't know about you two, but I'm knackered,' he said, diplomatically making his excuses so the women could talk alone. Freya was relieved. Things were awkward between them since their earlier, devastating, conversation. It was all she could do to smooth things over enough to put Hattie at ease.

'I am so sorry—' said Freya and Hattie simultaneously, when he had gone.

'Not again,' joked Freya. 'I—'

'No,' interrupted Hattie. 'Let *me* talk.' She gave Freya a pleading look.

Freya nodded her agreement and pressed her finger to her lips to signal acquiescence.

'I was hard on you,' said Hattie. 'At New Year's Eve . . . I wasn't being fair, those things I said. And it wasn't ever really about that stupid text full stop thing, that was a red herring. I was insulted at the time, but I know I was being too sensitive. And then, all that waiting for you to make the next contact rather than me doing it myself. It was childish, I know that now. I was just looking for things to be offended about and I'm sorry I made you feel bad about it. Like I admitted at the time, I'm basically envious, that's all. You've escaped Portneath and made your own success. I should be applauding that. So, well done. And as for being jealous of you and your relationship with your mum, I had no right . . . you were both really kind to me when we were younger, when I was falling out with my own mum all the time. When she was too busy with her boyfriends to be there for me, Anna was truly amazing. I will never stop being grateful for that.'

'She did it because she loved you,' said Freya.

'No,' Hattie told her, matter-of-factly. 'She did it because she loved *you*. And that's OK,' she went on hastily. 'I adored and admired your mum for supporting me like she did. It's crazy for me to be envious, just because you're her daughter and I'm not.'

Freya drew in breath to reply, but Hattie held up her finger. 'Still talking,' she said, and then smiled her apology. 'I just need to get this out.'

Freya nodded, taking a gulp of wine to silence herself, the gutsy, resinous red filling her mouth and warming her soul.

'I need to say,' Hattie went on, 'that when I had a go at you for not being there for your mum before she died, it's actually because I'm feeling kind of guilty myself.'

Freya drew in breath to reply again, but then visibly restrained herself.

'Yeah, so,' Hattie went on, looking down at her hands, 'I feel guilty because whilst you were hundreds of miles away, I was actually right here and I didn't even know she was ill again. I didn't keep in touch, just to see how she was, and I should have been doing that. I was too wrapped up in my own life, Freya, feeling miserable because it's all a bit of a dead-end pile of crap, and I definitely didn't want to admit to your mum I wasn't up to much, especially with your stellar career in contrast. I was keeping out of her way,' she sighed, 'and that was unforgiveable of me.'

Now Freya insisted on interjecting. 'Listen, that's something we both feel crap about, and I can't fix that for you any more than I can for me, although I do think you're wrong to be so down on yourself. What Diana said – and this sort of resonates for me – is that Mum didn't want us to know. She deliberately hid it. I don't think we will ever really understand fully why she made that choice, but she did. And I made it far too easy for her to do that because I was so wrapped up in my own life – and that's where I let you down too,' Freya added. 'The truth is, me and Mum hadn't seen each other for a while, not since last spring, and she seemed all right then, although she already knew it had come back, knew she didn't have long . . .' Freya gazed into space, remembering, but then she shook herself and continued. 'But we spoke on the phone often enough, and I *still* didn't realise. She sounded fine,' said Freya, remembering how her mother – always so honest – had deceived her, hiding her physical deterioration behind a bright, happy voice. 'So, yeah, I'm guilty too. I might have been a tiny bit self-absorbed. I might have talked about myself too much when we did have contact. I definitely – probably – forgot to ask her about her own life and how she was. I'm sure I did that, but, as Diana says, that's what kids do with their parents. I mean, let's face it, if you can't be a selfish brat with your own mum, who can you do it with?'

'Actually, not you, obviously,' Freya teased gently, answering her own question. 'With you and your mum, she's the selfish brat, natch.'

Hattie snorted gently. 'You're not wrong.'

'And I can't be too angry with her for not telling me,' Freya went on sadly but with absolute emotional clarity at last, 'because she totally did it for me. And you. She didn't want her illness to weigh us down and stop us getting on with our lives.'

Hattie wiped away a tear, and then another.

'I know,' said Freya, doing the same. 'I feel like I'd do anything in the world to have spent a bit more time with her. Just another day. Another hour, even.'

'I think that's bargaining,' said Hattie, sniffing.

Freya looked blank.

'It's one of the stages of grief – bargaining,' Hattie explained. 'It's where you end up torturing yourself, thinking exactly how much you would be prepared to give up for the person not to be dead or even just how much you'd have paid for more time.' She looked down at her hands. 'I've been doing it too. Regret's a bitch.'

'Then let's not have the regret of losing our friendship too,' said Freya, quietly, holding out her hand.

Hattie took it and squeezed tight, smiling crookedly through her tears, and after that the two women talked and laughed and cried, reminiscing for hours, polishing off the first bottle of wine and doing serious damage to a second. Their bittersweet memories tumbled out one after the other. They frequently burst into giggles, and then frantically shushed each other, worried about waking Finn. Eventually, regretfully, at nearly one in the morning, Freya managed to persuade Hattie to let her call a taxi. 'I've got to cook a banquet for thirty people tomorrow – I mean, today,' she said. 'We've not got my mum to make us be sensible now. It's up to us,' she told Hattie with owlish solemnity. By then, even this was enough to make them catch each other's eye and dissolve into hysterics. Freya was still stifling laughter when she fell, exhausted, into her bed. She felt so much lighter at having salvaged her precious friendship, even in the face of all this terrible loss, not least the car-crash conversation with Finn. It had to happen, mind, but she could have handled it better. Still, with the warmth of her relationship with Hattie wrapped around her like a warm, cosy blanket, she drifted off to sleep with a smile on her face.

Finn was shattered. He had been kept awake by the racket from the girls and had barely slept even after Hattie left. Eventually giving up the struggle, he had got up at the crack of dawn and had spent most of the morning so far being furious with himself. He had behaved like a complete knob, just before Hattie arrived, throwing a wobbly because Freya wouldn't commit to their relationship until she knew about this cancer gene thing.

What she'd needed in that moment was for Finn to provide non-directional, non-judgemental support, and what had he done? Had a tantrum because she wasn't involving him enough, that's what. He, Finn, who had only really got to know her properly since Christmas Eve, just twelve, short days ago – God, it was no time at all! He was in trouble here. And it was no good trying to tell himself – he had even tried telling her, for goodness' sake – that, in fact, they had known each other for longer just because they happened to be in the same room a few times when they were in their teens. Ridiculous. He should have stuck to his guns when he told her he was too busy for relationships, because that was the truth of it.

All this was the last thing he needed. If his stupid behaviour had been the last nail in the coffin, in her deciding to go back to France after all, then it served him right. Only that was the last thing he wanted for her. OK, even if he'd blown his chance of a relationship, staying in Portneath would be a better result for her, he was certain of it. Better still, if Gabriel changed his mind about handing the café space to the appalling Sharmayne for her puddings – which would be miraculous as Gabriel rarely changed his mind about anything – then all of that would be a million times better than going back to be ground into the dust by a lowlife like Andre, even if he was some famous, poncey chef with a reputation for brilliance. Freya was brilliant. He, Finn, thought so, anyhow. She was tough, and dogged, and funny – and beautiful . . .

Anyhow, what he needed to do now was help her to get through what was probably the second toughest day of her life after the funeral yesterday. The memorial dinner was the priority now. The rest could wait.

Freya heard him come up the stairs and sat up abruptly, banging her head on the sloping ceiling, yet again.

'Christ, what was that?' asked Finn, as he nudged open the door to her room with his foot and carefully put the latte and the apricot Danish pastry on the little chair next to her bed. 'Was that your head I just heard? Mind my ceiling, can't you? This building's listed.'

Thank goodness he didn't seem angry about the previous night, Freya thought, with relief.

'Finn . . .?' she said.

'It's all right,' he replied, cutting her off. 'You don't need this now, of all days, I get it. We'll shelve it, yeah? I'm really glad you've made it up with Hattie.'

Freya sighed with relief. 'We must have kept you awake,' she said, guiltily. 'I'm really sorry. What time is it?' She picked up the mug with a moan of gratitude and took a sip.

'Early. But I thought you'd want to make a start. The majority of the ingredients you asked for have arrived. We're still waiting for the last of the dairy stuff, except the sheep cheese from Holly Tree Farm, Ciaran's already dropped that by. We'll have the lot by nine o'clock.'

'It's amazing you've got it all,' she said. 'Given the amount of notice . . .'

'What notice,' he joked, weakly. 'But yeah, it's all going to be there. And Diana's already called to say she's coming in to finish setting up this afternoon. She's rounded up some helpers to give her a hand, so all the front of house stuff's sorted.'

'Thank you,' said Freya, making eye contact over the top of her mug. 'I really am *so* grateful.'

'Yeah,' he said, neutrally. 'You should be.'

'You need to keep a tally on costs,' she reminded him. 'I owe you.'

'You don't,' he said, firmly.

'I've got the money. Or I will have when I inherit. I've asked for some expensive stuff.'

'I don't want your money,' he said, standing up.

'I can't let you do that for me.'

'Then let me do it for your mum,' he said with finality, as he left.

Chapter Twenty-Eight

Twelve Drummers Drumming

Thirty minutes later, Freya was showered, dressed and down in the café kitchen with her knife roll open on the newly scrubbed work surface. She didn't have her chef's whites of course, but with her hair scraped back into a bobble and in clean T-shirt and jeans, with one of Finn's blue-and-white striped aprons over the top, she was in work mode.

The shopping list she had given Finn yesterday had been extensive and, providing the quality of all the ingredients was up to scratch, she had an ambitious schedule for the day's work. Using her own copy of the list, she carried out an inspection; first, the fridge, which was full of meat and dairy, including the partridge breasts, already neatly butchered and vacuum packed in pairs. Next, she had several pints of the fabulous Holly Tree Farm cream to whip and flavour for the meringue swans. Everything was present and correct, so far.

The wooden trays of fruit and veg were looking great. The pears were firm, unmarked but gently yielding to pressure. Perfect. The spring greens she had asked for – she was going to serve them with the partridge and pears – were beautifully fresh and would provide a vibrant flash of colour on the plate; first she would boil them so they were half-cooked and then she would plunge them into iced water to make sure they stayed bright green, and then, later, they would be tossed in sesame oil with lardons. They would be delicious, providing a hint of bitterness to offset the rich meat and the honeyed sweetness of the pan-fried, caramelised pears. There were big bunches of fresh herbs too; dill, thyme, chives . . . Freya picked up the bundles and sniffed them one by one, crushing a stalk of each between her fingers. Heaven.

Then there were the pomegranates, the shiny red globes with their tiny papery crowns. Freya would have to break them open and tap them sharply with a wooden spoon to release the ruby seeds from their carapace within each fruit's silken-white pith and tough, varnished skin. She took a moment to admire their beauty. She had cheated and got Finn to source her a bottle of pomegranate molasses too. She was going to use just a dab of this on the pudding plates. Normally she would make everything herself, but she had a mountain to climb today without that.

The rest of the ingredients came from stocks in Finn's deli, and she was impressed anew at the range. She had asked for some pretty wild stuff – smoked sea salt, wasabi, anchovies, sun-dried tomatoes and polenta flour . . . all were in the box Finn had left for her.

First, Freya got on with her special project. It was a last-minute idea – madness given everything else she had to do – but she had done her research and was determined. The idea was to make a Bolo Rei – the King Cake Diana had been talking about. She had heard about them vaguely in the past as a Portuguese delicacy, traditionally eaten on the twelfth day of Christmas. OK, so tonight was about her mother, but it was also the last day of Christmas for another year and Freya wasn't going to let it go uncelebrated. She quickly googled and brought the recipe up on her phone, propping it up on the worktop for easy reference. Basically, it was a fruited yeast bun, formed into a ring and studded with crystallised fruit.

Freya liked working with yeast – it never ceased to amaze her how the dough would rise, like magic, and there was no better smell, in her opinion, than the delicious aroma of bread baking. She had found a large baking tray that was just the right size to fit in Finn's oven, and she was making a big one – it had to feed more than thirty people, after all. She didn't have the powerful mixer she was used to working with in Paris, but handling the warm, soft dough, and losing herself in the rhythmic, repetitive movements of kneading was calming. Once the dough was stretchy and soft, she incorporated the port-soaked dried fruit and then placed the ball of dough gently into an oiled mixing bowl, covering the top with cling film. Running up the stairs to Finn's flat she had to move a pile of towels out of the airing cupboard so there was room to slide the bowl carefully in. Hopefully, it would be warm and cosy enough for the dough to rise well.

There was plenty to do in the meantime.

Downstairs in the café kitchen again, Freya prepped the main course. Soon she had a basinful of finely chopped greens resting in cold water and she had meticulously peeled, cored and quartered the pears, dousing them with a good squeeze of lemon juice to stop them from going brown, ready for frying in butter in small batches in the pan. They should caramelise nicely. The partridge breasts just needed marinading and, once that was done, she was happy she was on top of the main course, at least. The nerves would start again when she had to cook them tonight, especially as she was really missing the endless supplies of seasoned, black cast-iron pans she used for pretty much everything in Paris. Finn's single, trusty heavy-based frying pan was going to have to do. At least she was offering a fixed menu.

The meringues she'd made the day before had dried out completely now and just needed to be filled with the cream.

She whipped this next, sweetening it with icing sugar and delicately flavouring it with vanilla, almond and the merest hint of rose – too much and it would taste soapy. She was hoping for a steady hand when it came to assembling them into swans, which couldn't be done until just before they were served. She was going to have to work like lightning this evening.

All that done, she made herself a cup of tea and, while she was drinking it, got herself into the right mindset for the biggest challenge of all: to honour her mother and – she was happy to admit it – showcase her cooking skills to her friends (including Finn) she was going to produce canapés to stun and amaze. Each one would be tiny, intensely flavoured, complex and beautiful. Freya was determined that the colours, the shapes and textures would all be perfect.

For thirty guests to have canapés as a starter, around two hundred and fifty divine little mouthfuls were required. She would do six types, three dozen of each, and she had it all planned out. Prawn with wasabi and avocado; local smoked trout – like smoked salmon but more delicate – with creamy chives and dill; and then there were the hot, three-cheese and herb soufflé bites, the perfect showcase for Martha's sharp, crumbly sheep cheese; canapés with tender beef fillet from Holly Tree Farm, garnished with wild mushrooms and Parma ham on a crisp, puff pastry base with all the flavour of tiny beef Wellingtons – an absolute classic . . . That last one was the nearest to the vol-au-vents Diana had suggested but the whole production was a darned sight higher concept than vol-au-vents and cheese straws! They would bring into play every skill she had learned, with three different types of pastry, soufflé, pâté and a host of other complexities, all on a tiny scale . . . She was just about to get started when there was a tentative knock.

'Jess!' Freya exclaimed as her new friend shyly poked her head around the door.

'I came with the veg for the Lord Woolton pie,' she said, offering a cotton tote bag with verdant carrot tops sticking out of it like green dreadlocks.

'Thank you *so* much,' Freya was so touched, her eyes filled with tears. What was it with all this crying? For ten years she didn't cry, and now, after yesterday's meltdown, she couldn't stop. 'It all looks amazing,' she said, unpacking the bag onto the table. 'What a privilege to be cooking with such incredibly fresh and local ingredients,' she went on. 'It's every chef's dream, truly.'

'Really?' said Jess, shyly. 'I thought afterwards it was a silly offer, because of course you can easily get fruit and veg. Finn must have loads of good suppliers.'

'Yes, but it means a lot to use yours,' said Freya, with genuine gratitude.

'It means a lot to give it,' admitted Jess. 'Your mum was so kind to me. I've not lived in Middlemass long, but she was so welcoming. I work in the primary schools around here and – as of course you know – your mum was a reading volunteer in Middlemass primary.'

'I didn't know, actually,' said Freya, sadly. 'Not until Diana said in church yesterday. I've not been here much. And I'm loving hearing all the stories. Thank you.'

Jess was shuffling on the spot. 'Anyhow, I should let you . . .' she said, backing towards the door. 'I'll see you tonight,' she said, as she disappeared and after that, Freya's focus was total. Thankfully, she had found a stack of round, metal trays, left behind by the Marconis. In Paris, Andre liked to serve canapés on mirrors or on slabs of wood or slate. Freya just had trays, but she thought they would work well once she had given them a good wash and polish. Another treasure trove was a drawer full of small, green cocktail napkins. Freya put a stack of them in the middle of each tray and laid out her canapés around them. Providing napkins might seem mundane, but practicalities were important too and she wanted her guests to be impeccably looked after. That was the key to providing a memorable experience, not just the food but the whole ethos of hospitality.

Three intense hours later, Freya had made at least a start on all the canapés. She stood back, hands on hips to survey her work. There were finishing touches that she would need to do later – a single blade of chive on each of the smoked trout ones, a tiny sprig of thyme on the beef Wellingtons – but she was pleased with her progress and had assembled them with a painterly eye. Andre had always praised her delicacy and precision. 'Small hands,' he would say. Ideal for the fiddly jobs. Of course, in that macho world, being physically tiny had mainly been a disadvantage, despite Freya doggedly showing her strength, never ducking out of the heavy lifting when it needed doing – bringing in the heavy trays of meat and vegetables as they arrived, even carrying the huge bags of flour. She had earned her place on that team, fair and square, she remembered, however much it made her back ache when she finally got to her bed each night.

Finn brought her a toasted cheese sandwich for lunch and inspected her work. 'Amazing,' he said. 'You'll wow them, for sure.'

They were both being carefully polite with each other.

'Am I going to have to say something to everyone?' she asked, anxiously. 'I'm worried I won't be able to, plus I'm going to be running around in here. I'm not sure I'll have time.'

'Let's play it by ear,' he reassured her. 'And that other thing . . .'

'Not now,' she implored. 'I know . . . but not now.'

Chapter Twenty-Nine

'Never fear, the cavalry is here,' announced Diana as she swept in with Mungo in tow. 'Do I detect an atmosphere?' she said, sharply, looking at the two of them in turn.

'Nope,' said Finn, getting up and picking up the toastie plates. 'Nothing to see here.'

'Hmm,' said Diana, unconvinced. 'Anyhow, we are here to transform this venue into a posh restaurant worthy of your fabulous culinary skills,' she told Freya, taking the box that Mungo was carrying and plonking it on the table where they had just been having lunch. The rest of the tables still had chairs balanced on them and the little café was looking chilly and unloved. Freya struggled to see how it could be turned into a warm, welcoming space for the guests in just a few hours' time, but if anyone could do it, Diana could.

'First,' said Diana, 'let's sweep this floor and then get the chairs down. I have those tablecloths, but I've had to bring a couple of white bedsheets too, to make up the numbers. And I've been around the neighbourhood collecting white napkins from people too. Martha had a dozen, so that helped a lot. They're all ironed and ready to go.'

As she was talking, she was disappearing into the kitchen, reappearing with a broom which she handed to Mungo.

He obediently started to sweep.

'Now,' said Diana quietly once Finn had gone, 'how are you, my darling?'

Freya nodded and ducked her head. 'OK,' she mumbled.

'What's up between you and lover boy?'

Freya's head shot up. 'Nothing,' she said, and then – when she met Diana's piercing gaze, 'It's just . . . it's me . . .'

'So, are you going back to Paris on Monday?'

Diana had been the one who had created that option, of course. Freya didn't want to seem ungrateful. 'I don't . . .' she said.

'I'm getting a strong impression your future lies here in Portneath,' surmised Diana. 'I have a feeling for these things. And with a certain someone, perhaps too.'

'Look,' said Freya, 'I think I'm going to say "possibly" to the first and "almost certainly not" to the second. Listen,' she said, suddenly thinking of something to distract Diana with, 'I know this is an odd request, but I need something small and sparkly that will survive being cooked.'

'Definitely one of the odder "asks" I've had recently,' said Diana, thoughtfully. 'Will this do?' she said, pulling a dramatic-looking silver ring off her finger and holding it out to Freya.

'I can't take your ring,' Freya protested.

'It's just paste. That stone isn't diamond, it's glass. I bought it to annoy Mungo because it was so flash and even *he* thought it was tacky – the man who makes Liberace look like Oliver Cromwell. It's all yours if you want it; in fact, you'd be doing me a favour.'

'It *would* be perfect,' Freya admitted, taking it and turning it to admire it in the light.

'Sorted,' said Diana, briskly, standing up and brushing dust off her hands. 'Right. Onward.'

Freya was relieved and delighted to see the fruited dough for her Bolo Rei had risen beautifully. She carried it carefully down to the café kitchen and pummelled the air out of it again before carefully incorporating a single dried kidney bean into the mound of dough along with the sparkly silver princess ring with its gaudy pink glass diamond. This time, she was going to shape and decorate the dough. Once it was formed into a ring, she found a steep-sided cereal bowl to put in the centre. If she left out this step it was likely the hole in the middle would disappear as it rose. It was a quick job to glaze the top and decorate it with crystallised fruit and sugar nibs. She would rest it so it could rise again and then put it in to bake. It should still be faintly and deliciously warm when she served it at the end of the meal.

The Bolo Rei dealt with, Freya turned again to her canapés. She needed a steady hand, but her mind was churning things over and over and so even simple tasks were taking twice as long, because she was distracted. Time passed and it seemed like no time at all when she took notice of her surroundings again. She looked up to see the sky had darkened outside and it was nearly five o'clock – just an hour until people would start to arrive. Freya wiped her hands on the tea towel tucked into her waist ties and then pushed her hair off her face with the back of her hand. It had gone quiet at the front of the shop, and she poked her head around the door, curiously.

'I wasn't expecting this!' Freya exclaimed.

The transformation of the dull, grubby little space was astonishing. Mungo and Diana were polishing the windows on the outside with scrunched up newspaper and it was obvious they had already done the insides because the dozen or more strings of fairy lights they had strung across both expanses of window on either side of the door were doubled in impact by their reflections in the glass against the indigo night sky.

The five tables, each with seats for six guests, were precisely placed towards the windows, with just enough circulation space around them for servers to get around. That left a generous area closer to the kitchen for people to mingle and chat while they ate the canapés. The tables were covered in pristine white cloths and, at the centre of each table was a grey, Moorish pierced tin lantern, each one glowing with tea lights throwing tiny, twinkling beams of light into the room. Mungo had provided wine and water glasses, polished until they, too, were sparkling in the candle glow. A trio of hellebores – pure white, with green stripes – were precisely placed in pretty, pale green bud vases in the centre of each table next to the lanterns. The effect was simple, classy and almost ethereal – evoking the cosiness of a Parisian brasserie with the sense of occasion of a wedding marquee. The chequered black-and-white lino looked like marble in the warm light, and even the stainless-steel knives and forks – a handy legacy of the Marconi era – were polished so they gleamed softly, like the best silverware.

'So?' said Diana, coming back inside.

'Miraculous!' exclaimed Freya, grinning in wonderment. 'You have literally done absolute miracles. Extraordinary, really – I can't thank you both enough.'

'Nothing to thank us for,' said Mungo, dismissively. 'Now,' he went on, rubbing his hands, 'I've got the claret for the mulled wine back at home. I'll go back for it shortly and bring it straight down. Obviously, there's red and white for the meal too. I've got the white on ice already, so I'll be bringing it chilled. I imagine there's no room in your fridges for it?'

'There isn't,' said Freya apologetically. Every inch of fridge space was allocated, with the canapé trays carefully stacked and taking up most of the space.

'That's what I thought,' said Mungo. 'We'll manage just fine.'

'So,' said Diana, 'I'm going to push off and refurbish myself and I'll be back at six o'clock without fail, so don't worry. I'm front of house, Mungo's sommelier because we've got to give him *something* to do, but he's got an easy job, because all we're doing is putting a bottle of red and a bottle of white on each table so people can help themselves. Really, it's just his role to slosh mulled wine into glasses and make sure empties get replaced. Hattie is going to do the waitressing and Finn will find something useful to do, I'm sure. All you've got to do is cook like the wind and then take the applause at the end.'

Freya looked doubtful.

'Your mother would have been immensely proud,' said Diana gently.

Tears flooded Freya's eyes and she blinked them back rapidly, impatiently. Her eyes were still swollen from yesterday's meltdown – she couldn't afford to get into that state again now. She had things to do.

Chapter Thirty

Freya had popped upstairs to wash her face and put on a fresh T-shirt. By the time she came back down, Mungo was in the little kitchen, stirring the huge, gently steaming pan of mulled wine and sniffing it appreciatively. There was a tray of empty glasses to his side, ready for him to press a glass of mulled wine into everyone's hands on arrival. Diana was there too, looking glamorous in a floaty green dress and Hattie had arrived, clad in a black skirt and a pristine white shirt. 'I'm your waitress,' she told Freya, giving her a little bob and an irreverent grin. 'Do I look the part? Diana's going to help me do the canapés and get people sitting down a table at a time, then I'm going to bring out the food, if you tell me what to do.'

'Not much to tell,' said Freya, gratefully. 'I'll do the main course and puddings in batches of six and it'll work just fine.' She took a deep, shuddery breath, crossing her fingers behind her back.

In the kitchen, she took the Bolo Rei out of the oven and put it to rest on the side. The aroma was heavenly, all the rich, heady Christmas spice, mixed with fresh, yeasty bread. She would slice it just before serving. She must warn people about the ring and the bean. The ring was supposed to bring good luck and the bean was kind of the booby prize. The tradition was – she had read – that the person who ended up with the bean had the job of baking the

Bolo Rei the following year; bad luck if they weren't keen bakers, she thought.

Now, with a spasm of nerves, she could hear Diana and Mungo starting to greet people. She needed to get the canapés out there. It was judgement time. She did one last check of the first tray and handed it carefully to Hattie.

Peeking around the kitchen door a few minutes later, Freya could see Diana was far too busy intercepting people as they came in and facilitating introductions to be helping Hattie, so, gathering up her courage, she launched into the crowd with one of the trays herself.

It was all right once she got started. People seemed to know who she was and were keen to chat and share their memories of her mother. A gaggle of slim, fit-looking older ladies told her about the yoga class her mother attended in the Middlemass cricket pavilion every Wednesday morning with coffee afterwards. The gossip was filthy and the jokes came thick and fast. The class was clearly a riot and Freya wondered if they got any yoga done at all.

A sweet older lady in a neat, shirtwaister dress told Freya how she knew her mother through the flower arranging at the church. Freya would never have guessed. Her mother had always loved flowers, but she was anything but devout. Also, she was amazed and touched to hear from a couple of distinguished older gentlemen she recognised from church, that her mother was a member of the churchyard working party who cut the grass and weeded the paths in the churchyard every Tuesday morning. She was glad that her mother's commemorative plaque in the churchyard would be kept tidy by people she had known.

And then there were her mother's work colleagues; most recently, Anna had been working part-time as office manager in an estate agent in Portneath. Helen, a shy-looking girl about Freya's age, was visibly upset as she told Freya how Anna had been a second mother to her, brightening when she remembered what fun they had had celebrating her last birthday before she died. There had been a memorable work trip out that evening, with pizza and bowling. That story nearly got Freya crying again, remembering how she had nearly forgotten to call her mother on her last birthday. It was so late by the time she remembered she had been tempted to leave it. Thank goodness she did make the call, recalling how her mother was clearly in the midst of a rowdy crowd of friends when they spoke.

The canapés and mulled wine seemed to be going down well. She even saw the usually stormy-faced Gabriel, Lord Havenwood as he *wasn't* known, looking approvingly at the trays as Jess circulated with them. He was deep in conversation with Finn and didn't look Freya's way and she wondered if the conversation was about renting this space to Sharmayne. They both looked serious enough.

Martha and Ciaran were there too. Martha was absolutely glowing, and – Freya was *so* relieved to see – Ciaran was standing, relaxed, next to her with his hand solicitously in the small of her back. She caught Martha's eye and Martha returned her questioning look with a tiny nod and a beaming smile.

The canapé trays were starting to come back to the kitchen empty now, with Hattie piling them up in the corner out of the way. It was the sign Freya was looking for. She had to start doing the partridge and pears. She laid out the first six white plates and was quickly absorbed in the task of building the dish on each of the plates; the neat, circular mound of creamy mashed potato, the partridge breast fillets piled on top with the pears alongside, all united with a dribble of jus, poured onto each plate just so and then, finally, the warmed-through greens with lardons piled on the side. Freya's concentration was intense. By the time the second and third tableful of plates were going out into the restaurant, Freya was wiping the sweat from her glowing, red face. Just two more tables to go.

Diana had been doing a brilliant job persuading people to sit down when Freya was ready to feed them, linking arms and leading some physically when she failed to stem the flow of chatter.

Mungo, Freya saw, was removing and replacing empty wine bottles with aplomb, always combining the action with a hand on the shoulder of one guest, a comic comment to another. Oh, Mum would have so enjoyed herself if she could have been here! But she couldn't afford to think about that now, Freya told herself, rubbing away a lone tear and clenching her fists to stem the flow. Not now.

The hubbub of chatter was continuing even now people were sitting down, but at a lower volume with the distraction of food. Mungo was circulating assiduously, topping up glasses too. Most guests had gone for the red wine – a full-bodied Barolo – but a few had chosen the Chardonnay instead. Freya was no snob when it came to wine. She was all for people drinking whatever they preferred. Andre's sommelier, Tobie Charpentier, had been much more prescriptive, turning up his nose disdainfully at guests who did not accept his recommendations, which were usually from the top end of the wine list. Freya would not miss *him* if she didn't return.

It was such a pleasure to see people eating happily, but she couldn't enjoy it for long; the first table was nearly ready for pudding now. The delicate meringues, the scented cream, the sprinkling of juicy, crunchy pomegranate seeds and then the perfectly placed dribbles and dots of pomegranate molasses evoking the ripples on the water . . . it required precision and concentration. Keeping her focus, her hands stayed steady, thankfully, and the dish was coming together beautifully, looking just as pretty as Freya had hoped as she worked her way along the row of plates methodically. It was so pleasant to be in a kitchen environment with no shouting and swearing. In Paris, her hands often shook with nerves, and her concentration would be broken by sudden bellows of rage. It was an environment which Andre – and several of the others – seemed to thrive on, but not Freya.

How lovely it would be to run a restaurant like this. To have a little, happy team working to produce hearty, local, seasonal food with a small menu, changing daily depending on what was available and fresh; Freya's spirits soared at the thought. Then she remembered Gabriel's insistence that Sharmayne's Pudding Club was down to occupy this space, not her. She was determined not to be downhearted, though. She would enjoy the moment because who could say what the future held?

Before she knew it, all five tables had had their puddings and Hattie was clearing away the plates as people, replete, leaned back in their chairs, finishing their wine as the conversation rose in volume again. The low, twinkling light of the lanterns and fairy lights made the little room glow with warmth. Some people were table-hopping too, slipping into empty seats or leaning on the backs of chairs, chatting animatedly.

There was Jake, having an intense conversation with Aidan now, while their partners Kylie and Jess chatted together over the last of their wine. John Makepeace, she saw with pleasure, was sitting next to Diana who seemed to be telling him a story with much drama and animation, while he watched her with an expression of quiet amusement, the crow's feet around his eyes crinkling as his eyes twinkled. He was an attractive man, Freya realised. What a shame he didn't seem to have anyone in his life. Of course, that might be because he was a little shy and awkward. Freya hoped it wasn't because he had always held a candle for her mother. The last thing her mum would ever have wanted was for him to be limited by that. She had always wanted everyone to be happy. Looking at them together, Freya could imagine John and Diana becoming friends – perhaps there would even be a little romance? After all, there weren't *so* many years between them, and maybe a dose of Diana's outrageousness was just what he needed to break through his reserve.

Freya thought she was watching unobserved, but then Martha caught her eye and beckoned her over to the empty seat beside her. Freya went diffidently, wiping her hands on the tea towel tucked into her apron ties. She bobbed her head as hands came out to squeeze her arm and shake her hand, congratulating her on the meal. By the time she managed to slip into the empty seat and greet Martha with a kiss on both cheeks she was flustered and flushed with pleasure.

'So, you told Ciaran about the baby?' she enquired.

Martha beamed and nodded.

'All good?'

'All *very* good. Of course, he was thrilled,' Martha said, happily. 'OK, shocked, then thrilled,' she amended, with a shrug. 'I don't know what I was worried about. I think I was just in a weird place when I saw you last, thinking he wouldn't want to keep it. I mean, for heaven's sake!' she exclaimed at her own stupidity. 'Put it down to pregnancy hormones.'

'I'm so pleased,' Freya said, sighing with pleasure and relief.

'And . . .' Martha went on, pausing to keep Freya in suspense, 'I had no real clue how far along I was, so our GP sent me – us – for a dating scan, which is where we shot off to yesterday after the funeral.'

'When's it due then?'

'Mid-April! I can't believe I didn't cotton on much sooner, and . . .' she said, pausing again, making Freya bounce in her chair with frustration.

'What? What? Is it twins? What?' Freya interrogated her impatiently.

Martha's face registered horror, 'God no, that would be a nightmare – not twins again. No, but I *can* tell you this . . . It's a girl,' she said delightedly. 'Ta da!'

Freya gasped. 'A girl! How gorgeous!'

'I know,' agreed Martha, brimming with pleasure. 'She's going to have her work cut out for her, getting all my boys under control.'

'I bet she'll be twisting them round her little finger.'

'She'll certainly have her father around her little finger,' said Martha. 'He's just so thrilled!' Martha sagged in her chair, smiling the secret, inward smile that pregnant women so often have.

'Have you been hearing the news from my beautiful, clever wife?' asked Ciaran, suddenly appearing and dropping a kiss onto Martha's head, his hands on her shoulders in a gesture of proud ownership.

'I have, I have,' declared Freya. 'No sleep for you from this summer.'

'I'm used to it. I've not had a good night's sleep in weeks. Years.'

'Lambing, still?' asked Freya.

He nodded, grinning ruefully. 'Great grub, by the way,' he added. 'I'm not a big one for puddings but those swans were stunning. And the canapés . . . amazing. Really.'

'Thank you,' said Freya, feeling another pang that her dream of opening a restaurant – at least here – was going to be thwarted by mass-produced steamed puddings. 'Sadly, this place is soon going to be named after you,' she told Martha.

'What? "Martha"?' she replied, puzzled.

'No, "The Pudding Club",' explained Freya. 'That's what Gabriel's planning.'

'When I want a publicity officer, I'll be sure to let you know,' boomed a voice to her left.

She turned to see Gabriel, scowling, having slipped into the chair on her other side. 'Taking my name in vain?'

'I wouldn't dare,' muttered Freya mutinously, but too low for him to hear. Then she saw his frown soften into a grin of approval.

'Impressive work, tonight,' he told her.

'Not as impressive as a jam sponge though, apparently,' she replied, naughtily. 'Sharmayne?' she elucidated, seeing him look confused.

'And is this what I'm planning?' he asked.

'Well yes, I thought so,' said Freya, not so confident now. 'I saw you and Finn plotting earlier.'

'And that's what you think? I was just about to say more nice things. I'm not so sure I will now.'

'Oh no, don't let me put you off,' she pleaded.

'OK,' he said slowly. 'Well, I just wanted to say I hadn't appreciated previously what a high level you were working at. Those canapés were exceptional. You could teach the catering team at Middlemass Hall a thing or two. In fact, I wish you would. They're looking for some consultancy and I was wondering if you would like me to steer them your way?'

Freya was taken aback. 'Really?'

He nodded, amused.

'I'm not sure . . .' she said, confidence ebbing away.

'It's up to you, of course, but you'd be doing me a favour,' he pressed. 'Really, they're pretty awful at the moment. It's a conference and events firm I rent out the Hall to and the catering outfit's developing a reputation for all the wrong reasons. But it's my reputation too, at the end of the day. I need them to be better.'

Freya felt a huge bubble of joy forming in her chest, but then it evaporated. 'There won't be time,' she said, with disappointment. 'As things stand, I really should go back to Paris on Monday. There's nothing for me here.'

'How about you didn't do that?'

'I have to work.'

'So . . . what if I said that this space could be yours, to rent. For you and Finn to set up whatever it is you want to set up – local ingredients and all that jazz?'

'What about The Pudding Club?'

'Sharmayne is going to have to look for somewhere else.'

'She'll be livid,' said Freya, awestruck.

'Tough,' said Gabriel. 'She strikes me as a woman who gets what she wants often enough. She'll cope, but it's for me to decide, not her. That's if you and Finn want it, of course.'

'I – of course we do! At least *I* do,' said Freya, hurriedly. 'I can't speak for Finn.'

'I think it would be fair to assume he'd be interested. He goes on enough about it. And you.'

This was such a conversation stopper, Freya just sat staring at him with her mouth opening and shutting. It was Diana who broke the spell.

'Come on you,' she said. 'We need to call people to order. Are you going to say a few words, or shall I?'

'You,' said Freya, firmly. 'Also, I've got to deal with the Bolo Rei, I'll just go and get it.'

'Ah,' said Diana, 'no more plates.'

It was true. The Marconis' legacy chinaware had only stretched to a main plate and a dessert plate each and they were now all piled up in the kitchen needing a wash.

'I'll just hand out slices in paper napkins,' said Freya. Thank goodness they had some left over from the canapés.

Mungo was now going around with a bottle of port in one hand and brandy in the other, sloshing generous amounts into wine glasses for those who wanted it. Freya brought out the cake with one of her chef's knives and started slicing into it, getting a production line going with Hattie, who held out the napkins and passed the filled ones down the line.

'This one's for you,' Hattie said, jumping forward and pressing a piece of cake into Finn's spare hand as he came past with a stack of dirty plates. 'And here's yours,' she said to Freya, handing her a piece Freya had already cut. 'You can stop now, that's everyone I think.'

Diana waited until most people were tucking in and then smacked her fork a bit too forcibly against her glass until everyone hushed.

'We are gathered here tonight in memory of Anna,' she said as the chatter died down to a hum. 'She was a woman who made a positive impact on so many lives in Middlemass – I am one of many who had the privilege of calling her a friend. But, as much as we are doing this in Anna's memory, there is an even more important reason why Anna would want us all to gather here like this – and it's to provide support, in grief, for her beloved daughter, Freya.'

She paused, looking around the room as several people nodded.

'It was Kahlil Gibran who first said, *"if you love somebody, let them go,"*' she went on, 'and that sentiment could have been written for Anna, because *she* loved Freya enough to let her go. That is why Freya left our little community, nearly ten years ago. As many of us in this room know, Anna felt Freya's absence keenly, but she was sustained by knowing Freya was following her dreams and honing a talent we have all benefited from tonight.'

'Hear, hear,' came the murmur.

'Freya,' Diana said softly, turning to Freya, who was pressing her back into the wall in the hope she could hide the fresh wave of tears that had suddenly assailed her, 'your mother was quite justifiably immensely proud of you, not only because of your talent and your hard-earned skill, but also because you are a delightful person. We are very lucky to have you back among us. Dare we hope we will be enjoying your company for years to come?'

Freya muttered something non-committal as she sniffed and swiped the tears with the back of her hand, putting her piece of cake on the table next to her. Despite the pain of yet more tears – would she ever stop? – there was a warm glow of acceptance creeping into her soul, looking around the room at all the people who had filled her mother's life for her last few years. Maybe Freya had been right to go away after all. It would seem her mother *did* have happiness and fulfilment in her final years. Tonight was a testament to that.

'Here,' said Hattie quietly, pressing a clean napkin into her hand to dry her tears and then giving her back the slice of Bolo Rei. 'Eat your cake,' she said.

Obediently, Freya tucked in, carefully assessing whether she had achieved the ideal balance of cinnamon, clove, nutmeg and ginger; it was so easy to allow the clove to dominate, but – chewing thoughtfully – she decided it was reasonably good.

Good grief, some of the dried fruit was tough going, though. There was one great hard lump that just wasn't giving in, she thought, chewing away doggedly.

'What is it?' asked Hattie.

'Just got . . .' mumbled Freya, trying to discreetly spit it out. 'Must be a bit of stalk or something.'

'That's the bean,' announced Hattie happily as Freya spat it into the napkin. 'That means you're the one who's got to make it next year.'

'Thank goodness for that,' chimed in Diana. 'I was worried it might be me. Actually, *everybody* was probably worried it might be me – it's a well-known fact I can't bake for toffee. Plus, it answers my question about whether you're planning to stay. Now you'll have to, won't you?'

'I take it my getting the bean was pure chance and everything?' Freya said, giving Hattie a suspicious look.

'Totally,' said Hattie unapologetically. 'Also, she made me,' she added pointing at Diana, who didn't look apologetic either, Freya noticed, but neither of them was looking at her, instead their eyes were fixed on Finn, who was eating his slice and talking intensely to Gabriel on the other side of the room.

Suddenly he winced. Diana and Hattie winced too.

'Maybe we should have warned him,' Hattie said anxiously.

'What have you two been up to now?' asked Freya. 'Oh, you are *kidding*,' she added, watching in disbelief as Finn took something out of his mouth and held it up to the light. It glittered.

'Some people are just never grateful,' said Diana, sniffily, as Finn frowned darkly and then suddenly laughed, looking over at her with his eyes narrowed. 'Also, I was quite fond of that ring. I'd have thought he'd be pleased to have a bit of good luck.'

'Good luck?' queried Freya. 'The poor man's probably cracked a molar. You are wicked women, both of you.'

'Needs must,' said Diana, enigmatically. 'Now off you go, you and Finn, there's a mountain of washing-up to be done. You can wash, Finn'll dry. And talk, both of you, for heaven's sake. It's long overdue.'

Freya was a bit put out that Diana expected her to wash up on top of all the cooking, but the older woman was clearly confident of her authority.

Gabriel and Finn were still in conversation but, as she watched, they both turned and looked at her. Gabriel patted Finn on the shoulder encouragingly and the next thing Freya knew, Finn was coming towards her.

'Come on you,' he said, taking her elbow in no uncertain terms, 'I've got a proposal for you.'

'Ah yes, I gather *that's* what you and Gabriel were talking about,' said Freya, relieved, allowing herself to be steered, not in the direction of the kitchen as she had expected, but to the door onto the street. *No time like the present,* she thought. The really big issue would be whether the rent was affordable. They already knew Gabriel was after a big hike on the rent he had been charging the Marconis and they would need to do a really careful budget to make sure they could actually afford it. She would have to write to Andre, of course, explaining why she wasn't coming back. She actually thought he would approve once he stopped being livid. And she owed him a lot. He deserved a proper thank you. But, she continued, telling herself in no uncertain terms, this was just about her and Finn going into business together. The relationship thing – well, that was another issue entirely. He had made it pretty obvious he wasn't going to accept any compromises. The gene thing had got him running scared and it was fair enough, but it spoke volumes about their little fling, which was clearly all it was. Deep in her deliberations, she barely noticed the flurries of tiny snowflakes, tumbling down through the still, sharp air.

'Now,' said Finn, cutting into her thoughts, 'hear me out, OK?'

'Sure,' agreed Freya, but the next thing she knew, Finn seemed to stumble.

'Whoops,' she said, reaching down to him, but Finn, gazing up at her, pushed a lock of dark hair off his face and then caught her little hand in both of his own, large, strong ones.

'Freya,' he said. 'I've never done this before, so . . . well, bear with me?'

She nodded, stunned.

'OK, listen,' he said, intensely. 'You are the toughest, sweetest, most determined woman I have ever met. Obviously, you're clever – even though you do some pretty stupid things sometimes – and it goes without saying you're so talented, and funny and beautiful, and . . . oh, God knows you're stubborn and that's why I think you're going to struggle with this—'

'Finn!' implored Freya, unable to listen any longer, she pressed her finger against his lips, 'don't, please . . . this just can't work . . .'

'No, I haven't finished,' he insisted. 'You're going to say about the gene, but – don't you see? I don't care! I want to be married to you, whatever our future holds, so don't you *dare* open that envelope before I've asked you to marry me,' he insisted, his green eyes flashing with rage and frustration. 'I refuse to allow you to find out something so important to us *both* on your own. This gene – whether you have it or not – we deal with it together, right? That's what marriage is, for heaven's sake. The rough with the smooth, in sickness and in health. Listen, getting married isn't what someone like Sharmayne thinks it is – it's not the destination, it's . . .' his voice dropped to a murmur, 'it's just the beginning. Of everything.'

'But Finn,' she interjected again, and this time he let her speak, 'it's too late,' she said, remembering how she had opened the yellow envelope with trembling fingers when she had been in her room getting changed earlier.

Finn paled, squeezing her hands so hard she gasped, his knuckles as white as his face. 'What do you mean? Oh God, you've got it, haven't you . . .? You're positive.' He nodded grimly, his mouth a straight line. 'But that's OK Fred, we'll handle it,' he insisted.

Slowly, a sweet, calm smile crept across her face as she held his gaze, serenely looking into his eyes and beyond, at their long, happy future together.

She couldn't fight it any longer and she didn't need to. He was the only man she would ever want to spend the rest of her life with. If there were battles to fight then she wanted him beside her, shoulder to shoulder, but this – the fear and uncertainty, the question mark over her health and her chances of motherhood – of having children who would be free of the terrible burden her mother bore – this was a battle that was already won.

'Yes,' she said. 'I opened it.'

'And it's . . .?' His frown melted away.

She nodded, laughing.

Finn closed his eyes and hung his head for a long moment. Then, looking straight at her, he smiled. 'Until we can get something better,' he said, standing, taking Diana's ring and slipping it onto her fourth finger.

'It's perfect,' said Freya, turning her hand to make the pink glass twinkle in the lamplight. 'But I think Diana might want it back.' She glanced into the café to see a blur of faces looking out at them both.

'We seem to have an audience,' she said, wryly.

'Then we'd better give them something to look at,' he replied, bending his head to kiss her.

There was a chorus of cheers and whoops, followed by a round of applause . . . But neither of them heard a thing.

RECIPES

If I had to list all my favourite things, Christmas and food are two that would come close to the top, so writing this book has been the perfect opportunity to spend several months steeped happily in both. I am definitely a cook, not a chef, so my culinary skills are not nearly as extraordinary as Freya's. It has been a pleasure to imagine dishes inspired by the '12 Days of Christmas' carol and having my characters cook and eat them has frequently driven me into my own kitchen to experiment.

The following recipes are my keen but completely amateur take on the food in the book – some basic, others a little more exotic – so, if your mouth has been watering as much as mine as we followed Freya's journey, I urge you to give a couple of them a go!

On the first day of Christmas . . .

Roasted partridge with sautéed pears

This is the first dish Freya cooks for Finn and this version makes a special supper or dinner party dish. But there is a difference between the demands of restaurant cooking and domestic cooking. In the story, Freya uses a cast-iron skillet pan to fry just the breasts of the partridge whereas, on the rare occasion I cook partridge, I have the luxury of time and prefer to cook a whole bird per person, roasting them in the oven, which takes a little longer.

For each person you will need:
1 plump, oven-ready partridge
1 small, barely ripe pear (one of the firmer types, such as a
   conference pear is ideal)
2 rashers of unsmoked, streaky bacon (dry-cured, ideally)
A small handful of fresh thyme
A knob of butter

Rub a generous amount of butter onto the skin of the
partridge, especially the breast, and stuff the thyme – stalks
and all – into the cavity.

Stretch and wrap two rashers of bacon around each bird,
tucking the ends underneath as you place the bird in the
roasting dish.

Put the tin in the middle of the oven at 220°C/Fan
200°C/Gas Mark 7 for 45 minutes to an hour.

Peel and quarter the pears.

After about half an hour, once it has gone crispy, push
the bacon down into the pan to avoid it burning and give
the breast a chance to brown. At the same time, place your
pear quarters alongside the birds.

Check whether the juices run clear when you poke a knife
into the gap between the thigh and the breast.

As soon as they are done, lift the birds, bacon and pears
onto a warmed serving dish to rest.

The buttery, peary juices in the pan make a good, simple
gravy. Just deglaze the pan with a glass of white wine and
spoon over the birds as you serve.

If you prefer a thicker gravy, whisk in a little cornflour
and bubble the mixture on the hob for a few minutes to
cook through – I don't bother with the thickening bit as
long as there is plenty of mash or bread to mop up the
juices!

To serve:

The roasted partridges are gorgeous served on or with a mound of buttery mashed potato, along with the pears and gravy and perhaps a pile of collard or spring greens, sliced and sautéed in sesame oil until they are wilted and softened but still a brilliant, emerald green.

Another perfect accompaniment is a dollop of sharp, fruit jelly. In our garden we have two prolific trees which produce loads of crab apples. We make batches and batches of crab apple jelly each autumn – no visitor gets away without a jar of the stuff pressed into their hands – but redcurrant or cranberry jelly left over from the turkey will also do very well with this dish.

On the second day of Christmas . . .

Raised pigeon pie

A raised pie with a hot water crust is a magnificent thing. I usually make a raised pie as part of my Christmas food, as a thick slice of it can be the basis of the kind of meat, salad and baked potato meals that are popular in our house after the great Christmas Day blow-out. It's also superb as a sneaky supper on its own with a dollop of good chutney or perhaps a smear of mustard if that's more your thing.

Please don't be discouraged by the long ingredients list and instructions. It really isn't difficult to make, just a bit of a fiddle. And if you can take your time, it is a relaxing project to potter around the kitchen doing on a cold, rainy afternoon. This pie will keep for a week in the fridge and is well worth the effort.

Freya managed without a special raised pie tin in the book, substituting a round cake tin with high sides and a loose bottom. You may be able to find a proper raised pie tin but they can be pricey and I admit - if you only use this once a year - it's difficult to justify giving it space in the kitchen cupboard.

For the pastry:
500g strong white bread flour
1tsp salt
120g water
170g lard
A beaten egg for glazing

For the filling:
250g streaky bacon – dry-cure is best, smoked or unsmoked depending on your preference
4 pigeon breast fillets
300g good quality sausage meat or an equivalent-sized pack of fresh chestnut stuffing (supermarkets stock this around Christmas and I always buy extra to shove in the freezer)

For the jelly:
A dense, meat stock jelly is traditional here, but – in the book – Freya uses crab apple jelly. Great if you have some, but redcurrant jelly would do nearly as well.

The pastry:
This is an easy and accommodating pastry to make and use.

Heat the water until boiling, then add the lard, stirring on the heat until the lard is completely melted.

Mix the salt and flour in a large mixing bowl and make a well in the centre.

Pour the water and lard into the well, mixing the ingredients together, first with a knife and then, as the mixture cools, with your hands, until you have a pliable ball of dough.

Put aside a third of the dough for the lid of your pie.

Roll out the remaining dough and place it in the pie dish or tin you are using, pushing it into the corners with your fingers, making sure you have a complete shell so no pie filling can leak out anywhere.

The filling:

Line your pastry by laying slightly overlapping rashers of the streaky bacon into it and draping the ends over the edge of the pie tin to tuck in later.

Now push in half your sausage meat or chestnut stuffing, followed by the trimmed pigeon breast, followed by the second half of sausage meat/stuffing, before rearranging any stray bacon rasher ends to cover the top. You can be as fiddly or as casual with the arrangement of filling as you like, but I do like to aim for definitive layers, so there are attractive stripes of filling when the pie is cut.

Roll out and lay on the pastry lid, trimming the excess and then crimping the edges to form a good seal.

Use the scraps to decorate the top of the pie with turtle doves, holly leaves or whatever you fancy, using a brush of beaten egg to make sure the decorations stick. Brush the remaining egg over the top of the pie when you are done.

Push a wooden spoon handle into the centre to create a steam hole and access point for jelly later.

Cook at 180°C/Fan 160°C/Gas Mark 4 until well browned and piping hot all the way through. Use a meat thermometer to check.

When the pie is cool, melt the jelly you are using in a pan and pour it carefully into the pie through the steam hole. In my cooking trials for this book, I admit there was so much filling crammed in, even the shrinkage achieved by cooking left little room for this step and I could get hardly any in.

In this case, you could always serve it on the side as I did. Refrigerate well before serving.

On the third day of Christmas . . .

Coq au vin

Apologies for the unforgiveable word play, but no apology for the recipe which is fabulously worthwhile. Coq au vin is one of the French classics that Freya would have cut her teeth on in Andre Boucher's kitchen. In the French cooking bible, *Larousse Gastronomique*, there are no fewer than three recipes for Coq au vin but – you know what? – at the end of the day it's just a chicken stew. That said, a quick word about the chicken you use: the key ingredient traditionally would be the cockerel who is no longer up to doing his duty in the farmyard – and a tough old bird like that would need long, slow cooking. For most of us, though, a medium-sized free-range chicken will do an even better job and is worth paying a little extra for. I would avoid those flabby, white, intensively reared birds that make me feel sad at the same time as tasting of very little and giving off an unhealthy amount of fat as they cook.

To feed four . . .
A whole, free-range chicken around 1.75kg in weight
50g butter
A little vegetable oil
100g bacon lardons, unsmoked
A couple of generous handfuls of pearl onions or shallots
A couple of generous handfuls of small, chestnut mushrooms
A bouquet garni (a teaspoon of dried mixed herbs will do, at a push)
A bottle of cheap red wine
Cornflour (optional)

The ideal pot to use is one of those heavy, enamelled cast-iron ones; if your casserole pot is ceramic you will need to fry your ingredients in a heavy frying pan first and then transfer them into the casserole pot.

Peel the pearl onions or shallots and fry them whole with the butter and oil until they are becoming translucent and just starting to caramelise. Do just use chopped onions here instead if you don't have pearl onions or shallots available, although they won't be so pretty in the finished dish. Put them to one side.

Adding a little more oil and butter if necessary, fry the mushrooms, whole if they are small, quartered if larger, and let them sweat down a little. Put them aside with the onions.

Fry the lardons until they are starting to brown and put them with the onions and mushrooms.

Turn the heat up high and put in the chicken, turning it as necessary with tongs until the skin is browned and the fat is starting to run.

If you are using just one pot, now just chuck everything back in, with the chicken, breast side up, resting on top. If you are using a frying pan then do deglaze it with a little red wine and pour the result into the casserole pot.

Add enough red wine so that it is just coming up to the level of the chicken, season and simmer gently for two hours, removing the lid for the last half hour to brown the chicken skin.

When the chicken is cooked through and coming off the bone easily, take it out and put it on a serving dish to carve – if carving is the right word! You should find the meat just falls away.

If you like a thicker sauce, take a cup of the liquid and whisk in a tablespoonful of cornflour until it's incorporated without lumps and then add this back to the pot, stirring well. I often don't bother.

To serve:
This casserole is excellent served with simple side vegetables such as carrots and peas, along with mashed potato or some good bread to soak up the juices.

On the fourth day of Christmas . . .

Apple pie

Everybody has an opinion about apple pie. The essential quality – for me – is short, crumbly pastry that is in no way soggy, and *definitely* doesn't have even the slightest suggestion of stretchy goo from uncooked flour anywhere. In fact, the guaranteed way to avoid a 'soggy bottom' is to use a proper enamelled metal pie tin as it conducts the heat really well.

The other benefit of a traditional pie tin is the wide lip to support the pastry top and that, along with the cute little ceramic calling bird steam spout in the middle, more or less guarantees a crisp crust.

Freya uses four of the little, traditionally designed blackbird pie funnels but obviously just one will do. They are just a few pounds to buy and easy to find if shopping online – just google 'Blackbird Pie Funnel'. Other than that, my only requirements for this recipe are lots of tasty apple filling, with or without a Christmassy addition of cinnamon.

To feed two greedy people or four polite ones . . .
For the filling:
3 eating apples
30g butter
30g caster sugar
A sprinkling of cinnamon if wanted

For the pastry:
250g plain flour
50g icing sugar
125g butter, chilled
1 lightly beaten egg
A little milk to bind together
A second lightly beaten egg
A dessert spoonful of caster sugar to sprinkle on the top

For the filling:
Peel, core and chop your apples into pieces around 3cm across. Don't get too hung up – for a medium-sized apple, I cut each quarter in half to make eight evenly sized chunks.

Melt the butter in a frying pan and stir in the sugar, stirring until the sugar is melted.

Throw in the apples and toss them in the sugar and butter until they are coated and caramelising a little but not mushy.

Put aside to cool.

The pastry:
Combine the flour and sugar, then cut the cold butter into cubes and rub in. I use the bowl and blade of a food processor to do this.

Lightly beat *one* egg and add to the mixture, then add the milk a little at a time until the mixture comes into a ball of dough, being careful not to overwork it.

Wrap the dough in cling film and leave to rest in the fridge for at least half an hour.

To construct the pie:
Roll out the dough, handling it as little as possible, and – using the pie dish as a guide – cut a circle of dough out that's a little bigger than the rim of the dish, for the top

of your pie, and place to one side.

Roll out the remaining dough, drape it into the pie dish, making sure it goes right into the corners and then trim off the excess with a sharp knife.

Put your calling-bird steam funnel into the middle of the pie dish, followed by your cooled filling.

Using a pastry brush, paint a little of the second lightly beaten egg around the pastry on the rim. Drape the pastry lid over your pie, cutting a small slit for the beak of the funnel to emerge. Pinch the two layers of pastry together with your fingers, crimping as you go around. The egg will help them to stick together and form a good seal.

You might want to use the remaining scraps of pastry to decorate your pie. It doesn't have to be elaborate. I stick to making two or three simple leaves to decorate the hole in the centre of the pie. A light brushing of beaten egg will help them to stick.

When you are done, lightly brush the pie crust with the remaining beaten egg and sprinkle on some caster sugar to make a sparkling, golden crust.

Cook at 200ºC/Fan 180ºC/Gas Mark 6 until golden brown.

To serve:
This is best served warm with a generous pouring of double cream or a dollop of crème fraiche. With the sweetened shortcrust and sugar on the apple this is already a sweet dish, but I would have no objection to a scoop of good vanilla ice cream with this either.

On the fifth day of Christmas . . .

Tempura calamari with dipping sauce
I expect for a lot of us, the idea of cooking a) seafood and

292

b) Japanese-style might seem a bit daunting but honestly, this is the simplest and most accessible of dishes. I'm not saying you should prepare your own squid – although you are very welcome to! – but a good fishmonger will always do this for you. You could even use defrosted frozen squid rings.

To generously serve four as a starter or two as a main course, you will need:
500g squid rings
Vegetable oil, plus sesame oil if using

For a single batch of batter:
75g cornflour
25g plain flour
Pinch of salt
100ml sparkling mineral water, ice-cold

These are the measurements for a single batch. You will very likely need to make more, but don't be tempted to make a giant batch, instead just make it as you go.

For the dipping sauce (Tentsuyu):
4tbsp soy sauce
2tbsp rice wine
2tsp sugar

Whisk together the ingredients for the dipping sauce and put to one side.

The critical thing with this dish is the light, bubbly tempura batter which needs to be thin, crisp and barely there. Don't make it until just before you use it.

You will need to fry your calamari in at least two centi-metres of oil, so a deep fat fryer is fine but not essential – a wide-based heavy saucepan will do. Use a neutral-tasting vegetable oil such as rape or safflower and you can flavour it with a spoonful of lovely, fragrant sesame oil, if you would like to.

Before you start, defrost, drain and pat dry your squid rings.

When you are ready, lightly whisk the batter ingredients, being careful not to over mix, as this activates the gluten in the flour which will stop the batter from crisping properly.

Dip the dry calamari rings quickly in the batter, in small batches, and drop immediately into the oil. They will take only one to two minutes to cook – too long, and your squid will be chewy.

The temperature is a matter of trial and error. A thermometer is not necessary – you just want the calamari to sizzle and rise to the surface immediately it is dropped in. You will soon get the hang of it.

As each batch is done, scoop them out and pop them onto a cooling rack with a plate underneath to catch the oil as it drains. The critical thing is to ensure they are not sitting in a puddle of steam as that will make them soggy.

To serve:
Serve immediately with a little dish of dipping sauce each and if you are serving as a main dish, I recommend rice or noodles to accompany.

On the sixth day of Christmas . . .

Fried goose egg with bubble-and-squeak and crispy bacon

Bubble and squeak is the archetypal dish without a recipe, because it's very definition is leftovers – usually mashed potato and cabbage. That said, I insist on including this as a recipe, purely so I can be prescriptive. My favourite version is made using collard greens (*nearest British equivalent would be spring greens or kale*) with leftover roast potatoes and parsnips from the Sunday roast. In fact, I would even say half the pleasure of roasting potatoes and parsnips is the joy of anticipating bubble and squeak the next day, so I always make sure I do plenty. If you think about it, the crisp, brown bits you get from frying are the making of the dish, so it makes perfect sense that using really well-browned roasties in the first place is a brilliant start.

It might surprise you to know goose eggs can be used in any context where you might normally use hen eggs, allowing one goose egg to every three medium-sized hen eggs. A word of warning: the flavour is that of a chicken egg but somehow generally eggier – and this, along with the comedy size of the thing, might put all but the most ardent egg lovers off.

You will need, per person:

75g of cooked green, leafy vegetable – greens, cabbage, spinach and even broccoli or spinach are all suitable.

150g roughly chopped roasted starchy vegetables – such as a mixture of potato, parsnip, and sweet potato (and do chuck in a roast onion or two if you have them)

A little vegetable oil for frying

1 goose egg

3 rashers of smoked, streaky bacon

Roughly chop then mix and mash the roasted and green veg together in a bowl. It doesn't have to be too finely done – in fact, stop short of total pulverisation – and then place in a frying pan which already has a little vegetable oil heating in it, cooking in batches if necessary.

Press the mixture down into a rough patty and then, using a fish slice or spatula, turn it periodically, making sure to scrape up all the caramelised bits off the pan as you go. Once it is piping hot and marbled throughout with lovely crispy brown bits, put to one side to keep warm.

Add more oil to the pan and carefully break your goose egg into it, remembering that the lower the oil temperature, the neater the look of the fried egg. I have a morbid fear of the 'snotty egg' so I am personally keen to take all the time necessary to ensure the white is properly firm all the way through.

Meanwhile, get the streaky bacon good and crispy under the grill. I like mine nearly burnt and crispy enough to shatter satisfyingly into shards of salty deliciousness.

To serve:
I hardly need to tell you how you arrange everything on the plate, except to mention that – if it were Freya – she would probably have a neat round of bubble and squeak, topped with the egg with the rashers of crispy bacon criss-crossed on top.

Heaven on a plate!

On the seventh day of Christmas . . .

Swan meringues
I'm really not the kind of cook who is fixated on fancy presentation, but even I am prepared to have a stab at these little meringues, which are surprisingly simple to do – honestly.

For seven swans, you will need

Meringue:

3 egg whites from medium eggs
90g caster sugar
90g icing sugar
½tsp lemon extract
½tsp rose extract

Filling:

450ml double cream
100g icing sugar
½tsp lemon extract
½tsp rose extract
1 whole pomegranate or 100g seeds already removed from the shell

Equipment:

Parchment paper for baking
Baking tray
Disposable piping bag with small, round nozzle

The thing to remember, with meringues, is that you always have 60g of sugar for each egg white.

First, whisk the egg whites until they are stiff peaks and then stop! Do not continue until they are crumbly looking – when they get like this, they are a little overbeaten and less structurally sound – so keep a close eye out.

Gradually add the caster sugar, whilst continually whisking, a spoonful at a time.

When the caster sugar is all gone fold in the icing sugar gently but thoroughly.

I use a mix of caster and icing sugar because otherwise, no matter how long I whisk, I tend to end up with gritty meringue filled with undissolved sugar, whereas what you want is stiff, voluminous, glossy white meringue which feels smooth when rubbed between finger and thumb. When the sugar is all incorporated, sparingly fold in the rose and lemon extract, being careful not to beat too much air out of the mixture as you do so.

Line the baking tray with the parchment paper.

Spoon some of the mixture into the piping bag and pipe out ten swan necks, aiming for an opened out 'S' shape. You are doing a couple of extra ones for safety (and perhaps for sampling?).

With the remaining mixture, you just need to shape some classic meringue nests but, in this case, aiming for an oval shape rather than round. You could always pipe these too, but personally I think the spiky, casual texture you get with working freehand does the job perfectly well, if not better. My method is to scoop up a dessertspoonful and then push it out onto the parchment paper with the back of another spoon, giving you a neat, oval mound to start with. Then, with the back of a spoon, shape a hollow in the middle of each one which helps the meringue to dry out successfully and also leaves room for your scented cream.

I cook on an Aga so cooking and drying out meringues is more of an art than a science, but in a conventional oven I would put them in at 100ºC/Fan 80ºC/Gas ¼ for 1.5 hours or until you can lift one off the parchment cleanly, tapping the bottom to check it is crisp all the way through.

Whisk the double cream, aiming for soft peaks that hold their shape. Gently fold in the icing sugar and add a little lemon extract and rose extract to taste. Don't overdo it! The rose, in particular, can taste a little soapy if you are too generous.

To serve:
You can't construct these too far in advance or the moisture in the cream will melt the meringue so, just before you serve up:

Drop a spoonful of the cream into each nest.

Position the 'neck' in the cream at one end of the oval to make your swan.

Sprinkle a handful of pomegranate seeds onto and around each one and serve immediately.

These beautiful little seeds are the epitome of Christmas for me, what with the gorgeous jewel-bright red colour and their being available only in late autumn and winter – their relative scarcity makes them even more special.

Rose-scented meringue swans are a wonderful summer dessert too, in which case I would be tempted to dress them with a scant sprinkle of rose petals instead of pomegranate. Raspberries, along with a drizzle of raspberry coulis, would work beautifully too.

On the eighth day of Christmas . . .

Maid of honour tarts

These little individual tarts filled with cheese curds are an old British recipe dating back at least to Henry VIII, who is supposed to have named the little tarts after the ladies of the court when he found them eating them one day.

I think of these as the love child of a Bakewell tart and a pastel de nata, the delicious, traditional, custard tart that Portuguese people are justifiably proud of. We can now buy these widely in the UK but, for the very best in the world, head to the Belem district of Lisbon and eat them warm from the oven in the Pastéis de Belém café, just a stone's throw from the quay . . . but that's another story! There is, incidentally, a special place in hell for whoever invented the standard English custard tart with its chilled, claggy custard, cardboard pastry and horrid sprinkling of nutmeg. If there was a Portuguese, British 'tart-off' the pastel de nata would win, hands down, but I digress again . . .

As for their appropriateness in Freya and Finn's story, according to the magnificent Nigella Lawson – of whom I am a huge fan – these cheesy, almondy little cakes are a legitimate Christmas offering, being an alternative to mince pies for the many among us who don't like dried fruit. Her recipe, using double cream instead of curds, is in the Christmas section of *How To Be A Domestic Goddess* and is well worth a go.

To make a dozen tarts you will need:
A 375g packet of ready rolled flaky pastry (life is too short
   to make your own)
100g of curd cheese if available, but quark is very close
75g butter, softened
1 egg, beaten
75g caster sugar
50g ground almonds
Grated zest of one lemon
¼tsp almond essence
12-hole cupcake tin

These tarts are often made with shortcrust pastry, but I prefer flaky. I am going to encourage a strange way of using the flaky pastry that I have nicked from the makers of pasteis de natas because it works brilliantly here:

Take out the ready-rolled pastry, unroll it, remove the greaseproof paper and then roll it back up again tightly. Then, slice the roll into twelve equal 'coins' of pastry.

Push a coin of pastry into each of the bun holes and squish it outwards with your fingers until it forms a neat lining with no holes. Obviously, unlike rolling out and cutting rounds in the conventional way, there is no waste pastry with this method and the flaky leaves of the pastry really are organised optimally. Honestly, it's the way to go.

To combine the filling, first cream the butter and quark together. Add the egg, beating to mix, followed by all the other ingredients, beating until well combined. Distribute the mixture evenly among the twelve pastry cases.

Bake for 20–25 minutes at 180ºC/Fan 160ºC/ Gas Mark 6.

Cool on a wire rack.

On the ninth day of Christmas . . .

Bavarois – or my version of a charlotte russe

I fondly imagine that fancy puddings like these have a place on a groaning Regency supper table, with ladies in flowing dresses fanning themselves and Mr Darcy types glowering from the sidelines. Cooks in big houses at the time were huge fans of gelatine, using it to turn pretty much any food they could think of into an elaborate moulded jelly. However, gelatine was my nemesis until I discovered that everyone else was using gelatine sheets instead of powder – the sheets are a *lot* easier and more reliable to use.

The ladyfinger biscuit element of this pudding is traditional when paired with a fruit bavarois, both becoming the classic combination called a charlotte russe. I'm not sure if making the custard/mousse element coffee-flavoured rather than fruit stops it from being a charlotte russe. Probably. Instead, the coffee and chocolate direction that Freya takes owes much of its inspiration to tiramisu which isn't particularly Regency England – but who doesn't love a combination of coffee, chocolate and booze?

Biscuit outer layer:

Kahlúa to taste

250ml strong coffee (espresso)

A 400g pack of ladyfinger biscuits (Savoiardi) you will probably have some left over

Bavarois:

8 egg yolks

300g caster sugar

300ml whipping cream

750ml milk

250ml strong coffee (espresso)

4 sheets of gelatine

Decoration:

A little whipped cream

50g plain chocolate for grating or curls

A deep 8-inch cake tin with removable base

Start by mixing a decent slug of Kahlúa with your first 250ml of coffee.

Briefly dunk each biscuit (both sides) in the coffee, then use them, upright like soldiers, to line the edges of your cake tin, trimming them to fit if necessary, placing the cut ends down so the pretty, curved ends are at the top. Be careful not to get them too soggy or they will collapse before the bavarois mixture goes in.

To make the bavarois, first beat the egg yolks with the sugar until pale and the mixture is doubled in size.

Submerge the four gelatine sheets in cold water and leave to soak.

Meanwhile, heat the milk with the coffee until just short of boiling. Take off the heat and cool slightly before pouring in a stream into the eggs, whisking all the while. When the two elements are combined, pour through a sieve back into the saucepan and heat on a low heat, stirring constantly, until the custard coats the back of a spoon.

Squeeze out the gelatine sheets and add, one by one, to the custard, whisking to combine thoroughly, then put aside to cool, stirring every once in a while so a skin doesn't form.

Whip the cream and put a little aside in a piping bag for decorating the top of your bavarois later.

Fold the remaining cream carefully into the cooled custard, mixing gently to retain the air. When the mixture is evenly combined, pour into your cake tin.

Cool in the refrigerator for several hours until completely set.

Remove from the tin (anxiously holding breath is optional at this stage) and – when safely on your serving plate – decorate the top with the retained whipped cream and a good sprinkle of grated chocolate, or do proper chocolate curls if you're feeling fancy and are prepared to do something a bit more technically demanding. That said, if I can manage them, I am sure you can.

On the tenth day of Christmas . . .

Lord Woolton Pie

During the Second World War, severe food shortages, rationing and the 'dig for victory' food production push were major issues. There was even a Ministry of Food set up to make sure the country was fed and many recipes were issued by the Ministry to help people make good use of what few ingredients they could get hold of. This hearty recipe for vegetable pie, with a potato pastry top, was conceived by the head chef at the Savoy and named after Lord Woolton, Minister for Food from 1940.

Serves four

For the filling:
450g cauliflower
450g parsnips
450g carrots
450g potatoes
Bunch of spring onions, chopped
2tsp Marmite (yeast extract – or you can use a vegetable stock cube)
1tbsp rolled oats
Salt and pepper to taste once cooked
A small handful of parsley (fresh or dried)

For the pastry:
225g wholemeal/wholewheat flour
110g mashed potato
75g margarine or lard (in these non-rationed times I'd probably use butter)
2tsp of baking powder
Couple large pinches of salt
Dash of water if needed

Chop the vegetables into chunks, cutting those that take longest to cook into smaller pieces.

Place in pot and bring to simmer with just enough water to reach 3/4 of the way up the veg in the pot.

Add in Marmite and rolled oats, salt and pepper and cook until tender and most of the water has been absorbed.

Place mixture in deep pie dish and sprinkle with fresh parsley (or add dry parsley and mix in).

Make the pastry by mixing the flour with the baking powder and salt and then rubbing in the margarine/butter.

Mix the mashed potato in to form a dough and knead (add a little water to the mixture if too dry).

Roll out to form pie crust, place on top and decorate then brush with milk.

Place in oven at 200°C/Fan 180°C/Gas Mark 6 for 30 minutes or so until top is firm and nicely brown.

On the eleventh day of Christmas . . .

Haggis, neeps and tatties with whisky sauce (bagpipes optional)

First, take your sheep's stomach . . . just kidding. An ancient Scottish dish, haggis is basically a mixture of offal and oats, all contained in a handy sheep's stomach to keep it all together while you boil it. It's very much tastier than it sounds!

Practically no one makes their own haggis these days and popular brands are stocked in most UK supermarkets (there's even a vegetarian version) although you may find it is only stocked during January as it's traditionally eaten at New Year's Eve and at Burns Night on 25 January. My family tried the Simon Howie brand in the testing of recipes for this book – and despite being deeply conservative in their tastes they were impressed.

The final element of the meal is the delicious whisky sauce, which is dead easy to make and a useful option to have up your sleeve, not just with haggis but on a good steak, too.

Whisky sauce for four:
50g butter
2tbsp olive oil
2 shallots or 1 medium onion, finely chopped
2 garlic cloves, peeled and crushed

100ml whisky
400ml double cream
1tsp Dijon mustard
2tsp wholegrain mustard
A squeeze of lemon juice

Fry the onion and garlic in the butter and oil until translucent.

Add the whisky and fry off to evaporate the alcohol (you can set fire to it at this stage if you have pyromaniac tendencies).

Stir in the mustards and then the double cream.

Simmer gently, stirring occasionally until thickened.

Add a squeeze of lemon juice before serving and season to taste . . . with maybe an extra slug of whisky if you feel it needs it, which I generally do.

To serve:
Haggis with whisky sauce is traditionally served with mashed swede and mashed potato and I hardly need give you a recipe for these except to recommend lots of butter in the mashing.

On the twelfth day of Christmas . . .

Cheese straws two ways
The fancy canapés that Freya wowed everyone with are the perfect example of where Freya's skills and mine diverge. I am in awe of people who can produce such things, but people attending a drinks party at my house have to make do with something a lot more basic. These cheese straws are barely even a recipe, but they always seem to be appreciated, so either I do very good cheese straws or I have very polite guests. Give them a go.

A 375g packet of ready rolled flaky pastry (yes, again – I really love the stuff)
200g extra-mature Cheddar
2tsp Marmite
1tsp smoked paprika

Spread out the ready-rolled pastry and cut into two rectangles.

Grate a generous amount of cheese onto one half of each rectangle.

Spread the remaining half of one rectangle with Marmite and the other with smoked paprika. Fold each rectangle in two, covering the cheese, then roll each one fairly lightly with a rolling pin to squish it all together a little.

Slice each rectangle into long, narrow 'straws'.

Pick up by either end and twist each straw twice before laying gently onto an oiled baking tray and pressing the ends down fairly firmly to keep the twist in as they cook.

They will need about twelve minutes in a hot oven, 220ºC/ Fan 180ºC/Gas Mark 7, but keep a close eye on them so they don't burn. The cheese will ooze out as they cook, but they shouldn't stick if you have oiled the tin enough and those toasted, bubbly edges are the best bits.

Leave to cool for a couple of minutes before moving them carefully off the tray onto a cooling rack. These are best served warm but will keep fresh for a few days in an airtight container.

Acknowledgements

Writing Freya and Finn's story has been a joy, not least because it has felt like Christmas for months during a time when we could all do with a bit of cheering up.

It has been an absolute pleasure to work again with the lovely crew at Orion, a large team of people (I will inevitably forget someone) who each play a vital part in bringing a story like this to the world. From my delightful editor and chief cheerleader Charlotte Mursell ably aided by Sanah Ahmed and co; to Ellen Turner and Tanijah Islam who beaver away on publicity and marketing; the fabulous audio team; the stellar rights team; my copy editor Kati Nicholl for a laser-sharp edit; and never forgetting my superb agent and friend Julia Silk from Charlie Campbell Literary Agents who tirelessly administers solace and backside-kicking as required. Of course, when it comes to bringing a book out there would be few readers without the kind and supportive work of a multitude of bloggers and reviewers who are not only critical to the process but a delight to interact with too. For this particular book a special mention must also go to the universally charming team at Mumford & Sons who were perfectly within their rights to ignore me that particular week, but didn't.

Writers are probably some of the worst offenders when it comes to bringing work home with them; almost no-one in my day-to-day life is spared my writing angst, not even the dog who is only really interested in walks and food and the teenage son who is only really interested in food. Thank goodness I have such good friends who kindly pretend to care about my tiny writing woes and who genuinely come up with gold dust suggestions. I couldn't do any of it without the Gin Dog Bitches; Clare, Helen, Hélène, Louise, Sharon and Caroline. And then there are the other loyal friends who get sorely neglected and are kind enough not to be offended; Lisa, Alex, Charlie, Lizzy, Anna... you know who you are. Of course I could never forget the many mentors and allies amongst my writing compatriots, always ready for anything from a fleeting social media hangout to the – all too rare, lately – real-life cake and wine; Sue Moorcroft, Sue Fortin, Wendy Clarke, Carol Thomas, Wendy Clarke Angela Petch, Mandy Baggott (for the character name), Laura Pearson (for the personal insights on the BRCA gene mutation) Catherine Miller, Laura E James, Angela Petch, Liz Harris, Alison May, Janet Gover, Jules Wake, Immie Howson, Kate Johnson, Kathryn Freeman, Christina Courteney, Liz Fenwick - basically, everyone at the Romantic Novelists' Association – honestly, I don't think any of you know just how much belonging to such a generous and talented group means to me.

And then, of course, there is the man who suffers the most from my preoccupations, my wonderful husband Jonathan who has shared the highs and lows for an astonishing number of years already and will hopefully do so for many more.

Thank you all.

Credits

Poppy Alexander and Orion Fiction would like to thank everyone at Orion who worked on the publication of *The 12 Days of Christmas* in the UK.

Editorial
Charlotte Mursell
Sanah Ahmed

Copy editor
Kati Nicholl

Proof reader
Laetitia Grant

Audio
Paul Stark
Jake Alderson

Contracts
Anne Goddard
Paul Bulos

Design
Debbie Holmes
Joanna Ridley
Nick May

Editorial Management
Charlie Panayiotou
Jane Hughes
Alice Davis

Finance
Jasdip Nandra
Afeera Ahmed
Elizabeth Beaumont
Sue Baker

Production
Ruth Sharvell

Marketing
Tanjiah Islam

Publicity
Ellen Turner

Rights
Susan Howe
Krystyna Kujawinska
Jessica Purdue
Richard King
Louise Henderson

Sales
Jen Wilson
Esther Waters
Victoria Laws
Rachael Hum
Ellie Kyrke-Smith
Frances Doyle
Georgina Cutler

Operations
Jo Jacobs
Sharon Willis
Lisa Pryde